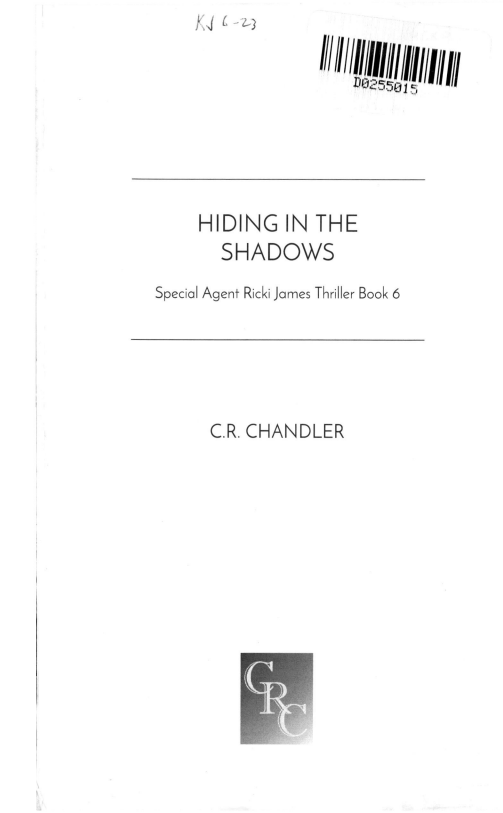

HIDING IN THE SHADOWS

Special Agent Ricki James Thriller Book 6

C.R. CHANDLER

Also By C.R. Chandler

SPECIAL AGENT RICKI JAMES
(Mystery/Thriller)

One Final Breath October 2020

One Last Scream January 2021

One Life Gone May 2021

Waiting In The Dark October 2021

Running In The Night February 2022

Hiding In The Shadows July 2022

Colder Than Ice Fall, 2022

Under the Pen Name: CAT CHANDLER

FOOD AND WINE CLUB MYSTERIES
(Cozy Mysteries)

A Special Blend of Murder 2017

Dinner, Drinks, and Murder 2017

A Burger, Fries, and Murder 2017

Champagne, Cupcakes, and Murder 2018

Tea, Dessert, and Murder 2018

Chapter 1

THE OVERCAST SKY couldn't decide if it should open up into a pouring rain, so it settled for dropping a steady blanket of mist on the forest below. Two lone figures made their way down the steep trail leading from the upper ridge to the oval-shaped lake, nestled in a picturesque valley. The lake wasn't big, and neither was the valley, but the views it offered of the mountains beyond were enough to stop even the most seasoned hiker in their tracks.

The pair of hikers halted their descent toward the lake to cut over onto a small path, overgrown and barely the width of a sturdy pair of boots. Another five minutes brought them to the edge of a small clearing.

"It looks like we found the place." Special Agent Cooper Warner didn't break his stride as he crossed the clearing and headed for the opposite side. The shoulders of his deep green parka glistened with moisture from the cold mist swirling in the air. His now thoroughly wet wool cap completely covered his wavy brown hair, with only a fringe curling up from under the hat's edge.

Ricki James entered the clearing right behind him but stopped on the perimeter of the oblong space to take a careful look around. Dark-blue eyes swept over the campsite then shifted to scan across the line of trees surrounding it. With only a narrow footpath acting as a tenuous link to civilization, the compact clearing was occupied by a single tent with nothing else in sight, giving it the feeling of being abandoned in the middle of the wilderness.

Tall, with long legs and a slender build that marked her as a natural athlete, Ricki tucked a strand of long dark hair back under the brim of her cap. Wearing a winter parka in the same olive green as the one Cooper had on, she rolled her shoulders back and forth. The movement helped generate heat inside her coat as she stood and studied the barren campsite.

Thinking the rest of the gear was probably in the zipped-up tent to keep it away from any foraging animal that wandered by, Ricki started across the clearing. She kept a careful watch on the silent trees since you never knew what they could be harboring. Even now, one of those animals hoping for an easy meal could be hiding and watching from under the protective covering of the surrounding forest. And then there was the much more dangerous animals of the two-legged variety, who owned the tent and might take issue with having their private space being invaded.

Even knowing that, Ricki walked over and unzipped the tent and took a peek inside. There wasn't much there. A pair of sleeping bags and some heavy-duty flashlights, along with a couple of small cooking pots and personal items. Not nearly enough to fill up the two large backpacks standing in their frames. The kind of gear that serious backcountry hikers used. Zipping the tent back up, Ricki kept her rifle cradled in one arm and her eye on the trees as she joined her fellow agent.

Cooper stood with his legs braced apart and his own rifle tucked into the crook of his arm, with the barrel pointing toward the ground. He was leaning slightly forward as he studied a notice encased in a plastic bag nailed at eye level to a tree.

"Nice of them to camp where the permit allows them to," Ricki commented as she too quickly scanned the permit. "I take it the name listed there is one of our guys?"

"Alan Barry. Yeah. He's one of them." Cooper tapped a lean finger on a line farther down. "And just like we were told, this permit is for two people." He straightened up. His dark-eyed gaze moved over to a rope tied off around the narrow trunk of a nearby tree. "They have a permit on display and their food hung a good twelve feet off the ground, so right offhand, I'd say they're model campers following all the rules."

"Maybe," Ricki conceded. She spotted a square metal box ten feet away and set back into the trees. "But a little weird, since there's a food storage locker right there."

Cooper nodded. "Yeah. I saw that." He walked over to the locker and opened it, pushing the door wide enough so Ricki could see for herself that it was being used. "They have some personal hygiene items in plastic bags, along with freeze-dried meals." He glanced over his shoulder. "Enough to keep them going for a few days, but not the full five they took the permit out for."

"And the locker isn't full," Ricki observed. "So they probably intended to snag some other food along the way."

Carefully securing the locker door, Cooper walked back to where Ricki was standing. "It could mean that Barry's wife was giving us good information about her husband and his buddy intending to do some hunting inside the park."

Ricki shrugged. It was certainly pointing in that direction, but she hoped not. "Her *ex*-husband, and there are other sources of food here besides hunting."

Cooper looked around as an icy finger of wind rushed around and between them, twisting through the trees and over the patches of snow that dotted the forest floor wherever there was an opening in the thick canopy above. "It's a little late in the season to be picking berries or gathering nuts."

Ricki laughed. "I was thinking more along the lines of fishing." She thought of the small oval-shaped lake. The view of the lake from the trail, with its turquoise-colored water and backdrop of tall snow-covered peaks, had made her stop and stare at the sheer beauty of the picture it made. The overcast skies and thin veil of rain had given it a mystical quality, but the small lake was fed by snow melt seeping through the ground rather than a mountain stream. The odds of it being well stocked with fish weren't great.

"But there are better places to fish, if that was their intention." She looked up and pointed with her free hand to the large trash bag hanging overhead. "Which makes me wonder what's inside that."

"You've lived here longer than I have," Cooper said. "I know you grew up next to Olympic Park, but how about this one? Spend any time in the North Cascades?"

Ricki looked beyond the campsite, toward the lake lying peacefully under the gloomy sky, as the memories flooded over her. Oh yeah. She'd been to this park before, and even to Egg Lake. She, her dad, and her Uncle Cy had broken up several of their backpack trips by camping overnight at Egg Lake.

After her dad had passed away when she was sixteen, her uncle had still brought her to North Cascades Park for long weekends. It had always been a favorite of theirs, maybe because of the memories it held of her dad and for its natural beauty. She'd even brought her son with her a time or two. But whatever the reason, beauty or nostalgia for a childhood long gone, she knew the park and was familiar with the back trails.

When she caught Cooper's stare, she brought herself back to the present and the question he'd asked. "I've spent time here." She nodded.

Her fellow agent grinned. "Great. Got any guesses which way our guys might have headed?"

That had her lips curving into a smile. The odds of her knowing that were ridiculously small, and it was just like Cooper to ask anyway, with that hopeful note in his voice.

She'd known him since her rookie year as an investigative agent with the National Park Service. They'd had an on-again, off-again friendship for a decade, starting with the occasional drink together when they were both stationed near Washington DC, and then reconnecting again recently when he was transferred to a district west of the Rocky Mountains. Their paths had crossed twice in the last month, and both times at North Cascades National Park, which suited her just fine.

She was fond of Cooper. He was like a favorite cousin who you didn't see very often but always enjoyed spending time with.

"No idea," Ricki said. "Maybe they aren't hunting but are just out for a stroll in the forest."

"I guess the best way to find out is to look inside that garbage bag." Cooper rested his rifle against the thick trunk of a tree and walked to the knotted rope. Easily undoing the loop, he slowly lowered the black plastic bag, his arm muscles straining underneath the protective layer of his parka. "Close to fifteen pounds, if I had to guess."

Mentally crossing a deer carcass off the list of possibilities, Ricki set her own rifle next to Cooper's and waited until the bag was on the ground. While Cooper kept a firm grip on the rope, she kneeled beside the bag and carefully opened its top, tilting it slightly to get a better look inside. At first all she saw were several clear plastic bags filled with snow, but when she reached her hand in and moved them aside, two dark eyes stared back at her.

She let out a resigned sigh. That figured. Why couldn't it have been a bag full of trout? Fishing was perfectly legal inside the park. She reached in with both hands and pulled out the clear plastic bag encasing the bird. Cooper got a good look at it, with the wings, legs, and neck neatly tied down to its back and sides.

"Canada goose," she said in a clipped tone while Cooper let out a soft whistle.

"I'm guessing they probably didn't find it just lying around dead from natural causes."

"Not likely." Ricki returned the bird to the bag and its final nest of packed snow. Once she'd tied the top back up, she waved an arm at Cooper. "You'll need to haul it back up to its hanging position. The local wildlife won't care if it was a legal kill or not if they catch its scent."

"I hear that." Cooper tugged on the rope until it went tight, then pulled hand-over-hand, stopping when the black bag was once again a good twelve feet off the ground. Tying off the rope the same way he'd found it, he picked up Ricki's rifle and handed it to her. "I'm betting they brought in a pack that was mostly empty."

"I'd say that's a good bet." Ricki pulled her wool cap down over her ears. "And I'd also bet that a goose wasn't what they hiked all the way in here for." Deer meat would weigh a good deal more than fifteen pounds and would have to be removed from the carcass in order to get it out of the park. But despite that, a smaller buck or doe could be field-dressed easily enough. And a couple of grown men, like the two they were tracking down, could carry out fifty to sixty pounds of meat between them. Especially with very little gear and very big backpacks.

"I'm thinking that the tip that the ranger office received from Alan Barry's wife about them going deer hunting was right on the money," Cooper said, picking up his own rifle and joining Ricki in scanning the area beyond the small clearing.

"Ex-wife," Ricki corrected again. "Which is why we received the tip." It seemed that the former Mrs. Barry was going to score in the game of divorce one-upmanship. And since the ex-Mrs. Barry's claim that her former husband and his good buddy were planning on hunting while in the park was actually true, she and Cooper were there to escort the two men straight to jail. Hunting in North Cascades Park was illegal, just like it was in every other national park.

The only fly in that ointment was that they'd have to find the two men first. Not a sure thing in a park nestled inside a mountain range.

North Cascades National Park covered over half a million acres, carved out of an untamed wilderness. Ragged mountain peaks towered over lush, forested valleys that sheltered an extensive network of rivers and streams that were constantly fed by the hundreds of glaciers nestled in the deep crevices and ravines of the Cascades. It was a beautiful and potentially deadly stomping ground for all sizes of wildlife, and only experienced hikers could successfully face the challenging terrain Their reward was some of the most spectacular views in the country, especially in the large and barely touched areas of the northern stretches of the park that reached up to and over the Canadian border.

Broken into two sections separated by the Skagit River, the park's northern section had a stingy pair of roads, each with limited access to the interior, and neither was close to the trail the two hunters had taken. Following a day behind them, Ricki and Cooper had started off on the trail leading into the park just before dawn, with their light packs and rifles secured to their backs. They'd made the steep climb over four miles up to Hannegan Pass and then another mile down until they'd crossed the boundary into the park, traveling the overgrown Copper Ridge Trail through dense forest until they reached the turnoff to the small but scenic, and appropriately named, Egg Lake.

According to the visitor log at the ranger station, Alan Barry and his friend, Mark Thurman, were the only hikers who had applied for a backcountry permit covering this midweek stretch of days. Which didn't surprise Ricki. It was early November, and late in the season to be camping in the park. Only an unusual warm spell had kept them from chasing after the two men through knee-deep snow, although the mounds that had accumulated in the dense shadows beneath the trees were a reminder of what was coming. Once the weather returned to normal, winter would hurl itself at the Cascades in earnest, making the trails, and most of the northern section of the park, inaccessible.

But so far their luck had held, and they'd made it to the camp without fighting their way through one of the sudden whiteouts that these mountains were so infamous for. As she mentally crossed her fingers that they could track down their quarry and get back to the ranger station before the next storm, Ricki's gaze quartered the area beyond the campsite.

"I'm going to check around the outside of the tent," she said before turning in that direction. "I've taken a look inside and there isn't enough there to bother going through."

"Okay. I'll be the lookout while you check around," Cooper agreed. "Barry's wife said he had a gun permit, and we've got a dead goose, so it's a sure thing both men are armed." He used a single hand to pull his wool hat farther down his forehead until it covered his eyebrows. With brown hair, brown eyes, even features and a medium build, Cooper was easy to overlook in a crowd, unless he caught you in a stare so intense you would swear the man was looking right through you.

Glad he wasn't aiming that brutal stare at her, Ricki made a slow circle around the tent. Nothing appeared out of place. The two men they were tracking could simply be off on a day hike in the rugged backcountry of the park as far as she knew. But she doubted it.

"Probably wasn't too bright of Barry to let his ex-wife in on his plans," Ricki said as she walked back toward Cooper.

The corner of his eyes crinkled in amusement as he grinned at her. "Meaning what? Ex-wives can never be trusted?"

"I wouldn't," Ricki said, moving to stand beside him.

Cooper laughed. "Oh, really? Aren't you an ex-wife?" When Ricki looked back at him and rolled her eyes, he wiggled his eyebrows, making his wool cap jiggle up and down. "Are you saying you might rat out Bear if the opportunity presented itself?"

Bear was the high school nickname of her ex-husband, bestowed on him long ago by his football teammates. Only his mother called him Benjamin. Everyone else in the three small towns that made up the Bay had called him Bear from the moment he'd first stepped onto a football field, and they still did. Including Ricki. And even though Bear's football days were far behind him, some habits just weren't worth breaking.

"Bear's an open book. No ratting out would be necessary," Ricki stated, because it was the simple truth. Her ex-husband couldn't keep a secret to save his soul.

"How's he doing?" Cooper asked.

Ricki stiffened slightly, then forced her shoulders to relax again. Her ex-husband, and the father of her teenage son, had been shot by a killer determined to murder everyone on a camping trip that Bear had been hired to guide through the enormous park on the western side of the state. Her ex had been critically wounded and was lucky he'd escaped at all. It had not only been her job but her mission to catch that killer, which she had. And it was one of the few times she was looking forward to testifying in court when the case made it to trial. That was one prison cell door she wanted slammed shut and locked for a very long time.

"So, I guess we just sit and wait for our guys to come back?"

The words were barely out of Cooper's mouth when the sound of a gunshot bounced through the trees. Both agents raised their rifles and then went still, their backs to each other. When a second bullet sounded, they turned in tandem and faced in the same direction.

"Did you hear that echo?" Cooper asked once the sound had faded away.

"I heard it," Ricki confirmed. "To the northeast and not too far off."

"Agreed," Cooper said.

Ricki drew in a deep breath. "Okay. Let's go."

Chapter 2

RICKI TOOK her global compass out of her pocket and checked their exact position while Cooper did the same. A smile drifted across her lips at the flash of a memory when she'd told Clay, the chief of police back in the Bay, that if he was going to live in the mountains, he should never leave home without it. Since their relationship had advanced far beyond giving advice about essential hiking gear, she admitted to herself that she missed having him there. They'd worked a lot of cases together, but those had all involved murder and this one didn't. It was also strictly park business, so she'd made the trip without him.

"Okay. I've got this location tagged," Cooper said. "At least we won't get lost coming back."

Ricki smiled and replaced the compass in her pocket. "Always a good thing. Let's go."

They moved silently through the trees side by side, their rifles ready, their gazes constantly scanning the area in front of them. Since she knew the terrain better than Cooper, Ricki was slightly in the lead, but made sure she kept the other agent within her peripheral vision.

Strength in numbers, she thought as she strained to hear any sound that didn't belong there. The high branches had dark and light patches dancing across the forest floor as the wind wove in and out of the treetops, playing a melody unique to the towering pines. Ricki carefully moved through the shadows, heading northeast. She skirted boulders left long ago by a retreating glacier and stepping over fallen logs reduced to a line of chunky pieces of bark covering a mound of wood chips and lumber dust.

They'd been looking for a good half hour when another shot rang out. Both agents immediately dived for the nearest tree. Ricki's rifle was up and aimed before the echo of the shot had faded away. She shifted her attention slightly to her left as her gaze quartered the area through the lens of her scope. A sound caught her attention. Nothing specific, just something that wasn't part of the forest. She drew in a shallow breath and held it, straining to hear. Her patience was rewarded when the sound drifted through the trees again. Voices. She was hearing voices.

Slowly standing, she looked over her shoulder and gestured at Cooper. He nodded back and also stood, then followed her when she moved forward, adjusting his direction to hers as he took up his position beside her once again. After another ten minutes, Ricki stopped. The voices were now close enough to make out two of them, definitely male, and raised in an argument. It also sounded heated enough they probably wouldn't notice anything going on around them. Ricki glanced over at Cooper, who raised a closed fist, then used a single finger to point to the left. Ricki nodded, watching him move off before slowly starting forward again.

"I'm telling you, I saw something in the trees, and we need to get out of here," one of the voices insisted.

"Is that why you're popping your rifle off all the time, because you think you saw something?" the other responded with a distinct sneer.

"I *did* see something."

Ricki moved forward another ten feet, then sank to one knee behind the thick trunk of a Douglas Fir. She peered around it into the small clearing. Two men had their backs to her. One was standing and the other was sitting on the ground with one leg bent as he massaged his ankle.

"You saw an animal, that's all." The man standing up used the toe of his boot to nudge his friend's outstretched leg. "We need to get going. I don't know what you saw, but I'm not staying any longer than it takes to pack up and get the hell out of here."

"I'm right there with you," his friend muttered, still rubbing his ankle.

"Then let's get going." The impatient demand was followed by another nudge with his boot.

His companion glared up at him. "Stop doing that. I told you, I can't walk on this ankle any longer. It's on fire. I think I might have broken something, Al."

"Well, you wouldn't have if you hadn't taken off running like that."

The man on the ground let out a loud snort. "Ha. Like you weren't right there with me. That dead guy scared you just as much as he scared me."

Ricki frowned. *Dead guy? What dead guy?* Wondering just how long the men had been out in the woods, Ricki moved in closer, settling into a spot behind a tree right on the edge of the clearing. Despite the nip in the air, she unzipped her parka so the gold badge attached to her belt was clearly visible. Waiting another minute to be sure Cooper was in place, she took a deep breath and let it out slowly before stepping out from behind the tree.

She took three steps forward and then stopped, her gun raised and her voice low and calm. "Federal agents. Put your hands up, nice and slow."

The man on the ground looked over his shoulder, his mouth gaping open while his friend whirled around. When he started to lift his gun, Ricki didn't take any chances but lowered her barrel and put a round into the ground a good two feet from his boot. He was in no danger, but the warning was clear. He dropped his gun and let out a high-pitched squeal before jumping backwards and tripping over his friend's outstretched leg. He fell on his backside as his friend's empty hands shot up into the air, palms facing out.

"I'd be careful if I were you, Mr. Barry. Or Mr. Thurman, whichever one of you is which," Cooper called out as he appeared at the edge of the tree line behind them. "It's my turn to shoot next, and I'm not as good as she is. I'd probably hit your boot or some other larger body part."

The man sprawled on the ground sat up and lifted his hands high into the air as he stared wide-eyed at Ricki. "Are you crazy?"

She smiled at him. "No, sir. I'm Special Agent Ricki James with the National Park Service."

While Ricki kept her rifle up, Cooper lowered his and walked forward until he was standing over the two men. "And I'm Special Agent Cooper Warner, and you two are under arrest. Now, which one of you is Alan Barry?"

The man who had been rubbing his ankle jerked his head toward his friend. "He is."

Alan shot him an annoyed look before aiming his gaze up at Cooper. "And he's Mark Thurman."

"He already knows that, Al," Mark said in a dry tone. "Didn't you hear him call out our names when he threatened to shoot you?"

Alan shrugged, his eyes still on Cooper. "Fine. Then what are we under arrest for? It isn't illegal to carry guns in the park."

"No, it's not. But it is illegal to hunt in the park." Cooper took a step back and picked up the man's discarded gun before looking over at Mark. "Where's your gun?"

"I dropped it," Mark said. "And was too busy running to pick it up."

Cooper frowned. "Running from what? Did some of the wildlife object to you taking potshots at them?"

Mark clamped his lips together and exchanged a long look with his friend. When neither man spoke up, Ricki sighed and lowered her rifle.

"I heard them mention something about a dead guy."

Her fellow agent blinked several times before his eyebrows winged upward. "A dead guy?"

Ricki nodded. "That's what they said." She turned to look at Mark, who was rubbing his ankle again. "Isn't it, Mr. Thurman? You hurt your ankle running through the woods, and apparently dropped your rifle as well, trying to get away from a dead guy? Is that right?" She'd tried to keep her voice as neutral as possible, but some of her skepticism must have bled through because Mark tossed a disgruntled look at her.

"We know what we saw. It's Agent James, right?" At Ricki's confirming nod, his chin stuck out and his mouth settled into a stubborn line. "The guy was dead. He had a hole in his back and another one in his head. Definitely dead."

Cooper cocked his head to one side and studied Mark until the man squirmed under the intense scrutiny. "What do you think?" Cooper asked Ricki without taking his gaze off Mark.

She thought it was probably a waste of time, but it had to be checked out. She looked at her watch and then back up at the sky. The sun was masked by the gray clouds crowding together overhead, but Ricki could feel the gathering darkness just beyond them. At this time of year, sunset came early to the Northwest.

"Where did you find this dead man?" she asked Mark, but it was Alan who spoke up.

"Almost due north of here. That's the way we were traveling, and we pretty much followed the same path back."

Ricki let out an audible sigh. "Pretty much? How close were you following the same route back? Because you're northeast of your campsite."

"Well, shit," Alan swore softly. "I thought we were on the same track."

Ricki shook her head in disbelief. These two morons might be experienced hunters, but clearly not in this kind of wilderness. Running blindly like that, they were lucky they didn't get completely lost out here. Then she and Cooper would have been mounting a rescue mission as well as hauling their butts into jail.

Ricki looked past Alan, her gaze studying the tree line to the north as she considered the options. "Never mind." She glanced over at Cooper, who had taken a pair of zip-tie handcuffs out of his jacket pocket. As the agent with the most seniority assigned to the case, he would do the arresting. Which was fine with her. That also meant he'd be doing all the paperwork.

"There's enough snow on the ground, I should be able to follow their tracks." Ricki took another quick glance up at the sky. "It probably won't snow tonight, but it should be cold enough to keep the tracks from melting away."

"I wouldn't do that." Mark's voice was soft, with an underlying note of fear. "Someone's still out there."

Both agents turned to face the hunter and scowled at him.

"What are you talking about?" Cooper asked while Alan slapped a palm against his head and groaned.

"I saw him," Mark insisted, glaring at his friend. "He was there, watching from the trees. He probably killed that guy we found, and if you go back there, he might kill you too."

Chapter 3

RICKI WOKE the following morning to skies clogged with heavy clouds colored in varying shades of gray. Despite the lack of any sign of the sun, the glowing face of her digital watch assured her it was time to get up. That and the vocal complaints of the men enclosed inside the tent demanding a bathroom break.

She and Cooper had emptied the tent of everything except the two sleeping bags that Alan Barry and Mark Thurman had brought along. Then after zipping the two hunters inside the tent, they'd laid their own bags in front of the entrance. It had made it impossible to exit the tent without stepping on one of them, although she hadn't been entirely sure the two captives couldn't have managed it.

After the long hike in, added with chasing down Alan and Mark, both agents had been tired right to the bone. Enough so that a herd of elephants might have trampled over them and they wouldn't have noticed. Fortunately for them, Alan was just as tired and Mark couldn't walk three steps on his own, so they'd made it through the night without anyone escaping and forcing her and Cooper to run them down again.

When the voices coming from the inside of the tent became more strident, Cooper stuck his head out of the top of his sleeping bag and blinked at her with bleary eyes. "Are you awake, James?"

She sat up and did a quick stretch of her arms overhead before pulling her mummy bag up over her shoulders. The bag was narrower at the bottom, well insulated, and made for cold weather. Which was a good thing because damn, it was cold. Wondering if they were in for a bout of snow after all, Ricki wiggled in her bag, groping around with one hand until she latched on to a hiking boot.

Even if they'd managed to get away, it wouldn't have done them any good, Ricki silently mused. Sitting up, she pulled on one boot then grabbed the second one as she looked around at the dense forest.

Where would they go? It would take them hours to hike out of the park and back to their car, where park rangers would be waiting for them, courtesy of a call Cooper would have easily made on the satellite phone. Besides, the worst the two hunters would probably get was a fine and some unsupervised probation. Especially if it was their first offense. And killing animals wasn't considered enough of a "shocking" crime to cause Alan to lose his law license.

Unless they got an unfriendly judge who considered their actions as poaching. Then it would be a very different story.

Ricki pulled on her boot and sighed. One could only hope. But since handing out jail time to bad guys wasn't her job, she dismissed her internal "what happens next" debate and stood up before stepping out of her sleeping bag. She grinned at an annoyed Cooper, who had grudgingly pushed himself to a sitting position and was glaring at the closed entrance to the tent.

"All right, all right," he growled out. "Hold your horses. We're up." The agent unzipped his own mummy bag, stood up, and then stepped out fully dressed—parka, boots, and all.

Ricki had to admire that. She'd slept in her clothes, too, including her parka, but she'd never been able to master sleeping while still wearing her heavy hiking boots.

When another complaint came from the tent, Cooper rolled his eyes. Reaching into his jacket pocket, he pulled out a pair of heavy gloves. "Come on out and we'll find some place for you to freeze your nuts off while you pee."

There was the grating sound of a zipper being lowered. Alan stuck his head through the tent opening and glared up at Cooper. "I don't appreciate your attitude or your language, Agent. Neither of which is necessary."

Cooper shrugged. "I don't appreciate having to make this trip at all, Mr. Barry, which also wouldn't have been necessary if you'd felt like obeying the law."

The lawyer cast a sideways glance at Ricki before moving past her with Mark close on his heels, hopping on one leg and clutching Alan's arm for support. "It was a bird, Agent Warner." He turned to face Cooper. "A very *common* bird," he said, emphasizing what he clearly intended to make as his main argument in front of the judge. "Hardly an endangered species."

Ricki sent Cooper a warning glance, silently relaying the message that there was no use in arguing with a lawyer. Cooper's eyes narrowed for a moment before he sighed and shook his head.

"Save it for the judge, Mr. Barry." He picked up his rifle and gestured toward the tree line. "You were the one in a big hurry, so let's get going. And help your friend." He looked back at Ricki. "The satphone is in my pack if you want to make the call."

Ricki nodded, immediately reaching for Cooper's backpack as the three men made their way into the trees. The phone was on top. Pulling it out, she made the call to the park's headquarters, explaining their situation and arranging a helicopter extract for Mark Thurman. She would have liked to have put his buddy, the lawyer, on that same helicopter, but they weren't to be used for a convenience flight. Since Alan Barry was unfortunately capable of walking out of the park under his own power, she and Cooper would have to be his escorts, which meant spending the best part of their day listening to his complaints about being arrested at all. Lucky them.

Hearing the men returning, Ricki replaced the phone and went to her own pack, taking out a small pad of paper with a pencil stuck in between the pages. Old fashioned as it was, she considered it an essential part of her equipment. It was amazing how often this very low-tech way of communicating came in handy. As the men approached, Ricki waited until Mark was sitting in reasonable comfort on a flat rock before handing the pad and pencil to Alan.

"Here." When he automatically took the open notepad but simply stared back at her in confusion, she tapped on the small circle she'd drawn at the bottom of a blank page. "This is where we found you. Now give me an idea where that dead body is."

The lawyer bent his head and drew a circle at the top of the page, and then a straight line connecting it to the one Ricki had drawn.

"Due north of where you found us." He kept drawing as he talked. "I had a global compass with me but didn't stop to check it." He looked up as he handed the pad of paper back to her. "We were too busy running once we saw the dead body. I was about to look at my compass when you and macho-man over there happened to come across us."

Ricki only smiled at the calculating look in the lawyer's eyes. "That was a bit of luck, wasn't it?"

"Phenomenal luck," Alan shot back. "Especially since the two of you aren't even park rangers, are you? Park rangers don't call themselves special agents."

"No, they don't," Ricki agreed amicably, her smile

growing a fraction of an inch at the glare Alan tossed back at her. "What's this thing you drew?" She pointed at two small circles with a line in front of it.

At first Alan simply looked away, keeping his mouth firmly shut. One of Ricki's boots started to tap against the ground as she waited for the lawyer to figure out that it would be smarter to cooperate than land in an even bigger hole he'd have to dig himself out of.

"A landmark of sorts," Alan finally got out between gritted teeth. "We walked around two huge boulders with a fallen tree in front of them and the body was about ten yards from there."

Ricki pocketed the small pad of paper. "Okay. Thanks."

Alan sighed and ran a hand over the top of his thinning hair. He glanced over at Mark, who nodded back at him before turning his gaze to Ricki. "Look. There probably was someone else out there. Mark says he saw a guy, and he has a real sense for that kind of thing." He cast another quick look at his friend and sighed again. "And there was more than one set of tracks."

Ricki blinked several times before slowly pulling her hand out of her pocket. "You saw different sets of tracks?"

"Why didn't you mention that before?" Cooper demanded.

"I didn't think you were serious about going back to take a look." He pointed an accusing finger at Cooper. "Especially on her own, unless you intend to tie us up and leave us here while you both go chasing after some phantom."

"A phantom?" Ricki lifted an eyebrow. "I thought you said that Mark had a real sense for this kind of thing?"

"He does," Alan groused. "And I don't want you to say you weren't warned."

Ricki snorted at that. "I'm not going to sue you, Counselor, so relax. But I need to know if you saw multiple sets of tracks or not?"

"I saw them." Alan inclined his head toward his friend. "We both saw them."

"Walking off in different directions," Mark supplied. "Like they split up or something."

"The tracks are how we found the body. We came across them, and what looked like drops of blood. Then there were more tracks, and they all led us around those boulders and to the body." Alan shrugged. "I saw two sets of boot prints, heading off in different directions." His gaze drifted down until he was staring at his feet. "That's all that registered before we started running."

Ricki frowned, thinking it over. "When did you see, or think you saw, someone else?"

"While we were following the tracks." Mark spoke up. "Back in the trees. I didn't see anything after we started running until I tripped and hurt my ankle. Then I saw him again. He was following us. I'm sure of it."

Cooper blew out an audible breath as he and Ricki exchanged a look. "Stay here," he told the two men before jerking his head to the side. Carrying their rifles, Ricki and Cooper walked off, stopping at the edge of the campsite where they still had a clear view of Alan and Mark. The two friends were sitting side by side with their heads hanging down.

"Multiple tracks and dead bodies? I don't like it, Ricki," Cooper said. "You need to wait until the helicopter gets here. If they send some rangers along, they can start walking out with Barry while we go together."

Ricki considered it, then shook her head. "If we do that, we'll be camping out here another night. The rescue copter won't be here for another three or four hours." She looked off to the north and studied the mountains in the distance. "I'm only going to go in, take a quick look and some pictures to verify their story, and then head back. Even if there was a body, it might not be there anymore. Some animal could have gotten to it, and probably has." When Cooper started to protest, she frowned at him. "Maybe they saw a dead body, but why would someone be watching a body that's been dead who knows how long? And if there is, he didn't take any shots at Barry and Thurman when they stumbled across it, so if this man they think they saw is still out there, then he doesn't act like he's dangerous. But I'll keep an eye out." She cradled her rifle and stamped her boots to warm up her feet. "I have my compass, so it won't take any time to travel the half mile back to that clearing where we found the two stooges over there." She gestured toward the pair of men sitting on the flat rock. "And I doubt if they went much farther in. Another mile or so at the most."

Cooper rubbed a tired hand over his cheek before finally nodding. "Okay. But if you haven't picked up anything after another mile or so, come on back. If somebody is out there, he won't be any less dead if we don't find him for a few days, and I don't want to have a heart attack worrying about you." He pulled the sleeve of his parka back and glanced at his watch. "If you do that, you should be back here before the rescue team shows up."

Ricki reached out a gloved hand and did a fist bump with Cooper. "Deal."

Chapter 4

RICKI STOPPED BY A LARGE TREE, its branches spreading out wide overhead. Leaning back, she propped a boot against the thick, rough bark and pulled out her compass to check her direction. It was just a precaution, since she was sure she was on the right track.

Yesterday, both she and Cooper had left signs on the way back to camp, and she was simply following them, using the compass to verify her direction of travel. The air was crisp and clean, with a bite to it sharp enough to keep her moving but not uncomfortable for a hike in the woods.

Replacing her compass, Ricki followed the upward slope of the land, keeping an eye out for the broken branches and piles of twigs and stones they had used to mark their passage the day before. There were also boot prints left in the small drifts of snow between the trees. Altogether, it was like walking on a wide road with signposts along the way.

It took her less than forty minutes to reach the clearing. She smiled in satisfaction when she broke through the trees and stood at its edge. Without human beings cluttering the landscape, it was a pretty little place. Patches of grass still showed here and there despite winter rapidly closing in, and the entire area was open to the sky. Ricki waited where she was for a full minute, listening carefully to the noises around her. The occasional bird calling out and the breeze dancing over the treetops were the only sounds drifting into the clearing. She'd heard that soothing combination of wind and wild creatures a thousand times before. More importantly, there wasn't anything to indicate another human being was close by.

Deciding it was a toss-up on whether the man had gone on his way or Mark Thurman had imagined the whole thing, Ricki quickly crossed the open space. She headed directly for the spot where they'd first come up on Alan Barry and Mark Thurman.

Once her boots were occupying the same space Thurman had been sitting the day before, her gaze went carefully over the surrounding ground, looking for something that would tell her what direction they had come from. Not seeing anything obvious, she slowly stepped out, keeping north as she continued to scan the ground.

About eight feet out, she spotted the boot print embedded in a melting patch of snow. Backtracking from the direction it was pointed in, she continued on until she came to another patch of snow with a boot print. Holding her compass in one hand, and keeping her rifle ready with the other, she methodically made her way north, veering slightly to the east and then back again to the north as she followed the tracks left in patches of snow or an occasional strip of mud by the two fleeing men.

Once another forty minutes had passed, she knew she was coming up on that mile mark she'd agreed on with Cooper. Knowing she could not go much beyond that point, she let out an exasperated sigh even as she spotted another boot track. She'd been walking with her gaze glued to the ground, causing a slight cramp in her neck.

Absently rubbing the ache, she looked up, and a smile bloomed on her generous mouth. Through the trees, and not too far ahead, she could make out the shape of two large boulders. Just like Barry had penciled onto his crudely drawn map.

Nodding in satisfaction, she headed in that direction, making a beeline for the rocks. As she drew closer, she could see the fallen log in front of the boulders, confirming that this was indeed the spot that the two hunters had passed on their way to finding a body.

When Ricki reached the log, she came to a sudden stop. Not two feet away was a large dark stain on the ground.

She walked over and slowly squatted down. Placing her compass back in her jacket pocket, she pulled off one glove and gingerly reached out to touch the dark surface. Most of whatever had once pooled there had soaked into the pine needles covering the ground, leaving behind an irregular shape that looked almost black against the lighter-colored needles. The dark spot was completely dry, so while she couldn't be sure, she was betting it was blood.

This must be where the guy got shot, she thought, staring at the spot until her gaze picked up the dark splotches leading off past the boulders. It looked like a bullet hadn't kept him from running. Standing up, Ricki kept her glove off as she carefully followed the grisly trail around the edge of the two boulders.

She heard the slight buzzing of insects first. Drawn by the noise, Ricki walked in that direction. She'd covered another ten feet before she saw the flies clustered in the air over a bump on the ground. Her expression turned grim. She wished the two hunters had made the whole thing up even as she crossed over to the body lying face down in the dirt.

Ricki stood over it for a long moment, staring at the lifeless form. From the shape of the torso and hips, as well as the shaggy ends of dark hair that reached over his collar, it was a male. And there was definitely a bullet hole in the man's back, so the two men who'd found him first had been right about that. They'd also been right about a second bullet hole in the man's head.

The gaping wound at the base of his skull was larger than the one in his back and from the amount of blood that had pooled out from beneath the head, had likely shattered the front part of the skull. Ricki frowned. That meant the head shot had been taken at a closer range.

The victim's bright-red wool cap was lying a good two feet in front of him and must have flown off when he fell, but other than that, he was fully dressed. His faded blue jeans bulged out enough down his thighs that Ricki was sure he had a couple of layers of long underwear on. A black parka went halfway down his thighs, and the lower part of his legs was covered with a white powder. So was the back of his jeans as well as his dark hair and upper arms.

Studying the large square space on the man's back that was powder free, Ricki's eyes narrowed as her gaze cut to the right. Next to the victim's torso was a solid line of drag marks. Ricki eyeballed it to be almost two feet wide. It continued away from the dead man toward the surrounding trees.

Leaving that to explore later, Ricki slowly walked around the body, examining it from all sides as she snapped a continual string of pictures with the camera on her cell phone. When she reached the point where she'd started, she kneeled down. Tucking her camera away, she gingerly laid her rifle on the ground next to her, then pulled out a pair of latex gloves she'd stuck into the back pocket of her jeans.

Never leave home without them, Ricki thought with a grim smile as she pulled the gloves on and went through the dead man's pockets. She pulled out a wad of US twenty-dollar bills, along with a foreign currency. Ricki frowned. Pesos. She'd been to Mexico on several occasions, so it didn't take much to recognize its national currency.

Retrieving a plastic evidence bag from her pocket, Ricki dropped all the paper money into it and continued her search.

The only other items in the man's various pockets were a book of matches and an international driving permit. She studied the permit, which was attached to a Mexican driver's license with a paper clip.

"Santiago Garcia, twenty-three," Ricki read out softly before dropping the license into the evidence bag that held the paper money. Shaking her head over the loss of such a young life, Ricki murmured to herself, "Well, Mr. Garcia, you're a long way from home and in a very strange place. Especially with no equipment."

She looked at the drag mark leading away from the body. Or at least Santiago didn't have his equipment with him anymore. The width of the drag marks was about right for the bottom bar of a large backpack, and judging by the depth of the gouge, not only a large pack but a heavy one, too.

"So, what?" Ricki asked the silent man on the ground. "Someone came out here and killed you, then stole your pack? Seems like a lot of trouble to go to for some camping gear." She leaned back and rested her hands on top of her thighs, her gaze roaming over the dead Santiago Garcia's back. The clean space on his parka was right where the pack would have been, assuming Santiago had been wearing it when he was shot. Which meant that whatever the bullet had hit had caused it to spray all over Santiago's arms, legs, and hair.

Reaching out a finger, Ricki ran it along one of the young man's shoulders, transferring the white substance from the dark parka onto the tip of her glove. Raising her finger to her mouth, she took a small taste, her nose instantly wrinkling in disgust. Bitter. Very bitter. Ricki's eyes narrowed. Withdrawing her second, and last, evidence bag, Ricki scraped a large sample of the white powder from Santiago's clothes and into the bag.

Standing up, she took out her phone again and snapped a few more pictures before zipping it back up in her parka and turning her attention to the drag marks. Picking up her rifle, she started to follow them, then suddenly stopped. Something had flashed on the edge of her vision. Whatever it was had moved from behind one tree to another. She stood with her head bent slightly forward and her gaze sharp as she slowly scanned the tree line, trying to see what was hiding in the shadows.

When she didn't see anything out of place, her shoulders relaxed. Then she heard it again—the faint crackle that was out of sync with the surrounding forest. It was the sound made by a boot stepping on dry pine needles. She waited, barely breathing, and then heard it again.

This time it was farther on her left, as if whoever, or whatever, was making the sound was trying to move behind her. It could be a deer, or some other four-legged animal, but the shape of a deer was not the impression she'd got in that brief glimpse of something among the trees. The length had been more vertical than horizontal. Like a bear standing on its hind legs. Or a human being.

She slowly walked in a large circle, her back to the dead body and her eyes trained on the trees in front of her. Halfway around, she saw the set of tracks in a long patch of snow, with the boot prints pointing north and heading away from the body. She kept on moving, not quite completing a full circuit before there was a loud snap. Her gaze instantly shifted in that direction as her rifle came up.

She spotted the man for a split second, standing next to a huge tree trunk. He disappeared in the blink of an eye, and then the forest went silent once more.

"What the hell?" Ricki said under her breath. She'd never seen anyone just poof into nothing like that. If the man's intent was to spook her, he'd done a good job of it.

Locking her knees into place, Ricki moved away until she had a tree at her back. With one side of her protected, she continued to scan the tree line in front of her as she called out. "Hello? I know you're out there. I saw you plain as day."

When she was met with silence, she tried again. "I'm Special Agent Ricki James, with the Investigative Services Branch of the National Park Service. I'm standing next to the dead body of Santiago Garcia. If you know anything about what happened here, I'd like to talk to you."

"No. You just fix it. Or pay the price like the rest did."

The voice sounded far away and had enough of an echo as it bounced through the trees that it was hard to tell what direction it was coming from, or even if it was real.

Almost wishing it were a ghost out there, rather than a real human—maybe one with a weapon—that she couldn't see but who could see her, Ricki tried again.

"I can fix it, but I need to know what happened," she yelled back. "Show yourself and we can talk."

Once again she was met with silence, but she could feel the change around her. Whoever he was, he wasn't there any longer. A moment later, she heard footsteps floating through the trees. They grew fainter as they steadily moved off. It was only a few seconds until she couldn't hear them anymore.

For a moment she considered going after the man, but then thought better of it. She'd been with Santiago Garcia's body for a while, and if she didn't start back soon, she'd be crossing into Cooper's self-declared worry zone. While she hadn't heard a helicopter overhead, she was sure it was on its way. There was also the fact that the man in the woods had managed to sneak up on her without her having any idea he was out there until he's decided to make himself known. Since she'd practically grown up in the forests of the Northwest, that was a very rare occurrence. And, she silently admitted to herself as she took one final look around, not a very comfortable one.

Chapter 5

AN HOUR LATER, Ricki was still brooding over her encounter with the disembodied voice in the woods. She absently walked into the campsite near Egg Lake, only to find it empty. Moving over to the tent, she unzipped the front flap and stuck her head through the opening. Cooper's backpack as well as her own was inside, along with the packs and gear the two hunters had brought along. Since it wasn't likely any of them would have left the area on foot without their packs, she took a step backwards, closed the tent and glanced at her watch.

She hadn't heard the approach of a helicopter, but according to the timetable Cooper had laid out that morning, it should be coming soon. Which meant he'd probably taken Barry and the injured Thurman to the clear area at the far end of the lake. Following the narrow track leading out of the campsite, Ricki turned right when it met the larger trail and headed down toward the lake.

Even with a frigid breeze freezing her cheeks and a gray sky poised with the constant threat of snow, it was impossible not to lose herself in the sheer beauty of her surroundings. The idyllic scene of blue-green water against the backdrop of trees and mountains seeped into her senses and soothed the jagged-edged nerves that had dogged her all the way back to the camp. When she reached the lake, she shifted into a slow trot, traversing the distance to the far end in fifteen minutes. She immediately spotted Cooper, standing with one hand cupped against his forehead to shade his eyes as he stared off to the west. Close to him were the two men they'd chased down, sitting cross-legged on the ground with their hands behind their backs.

Must have made use of those zip ties after all, she mused as she came up beside her fellow agent. "No sign of the helicopter?"

Cooper lowered his hand and glanced over at her. "Not yet. How did you make out? Find a body?"

"Yeah." She nodded a confirmation when Cooper's jaw dropped to his chest.

He shook his head in disbelief as his gaze met hers. "You aren't kidding, are you?"

At the faint sound of metal blades rhythmically slicing through the air, Ricki looked up. She couldn't make out anything flying against the gray sky, but she could definitely hear it. "It sounds like Thurman and Barry's ride will be here in a few minutes."

As the sound grew louder, Cooper returned his gaze to the west. "Yeah. And once we get them on their way, I want to hear all about this body."

There was a lot more to tell than just the dead man, but with the beat of the rotor blades growing louder by the second, it wasn't the time to get into it. Turning around, she walked over to where the two men were sitting and squatted down next to Mark Thurman.

"Are you ready to get out of here and get that ankle looked at?"

Mark dragged his gaze away from the approaching helicopter and took a slow look around. "I guess they won't be landing?"

Ricki shook her head, sending the long ponytail anchored

at the base of her neck sliding across her back. "No. There's not enough cleared area to do that, so they'll send down a basket." When Mark's shoulders hunched over, Ricki reached out a gloved hand and gave his arm a quick, reassuring pat.

"You'll be strapped in as tight as a sardine in a can. All you'll have to do is lie still." When he sent her a skeptical look, she nodded and smiled. "Once you're on your way, it might help if you close your eyes and count to one hundred. Before you're finished, you'll be safe and sound inside the helicopter."

The corners of his mouth twitched slightly upward. "Is that what you do?"

"I've put my share of people into one of those baskets, but I've never ridden in one myself." She let her smile grow a fraction of an inch. "It looks like fun, though."

The middle-aged man looked back up as the helicopter made a slow pass right over their heads. "Yeah, fun."

Hoping the transfer went smoothly, and that Thurman wasn't afraid of heights, which could lead to some serious problems while he was being lifted into the air, she left him to fret in silence. Her gaze then shifted over to the lawyer, who was watching her intently.

"Something on your mind, Mr. Barry?"

"Yes. I'd prefer to stay with Mark and ride out on the helicopter." His jaw set into a firm line when she gave him an amused look. "I have a right to do that."

"Oh?" Ricki kept her voice polite even as she rolled her eyes. "Which constitutional amendment would that be?"

"Common decency," he shot back. "I've been up here without any proper facilities or decent food for days and shouldn't have to walk almost ten miles over rough terrain to access services for my basic needs."

She tilted her head to one side and stared back at him. "Well, the permit you requested was for five days, as I recall. And this is your fourth day here, so I'd say you'll have to wait another twenty-four hours before you start making that demand."

Barry's face turned a bright red as he glared at her, fire spitting from his gaze. "And you expect me to hike out of here with your gun aimed at my back?"

"If we hadn't shown up, how were you planning on getting out of here?" Ricki wondered out loud, as if she were talking to herself.

His mouth thinned, but he kept it closed while he deliberately turned his head and stared off into the distance in a stony silence.

Feeling sympathy for any judge who would have to sit and listen to Alan Barry's load of crap, Ricki rose to her feet and stepped away to rejoin Cooper. They watched as the helicopter made its final sweep and came to a hovering position not far from where they were standing.

A man appeared in the open doorway and leaned out far enough to have Ricki drawing in a breath as he surveyed the ground below. He was dressed in a bright-orange jumpsuit overlaid with a black harness and wore a white helmet. From their angle almost directly below him, it looked as if he'd stepped out into the air. It wasn't until he was completely clear of the aircraft that they could see the line he was holding on to, attached to the harness on one end and a long-armed winch at the top. Both Ricki and Cooper moved forward as he was lowered down, intent on guiding him away from any large boulders or other embedded hazards so he could put his feet solidly on the ground.

Once he'd unhooked his harness, he gave a thumbs-up to his spotter, leaning out the door of the helicopter. As the line was retracted back up to the helicopter, he turned and nodded at the two agents, raising his voice to be heard over the loud clap of the rotor blades overhead.

"I'm Lieutenant Scott Vance, with the Search and Rescue Unit based out of Bellingham. Which one of you is Special

Agent Cooper Warner?" When Cooper lifted a hand, the lieutenant held out one of his. "Good to meet you, sir."

Scott was an inch under six feet, with wide shoulders tapering to a flat waist. With his helmet on, it was impossible to tell the color of his hair, but he had light-brown eyes set into a deeply tanned face.

"Not a 'sir,'" Cooper corrected as he bumped fists with Scott's gloved hand. "Just Cooper." He gestured toward Ricki. "This is Special Agent Ricki James. She came along to help track down the two suspects."

Scott glanced over at the two handcuffed men sitting on the ground. Both were watching them with wide eyes. His gaze shifted back to Ricki. "It looks like your hunt was successful." With the deafening noise still raining down from above, Ricki kept her response to a nod.

"Okay. Let's get this going." The rescue Ranger looked up and lifted another thumb into the air. "They're going to start lowering the heli-basket for your injured hiker. Start walking them over here one at a time. The injured man first."

Cooper frowned. "One at a time? I thought you were only taking one."

Scott shook his head while his eyes stayed glued on the basket being swung out, away from the helicopter's landing skids. "I have orders to take both of the suspects." He spared Cooper a quick glance. "And per your request, there will be officers in Bellingham waiting to arrest them both. Once we get the second guy on his way up, we need to have a quick talk."

Ricki only shrugged when Cooper tossed her a questioning look. She had no idea what Hamilton had told the rescue unit, but they'd have to wait until Barry and Thurman were on their way before they could hear it.

The next hour was busy with getting the two men up and in position, then safely secured for their trip up to the helicopter. Ricki ignored the smug look on the lawyer's face when she told him he'd also be getting a ride out. The jerk didn't deserve it, but those were Hamilton's orders, and he was the SAC--the senior agent in charge of the Seattle office. And, as Scott had pointed out, her boss. Since Seattle was the closest office to North Cascades Park for this operation, he was also Cooper's boss. At least temporarily.

It was just another thing that she couldn't do anything about, so Ricki concentrated on the job at hand: escorting the two men closer to the drop zone, where Cooper removed their zip-tie cuffs. Then they both steadied the heli-basket as Scott secured one man, and then the next, inside.

Because of his injury, Thurman went first, which left Ricki to put up with Barry's growing smirk longer than she wanted to. But it did give her mood a lift when she saw the white-knuckled grip the lawyer kept on the edges of the basket. What seemed like a permanent sneer on his face was replaced by a look of fear as he rose into the air. Maybe it was a little petty on her part to hope the ride up made him puke all over himself, but she figured she was entitled to a little spite for all the trouble he'd given her and Cooper.

Once the basket cleared the ground, with Barry clinging to it for dear life, Scott jerked his head to the side and moved off. Ricki followed him, with Cooper bringing up the rear.

When the lieutenant stopped, he took off his helmet and tucked it under one arm, revealing a short military-style buzz cut. He still had to shout, but not quite as loud, as he looked over and addressed Ricki. "My captain told me that Senior Agent Hamilton first wanted confirmation that you were here and in one piece." He grinned. "I'll relay that you're good to go. And I hope you'll fill me in on the story behind that." He sighed and pulled off his gloves, stuffing them inside his helmet. "He also said that there might be another extraction needed?"

Cooper nodded. "A dead body. Ricki found it earlier this

morning and has the location marked about two miles from here."

"A dead body," Scott repeated, the last of his grin completely fading away. "Okay. Let me take care of some business here." He strode off, leaving the two agents staring after him.

"I wonder what he's up to?" Cooper voiced aloud once the ranger was out of earshot.

"I'm betting Hamilton told him about the possibility of having to remove a dead body, and that's why he asked to give the snarky lawyer a ride. To get him out of our way."

While Cooper grunted his agreement, Ricki watched Scott set his helmet on the ground and then lift both arms into the air. He gave a quick series of hand signals to the crewman watching from the helicopter. Less than a minute later, a backpack was attached to the line and lowered to the ground.

Scott easily dealt with the wildly swinging pack, managing to corral it and get it unhooked before waving the helicopter off. As it headed west, the ranger kneeled and took a satphone out of a side pocket of his pack. He made a quick call, then tucked the phone away again. Shouldering the pack, he walked back to where Ricki and Cooper were waiting.

"I made a call to get a recovery team going," he said without preamble. "Since Hamilton gave us a heads-up about a possible dead body, I contacted the park's ranger office before coming out here to arrange for some of their guys to meet up with a couple of mine if there was a need." He paused as he drew in a breath. "And it sounds like there is. I spoke to Jonah, my team's lead, and he'll have the guys on the trail at first light tomorrow morning."

Ricki stuck her gloved hands into the large pockets of her parka and did a quick calculation in her head. By the time they got here, there wouldn't be enough daylight left to safely make the round trip to retrieve Garcia's body. Which meant that would be the task for the next day. And even then, once they had the body back at Egg Lake and ready for transport, there wouldn't be enough time to hike out of the park.

She glanced over at Cooper. "The time we'll need to get this done says we have at least another couple of nights here, and possibly three."

Cooper nodded his agreement. "Yeah. We won't be able to get started until the carry-out team is here, and by the time we get to the body, and then figure out how to get it someplace the rescue copter can pick it up, it will be too late to make the hike out." He pointed at Scott's backpack. "I hope you brought some food with you, or we might have to eat the evidence for our case."

Scott's forehead wrinkled as he looked from Cooper to Ricki. "Evidence?"

"Those two taking the cushy ride home were illegally hunting in the park. They shot a Canada goose," Ricki said. "If we eat the evidence, we won't be able to make our case, because super lawyer Alan Barry will deny the whole thing if he thinks he can get away with it."

The ranger chuckled. "I have provisions, and the guys are bringing in more. We won't need to eat your goose."

"Do these provisions include coffee?" Cooper asked hopefully. "It's ice cold in the morning out here, and having no coffee is adding a shit layer on top of an already miserable start to a day."

"I brought coffee." Scott laughed.

He sobered quickly when he glanced over at Ricki. "So, what about our dead guy? Was it an accident?"

"No. He was shot," Ricki stated bluntly. "Twice." She pointed at the trail leading around the lake. "Your guys will be coming in on the main trail, which is not far from the campsite. Let's head that way and get settled, and I'll fill you both in."

Chapter 6

"GARCIA, Santiago. Male. Hispanic. Twenty-three years old. Approximately five nine, one seventy," Ricki said, her gaze flat as she stared at the ground in front of the small portable stove left behind by the two hunters. She'd given a lot of updates and reports on dead people and had never liked talking about any of them as if they were numbers on a statistics sheet. And this one was no exception.

She paused to take a sip from the steaming mug Cooper had handed to her. He'd fired up the stove and Scott had supplied the coffee, which was why they were all sitting on the ground and cradling a warm cup between their hands. It scraped away the surface chill of the day but still didn't make the bare facts of Santiago Garcia's death any easier to report.

"I guess he must have had ID on him?" Scott asked.

"An international driving permit," Ricki said. "Attached to his license, issued by the state of Jalisco in Mexico. The victim had two gunshots. One in his back, and one at the base of his skull. The one at the base had a larger entry wound than the one in his back, and a large enough exit wound to shatter the front part of the skull."

"So the shooter was closer when he put that second bullet

into Garcia," Cooper murmured. When Scott made a low sound in his throat, the agent looked over at him. "Since Ricki said she followed a blood trail, the first shot must have slowed him down, but not taken him down. The second one would have finished the job."

"Or the shooter waited until he collapsed, then walked up and killed him," Ricki said quietly. "Either way, Mr. Garcia was murdered here in the park."

"Twenty-three," Scott said quietly. "What a waste." He took a sip of his coffee, then sighed. "Any idea why he was out here by himself?"

"Someone killed him, so he wasn't by himself," Cooper said. "He might also have had a buddy with him who got away and is still hiking out to get help."

Ricki considered it, then shook her head. "Maybe," she said in a way that clearly conveyed that she didn't think so. It was a habit of hers. Like tapping her boot whenever she was irritated or focusing in on something. Which she was doing now. "But the odds of him being ambushed by a stranger that far off the main trail are very small. Add that to the fact that the blood was completely dry, and I'd guess that Garcia has been dead for at least three days. So, if he had a companion who is going for help, Santiago's buddy is either the slowest hiker on earth or completely lost."

"Or dead himself," Cooper pointed out, drawing a wince from Scott.

"Or that," Ricki agreed. "Next to the body was a solid track of something that had been dragged. And the track was deep, so whatever it was, it was heavy."

Cooper's eyebrows immediately lowered into a scowl. "Dragged? Away from the body."

Ricki let out a slow breath. "Yeah. And there weren't any marks that looked like the heels of a boot being dragged over the ground. Judging by the width and solid marking, I'd say it was the bottom frame of a backpack. It's either that or he was out there by himself with no equipment or supplies." She paused and reached down for one of the baggies she'd set next to her feet. "There was also a white powder coating his hair and shoulders as well as the backs of his thighs." She held up the clear plastic bag, the powdery contents inside easily on display. "I took a sample and had a taste. Bitter."

She handed the baggie over to Cooper when he reached for it. He peered at the powder, his gaze intense. "Bitter, you said? So, cocaine?"

Ricki nodded. "It needs to be tested, but that would be my guess. And I'm thinking it was in his pack. When the bullet hit him in the back, it must have caused some of the powder to explode outward. Which would explain why the back of his parka was clean while the areas around it were not."

"It would have to have been packed inside pretty tightly to cause that kind of reaction," Scott said quietly.

Cooper's face settled into deep lines, and his voice was harsh. "If coke exploded out of his backpack, then our victim was a drug runner? And he was smuggling drugs through the park?"

"Wouldn't be the first time," Scott's quiet response drew both their gazes. "I did a stint in southeast Texas, and one park we serviced was Big Bend, right there on the border. We heard stories about drug busts in the park. It was isolated, rugged terrain, and not overrun with visitors. It only drew about half a million a year, as I recall, which is peanuts compared to most of the big parks. And it's not as heavily patrolled as other areas of the border. The park service just doesn't have the manpower."

"Isolated and rugged terrain." Ricki nodded. That certainly fit the North Cascades, too. Not to mention the annual visitors here topped off at less than 10 percent of what went through Big Bend, making it even easier for a hiker to go unnoticed. "Which would make this park a target for smuggling drugs into Canada," she said, finishing her thought out loud.

Her fellow agent scuffed the heel of one boot through the dirt. "Well, isn't that a kick in the pants?" He handed the plastic evidence bag back to Ricki. "Do you think our vic was shot by one of his fellow smugglers?"

"I don't know." Ricki set the bag back down on the ground and stretched her long legs out in front of her, crossing her boots at the ankles. "Drug smuggling isn't one of my areas of expertise."

"Mine either," Cooper said with a sigh.

"I don't much like the idea of bringing my guys into a situation like this," Scott declared. "We're going to need more help." He leaned forward and rested his forearms on top of his thighs. "I don't suppose your boss would be willing to kick more of his agents free to tag along with my team?"

Ricki lifted her shoulders and stayed silent. She honestly didn't know. But with evidence pointing to drugs, not to mention a dead body, Scott had good reason to be worried, so it wouldn't hurt to ask.

Technically, North Cascades Park was in the Seattle office's district, which made Hamilton the person to ask. But it was a big district, and like everyone else, they were shorthanded. There was also the hard fact that dealing with drug running was way out of her wheelhouse. The occasional marijuana patches discovered inside a park were dealt with by that park's law enforcement unit. Or the FBI, if the park service chose to call them in.

The thought sent a cold chill down her spine. This would be just the sort of opening Dr. Jonathan Blake would jump at. She'd butted heads before with the famous FBI profiler and had already had the dubious pleasure of being manipulated into serving on one of his "inter-agency" task forces. A pet project of his that Ricki did her best to avoid.

The man had been a thorn in her side ever since he'd

unexpectedly shown up in her small hometown, offering his help and pitching his notion of a task force pulling from the expertise of different agencies. While the only one she'd served on had been a success, that didn't mean she wanted any part of it again. If that's where this was headed, Cooper was welcome to take on the investigation, and she'd be happy to go back and cool her heels in Olympic Park.

"How much cocaine do you figure this Santiago character might have been carrying?" Scott tossed out.

"He could have managed a forty-pound pack," Ricki replied.

"And forty pounds is forty pounds, no matter what makes it up," Cooper added. "I'd have to look it up to figure out what the street value is for that much cocaine, but I'll bet it's well over a million dollars."

Yeah, me too, Ricki thought as she turned the idea over in her mind. A million dollars was a lot of money. Certainly worth stealing. Or killing for.

"Anything else to share about your excursion this morning?"

Cooper's question jolted Ricki out of her own thoughts. She took a sip of coffee while she settled herself back into the present. "I was going to follow the drag marks but didn't get a chance. I was interrupted by a voice coming out of the trees."

Once again Cooper was gaping at her. "You're kidding? You heard Thurman's ghost?"

On the opposite side of the tight circle they'd formed around the small stove, Scott sat straight up, blinking rapidly as he stared at her.

Even though she'd harbored the same thought herself about a ghost, Ricki wrinkled her nose at both men. "No. I heard someone hiding in the trees. I caught a glimpse of him and he wasn't a ghost. But he didn't come out to introduce himself, either."

"So, this unfriendly not-a-ghost, what did he have to say?" Cooper demanded.

"Not much. Just 'you fix it or pay the price like the others did.' And then he poofed out of sight."

"Poofed out of sight?" Cooper frowned. "So he *is* a ghost?"

"No. That's just the best way I can come up with to describe it, and it seemed to be a well-developed skill of his. A pretty impressive one, too."

Scott's gaze jumped back and forth between them until it finally settled on Ricki. "What did he mean when he said, 'like the others did'? It sounds like there are more bodies out there."

"Wouldn't surprise me at this point. Drug dealing has a way of doing that." Cooper answered for her. He leaned forward and picked up a potholder lying next to the stove before grabbing the handle of the coffee pot. He poured steaming liquid into his mug before replacing the pot on top of the stove.

"Alleged drug dealing. We still need to get the powder tested," Ricki said absently. "I don't know what he meant by 'others,' Scott. And it sounded like a threat, but he didn't sound dangerous or menacing when he said it. He sounded like he was having a chat."

A loud snort escaped from Cooper. "A chat? Was he having this chat with a gun pointed at you?"

"I assumed so, but I didn't actually see one," Ricki admitted. "And we won't know for sure what's going on until Santiago's murder is investigated. Because whether or not he was a drug runner, he was still murdered in the park. Which makes it the ISB's responsibility."

Scott slapped his palms against his knees, then stood up. "Well, I'll leave that to both of you and your boss, but I'll say this. If we can't get more protection out there, I won't be sending my guys to get that body." He lifted an expectant eyebrow at Ricki. "Which reminds me, your boss is expecting a call, and he made it clear that it would be my head if you didn't make it. So now on top of giving him your report, you can let him know what I said."

She nodded her understanding. "I will. We'll work something out and keep your head intact while we're at it." She gave him a smile. "After all, you brought the coffee."

Looking satisfied with that, Scott relaxed his shoulders as he nodded at Cooper. "And thank you for making it. Mine never turns out quite right."

Cooper laughed, his gaze cutting over to Ricki. "Can't be worse than hers. Ricki's coffee is always some kind of cross between tar and sludge."

Scott's eyes shone with amusement. "Is that so?"

Ignoring Ricki's glare, Cooper also stood up. "True words. And she told me she owns a diner back in Brewster. Hard to imagine. The woman is such a disaster in the kitchen that warning notices were posted throughout the entire branch."

The ranger's grin spread until it reached from ear to ear, but he politely didn't utter one word.

Ricki got to her feet so she was on the same level as the two men, who were clearly struggling to hold back their laughter. "My hometown is Brewer, not Brewster, and I would remind you, Agent Warner, and you, too, Lieutenant Vance, that this 'woman' will be the one protecting your collective backsides when we go to collect Santiago's body. So, be nice."

Scott blinked, then pointed at Cooper. "Is that true?"

The agent grinned at Ricki, who gave him a bland stare. "Oh yeah. I'd swear on my mother's grave that Special Agent James over there is one of the best shots in the whole agency."

Ricki rolled her eyes upward. "His mother isn't dead, so that doesn't mean much, but I can guarantee that I'm a better shot than he is, Scott, so you'd better stick with me."

"Ouch. That hurt," Cooper declared.

"And on that note," Scott put in. "Maybe we can look at a

map and you can show me where the body is so we can tag several spots close by that might work for the helicopter? If we already know where we're going, it will save us time when the team gets here. And right now, it sounds like it's better if we spend as little time out there as possible."

She nodded. "It won't be easy, but I think we can narrow it down enough to make it doable."

Over the next hour, she and Cooper huddled around a map Scott had laid out on the ground. The ranger had already drawn an X on the spot Ricki had pointed out, and they'd radiated out from there, with Ricki giving her best guess on where the bigger clearings would be based on the topography of the map. She also drew on her general knowledge of what she remembered from her hikes on the main trail.

"Yeah. We'll need to check that one out first." Scott stared at the place where Ricki's finger was resting. "It's not too far. We don't want to transport the body over land any longer than we have to."

"Even at that distance, it isn't going to be an easy trip," Cooper said. "There's nothing soft about this park."

"No, there isn't," Ricki agreed. "And we have another immediate problem."

Cooper ran a distracted hand over the top of his hair. "Yeah. The park visitors. We might have a killer running loose. Those two things are not a good combination."

"It's the end of the season," Scott pointed out. "And I know this park doesn't get a lot of visitors anyway, so there shouldn't be many people roaming the trails this time of year."

"Even one is one too many at this point," Ricki said. Her boot started tapping against the packed dirt as she looked out over the ridge toward the small lake in the valley below. "We're going to need some help to do the walk-through."

Cooper crossed his arms over his chest. "We can get a permit list from the local ranger office."

Scott nodded. "I can have my guys pick it up on their way in."

Cooper's mouth pulled down at the corners. "This park is fairly new to me, but as I recall from the map, there aren't that many trails up here." He looked over at Ricki. "Only two main ones that I remember."

She nodded. "That's right. Copper Ridge and the Chilliwack Trail. I'm thinking the one that intersects Chilliwack farther south is the more traveled one. It heads toward Whatcom Pass."

Scott retrieved his map and folded it up. "Like I said, my two guys are coming this way with four rangers assigned to this park. Maybe they can help you out." He sighed. "When I call this in, I'll be sure to ask if we can stay on and help. But we're spread pretty thin, so I'm guessing we'll be told to leave the trail sweep to the local unit and hightail it back to our base." He nodded at Ricki. "You need to make a call, too. I have a satphone if you need one."

"Thanks, but I'm good. Cooper brought one for us." Ricki smiled when Cooper, taking the hint, immediately did an about-face and headed for the tent, where he'd left both their packs.

When he returned, Ricki took the phone and walked over to the far side of the campsite. She put in Hamilton's number, not surprised when he picked up on the second ring. The senior agent was dedicated to his job and made a point of always being available to his team.

"Hamilton. And it's getting late enough in the day this had better be you, Agent James."

She smiled. "It is. I made it up to the site and back in one piece."

"I've already been informed that you found a body up

47

there," Hamilton stated, his voice all business. "What can you tell me about it?"

Ricki shifted her weight into a more comfortable stance as she went through a quick report for her boss. He listened, not making any comment until she finished with "He didn't give the impression of being dangerous."

"Just your typical, friendly guy who hangs around a dead body in the woods for a couple of days?" Hamilton growled out. "You're going to have a hard time selling that one, Ricki." He blew out a breath strong enough it sounded like a windstorm over the phone. "We need help up there."

"I couldn't agree with you more," Ricki said. "Where can we get it from within the agency?" Ricki made sure to emphasize that last part. She knew how stretched the Seattle office was, which was why Cooper had been called in from another district to help. But she still didn't want to put any ideas into the senior agent's head about where to go looking for help. "We also need to alert any visitors in this section of the park."

"Agreed," Hamilton said. "But that part isn't your problem. I'll make a call to the ranger headquarters there and get that in motion. Your problem is a dead body and a missing backpack that's possibly filled with cocaine."

He continued to go over the various challenges the case was facing while Ricki listened. When he concluded by telling her she would be assigned to this case, along with Cooper, she didn't say anything, but gave a mental sigh. There were a lot of loose ends at home she was dealing with that would now have to be put on the back burner.

More than just a few, she thought with a mental groan. By the time she'd hung up the phone and walked back to where Cooper was waiting, she already had a list going in her head. He gave her a questioning look when she held on to the phone.

"So?" Cooper asked when she simply picked up her now

cold cup of coffee with her free hand and took an absent-minded sip. "What did the boss have to say?"

"Lucky you. He's going to arrange for you to be assigned to the case," Ricki said, feeling a tug of empathy when Copper's entire face slowly drooped. "Me too, if that makes you feel any better."

Her fellow agent immediately perked up. "It does." When a cold finger of wind lanced its way across the campsite, he shivered then stuck his hands into his pockets.

"You know, it used to get cold in the Appalachians," Cooper said, referring to his previous assignment before coming west. "But nothing like it does up here. I hope Hamilton had some idea of how long we'll have to be on scene if there's just the two of us working on this."

"Hamilton said he was going to get us some help, but since he didn't know where from and we've got to get started, he asked me to make a few calls, just to be sure."

Cooper barked out a short laugh. "Why? Do you have a personal army at your disposal?"

Ricki smiled as she lifted the phone and punched in a number. "Not an army." She waited, smiling when this call was also picked up on the second ring. "Hi, there. It's me. I can't talk long, but we've got something pretty serious going on here, and there's just Cooper and me to deal with it. So I'm hoping you can shake free for a few days and lend us a hand." She paused, listening, then smiled. "That's great. I'd appreciate it if you would get in touch with Hamilton. He has all the details." She paused again, long enough to grin at Cooper. "And ask my cook if he can come along, too."

Chapter 7

"Your cook? You asked your cook to come along?"

Cooper's question was overlaid with a heavy dose of curiosity—one that Ricki wasn't inclined to satisfy. He'd find out soon enough that her cook had skills that went far beyond the kitchen.

"He's an extraordinary cook," she said, quickly turning her back on Cooper so he couldn't see her grin.

"But a cook?" Cooper repeated. "Out on an investigation? Geez, Ricki. If you're afraid of poisoning yourself, I'll make your meals."

Scott stopped in the middle of pacing off the perimeter of the clearing and turned with his hands on his hips. "It's a recovery mission first, and this area is too small." He gestured toward the surrounding forest. "One wild swing of the basket in this wind and it will be tangled up in the trees."

The threesome had started out early that morning to scout around for a good spot for the helicopter to pick up Santiago Garcia's body. The lieutenant hadn't been keen on just the three of them looking for a good extraction point, which meant going out on their own without the safety of numbers. But Ricki had pointed out that the smaller group could move faster and quieter than the entire team. The ranger had conceded her point but was still reluctant until Cooper had stated that the team would spend less time on the recovery, and therefore less time out in the field as a target, if they knew exactly where they were going. Once Scott had agreed, it hadn't taken them long to get going.

Since Ricki had already traveled the route several times, she led the way. Their small group reached the murder site in forty-five minutes. Ricki had made a point of bringing along a plastic tarp left behind by the hunters to cover the body. Once she'd done that, and weighted the corners down with four separate piles of rocks, they headed north toward the first site they'd marked on the map as a possible extraction point.

But, with the limited information from the map, the spot had turned out to be little more than a sliver of an opening in the trees, so they'd quickly moved on. Their second stop had been more to the east, and while it had a good open section, it would also mean climbing up a steep embankment. It wouldn't have been an issue for any member of the team to do on their own, but hauling a body with them would have been a challenge, and more importantly, it would take more time than Scott was comfortable with.

Now, they were standing on the last marked place on their map, and it was plain that the ranger still wasn't happy.

Scott walked back to where the two agents were standing and shook his head. "So, do we keep looking, or will I have to settle for that last site up on that ridge?"

Ricki glanced over at Cooper. "How far out do you think the body is from the lake?"

"Right now? Somewhere under two miles." He paused, his forehead wrinkled in thought. "It wasn't a bad hike until we started coming farther north." He lifted an eyebrow at Ricki. "Are you thinking what I'm thinking?"

Certain that they were indeed on the same page, Ricki nodded. "Yeah." She centered her gaze on Scott. "At this point we know a helicopter can safely drop the basket near the lake, and we know the way from the location where Garcia was killed back to our campsite. It isn't a difficult hike, and there aren't any ridges to climb."

"I know where we're standing is less than half that distance from the body," Cooper put in, "but it's a more difficult route than simply retracing our steps back to camp. And like you said, we haven't found a good place for the extraction yet, so if we keep looking, there's no telling how much farther out we'll have to go. Not to mention the time we'll burn taking some stabs in the dark to find another spot."

"We can get to the crime scene, pick up the body and haul our tails back in no time by making the trip in quick shifts." Ricki added a firm nod when Scott's expression turned thoughtful. "Even carrying a stretcher, I'll bet we can make the run back in an hour."

"An hour and a quarter, tops," Cooper chimed in.

Both agents waited, letting out a collective breath when Scott slowly nodded.

"Yeah," the ranger said. "Yeah, I can see that. The helo pilot will know exactly where to go, and if we get an early start, it should leave us enough time to hike out of here." His lips twitched when he looked over at Ricki. "And we won't have to put your cook out, getting a meal ready for the extra mouths." He tilted his head to the side. "Providing, of course, he's willing to take on the cooking duties for the whole team."

Cooper laughed. "What duties? Boiling water to add to our freeze-dried meals? Unless you're thinking we should cook that goose after all."

"It's been hanging for at least three days in a bag of ice that's probably melted and refrozen at least twice," Ricki pointed out. "I'll pass on the goose." She returned Scott's smile. "So we're agreed on taking Mr. Garcia's body back to Egg Lake?"

Scott nodded. "Agreed." He cast a quick look around. "I'll

make the arrangements for the airlift when we get back to camp. Now let's get out of here. I'm seeing ghosts behind every tree."

Having no problem with that, Ricki cradled her rifle and started off toward the east. When Cooper yelled out, she looked over her shoulder and saw him pointing in the opposite direction.

"We came in that way," he said.

She countered by lifting her free hand and pointing to the east. "I know. But we've come far enough that I'm guessing the main trail is less than a half mile or so that way, and while it will take a bit of climbing, it will be much faster than that cross-country route we took getting here."

Cooper immediately switched directions, with Scott falling in behind him. Ricki had already taken out her compass, and kept it in her hand, following as straight a line as she could. About halfway to the main trail, Ricki stopped, causing Cooper to step quickly to the side so he wouldn't plow into her back.

His intense, dark-eyed stare swept across the forest in front of them. "What's up?"

Ricki looked off to their left, then stepped forward to peer around Cooper. When he repeated his question, she pointed to the ground. "It looks like someone has come through here recently." She frowned as her gaze followed the faint path until it disappeared into the trees.

"I'd say you're right, but anyone could have come through here," Cooper said. "Are you thinking it's our ghost?"

"It could be," she said, still studying the ground. "And for the record, he's *your* ghost and *my* flesh-and-blood human being."

"Who moves like a ghost," Cooper put in.

Silently agreeing, Ricki only shrugged, and after consulting her compass, started moving again. They maintained a brisk walk, breaking through the trees and onto the

Copper Ridge Trail twenty minutes later. The views were breathtaking everywhere you looked, but Ricki barely noticed them as she picked up the pace, intent on returning to the campsite before the rescue team arrived.

They made the two-mile trip back in good time, but it was already well past noon when they approached the trail branching off toward Egg Lake. As they came up on the campsite, Ricki heard the team before she saw them. When she rounded the last bend in the footpath leading up to the site, she called out to the group of men to alert them to their presence.

The small campsite was overrun with bodies. A few were moving around, but most of the guys were sitting on the ground, their packs all standing on end and neatly lined up in two rows next to the tent.

A tall man with dark-blond hair and gray eyes immediately got to his feet and walked over to meet her. He didn't hesitate, but curled his arms around Ricki's back and pulled her toward him. The move took her by surprise. It was an unspoken agreement between them not to put their personal relationship on display when they were on the job.

"Clay," she protested. That's as far as she got before his mouth settled on hers. Ricki quickly lifted her hand holding the compass and pressed her fist firmly against his shoulder. "Come on," she said, leaning back, straining to break his hold on her without looking obvious about it. "We're working here."

The look he gave her had her frown deepening. It was both apologetic and distant. There was something about it that was off.

"Sorry. I was taking a break," Clay said, his voice light, but the usual teasing note in it fell flat.

"And I'm carrying a rifle," she whispered back at him. His laugh had a hollow ring, but he immediately loosened his hold and took a long step back, putting a foot of space between them in a complete reversal of his previous move.

Wondering what was going on, she gritted her teeth at the sound of a low whistle from Cooper, who had come up behind her. Aiming a dagger glare at her fellow agent, she took a step sideways, putting even more distance between herself and Clay.

"So," Cooper said with a wide grin. "Is this why you wanted the cook to come along so badly?"

At the sudden spate of coughing from the group behind her, Ricki shot Cooper another warning glance. "No. And he's not the cook." She had to clench her mouth shut to keep from snapping out when one man behind her snickered. Taking a deep breath, she got her spike of anger under control. "This is Clayton Thomas. He's the chief of police in the Bay."

Cooper sent Clay an amused look as he shook the chief's hand. "I know what a police chief is, but how do you patrol a bay? In a boat?"

"Not a bay," Ricki corrected, her voice still tight. "*The* Bay. It's three small towns right along the highway that separates Olympic Park from Dabob Bay. And that includes my hometown of Brewer that you've insisted on calling Brewster for the last ten years."

Clay nodded but his smile was stiff. "Three towns, one police chief. Part-time now." He looked over at Scott. "You must be Lieutenant Vance. Hamilton filled me in on your recovery mission."

"Scott is good enough, Chief," the ranger said as he clasped Clay's outstretched hand. "And I'm glad to see you. We can use the extra eyes and protection on this one."

"I'm not on my police chief duty right now, so it's Clay, and I'm only part of your protection, not heading up the investigation." Clay tilted his head toward Ricki. "Cooper is, and Ricki's on protection duty too, along with that tree that's sprouted legs and is walking over here."

The man Clay had pointed to ignored the jibe as he stopped to give Ricki a quick, friendly pat on her shoulder. He really was built as solid as a tree stump, and had a couple of inches on Clay's six-foot frame. That put the big man half a foot taller than Ricki and Cooper, since the two agents were about the same height. The big man nodded at Scott then stared at Cooper for a long, deliberately intimidating moment, before offering his hand.

"I'm the cook."

"You are?" Cooper's voice came out half an octave higher than his usual mellow tone. He quickly cleared his throat as he shook the offered hand. "Um. I'm Special Agent Cooper Warner. Glad to meet you, Mister . . . ?

The man let the question hang in the air before he finally smiled. "Anchorman. I'm just Anchorman."

One park ranger who had been avidly listening to the exchange took that as a cue and strolled over. He clapped a hand solidly on top of Anchorman's shoulder. "I've been over to that diner Ricki owns and can attest that Anchorman here is a great cook. But I think he's here for his other skills." The thin, lanky man with a bushy mustache grinned at Ricki. "You were busy chasing down some serial killer the last time I was over your way, so we never got a chance to meet. I'm Darren Jenson, but everyone calls me DJ. I'm one of the rangers assigned here to North Cascades Park."

Ricki smiled as she shook his hand. "Glad to meet you, DJ. We'd appreciate it if you would introduce us to the rest of the team."

Darren quickly accommodated the request, with each man nodding or raising a hand in a casual salute as he called out a name. As the rest of the team went back to settling into the campsite, a slightly older man, with threads of silver weaving through his dark hair, stepped forward. His brown eyes sparkled with humor.

He shook Scott's hand first before both men turned

toward Ricki. "Special Agent James, like DJ said, this is Jonah Barnes. He's the lead for the team."

"It's good to meet you," Jonah said, offering his hand. "I've heard good things."

Jonah's smile was infectious, and Ricki couldn't help but return it. "Thanks."

Anchorman visibly winced at the sound of a yelp followed by the thud of the coffee pot hitting the ground. He glared over his shoulder at the offending ranger, who was blowing on his fingers. "I'll let you all talk shop." Without another word, he turned on his heels and strode over to the small stove, scooping up the potholder and then the coffee pot before talking in a low voice to the ranger, who was still waving his hand back and forth.

"Anchorman?" Cooper said, keeping his voice down so it wouldn't drift over to where the big man was standing, dumping out the remaining coffee and refilling the pot with fresh water. "Does he do a news broadcast along with being your cook?"

DJ let out a hoot of laughter. "Not hardly. That was his handle when he was in the Marines. Earned it because he always anchored his unit and made sure every guy got out of there. All of them did, and most were still in one piece."

"Ah." Understanding dawned in Cooper's eyes. "He's a good shot, too. That's why you wanted him to come along."

The gangly ranger's laugh got even louder. "A good shot? Dang, man. That Marine was a sniper." Still chuckling, DJ shook his head. "A good shot. That's funny."

"Yeah, I'm laughing," Cooper said. Now he was the one turning a glare on Ricki. "A sniper? Your cook is a sniper? Do you think you could have mentioned that?"

His annoyed tone lightened Ricki's mood over Clay's strange behavior. She stuck her tongue in her cheek and pulled off a nonchalant shrug. "Former sniper. So cook first, sniper second."

Jonah rubbed a hand up and down his windburned cheek. "I served in the Corps, and it's been a real pleasure to meet Anchorman. But I'm not sure a trained sniper would ever consider that his second skill."

"Since you've tasted his food, you know how hard it is to tell what he's better at, shooting or cooking," Ricki said.

"Shooting," DJ declared. From the reverent look on his face, there was no doubt he was sure of that. As the other men nodded, DJ looked over at Ricki. "The chief told me about that ghost you ran into."

Ricki blinked at Clay when he gave her shoulder a slight squeeze. "Hamilton told me the whole story," he said when she continued to stare up at him.

Not thrilled that the story could easily have grown out of proportion and made the carry-out team jittery, Ricki turned her attention back to DJ. "I'm getting a little tired of everyone calling him a ghost. I saw the guy and definitely heard him. He is no ghost."

Happy to go along with her assessment, DJ bobbed his head up and down. "Yeah. That's good to know, because I was wondering if he might be the hermit."

"The hermit?" Ricki echoed, her eyebrows drawing together. "Exactly who is the hermit?"

As the other men leaned in closer, DJ noticed the sudden silence and glanced over his shoulder at the larger group. Every man was staring back at him, causing a thin sheen of red to creep up his cheeks. "Well, I don't know exactly. It's a story my dad used to tell us. He still does, for that matter. My dad claims he went to school with the guy way back in the day."

"How far back in the day are we talking about?" Ricki asked.

"Well, my dad's in his midsixties," DJ said. "So we're talking at least forty years ago, but he's always sworn that the hermit is real." DJ paused, his teeth chewing on his lower lip.

"Still, we're a ways from where Dad says the hermit is living. I mean, if the guy's still alive. Dad figured his old classmate was holed up somewhere in the Mount Baker Wilderness."

Ricki shifted her weight, unaware of Clay's mouth curving up into a smile when she started to tap one boot. "The Mount Baker Wilderness? Along the western border of the park?" When DJ nodded, she considered it. "Where did your dad go to school with this guy?"

"My dad grew up in Glacier. It's just a speck of a town, down the 542, about a half hour from the trailhead."

"I know it," Ricki said absently. "I've driven through it several times." She'd even had a bite to eat at the small bakery there on more than one occasion. That had been years ago, though, when she was a young teenager, heading for a backpacking trip in the North Cascades Park with her dad and uncle. Unlike her dad, who had definitely leaned toward the quiet, scholarly side, her friendly uncle would always strike up a conversation with a local shopkeeper wherever they stopped. Ricki had always enjoyed listening in, and even though they'd stopped in Glacier less than a handful of times, she didn't recall any of the locals her uncle had chatted with mentioning a hermit living in the surrounding wilderness. That's the kind of story that would stick with a person.

"I've never heard of a hermit, or some guy making a home inside the park or in the Mount Baker Wilderness," Ricki said slowly.

"Dad said no one talked about him much after what happened. He heard about it from another guy who he kept in touch with over the years, but it must have happened some time ago because I heard the story from dad all my life. Anyway, I guess the hermit had a wife and they both disappeared. It could be they went up to Canada." DJ shrugged. "That's what I would have done if I'd been on the run."

Ricki frowned. *On the run?*

"What was he running from?" Clay asked before she could put the thought into words.

"Dad said he murdered a guy in a bar fight one night. When the sheriff got the whole story and went out to his house to pick him up, the hermit was gone." DJ lifted a hand and snapped his fingers. "Poof. Just like that. And no one has ever seen him again."

Cooper looked over at Ricki, his eyes narrowed in speculation. "Murders a guy and then poof, he's gone? Sounds familiar."

Chapter 8

Ricki watched DJ stroll off with Scott and Jonah. She waited until they'd rejoined the rest of the team gathered on the opposite side of the campsite before turning to face Cooper, her hands on her hips.

"Being able to disappear into the trees doesn't make him a killer."

"It doesn't exactly eliminate him either," the other agent countered. "Especially considering the trees he's disappearing into just happen to be near Garcia's dead body."

It was a good point, but not enough to lock someone up and throw away the key.

When Ricki continued to stare silently at him, Cooper shrugged. "Look. I'm not trying to railroad the guy just because he's different, or maybe living illegally in the park. But right at the moment, we can tie him to the crime scene, which isn't exactly in the middle of a suburban neighborhood. So he's the only suspect we've got."

"But no hard evidence to link him to the murder," Clay said quietly as Anchorman strolled up, juggling four mugs of coffee.

The big man passed them out, keeping one for himself. He

raised it to his mouth, looking at Ricki over the cup's rim. "That whole hermit-in-the-woods thing sounds like the urban legends we used to pass around when I was a kid." He took a long sip of coffee then lowered the cup again and smiled. "You know, like saying Bloody Mary three times in front of a mirror to make her image appear. Although my personal favorite's always been that before Mr. Rogers sang about a beautiful day in the neighborhood, he was a Navy SEAL." He chuckled at that while Ricki rolled her eyes.

"Okay." She held up a hand to stop Clay and Cooper from adding their legends to top Anchorman's. "Let's stick to what we know." Her eyes narrowed in thought. "Whether he's this hermit or not, I saw and heard someone out there. And if he is this hermit that DJ talked about, all we know about him is from a secondhand story that DJ's father heard at least several decades ago. And the odds are good it was distorted back then and even more now."

"And this hermit person is our biggest threat?" Anchorman asked. "Was he armed?"

"Unknown," Ricki said. "But we have to assume he is because if he's living out here off the grid, then he would need to hunt in order to eat."

"And not the only threat," Clay put in. "From what Hamilton told me, everything points to the vic being a drug runner, which means he might have buddies hanging around."

Ricki nodded. "That's also a possibility. But his backpack was missing, so it's probable that his buddies, or whoever killed him, already have the drugs."

Anchorman shifted his weight, settling himself more comfortably on one hip. "How much do you figure he was carrying?"

Cooper lifted his hands and spread them apart. "According to Ricki, the drag track was about two feet across." He marked the distance off with his hands. "If it was the bottom of a frame, that puts it at a forty-pound pack." He looked over at Clay. "Ever dealt with drugs, Chief? Do you have any idea how much forty pounds of coke is worth?"

Clay shook his head. "I was always a homicide cop, but I did my stint in a patrol car. From what I remember, I'd put that much coke in the neighborhood of a million dollars."

A soft whistle escaped through Anchorman's teeth. "That's enough to hang around for."

"Which is why we need to get back up there," Ricki declared. "We need to see how many pairs of footprints are following those drag marks."

Her fellow agent immediately shook his head. "We promised Scott and his team a quick in-and-out. We can't be hanging around or wandering off to follow a set of tracks."

"We might have to split up," Ricki said, bracing herself for an argument when Cooper didn't look happy with the idea.

He finally used two fingers to pinch the top of his nose, between his eyebrows. "Yeah. It's either that or make another trip back." He dropped his hand in favor of stamping his feet on the ground. "And the forecast calls for snow tomorrow afternoon, so we need to get in and out fast. The body is going to get a ride back to the Bellingham morgue, but we're going to have to hike out."

Anchorman stepped to the side and tossed the remains of his coffee into the trees. "DJ told me that he had a list of all the permits issued that were good for these last few days. He said there's only four of them, so he and some of the others are going to do a trail sweep." He folded his arms over his chest. "Not sure what that is, but it sounds like they're looking for the enemy."

Ricki smiled. "Not the enemy. Other hikers and overnight campers who are in this section of the park." She looked up at the rapidly darkening sky, a forewarning of the snowstorm that the latest weather forecast said would be heading into the mountains tomorrow night. The complete loop was close to thirty miles long, through some of the most remote and rugged areas of the park. Even the rangers wouldn't be able to go all the way around it in one day. With snow threatening, it was far from an ideal scenario.

"You're thinking we should go along with them," Cooper said quietly. When she nodded, he stared at the group sitting in a sprawled-out circle near the lone tent. "I was thinking the same thing. The body isn't going to be any less dead if we don't get it to the morgue for a day or two."

"If you go, we all go," Clay stated, his hard stare a clear signal there wouldn't be any debate over the matter.

"Second that," Anchorman said. "I'm in no hurry to get home." He stuck his hands into his jacket pockets when Ricki turned his way. "I need to see about getting some food started. I promised the guys a decent meal."

When he abruptly deserted them, Ricki did another quarter turn to give Clay a head-on look. "What's up with him?"

Clay shrugged. "He and Cheron had a disagreement."

"Disagreement?" Ricki looked over at Anchorman's stiff shoulders as he rummaged through a large pack.

"Who's Cheron?" Cooper asked.

"Dr. Cheron Garrison. She's a forensic pathologist, and Anchorman's girlfriend, if he can ever talk her into it," Clay said.

Cooper blinked. "Seriously? I thought women fell all over themselves for guys like Anchorman."

Ricki crossed her arms and gave Cooper a bland stare. "Is that so? Just what kind of guy do you think a woman can't possibly resist?"

"The kind that cooks," the agent said without missing a beat. "Hell, if his food is good enough, *I* might agree to be his girlfriend."

She laughed. One thing about Cooper, he was quick on his feet. "Good answer."

He grinned back at her. "Thank you. Now I think I'll see if he needs any help and call in our report to Hamilton."

"Ask Hamilton if Dan can do some research on our so-called hermit," Ricki said. Dan Wilkes had recently transferred from the ranger unit at Olympic Park, to the Seattle office of the ISB. Like Ricki, he reported to Hamilton, but unlike Ricki, he didn't specialize in field operations. Dan was a premier researcher, a skill he'd honed in his days as an analyst with the CIA. If anyone could uncover solid information on this hermit character DJ had told them about, it was Dan.

"I'll do that." Cooper gave a pointed look at the wide piece of ground between Ricki and Clay. "That should keep me busy enough to give you two a chance to catch up."

Not if it's going to lead to a fight, Ricki thought. She had a feeling in the pit of her stomach that's exactly where it would go. When she felt rather than saw Clay tense up next to her, she knew she was right. And this still wasn't the time or the place for a kiss, or to have it out with Clay about whatever was bothering him.

Shying away from a discussion about their relationship, she opted to go with Anchorman's rocky love life. "Did Cheron and Anchorman have a disagreement, or an all-out fight?"

"Cheron is half a foot shorter and can be blown over by a puff of wind, so it wouldn't be much of a fight," Clay said.

Tamping down her exasperation, Ricki drew in a slow breath. "I wasn't talking about a physical brawl. What were they fighting about?"

"Coming here."

Surprised, she uncrossed her arms in favor of putting her hands on her hips. "Cheron didn't want Anchorman to come? Why not?"

For the first time since he'd been in camp, Clay's mouth curved into his usual relaxed smile. "Oh no. She was fine with him coming, but as soon as he told her there was a dead body involved, she wanted to come too." His smile grew. "She informed him she was your ME and needed to be there to examine the body on the scene and then hear the Whatcom County ME's report."

Slightly embarrassed and amused at the thought of having a personal medical examiner, Ricki laughed. "I take it Anchorman objected?"

Clay clapped his gloved hands together to warm them up and rocked back slightly on his heels. "Aside from Hamilton telling us there was some unknown suspect hanging out in the woods, Anchorman didn't think she was able to make the trip."

"Not able to make the trip? As in, she's too fragile?"

"Yeah. Something like that."

Ricki rolled her eyes. She could just imagine what Cheron had thought about being told that. Her hardheaded cook had a lot of wonderful qualities, and she depended on quite a few of them, but sometimes he could be a complete idiot. "He knows Cheron is going to find a way to do what she wants, doesn't he?"

Clay laughed. "No. I don't think he does." He grinned at Ricki. "And this time, I'm not seeing how. She didn't follow us in here, and I half expected her to give it a try."

"Really?" Ricki wiggled her eyebrows. "I have five dollars that says she gets her way."

"Five dollars?"

She sniffed at him. "I'm a single parent. Take it or leave it."

"I'll take it," Clay said, then jammed his hands into the oversized pockets of his parka as his smile faded away. "I owe you an apology."

Ricki cast a quick glance at the rest of the team. Since they didn't appear to be drawing anyone's attention, she quickly nodded and lowered her voice. "We need to have a talk, but . . ." She trailed off to take another sideways look at the men slowly gathering around Anchorman and the stove he was manning.

The chief sighed. "I know. This isn't the time or the place to get into it."

"No, it's not," Ricki agreed softly. She stared back at him, seeing the sad look in his gaze. "But I guess there's something we need to get into?"

Clay's shoulders lifted in a restless movement. "I don't know. Probably. Maybe not." He shook his head. "I just don't know."

Despite her resolve not to open a can of worms with the whole team within earshot, words crowded into her throat. She swallowed them all when she spotted Cooper and Scott heading their way.

"I talked to Hamilton," Cooper said by way of a greeting. "He's not happy about the situation up here, but he agreed about Dan doing some research on the hermit. Or anyone else who might have some kind of chronic sighting in the park. He's also going to ask the ranger office to go through all the permits issued this summer and see if there's anyone who was reported missing or isn't accounted for."

"That's a good thought," Ricki said.

"I certainly agree with it. It will save you some work."

"Me?"

Cooper nodded. "Yep. Since North Cascades is in your district, Hamilton is assigning you to head up the investigation, and it turns out that I'll be heading back to Colorado after all."

"But Hamilton said you'd be assigned to this investigation," Ricki protested. "What happened?"

The other agent gave a helpless shrug. "I don't know, Ricki. That's what I was told. That I'm to head back to Colorado."

Clay let out a snort before a scowl settled on his face. "So Ricki is supposed to investigate this on her own?"

"No," Cooper said with a quick, decisive shake of his head. "I wouldn't have gone for that, Chief. Hamilton is sending more help, and he wanted me to tell you that he hopes you and Anchorman will stay on until the other two agents get here."

Ricki was fine with making a stop in Glacier. She'd intended to do that anyway to see if she could corroborate the story from DJ's father and find a longtime resident who could also remember the man that legend had turned into the hermit.

"Did Hamilton happen to mention which other two agents are coming?" she asked absently.

"No, he didn't. And he ignored me when I asked."

That got Ricki's attention. "He did?"

"Well, the phone was dying, and he wanted to let me know there was no reason we had to accompany the rangers on their trail sweep," Cooper explained. "It seems the farthest permit is for Copper Lake, and there aren't any for the Chilliwack Trail. They also stationed rangers at the Hannegan trailhead right after they got Hamilton's call, so they've been turning any day hikers away since yesterday."

Some of the tension eased out of Ricki's back and shoulders. That was good news. She hadn't been looking forward to the trail sweep and the accompanying delay in the investigation. Not to mention the thirty-mile hike around the entire northern loop along with an overnight in a possible snowstorm.

"I also talked to Scott about us splitting up tomorrow," Cooper went on, gesturing toward the lieutenant standing quietly beside him. "He's not keen on the idea, but he's willing to hear us out."

Ricki looked over at Scott, who nodded back at her.

"What do you have in mind?" he asked.

"Something I think will work for all of us," Ricki answered easily. Since she'd already thought this possibility through, she got straight to the point. "We all go in. Clay, Anchorman, Cooper, and I will keep an eye on the perimeter while your team prepares the body for transport. Once you're ready, the team makes a quick beeline to camp with Cooper and Anchorman watching your backs. Clay and I will stay behind and take a more thorough look around the area, then come in right behind you."

"The helo is going to be here at ten," Scott said. "We need to get the extraction done and be on the trail ASAP if the team is going to get out of here before dark."

Ricki nodded. "Understood, Lieutenant."

"I'll pack up all our gear and have it waiting so we can bug out as soon as Ricki and Clay get back."

Scott frowned as he thought it over. "No more than an hour behind us, Ricki. Any more than an hour, and I'll be having some serious words with your boss about putting the team in danger. We're all going to leave together, so the guys will be counting on you to get back on time."

She held off on agreeing to the ranger's terms before hearing from Clay since she'd volunteered him to stay back on the crime scene instead of taking the safer position of sticking with the larger group. "Are you okay with this plan?" she asked him.

The chief didn't hesitate to give her a quick nod before glancing over at Scott. "It sounds good to me."

Chapter 9

THE MORNING DAWNED with a sharp bite in the air and thick clouds overhead. The unbroken forest was bathed in a soft gray light as it braced itself for the coming storm. Despite the ominous look of the sky, the forecast called for only a light snowfall. But forecasts had been wrong before.

Ricki curled her gloved fingers around the sides of her tin coffee mug and allowed herself a moment of worry about the weather. Living in the Northwest, she was used to all kinds of changes in the climate, most of it involving some sort of rain, but she usually wasn't facing a five-hour hike in the snow. And it didn't make much difference if there was a lot of the white powder or just a bare dusting; it still meant temperatures below freezing—or worse, once the sun went down.

The team downed a gallon of coffee and small bowls of instant oatmeal. Although she wasn't fond of the lumpy stuff, Ricki ate every bite. Given the day ahead of them, who knew how long that bit of fuel would have to last? With an eye on the clock, equipment and personal gear were checked in record time.

It was seven thirty when they started out for the three-mile round-trip run. Over even ground, their two-hour window to complete the task would have been more than enough. But traveling over open country and hauling a 170-pound weight back with them was another story.

The team traveled single file, with each man tasked with keeping up with the man in front of him, and no one wasted any breath on chatter. Jonah set the pace, and he made it a fast one as they headed out, with Ricki and Cooper taking point and Clay and Anchorman bringing up the rear.

When they reached the clearing where the two hunters had been found, Ricki didn't even pause. She crossed over the spot and turned slightly more toward the northeast, following the compass in her hand.

Forty minutes after they'd left camp, she spotted the two huge boulders through the trees. Heading right for them, Ricki led the group to the left. As soon as she'd rounded the boulders, she heard that same buzzing sound of swarming insects, telling her that Santiago Garcia's body was right where she'd left it.

She immediately threw up an arm and stopped. Behind her, the sound of boots pounding against the ground grew silent. The rest of the team were still behind the boulders, blocking their view of the body, but also of anyone who might be watching them from the shadows in the forest. She raised her rifle as Cooper came up beside her and did the same.

"The body's about twenty-five feet out, near that tree, slightly off to the left."

The barrel of Cooper's rifle shifted. "I see it. So, should we establish a perimeter around that tree and keep the rest of the team inside it?"

"Sounds good," Ricki said. "Let's get Clay and Anchorman up here."

Cooper turned and trotted off, signaling to the two men once he came into their line of sight. As Clay and Anchorman approached, Ricki heard Cooper's low voice explaining to Scott what they would do while her gaze continually scanned the area around the body. She didn't see any movement, or a shadowy presence in the trees, but that didn't mean much. This hermit, or whoever he was, only let himself be seen when he wanted to be. The thought still left her jumpy enough that she had to give herself a stern silent warning not to get distracted.

When Cooper stepped up beside her again, Ricki crept steadily forward, then split off to the right with Cooper just behind her. From her peripheral vision, she saw Clay move to the left of the tree and slowly walk in an arc around it. Once the four of them were in place, Scott brought the rest of the team out.

They rapidly crossed over to the tree, four of them kneeling to remove the tarp. They spread it out on the ground then moved the body to the center, wrapping it up and cocooning it inside. They secured it with strips of rope they'd brought with them while the remaining two men of the carry-out team quickly assembled the stretcher.

With Ricki and her part of the team keeping a watchful patrol around the perimeter, the remains of Santiago Garcia were loaded onto the stretcher and strapped in to be taken back to the campsite. It had taken the team less than fifteen minutes before they were ready to make the trip in reverse. Scott approached Ricki and nodded in satisfaction.

"So far, so good," he said before holding her gaze with his. "One hour behind us, Special Agent James. And not one second more."

"Understood," Ricki said. She turned away, intent on corralling Clay to start backtracking the drag marks that were still visible in the dirt, when she came smack up against Anchorman.

"Hey," she protested, taking a quick step back. "You need to get going. Cooper's going to lead the way back."

"I'm going," her cook said evenly. "But I want it on record that it's under protest."

Ricki knew that annoyed tone, and it had her eyes narrowing and her boots digging in. "Two law enforcement types will stay to take a look around the scene, and the civilian is going."

Anchorman lifted his shoulders in a careless shrug. "One perk of being a civilian is that I don't have to take orders anymore."

Her lips pursed as she considered the former sniper. She really didn't have time to argue with him, but he could be as stubborn as a mule whenever he felt he was right. And when it came to not having to follow orders, he had a point. She couldn't even remind him he was her employee since she'd made him a full partner in the diner. Which left one argument in favor of him returning with the rest of the group.

"No, you don't have to follow orders," she said evenly. "But you agreed to come along as part of the team, which means you have to do whatever is best for the team. Right now, protecting them is our highest priority, and you are the best shot."

He frowned but didn't say anything, as Ricki was careful not to show even a hint of a smile. What could he say? He *was* the best shot.

When Scott looked as if he was about to come over and have a few words of his own on the delay, Ricki jerked her head in the direction of the stretcher, where the first shift to make the carry were waiting to start. "We're out of time, Anchorman. You make sure they get back to camp within the hour so they're ready when the helo gets here."

The former Marine blew out a short breath, then turned on his heel and strode off. Scott immediately gave the signal to lift the stretcher, and within a minute the team was heading out. Ricki watched them until they disappeared around the boulders.

"Where do we start?" Clay's voice was low and calm.

She turned and walked directly to the drag marks and

pointed at the ground. "We need to follow these. We'll see where they lead and then go from there."

When he nodded, Ricki stepped over the long gouge mark, keeping it between her and Clay as they slowly walked along. The trail went straight for a thicker stand of trees. Once there, the marks changed, traveling in a vertical line, rather than a horizontal one, as if the pack had been turned sideways before being dragged farther into the forest.

The trees had barely closed behind them when both Ricki and Clay abruptly stopped at the same time.

"Holy hell," Clay said under his breath.

Ricki's eyes were as wide as moons when she took another step forward and stared down at the rectangular pile under the far side of a tree. At first glance it looked like a stack of squared-off white stones, each one heavily wrapped in plastic. But she didn't need to test it to know what it was. Ricki slowly counted the number of plastic-wrapped bricks of cocaine.

Ten, she silently concluded before reaching over and carefully picking one up. She hefted the weight in her hand as she glanced over at Clay.

"About two pounds each, give or take," she said.

"Yeah. I count ten," Clay replied. "That makes about twenty pounds of coke." He whistled softly through his teeth. "You're looking at half a million dollars."

"Wonderful," Ricki muttered. She returned the brick to the stack and took a slow look around. "It looks like the drag marks end here."

"I'll scout around and see if there are any more," Clay volunteered.

Nodding her thanks, Ricki returned her gaze to the pile of cocaine left out in the middle of nowhere. If the intent was to steal it from Garcia, what was it doing here? She was still thinking it over when Clay returned, shaking his head.

"Nothing. Whoever dragged that pack back here must have unloaded it and then taken off with the pack." He poked at the plastic covering of the closest brick with the barrel of his rifle. "Maybe there was something else in that backpack more valuable than this."

"Maybe," Ricki said, giving her standard response when something didn't sit right with her. What could be so valuable it would be worth leaving half a million dollars behind? She shook her head and took a step back.

"What should we do with it?" Clay asked. "It's too bulky for us to take back zipped up in our jackets."

"Yeah. Maybe just one to test it, and hopefully raise some prints off the plastic." With a resigned sigh, Ricki reached for the bandanna around her neck that was keeping the cold air from traveling down her back. She hadn't even undone the knot when a voice came rocketing out from the trees.

"Leave it. I'll take care of it."

Her hand froze in midair as Clay swiveled around in one smooth move and lifted his rifle to his shoulder.

"Are you going to sell it?" Ricki called out. When she was met with silence, she slowly turned around and lifted her own rifle, tucking it firmly into her shoulder. "What? No answer?"

"I'm not going to sell it." The voice was deep and gravelly, the way it gets as a man ages.

Both Ricki and Clay took a step away from each other and adjusted the direction of their aim.

"I don't see any other reason you'd leave it here, unless you intended to come back for it," Ricki said, her voice raised to be heard over the wind scampering through the trees.

There was a short laugh, followed by a rustling sound. The man was definitely on the move, and making enough noise to let them know that he was.

"I told you. I'm going to take care of it. Now leave it be." The voice came from a different angle on their left, so Ricki once again adjusted her aim. She put an eye to her scope and slowly swept the rifle across the line of trees.

"Why don't you come out here and tell us what happened?" she asked.

"That's your job to find out, and you're wasting time getting to it. They shouldn't be bringing that poison into my home."

Now there was a good dose of impatience laced into the voice, but at least the man hadn't moved again.

"We're in agreement on that," Ricki shouted back. "Is that why you killed that man I saw back there?"

That was met with an even louder crack of laughter. "There isn't anything special in that. Those two fools dressed in camo saw him, you saw him, and now that whole gaggle you brought along has seen him. What I expect you to do is stop looking at him and start looking for the person who killed him. You take care of him and no more of that poison can get through these woods."

"Sounds to me like you have a pretty good chance of catching whoever killed Mr. Garcia," Ricki said. "Why don't you come and help us hunt him down?"

"Anyone who deals with that poison doesn't deserve the respect of being called a 'mister.'" The words were flat and hard, without a hint of compromise in them. "The world is better off without him."

Ricki pursed her lips into a thin line, her eye still glued to the end of her scope. "Come on. Move," she said under her breath.

"Who's with you?"

For a moment, Ricki considered ignoring the question, but the more he kept talking, the better the chances she or Clay would pinpoint his exact location. "He's helping me catch Garcia's killer," she said, careful to ditch using the word *mister*, since it seemed to agitate him. "He's Chief Clay Thomas, from the Bay. That's over near Puget Sound."

There was a long moment of silence before words came

pinging between the trees. "We don't need any police in these woods, either."

The impatience was gone, replaced by a thick layer of anger. Apparently whoever he was didn't care for the police any more than he did for her. But for that small moment, he seemed to lose some of his caution as well, and Ricki saw the slight movement between the trees. It was part of an arm and shoulder, barely clearing the edge of a wide tree trunk. Everything in her focused on that image. Now that she had him in her sight, she wasn't about to lose him again.

"That's too bad because police investigate murders. So do I," Ricki said. She was barely breathing as her gaze lasered in on the image in her scope.

"We aren't going to see eye to eye on that, then. So it's time for you to leave."

Ricki barely had time to shout when the arm suddenly disappeared, to be replaced by the barrel of a gun, pointed right at her. She reflexively pulled her trigger, hearing the bullet smack into the tree. Bark went flying as she shouted at Clay and dived for the ground.

A split second later, there was the whine of a bullet ripping through the air. It sped past her, less than a foot over her head as Clay opened fire. He laid down a rapid line of shots as Ricki quickly scooted backwards, scrambling behind the tree with the cocaine stacked next to it. Lifting her rifle, she laid down her own fire so Clay could get out of the open and find cover. Once he was safely behind a tree, she let up and an eerie silence fell over the forest.

She waited, her eye once again glued to her scope as she searched for the shooter. Several minutes passed, leaving her more tense by the second. Where was he?

The thought had barely finished forming when she heard the distinct pattern of boots, pounding in a quick, staccato rhythm, and moving away from them. Their echo had her quickly shifting her position around to face the direction the noise was coming from. He'd moved without a sound, coming up on her exposed side. Readjusting her gun into her shoulder, she held still, straining to hear. When the boot steps had faded away completely, she still waited several more minutes before calling out to Clay.

"He's gone."

"Yeah," Clay called out. He cautiously stood up and backed away, slowly making his way to where she was waiting.

"That's a helluva trick he has," Clay said. "Moving like that."

"Yes," Ricki agreed. "It is."

Chapter 10

PRESSED FOR TIME, Ricki and Clay pushed hard to reach camp before their allotted hour was up. But the passing time wasn't their only problem. The wind had picked up, relentlessly pushing the forecasted storm toward the park, threatening to abort the extraction effort if the helicopter couldn't make the trip. The possibility weighed on Ricki's mind as she trotted through the final fifty yards of trees separating them from their small camp on the ridge overlooking Egg Lake.

Her breath was coming in rapid spurts by the time she passed the food storage locker and stepped into the cleared-off circle surrounded by stones. Nothing was left in the campsite except the row of backpacks, now all lying on their sides to lessen the chance of being blown around by the wind.

Anchorman stood at the far end of the cleared-off space, looking out over the ridge. His feet were braced apart and his hands tucked into his jacket pockets as he watched the activity near the lake below. When Ricki and Clay stopped to catch their breath, both leaning over with their hands braced on their upper thighs, Anchorman looked over his shoulder.

"Glad to see you made it back in one piece." When he

didn't get an immediate response, he frowned and turned around to face them. "You are in one piece, aren't you?"

Ricki waved a hand at him before she slowly straightened up. "We're fine. It was a fast trip, and a lot of it uphill." She forced herself to draw in her breath more slowly, carefully easing it back into its usual rhythm. "Is Cooper down with the rest of the team?"

Her cook shook his head then tilted it to one side. "Nah. He's over there, just inside the trees, securing the gear we're leaving behind."

Guessing that would be the equipment that Alan Barry and Mark Thurman brought in with them, Ricki smiled her approval. "That's good. I don't want to carry out any more than we have to."

"Provided we carry out anything at all," Clay said. His breathing had evened out and he'd moved to stand beside her, his eyes on the roiling sky over their heads. "I'm not sure the helicopter can fly in this."

Anchorman strolled over and joined them, his gaze turned up in the same direction as Clay's. "Me either."

Even though she'd been having the same thought for the last thirty minutes, Ricki turned her face into the sharp wind and assessed the sky. She'd seen worse, and the rescue crews were good at their jobs. "We'll know pretty soon whether or not they can make it in."

"If they can't, what do we do then?" Anchorman asked. He looked past them when Cooper emerged from the trees. "How about it, Warner? Are there any regulations about leaving a dead body behind? Because I'm not hauling it back over that pass."

Cooper stopped next to Ricki and also scanned the sky. "I don't know. I've never had to deal with that before. What I do know is that we don't have the supplies to stay up here for more than another day or so, and camping out in the snow isn't my idea of a good time."

"We could put the tent back up," Clay pointed out. "It could provide a few of us shelter, and we could take it in shifts."

"Storm forecasts in these mountains can be fickle," Ricki said quietly. "What looks like a light snow that will pass over in hours can turn into a three-day fight with nature." She stomped her boots to warm up her feet. "It's up to the senior ranger to decide, and that would be Scott, but I think he'd put the team first. The prudent thing to do would be to stash the body and hightail it out of here."

"So no trail sweep either?" Anchorman asked.

Ricki quickly shook her head. "No. It's too dangerous for the rangers, and if the other hikers haven't headed for the southern section of the park or back out to the Hannegan trail, then they shouldn't be out here at all."

"There's no need to do the sweep," Cooper said. "I spotted a group of hikers coming this way when we first got back. They were heading south toward the park's border. DJ went up to check on them, and he said they accounted for all the people on the list of issued permits he had, so I'm guessing we're the only group of fools still hanging around."

"Never a dull moment." Clay smiled when Cooper gave him a sour look.

Anchorman suddenly straightened his back, craning his neck as his gaze searched the sky. "I hear a he-lo."

The foursome went quiet. Everyone held their breath as they waited and listened in silence. Several long moments later, there was the faint but unmistakable sound of rotor blades slicing through the air. They all rushed over to the edge of the campsite and peered down at the group gathered at the far end of the lake, where there was a burst of activity. Within minutes, the rescue helicopter swept overhead in a graceful arc before settling over the team waiting below.

Ricki could see the pilot in the cockpit, fighting to keep the aircraft hovering in one spot as a crew member quickly swung the basket out and lowered it to the ground. This time it took the combined strength of four men to control the wildly swinging basket. While they kept an iron grip on it, the other four men quickly strapped in the tightly wrapped body, anchoring it in place so it wouldn't slide out, even if the basket were blown upside down. On Scott's signal, all four men let go at the same time then ducked and ran, scattering into the wind. If any of them were hit by the untethered basket, the extraction mission would quickly turn into an emergency medical evacuation, provided whoever got hit survived it.

Once the body was safely on board the helicopter, the aircraft quickly headed east toward the base while the rescue team sprinted along the lake, then up the path toward the ridge. Ricki and the rest of her group grabbed their own packs and slipped them on. She paused long enough to empty her rifle before sliding it into its holder, attached to the side of her pack. She tightened the straps around her shoulders and waist, then checked her watch just as the bulk of the team reached the campsite.

They were leaving later than planned, but hopefully the snow would hold off. There was a jumble of arms as backpacks were hastily swung into place and the hiking line formed. Within five minutes, they were on their way.

DJ took the lead since he was the one most familiar with the trail back to civilization, and Cooper brought up the rear.

"Think we'll make it back before we get snowed in?" Cooper whispered when Ricki passed by him.

"I don't know," she said in an undertone. "I guess we're going to find out."

The next five hours were an exercise in perseverance. It was an exhausted group that finally rounded the last bend before reaching the parking lot at the beginning of the trail-head. They'd pushed hard for the entire hike out because they'd had to. Even with the tremendous effort that left legs burning and back muscles screaming in protest, it was dark when they finally exited the forest. The only cars in the parking lot belonged to them.

Vaguely thankful they didn't have to worry about any campers or hikers being stranded in the mountains, Ricki brushed the snow off the shoulders of her parka. The sun had disappeared an hour before, and the temperature had dropped right along with the vanishing light. Even with her heavy parka, wool cap, lined gloves, and a brutal amount of exercise, Ricki could feel the cold seeping into her bones. They hadn't beaten all the snow but were fortunate to get away with a light dusting. If they had left any later, they might not have been so lucky.

She tramped toward the cars along with the rest of the team and piled into Cooper's rented SUV along with Anchorman. Clay's truck was parked next to it, and he climbed into the cab as Scott and his crew headed for the eight-passenger van ten feet away. No one could manage much more than a wave of a hand as a last farewell.

A polite goodbye didn't concern Ricki nearly as much as getting the SUV's heater cranked up while they made the half-hour trip to the town of Glacier. Hopefully whoever Hamilton had sent to be their contact was already there, as promised, and had scared up someplace for them to eat and sleep. Both activities were at the top of her critical to-do list.

Cooper turned over the engine and slowly drove out of the parking lot, not gaining any real speed until he reached a paved section of the road. When the heater kicked in, Ricki made a low, contented sound of relief. She pulled off her gloves and held her hand up to the vent, letting the warm air thaw out her fingers before taking off her headlamp and tossing it onto the wide top of the dashboard.

"That feels like heaven, doesn't it?" Cooper asked, grinning while he kept his eyes firmly on the road. "And it looks like the forecast for this storm wasn't far off. The snow has already slacked off and there isn't much sticking to the ground, so it must be saving its biggest punch for the higher elevations."

"What we did get was still cold," Ricki said. "And I hope wherever we're going has hot food and iced beer."

"I second that," Anchorman chimed in. Ricki heard the leather seat creak as he leaned back and stretched his long legs out as much as he could. "The good news is that Glacier's close by. The even better news is that we don't have to make that two-hour drive to SeaTac."

"Ha, ha," Cooper replied. "At least I know for a fact that there's hot food and a cold beer at the hotel near the airport. You'll just have to take your chances you won't be stuck in an RV or a camper in the middle of the field because that's all there is out here."

"Bite your tongue," Ricki said before leaning back and closing her eyes.

"You haven't told me if you found anything when you followed those drag marks into the trees," Cooper said.

"We found something," Ricki said, her eyes popping open again when she turned her head to look at him. "Ten bricks of cocaine stacked under a tree."

Cooper's jaw dropped to his chest. "You're shitting me?"

"Nope. I brought one of them back even though our drop-in guest objected to it."

"Drop-in guest?" Now Cooper was gaping at her. "The hermit showed up?"

"Yeah, he was there," Ricki confirmed. "And not too friendly. He took a shot at us."

She heard Anchorman draw in a sharp breath. "He shot at you?"

"He shot in our direction, to be more precise," Ricki said, determined not to have their encounter with the hermit blown out of proportion. Anchorman still considered himself her personal protector, no matter how many times she'd shown him she was perfectly capable of looking out for herself.

"He let us know he was around and then disappeared," Ricki went on, ignoring the former sniper's fierce growl.

"He did that 'poof' act of his?" Cooper asked.

"That pretty much describes it. And when I asked him about murdering the drug runner, he didn't deny it," Ricki concluded and then frowned. "He didn't confess to it either."

Anchorman lightly kicked the back of her seat. "He took a shot at you. I'd say that's a confession."

"I second that," Cooper chimed in.

"Yeah, well, maybe he did and maybe he didn't, but I know one thing for sure, someone dragged a backpack into the trees and then unloaded those ten bricks of cocaine before taking the backpack with him." Ricki scrunched up her face in thought. "Clay estimated that it was close to a half million dollars that Garcia's killer left behind."

Anchorman grunted. "So it wasn't a robbery after all? Someone just wanted this Garcia character dead?"

"Listening to the hermit calling the stuff 'poison,' I'd say he wanted a drug runner dead." Ricki lifted a hand and stifled a yawn. "He seemed to have a real problem with drugs being brought into what he called his 'house.'"

Both of Cooper's eyebrows lifted in surprise. "He said that?"

"He did," Ricki said absently, staring out the front windshield as her thoughts went back to the drag marks and what they were telling her. "But I think we didn't see it all."

Feeling Anchorman's eyes behind her boring into the back of her head, Ricki caught Cooper's sideways glance before he returned his attention to the road.

"I think the drag marks are off," she explained slowly. "Those bricks weighed about two pounds apiece, and there were ten of them, so we're talking about twenty pounds of drugs."

Cooper shrugged. "Yeah, okay. What has that got to do with the drag marks?"

"You didn't have time to get a close look at them," Ricki pointed out. "If they were made by a backpack being dragged across the ground, then the bottom bar of the frame was about two feet wide, just like a told you."

Cooper made a sound deep in his throat. "Which is too long for a twenty-pound pack. Is that what you're thinking?"

She nodded. "Yeah. That's a frame for a forty-pound pack all day long."

"And only twenty pounds was left behind," Cooper speculated, drumming his fingers against the steering wheel. "So either the pack was half-empty, or we're missing twenty pounds of something."

Anchorman leaned forward and rested an arm on top of the front seat space between Ricki and Cooper. "Could have been filled with supplies. I mean, the guy was out there for who knows how long, doing something with all that coke."

"Going to Canada is my guess," Ricki said. "With a backpack full of cocaine. Clay agreed that the odds are good that Garcia was a drug runner."

Anchorman leaned back again. "Since there are such things as boats and planes, hiking through the mountains is kind of doing it the hard way, isn't it?"

"It happens. Scott heard reports of drug running going on in Big Bend Park, down in Texas," Ricki answered. "The usual entry ports are heavily watched and heavily traveled. The park is neither. All you need to transport the drugs are runners who are in good shape. And from the look of him, I'd say Santiago Garcia fit that bill nicely." She rubbed a hand across the back of her neck. Now that the cold had receded from her limbs, a headache was forming at the base of her skull. She kept up a steady circular motion, trying to ease the pain away before it got out of hand. It had been a long day, and she didn't need to deal with anything else.

A small sign announcing the town of Glacier flashed by, and Cooper immediately slowed the SUV. "According to

Hamilton, we're supposed to meet your contact at a diner-bar kind of thing called the Snowmelt."

Ricki laughed. "Really? The Snowmelt is still here?" She leaned forward and stared out the front window, intent on helping Cooper spot the place.

"You've been there before?" Cooper asked.

"A long time ago with my dad and uncle." She pointed at a barely lit blue neon sign farther down the road. There was a row of cars out front, and as they turned into the parking lot, their headlights bounced off the word "Snowmelt," emblazoned across the side of a large panel truck. "There it is. I didn't even notice it on the way up here."

"Snowmelt," Anchorman said. "Catchy name."

A wicked spark crept into Ricki's dark-blue eyes. "Oh, it got its name from the way the cook puts melted cheddar cheese over everything he serves. That's pretty much what makes the food edible."

When Anchorman swore under his breath, Ricki grinned into the dark. There was very little the man disliked more than poorly prepared food. The longtime establishment had actually come by its name from a drink the bartender had conjured up and made available on its opening day, but her cook would find that out soon enough. In the meantime, she was enjoying hearing him gnash his teeth in annoyance.

When Cooper pulled their vehicle to a stop, with Clay's truck taking the next space over, they all piled out and headed for the front door. Ricki pushed it open and was immediately greeted by the wide, friendly smile of a woman well into the upper range of middle-age. She wore a plaid wool shirt and faded blue jeans overlaid with a large chef's apron. Her white-blonde hair was pulled back into a bouncy ponytail that swayed as she walked toward them.

"Hi, there." Her gaze swept over the group before zeroing in on Ricki. "Are you Special Agent James, by any chance?"

Ricki smiled and slid right into the cadence of small-town habits. "Yeah, but please call me Ricki."

The woman's smile beamed back as she nodded. "And I'm Jo. Glad to meet you. Your friend has a table in back." Jo looked over at Cooper and smiled. "I'll be happy to bring you a burger and some fries." She shifted her gaze and winked at Clay and Anchorman. "For all of you. I understand you hiked out of the park today, so you must be starving by now."

"We are." Ricki pointed toward the long aisle extending the length of the diner as it ran right beside the equally long bar. Several patrons were manning stools there, blocking her view of the table at the far end. "My friend is down there, you said?"

"That's right." Jo waved her on. "You go on and have a seat and I'll get those burgers going for you."

"Not for me, thanks," Cooper said. "I have to get back to Seattle tonight."

"I'll have mine without cheese," Anchorman said, the slight edge in his tone causing Jo to give him a puzzled look.

Choking back a laugh, Ricki turned and strode through the diner, heading for the large table in the back. As the lone occupant came into view, Ricki skidded to a halt and stared in disbelief. The tall, thin woman had brown hair that was cut in a plain straight line that left an edge brushing against the top of her shoulders. She looked up and adjusted the oversized glasses on the bridge of her nose before offering the astonished Ricki a smile.

"Hello. I'm glad you made it. I was beginning to worry."

It took Ricki a moment to find her voice, squeaking out a "Cheron?" before she burst out laughing as Anchorman crowded in behind her.

Chapter 11

Anchorman gently pushed Ricki aside then stepped forward. He crossed his arms over his broad chest as he stared down at Cheron. "What are you doing here?"

Her first response was to roll her eyes before she pursed her lips into a tight, thin line. "It's nice to see you again, too." Dismissing him, she leaned over the arm of her chair so she could look around the big man and see Ricki. "Senior Agent Hamilton sent me. I have everything arranged."

"What do you mean he *sent* you?" Anchorman demanded. "Why did he do that?"

Huffing out a breath, Cheron folded her hands in front of her on the table and glared at him. "Because I'm now part of this team, so he gave me an assignment."

"Oh no," Anchorman ground out. "You are not part of this team."

Cheron only continued to glare. "And why wouldn't I be? I'm the closest forensic pathologist, and I was told there's a dead body involved." She drew in a breath, then turned her glare into a polite smile. "Which makes me a qualified team member." She unfolded her hands and tapped a finger against the tabletop. "And what makes *you* qualified to be on the team?"

"The fact people are shooting at us," Anchorman stated flatly, not budging an inch despite the sharp poke Ricki gave him in his back. "Which is why you are not going to be part of this team. And you're the closest pathologist to what? There's got to be a dozen between here and the Bay."

"I'm the closest one to where Ricki lives," Cheron said primly. "And I've worked with her before, if you'll recall, so that also makes me the best qualified." Her eyes narrowed behind the lenses of her glasses. "And who was shooting at you?"

Ricki finally abandoned her finger poking in favor of planting a shoulder against Anchorman's side and giving him a hard shove. It didn't knock him over, but she did manage to push him away, leaving her just enough room to pull out the chair next to Cheron's. Quickly sitting down, she ignored Clay's chuckle behind her as she reached a hand over to give the pathologist's arm a gentle, friendly jab.

"Hi. It's good to see you, and welcome to the team."

"She's not on the team," Anchorman repeated, having once again occupied the space Ricki had forced him out of.

"Oh, give it up," Clay laughed, giving the cook a shove of his own. Taken by surprise again, Anchorman took a step back and Clay slipped by him, calmly taking the seat next to Ricki.

As he regained his balance for the second time, Anchorman's fiery stare promised retribution, but Clay only shrugged in response. Still frowning, Anchorman stomped past Cheron and yanked out the chair on her other side as Cooper broke out into a laugh.

"Well, hell. I'm sorry I can't stick around to watch the rest of this. Whatever it is."

Knowing the agent would be calling her later to demand a full explanation for Anchorman's behavior, Ricki sighed, then jerked a thumb over her shoulder. "Cheron, this is Special Agent Cooper Warner." Her hand switched directions to wave at Cheron. "Cooper, this is Dr. Cheron Garrison. And like she said, she's a top-notch forensic pathologist."

Cheron beamed a smile at Ricki, then turned it on Cooper. "I'm pleased to meet you, Special Agent Cooper."

"Call me, Coop, Doctor. And I read all about your work on that Utah case."

Cooper's voice held a note of admiration that had Anchorman audibly grinding his teeth and Ricki rolling her eyes.

The man is playing with fire, Ricki thought. She might have felt some sympathy for Cooper, but she was certain he knew exactly what he was doing by poking at Anchorman that way.

When her cook's jaw visibly hardened, Ricki decided she did not want to have to explain to Jo why two grown men had broken up her place. She turned in her chair and gave Cooper a warning look. "I guess you need to be on your way."

Cooper shrugged. "I can spare a few more minutes."

Ricki gave a hard shake of her head. "No, you can't."

Grinning, Cooper finally switched his gaze from Cheron to Ricki and winked. "Maybe not." He shifted his smile back to Cheron. "It was nice to meet you, Dr. Garrison." When she nodded, he raised two fingers to his head in a breezy salute. "I'll see the rest of you some other time." His jaunty smile faded when he dropped a hand onto Ricki's shoulder, giving it a solid squeeze. "Good luck with the case. Call if your backup doesn't show and I'll hightail it back here."

Appreciating the offer, Ricki nodded. "Thanks. I'll do that."

Clay stood up and reached out a hand. "It was good working with you, Agent Warner."

Cooper clasped the outstretched hand and smiled. "You, too, Chief." He nodded at Ricki. "I'll get your packs out of the SUV and leave them up front."

As Cooper strode off, Clay retook his seat and cocked one eyebrow at Anchorman. "You asked for that."

The ex-Marine ran a hand over the top of his buzz cut, a style he'd never abandoned even after he'd left the military. "Yeah. I know it."

"Now then," Ricki interjected, determined to get away from Anchorman's bout of jealous stupidity and back to more practical matters. "When you said you had everything arranged, Cheron, I hope that meant somewhere for us to get some sleep. It's been a long day."

"That was the first assignment Agent Hamilton gave me." Cheron waved at Jo, who was bearing down on their table. The waitress expertly juggled three plates, each with a large burger and a pile of fries. "Jo has rented us one of her places for as long as we need it."

Ricki blinked up at the older woman, who winked back at her as she passed the heaping plates of food around. "You have a place to rent?" Ricki asked, putting her hand on her stomach when it growled from the deep aroma of fried food wafting in the air.

"Several," Jo affirmed as she produced napkin-wrapped silverware from the large pocket of her apron. "Along with this place, it keeps me busy."

"You own the Snowmelt, too?" Clay asked. He smiled, causing a slight blush to rise in Jo's cheeks. "It's a nice place."

"My, you are a good-looking one. Like a movie star." When Clay grinned, Jo laughed. "And I suspect you've heard that before. Thanks for the compliment about my place. I like it. Cheron has already looked the Airbnb over and has given it her approval, along with a deposit. So I gave her the keys, and you're all set." Her smile took in all four occupants at the table. "Now, what would you all like to drink? I'll have it here in two shakes, right along with Cheron's salad."

Jo laughed when they all asked for a beer, the soft sound lingering behind her as she headed for the bar.

"A salad?" Anchorman looked at the empty space in front of Cheron. "All you're having is a salad?"

"I'm not the one who hiked out of the park today," she said. "I'm fine with a salad. You just eat your own food."

Anchorman looked down at his plate and then over at Ricki. "I don't see any melted cheese."

Cheron's forehead wrinkled in confusion. "Why would you?"

Anchorman answered her while keeping his stare on Ricki. "Because I was told melted cheese was poured all over the food, and that's how the place got the name Snowmelt."

The doctor sighed. "Now, why would you believe something like that? Melted cheese doesn't look anything like snow, and this establishment shares its name with a drink that Jo's husband came up with. Jo told me he was the bartender here right up until he got sick." She pointed at Anchorman's plate. "Now everyone eat before your food gets cold."

"Yes, Mom." Ricki grinned at her chagrined cook before taking a big bite of her sandwich. While it wasn't as good as one of Anchorman's burgers, it was pretty damn close, and right now she was hungry enough to wolf down the whole thing.

Cheron's eyes were wide as she watched overfilled plates of food disappear in record time. Jo walked up with three beers and a salad just as the last of Ricki's burger disappeared. Anchorman and Clay had consumed theirs even faster and had already made a substantial dent in their respective piles of fries.

The owner set the salad in front of Cheron and distributed the drinks before taking a step back, her hands on her hips. "I'll just bring out a giant bowl of chili and three spoons, and I expect you all to keep eating until you're full. No one walks away from the Snowmelt hungry."

While Clay and Anchorman voiced their thanks, Ricki started in on her own fries. Her headache had disappeared once she'd gotten some fuel into her. Now that she was warm and fed, her thoughts turned back to the murder that needed solving. When Jo appeared with a casserole-sized bowl of chili, Ricki waited until Clay and Anchorman were happily digging into it before turning to face Cheron.

"The body is on its way to the morgue in Bellingham. The ME there is Dr. Robbins. I'll give him a call tonight and leave a message that you'll be coming along on a consult tomorrow." She tapped a slender finger against the long neck of her bottle of beer. "I'm assuming you'll want to come along?"

"That's why I'm here," Cheron confirmed. "That, and Agent Hamilton seems to think there might be more bodies."

Thinking that was a good call on Hamilton's part, Ricki nodded and took a long sip of her beer. If the murder had been an ambush because someone was after the cocaine, then where there was one dead drug runner, there could easily be two or three more.

The beer went down cool and smooth. Enjoying it, Ricki leaned back in her chair. "Did Hamilton fill you in on the case?"

"He mentioned something about drugs," Cheron said. "I guess the victim was dealing in them, and someone shot him?" She frowned. "Twice, from what I understand. Once in the back, and again in the head?"

"Yeah. The back shot looked like it was taken from some distance away. The one to the head was right at the base of the skull and taken a lot closer." Ricki lowered her voice. "The head was split open from the shot."

Cheron slowly nodded. "An execution, then?"

"Odds are good," Ricki replied.

"For the drugs he was dealing?" Cheron asked.

"He was probably a drug runner rather than a dealer, since it appears he was carrying cocaine in his backpack. And once again, the odds are good the drugs are what got him killed. Except there's a problem with that particular theory," Ricki said.

"Which is?"

Ricki took another sip of her beer. "We found a stack of cocaine bricks in the trees. It looks like someone unloaded them from the victim's backpack, then took whatever was left in the pack with him."

Cheron blinked then reached up to adjust her glasses. "That sounds very odd. What was left in the pack? More cocaine?" Cheron shook her head. "That doesn't make sense. Why not take all of it?"

"Hmm," was all Ricki said, still not sure what to make of it.

The doctor was quiet for several moments, spearing lettuce and some vegetables and chewing them slowly. She suddenly frowned, looking over at Ricki with her fork hovering halfway to her mouth. "Then who was shooting at you?"

Ricki's expression went blank as she watched a cherry tomato fall off Cheron's fork and back into her salad bowl. "What?"

"Chief Thomas said that someone was shooting at you? Obviously it couldn't be the drug runner, because he was dead when you found him, wasn't he?"

"Yeah. He was." As Cheron took another stab at the hapless tomato, Ricki picked up a french fry from her plate and popped it into her mouth. She chewed slowly and swallowed while she thought about the man they'd all dubbed "the hermit."

"There was a guy out there, hanging out in the woods near the body. I don't know how long he'd been camping out, or what he was doing there, but he was definitely watching us. And he knew about the drugs being smuggled through the park."

Cheron's hand came up to cover her mouth. "Smuggled?"

Ricki nodded. "Most likely to Canada. Anyway," she

continued. "One of the rangers who came along to help the rescue team said that his dad grew up here in Glacier. When we mentioned this guy we'd seen, DJ said his dad always told a story about someone he went to school with who ended up disappearing into the mountains. He claimed all the locals call him 'the hermit.'"

"How long ago did this hermit person disappear?" Cheron asked.

"I don't know." Ricki shrugged and then sighed. "At least a couple of decades ago. Supposedly he killed someone and then went to live off the grid to avoid being arrested. He's also rumored to have taken his wife with him."

"A few decades ago?" Cheron sounded skeptical, and Ricki couldn't blame her. As stories went, it was a hard one to believe. Especially if you threw in the claim that the same guy was still alive and now the primary suspect in a second murder.

"You don't believe that, do you?" Cheron asked. "Surely it's simply a local myth."

"It probably is," Ricki had to agree. "But Hamilton is having Dan put in some research time on it, and I thought I'd ask around while we're here. Maybe a longtime resident can tell me something about it." She shrugged. "I hope so, because right now we've got nothing but a dead body and a pile of drugs."

"The body might tell us a lot," Cheron declared. "But if you want to debunk that hermit myth, you might ask Jo. She and her husband both grew up here in Glacier. He passed away five years ago, but I'm sure Jo can tell you all about any local legends and how they got their start."

Ricki frowned as she thought it over. While Jo was a bit older, she still looked a decade short of being old enough to be DJ's parent. But then, with some good genes and a little hair dye, looks could be deceiving.

She lifted a hand to cover a yawn. It was worth a shot, but

not tonight. Right now she needed some sleep, and judging by the heavy eyes on both Clay and Anchorman, so did they.

"I'm hoping you have some transportation because Cooper drove off in ours, and Clay's truck only seats three," she said. When the doctor nodded, Ricki's shoulders tensed. "Please don't tell me you drove your own car here?"

Cheron's small, beat-up Toyota had patched-over seat covers and a peeling yellow paint job. It was the only car in the Bay that was uglier than Ricki's lime-green jeep. At least the jeep didn't look like it was going to fall apart at any moment. Cheron's little Toyota looked like it should have been put out of its misery years ago. It would also be a tight fit for them, plus their backpacks.

"I was going to bring my car," Cheron said, completely oblivious to Ricki's wince. "But Hamilton insisted I rent a better vehicle for the snow." She pressed her lips together. "You know. Just in case there's a big storm while we're here, and because we're expecting two more agents to arrive some-time tomorrow. My car won't seat six people."

It won't seat four, Ricki thought once she'd given a mental high-five to her boss. "Did Hamilton mention the names of these agents he's sending?" Ricki asked, hoping one of them was Ali Gibson, an ISB special agent assigned to the southwest district. She not only liked Ali but had worked with her before, and wouldn't mind at all if the tall, willowy blonde joined the investigation.

"He didn't say, and I didn't think to ask." Cheron's shoulders drooped. "I'm sorry. I should have asked. I just assumed it would be Agent Gibson, since she helped us in Utah, but I guess there are a lot of other agents Hamilton could have called."

"About thirty others," Ricki said, stifling another yawn. "If we're going to count all the agents in the ISB."

With fatigue rapidly settling in, Ricki garnered up enough strength to push back her chair and stand up. She grimaced at the stiffness in her legs and lower back. It had been a while since she'd covered eight miles of trail that fast. "I'm beat. Let's get our packs and head for Jo's rental." It might be another one of Cheron's very weird ideas of "quaint," but right at the moment, as long as it had a bed, she really didn't care.

Chapter 12

THE NEXT MORNING dawned clear and bright, with only a few wispy clouds drifting through the sky. The storm the night before had dropped less than two inches of snow on the western side of the mountains, making the ride into Bellingham easy going.

Only Ricki and Cheron made the trip in, leaving Clay and Anchorman behind to get some extra rest and to be there in case the two agents Hamilton was sending decided to show up early. They took the SUV Cheron had rented, with Ricki at the wheel, solely for her own peace of mind since she was all too familiar with being a captive of Cheron's driving.

The medical examiner's facility in Whatcom County was on a quiet tree-lined street. Set back from the curb, the two-story building had siding painted in a desert tan and an entrance made entirely of glass. Ricki led Cheron through the front doors.

Once Ricki produced her badge, a friendly clerk in the lobby directed them to the back of the building. The doors to the autopsy room were guarded by a young lab tech with spiked hair tipped in blue and two rows of polished metal studs in her ears.

Ricki had met Crystal the last time she'd been called out on a case at North Cascades Park. A body had ended up in the morgue on that case too. She smiled a greeting when the young girl looked up.

Crystal's mouth spread in a wide grin as she yanked out her ear buds and set her phone down on the desk. "Hey, Special Agent James. How's it going? I guess that body we got in from North Cascades yesterday is yours?" She didn't wait for an answer as her gaze bounced right over to Cheron. "And you must be Dr. Garrison?" She tapped a long nail painted in blood red against the screen of her computer. "I have you down as 'expected' on the visitor log, along with Agent James." She looked back at Cheron as she placed her elbows on the desk and propped her chin in her hands. "So, what kind of doc are you?"

Cheron took the unusual lab tech in stride, shoving her hands into the pockets of her overalls as she returned the girl's smile. "I'm a forensic pathologist."

When Crystal blinked and gave Cheron a thorough once-over, Ricki sent the doctor an amused look. "Cheron, this is Crystal. She helps Dr. Robbins. He's the ME here in Whatcom County."

"I've spoken to Dr. Robbins," Cheron said. No longer comfortable under the lab tech's intense scrutiny, she took a slight step backwards when Crystal continued to stare at her as if she were a specimen under a microscope.

"So, you're an ME too? You don't look like one," Crystal finally declared. When Cheron nodded, the lab tech grinned at Ricki. "You got your own ME? How cool is that?" Her gaze bounced right back to Cheron. "Do you work with Coop?"

"Agent Warner?" Cheron adjusted her glasses higher on her nose as she peered back at Crystal. "I've only recently met him. We've both been assigned to this case."

Crystal immediately stood up and craned her neck to look down the hall. "Coop is here? He's working this case too?"

"Um, no," Cheron stammered. "I meant he *was* working on this case, but now he's on his way back to Colorado. Ricki —that is, Special Agent James—will be leading this investigation."

The lab tech's face fell as she plopped back into her seat. "Oh. I was kinda hoping to see him."

"Maybe next time," Ricki said. She really didn't want to get stuck listening to Crystal sing the praises of the absent Cooper, so she gave a pointed look at the closed doors leading into the autopsy room. "Is Dr. Robbins in yet?"

"Sure." Crystal pointed at the ceiling as if the doctor were floating in the air somewhere over her head. "He's upstairs finishing some paperwork."

Ricki nodded and walked past Crystal's small desk. "Then we'll just wait for him inside." When Crystal opened her mouth, Ricki only smiled back. "I'm sure he won't mind since he's already talked to Dr. Garrison several times." She pushed through the door then held it open, waiting for Cheron to catch up with her.

The room was dark. Sensing movement, the lights flipped on, bouncing off the stainless-steel autopsy tables and countertops. One table held a sheet-draped body while the other one was thankfully empty.

"That was rather misleading. I've only talked to Dr. Robbins once," Cheron protested. "And it was a very short conversation."

"Once works," Ricki said with a shrug.

"That must be our victim." Much more interested in the body than the gum-chewing lab tech, Cheron pointed at the closest autopsy table.

Ricki crossed over to the end of the table and read the tag attached to a bare toe sticking out from under the sheet. "Santiago Garcia. Yeah. This is him."

Cheron wrapped her arms around her waist and slowly turned in a full circle. "It's a nice autopsy room." Lifting her nose into the air, the doctor took several, loud sniffs. "Very clean." She looked over at Ricki, the corners of her mouth pulled down into a frown. "Does Cooper know how bad a crush that young girl has on him?"

"Do *you* know that it's none of our business?" Ricki said, choking back a laugh. There was no way she was going to get involved in Cooper's love life. It would be exhausting. "Besides, I'll bet it's all in her head. Cooper hardly knows the girl."

"Well, I'm sure he flirted with Crystal since he tried to do the same with me."

Surprised that Cheron had even noticed, Ricki grinned. "And that didn't go over well at all with Anchorman. How long do you intend to keep him dangling with his heart on his sleeve, anyway?"

Cheron's expression turned very serious. "Oh, I'm aware that he's been hinting around at having a relationship. And I'm considering it."

Hinting around? The man was practically hitting her with a sledgehammer. Subtlety was not one of Anchorman's more prominent traits. "Try not to consider it for too long. He's getting hard to live with."

"Well, there are a few things I'm concerned about . . ." Cheron trailed off when the double doors opened.

A tall man with long legs and thin arms, the doctor walked over to Ricki with his hand extended in welcome.

"How are you, Ricki? I'm glad to see you again, but sorry about there being another death in the park." He turned toward Cheron. "I'm Dr. Robbins, and you must be Dr. Garrison? I heard about your work out in Utah. Very impressive. Jefferson County is very lucky to have you."

Cheron took the long, bony fingers of his hand in hers and gave it a good shake. "Thank you. And I'm pleased to meet you as well, Doctor."

He smiled before walking across the room. "Shall we get

started?" He picked up a clipboard and rapidly flipped through several pages. "I have a few preliminary results." He looked over at Cheron, waiting for her nod before continuing. "The victim is identified as Garcia, Santiago. According to his identification, he was twenty-three years old at the time of death and Hispanic. He's five feet, nine inches, black hair and brown eyes, and weighs 173 pounds. Subject appears to be in good shape with well-toned musculature, indicating a healthy diet and a proper amount of exercise. His skull was badly damaged. I understand the bullet that was recovered at the scene went right through it and was embedded in the ground. Judging by the amount of heavy stippling and traces of gunpowder around the wound, I'd say the head shot was fired at close range from a heavier gun. This is supported by the bullet and the cartridge that was recovered. It was a .30-30 Winchester cartridge, according to my lab tech." He looked up and tilted his head toward the closed doors. "Crystal is very good at identifying that kind of thing."

Since Cooper had recovered the bullet on the rescue team's trip to the murder scene, Ricki hadn't seen it. But the size of the cartridge had her eyebrows winging upward. "A .30-30 Winchester? Was Crystal sure about that?"

As Dr. Robbins nodded, Cheron's forehead wrinkled in thought. "Isn't that commonly used in a Winchester 1894? From my research on firearms, I know that's a very popular gun."

"Rifle," Ricki corrected. "A lever-action rifle, and popular? Yes," Ricki said, still puzzling over it. "For hunting large game in forested areas, mostly."

"Which is exactly where we were," Cheron pointed out.

"We were, and I wouldn't blink an eye if we'd found the dead body of a hunter. But Garcia was running drugs. And he didn't have a weapon on him, at least not that we found. And if he did have one at some point, I doubt if it would have been a Winchester 1894. That isn't exactly the gun of choice for the drug crowd."

When Cheron's mouth formed into a silent O, Ricki sighed. Another ill-fitting piece to a weird puzzle. She turned it over in her mind as Dr. Robbins prepared the body for autopsy. As he got to work, with Cheron happily acting as his surgical assistant, Ricki found a chair tucked into the corner and sat down. When she heard a clink of metal hit a glass plate, she got up and walked back over to the table.

Cheron pointed to a small dish holding a fairly intact bullet sitting in the middle of a small, gleaming table on wheels that had been pulled up next to the body. "We just took that one out of his back."

Ricki picked up the dish and turned it around in her hand, carefully studying its contents. Finally setting the glass petri dish back on the small table, she returned to her seat.

It took the two doctors several hours to finish up their work since they stopped frequently to not only discuss this body but exchange stories on other autopsies they'd performed. It was getting into the late afternoon by the time Cheron had a copy of the dictation tape Dr. Robbins had made during the autopsy. Ricki kept her in tow as they headed back to the Airbnb in Glacier.

Night was falling when they pulled up in front of the large A-frame house. Both Clay and Anchorman were sitting on the wide porch, enjoying a beer, as Ricki brought the car to a stop. Cheron popped out of the car and waved enthusiastically when both men stood up and moved to the railing surrounding the porch.

"We had an excellent day," Cheron called out.

Ricki shook her head as she followed in the doctor's wake, stopping when Clay offered her his beer.

"An excellent day at an autopsy?"

Ricki looked up at him as she took a long sip from his beer. After spending the entire afternoon in a room that smelled like formaldehyde and had lights bright enough to give you a headache, she needed a good, cold beer. "It takes all kinds," she said in a voice low enough that it wouldn't carry through the front door that Anchorman had left wide open when he'd followed Cheron into the house.

Clay gave her a sympathetic look as she handed him back his beer. "Well, Anchorman and I managed to make a trip to the nearest market and got everything on Cheron's grocery list plus a few extras, and now the place is pretty well stocked. He has an excellent pot of stew going, so maybe that will help smooth out your day a little."

Ricki smiled at the thought as she looked around the front yard. The only car in the driveway besides Clay's truck was the one she and Cheron had just arrived in. "I guess the other two agents haven't arrived yet?"

"Nope. Haven't seen anyone. Did you learn anything new from the autopsy?"

"Uh-huh. The bullets that killed Santiago were .30-30 Winchester cartridges."

"No." Clay shook his head. "That isn't right. Drug dealers don't use hunting rifles. Even up here in the mountains they'd have a semiautomatic." He stopped and rubbed a hand across the top of his head. "Unless this is a small-time mom-and-pop operation. But forty pounds of coke doesn't sound like a second-string outfit to me."

"Me either," Ricki said with a sigh. "I don't know. This whole case is wonky."

He smiled and gave her a friendly one-armed hug before dropping his hand back to his side and sticking it into the pocket of his jeans. "I say we eat something and go over our plans for tomorrow."

Slightly embarrassed at the suddenly awkward moment between them, Ricki quickly nodded. "That sounds good."

The rest of the night passed uneventfully, even if it was becoming painfully obvious that Clay was deliberately keeping his distance. When he said he wanted to stay up in case the new agents made an appearance, Ricki didn't say anything but went off to the bedroom by herself. She fell into a restless sleep, only to be rudely awakened just after midnight by Clay giving her shoulder a firm shake.

"Ricki, you need to wake up."

She rubbed her eyes and peered at him. He was standing next to the bed, fully dressed. Still groggy from her interrupted sleep, she frowned at the noise coming from the living room. "Why? What's going on?"

"Jo is here with a deputy from the county sheriff's department, and they're asking for our help."

She bolted straight up and swung her long legs over the edge of the bed. "Why? What's happened?"

"I'm not sure, but they said that the road is on fire."

"What?" Ricki shook her head, waving the question off as she pulled on her jeans. "Go ahead and get Anchorman and the rifles. I'll be there in less than a minute."

Chapter 13

THE HEADLIGHTS of the SUV cut through the night, transforming the trees next to the two-lane highway into a moving picture of stark branches and shimmery shadows. Clay's face was grim in the shifting light as he expertly guided the car through the curves, following the police cruiser one hundred feet in front of them, its lights flashing and siren screaming.

Ricki braced a hand against the dashboard as their vehicle cut around another bend, craning her neck as she stared through the windshield at the night sky just above the treetops. She had no idea what the deputy had meant when he'd claimed that the road was on fire, but up ahead, there was a concentrated glow rising over the towering trees.

They raced toward it, the tires screeching on asphalt as Clay muscled the SUV around another curve without losing any speed. Another police cruiser came into view, parked sideways across the highway, its headlights on and the light bar on top blinking like a Christmas tree. On the other side of it, she could make out the red and silver of a fire truck, and beyond that there was fire.

Clay slowed down, bringing the SUV to a stop five feet

away from the parked cruiser. All three of its occupants leaped out of the car at the same time, with Anchorman passing Ricki her rifle first, and then a second one to Clay. Picking up his own weapon, Anchorman trotted after Ricki, who was already standing next to a deputy with a soot-streaked face. He was talking to her at a mile a minute.

"We got the call, and three of the piles were burning when we arrived." He pointed at the nearest one, built in the middle of the road and burning with an intense heat. "There are two more just like it, and they all smell like gasoline was poured all over them. I've never seen anything close to this before. It's beyond weird." The deputy's voice was muffled because he'd zipped up his jacket and then turned up the collar until it covered half his face to protect it from the intense heat. "You can see the fire truck. It came out from Glacier and most of the crew are volunteers, but the station chief is here. You might want to talk to him."

Ricki coughed then pulled up the bandanna knotted around her neck until it covered her nose. She couldn't do anything about the burning sensation in her eyes. Her only option was to power through it.

"We don't know what caused this, but it sure wasn't an accident," the deputy said, his gaze shifting to look over Ricki's shoulder as Clay and Anchorman joined her. "And we found a note nailed to a tree farther down." He jerked his head in that direction. "It was addressed to Agent James." His red-rimmed, watering eyes came back to Ricki. "Someone sure wants to get your attention." He paused and waved a hand in the direction of the fire. "We've got a sergeant with us. He's over that way, talking to the fire chief."

"Okay," Ricki said. "Thanks." She headed for the fire truck, with Clay and Anchorman right behind her. Skirting around it, Ricki spotted the fire chief first, fully decked out in heavy gear, with the department emblem embedded on the front of his helmet. When she trotted up, both men turned in her direction.

"I'm Special Agent Ricki James," she announced as soon as she reached them. She did a half-turn and nodded at Clay. "This is Police Chief Clayton Thomas, from the Bay over on the peninsula, near Olympic Park. And that is Anchorman. Both of them are part of my team." She gestured toward the cruiser. "The deputy said something about a note."

The police sergeant was a big man, with large arms and a barrel of a chest. He sent Clay a nod before giving Ricki a quick once-over, then hooking his thumbs into the belt circling his waist. "Well, now, Special Agent Ricki James. Care to tell why you have a team here at all? You're far away from Quantico back in Virginia, aren't you?"

Ricki smiled without a hint of warmth behind it. She was used to the attitude toward female agents. It usually wore off in short order, but sometimes it hung around like a bad odor. She'd have to see where this one went. "And you are?" She was surprised when the sergeant suddenly looked chagrined, as if it had just dawned on him he was being less than professional.

"Sorry. I'm Sergeant Brian Crowder, with the county sheriff's department, and this is Fire Chief Gregory Newman, with Fire District 19 out of Glacier. We've both been on scene about twenty minutes."

Satisfied for the moment that Crowder wasn't one of the assholes who didn't like women in law enforcement, Ricki relaxed her shoulders by rolling them back and forth.

"I'm not with the FBI. I work for the ISB with the National Park Service. That's the—"

"I know what it is," Crowder cut in. "Their Investigative Services Branch." His mouth curved up into a smile. "Now I know why your name sounded familiar. Read up some on a couple of your cases that made the newspapers. You do good work. Not sure I could track down bad guys while running through the kind of rough country that you face doing it." He glanced over at Clay. "I've heard about you too. Law enforcement in this state is a tight community. You spent time as a homicide detective in Los Angeles, didn't you?"

Clay nodded back at the man. "Yeah. I did."

Crowder switched his gaze to Anchorman, slowly taking in his buzz cut and direct stare. "Are you in the military?"

"I was," Anchorman said, not elaborating any more than that.

With the initial ice wall broken and the introductions made, Ricki looked over at the fire chief. "I'd appreciate it if you'd bring me up to speed, Chief Newman."

A pair of light-blue eyes gazed back at her from beneath the brim of his helmet. "Unlike the sergeant here, I'd already heard that you were in town." Beneath a salt-and-pepper mustache, thin lips stretched into a smile. "I had dinner at the Snowmelt." He looked back at the fires. "Not much to tell. We're maintaining a watch on the perimeters of the three fires that are lit, to be sure they don't pose a danger to the surrounding area. When we got here, we weren't sure what we were dealing with, and hitting those bonfires with the pressure behind our water hoses would have scattered the burning debris all across the highway and maybe into the trees."

"The three fires that are lit," Ricki repeated. "Does that mean there are more than three and some are not lit?"

"There's one more," the chief confirmed. "And it's pretty interesting. You need to go down and look for yourself."

"I'll go with you," Crowder volunteered. "And show you where that note is." He fell into step beside Ricki, his thumbs still hooked under his belt. "I'd appreciate it if you would tell me what you're doing out this way."

"Have you heard about the killing up in North Cascades?" Ricki asked.

"You pulled that one? I was told that there was some guy out of Colorado working that case."

Ricki shook her head. "Not anymore. He was needed back in his home district, so I was called in."

"That's an unusual team you brought with you." Ricki could hear the smile in the sergeant's voice. "A police chief, a military guy—just about everyone but the FBI."

She shrugged. "Yeah. I guess so."

They walked the rest of the way in silence. Ricki, along with Clay and Anchorman, kept a careful eye on the trees standing on either side of them and stretching out well behind the arc of light from the fires. The fourth bonfire was built on a bed of branches, leaves, and twigs. More logs were stacked on top, standing on end and leaning against one another, forming the shape of a teepee, and from the strong smell, they were thoroughly soaked in gasoline. Around the base of the teepee were square shapes that looked like gray bricks.

You've got to be kidding me, she thought before turning and holding out a hand to Anchorman. "Can I borrow your knife?"

The former Marine bent down and pulled a wicked-looking blade out of his boot. Flipping it over, he handed it to Ricki hilt first. All three of them walked over to the unlit pyre, with the men watching as Ricki kneeled down and ran the knife over the top of the plastic that was covering one of the bricks. The white powder gleamed in the dark as Ricki gingerly took a sample onto the tip of her finger. She raised it to her mouth and tapped it against her tongue. The bitter taste was unmistakable.

She stood up and looked at Clay. "I'm betting this is our coke."

Sergeant Crowder made a choking sound. "Coke? Someone is out here setting fire to a fortune in cocaine?"

"Looks like it," Ricki said, glancing around. "Where did you say that note was?"

"What's that much coke doing out here? And why did you

say it was yours?" Crowder asked, his gaze fixed on Ricki. "Does this have anything to do with your dead guy?"

"Maybe," Ricki hedged. "I still need to see that note, Sergeant."

The big man took one last look at the bricks of cocaine piled around the stacked logs. "How much coke do you figure is on there?"

"Nine bricks," Clay put in. "I've counted them. So, eighteen pounds, which comes out to just under half a million."

The sergeant whistled in surprise and then let out a long sigh. "The note is down this way." He walked another twenty feet down the road before stopping to have a short, low-voiced conversation with the deputy standing guard over three sticks arranged on the road in the shape of an arrow.

"Not real subtle," the sergeant commented as he stepped off the road and walked across the small stretch of grass separating the road from the tree line. He approached the nearest tree, stopping a few feet away. "There it is. A message from one of your admirers."

Ricki went past him until she was barely a foot away from the tree. A notebook-sized piece of paper was nailed about five feet up. Along with her name, there were four words written with a thick black marker.

The clock is ticking

"Not much of a poet either," Crowder said dryly.

Anchorman leaned forward and peered over her shoulder. "Clay filled me in on what that hermit said to you up in the park. I'd say he's definitely warning you."

"Yeah," Ricki agreed. "He also said he'd take care of the cocaine we found." She looked back over her shoulder toward the burning fires. "I guess he did" Her gaze settled on the lone, unlit teepee of wood and gasoline. "Or at least intended to."

She took an evidence bag out of her jacket pocket and using Anchorman's knife, pried the nail away from the tree, then slipped the note into the plastic bag. "Maybe he left a print on this and he's somewhere in the system."

"Care to let me in on who you're talking about?" Crowder asked. "Who's this hermit person?"

Ricki tucked the evidence bag away and turned to face the sergeant. "We only call him that because we don't have a name for him. He's a guy we saw in the park that wasn't real happy that we were there."

The group walked back over to the road. They were about ten feet away from the unlit fire when there was a whistling noise in the dark. It sounded like it was coming from the trees on their right. Ricki had barely turned to look that way when a flaming comet whizzed past her, immediately followed by a small explosion. Smoke and sparks lifted into the air as the fourth pile of logs shot up in flames. Ricki threw up her arms and staggered backwards, knocking into Clay, who put his hands on her shoulders to hold them both steady.

"Are you all right?" His voice was close to her ear.

"I'm good." She immediately looked over at Anchorman, who was standing, his feet braced apart and his mouth open. "What the hell?" he said loudly, then blinked. In less than a second he had his rifle tucked into his shoulder and aimed at the trees on the other side of the road.

Ricki and Clay automatically followed suit and so did the sergeant and the deputy standing next to him with their sidearms.

"I saw movement," Anchorman stated flatly. "Two o'clock."

Ricki shifted the barrel of her gun and looked through the site. Unfortunately, most of her view was obscured by smoke.

"How'd you see any movement through all this shit?" Crowder asked.

"I saw it," Anchorman said slowly.

Like everyone else, the deputy standing on the far edge of the group had his gun raised when he let out a loud shout.

"Hey. There he is." Without hesitating, he fired his revolver, discharging it several times into the dark. "I know where he went."

When the deputy took off, Ricki remained frozen for half a beat before leaping forward. She hit the ground at a dead run. "No," she yelled out. "No, don't go into the trees." When the deputy didn't stop, Ricki pumped her long legs even faster. "Stop! He'll kill you if you go into the trees."

That did the trick. The deputy skidded to a stop so fast that Ricki ran right past him before she could put her forward motion completely into check. She spun around and marched back to the deputy, latching on to his arm. "Come on. We need to get back to the others."

Both Clay and Anchorman had stopped just a few feet away. They waited until Ricki was past them with the deputy still firmly in tow, before walking backwards, facing the forest with their rifles raised. When they reached the road, the deputy made a beeline for the sergeant, whose frown turned fierce as he listened to what he was being told. After a minute, Crowder waved the deputy off, sending him back toward the cruiser as he stomped over to Ricki.

"You said that hermit of yours would kill my deputy if he set foot into the trees?" Crowder demanded.

Ricki drew in a breath and reminded herself to stay calm. "I don't know if it was the same guy we saw in the park or not. I didn't get a look at him."

"Still, you think there's someone running around out here who is willing to kill cops?"

She gave him a level look. "I think he's an expert in the forest, and he considers anyone in law enforcement a trespasser in his domain."

Crowder stared at her for a moment, frowning. "Then I'd better put out an alert. What about the firefighters? Are they in danger too?"

"I don't know," Ricki said honestly, watching the six men

who had come running with portable extinguishers the minute the fire had exploded into life.

"Okay, then. I'll repost the men along the road and tell them to keep their weapons drawn." He stared at the fire for a moment, his eyebrows lowered. "How did he get that thing lit, anyway?"

Ricki followed the direction of his gaze. "I heard an arrow."

"And I saw it," Clay said. "The tip was wrapped in something and on fire. When it hit that gasoline, it blew up like a bomb."

"That part I saw," Crowder declared. "It would've been quite a show if I hadn't been so busy trying not to go up with it."

"A 'show' is a good word for it. Glad we arrived in time to see it."

The female voice came from behind Ricki, and when she turned around, she came face-to-face with an amused smile. What was it with everyone lately? Soundlessly sneaking up on a person like that?

The woman was medium height, with thick brown hair that glinted with red highlights in the firelight. She had a sprinkling of freckles across her nose, and eyes the color of dark moss stared back at Ricki. If it weren't for the edge in her gaze, she might have stepped right off the pages of a travel advertisement for Ireland. But there was something about the look in her eye, and the way she stood with her feet apart and her hands in the pockets of a puffy black parka, that told Ricki she was a cop.

A tall, lean man stood next to her, his hands clasped behind his back. His straight black hair was neatly groomed, and a perfect match to his dark eyes. But despite the fact that he looked like he'd come off the cover of a high-end fashion magazine, he had the same flat look in his gaze as his female companion.

Another cop, Ricki thought. She studied them for a moment in silence. She figured they were either detectives with the county sheriff's department or Hamilton's missing two agents. And since she didn't recognize either of them, she was going with the county detectives.

"I'm Special Agent Gin Reilly, with the FBI." She tilted her head to the side. "And this is Special Agent Stephen Jones. Also with the FBI and my partner."

Somewhere behind her, Ricki heard a soft chuckle.

"Well, I guess you brought the FBI after all," Crowder said.

"How about that?" Ricki replied flatly.

Gin's smile didn't falter. "Senior Special Agent in Charge Hamilton sent us."

"Did he?" Ricki shifted her weight but didn't move one inch forward to greet the woman.

Gin matched Ricki's stance and lifted one eyebrow. "In a roundabout way, but regardless, your boss has assigned us to this case."

Chapter 14

IT WAS another two hours before the weary group headed back to Glacier and their rental, with everyone hoping to grab a few hours of sleep. Gin and Stephen followed in their own rental, and Ricki could see their headlights every time she glanced over at the side mirror. Without saying a word once she'd slid into the front passenger seat, leaned back, and began silently alternating between anger and brooding.

Blake's agents, she mentally fumed. Hamilton had sent her two of Blake's minions to be part of her team. She didn't want the services of Special Agent Gin Reilly. Why hadn't he sent Dan? Research might be his strong point, but he was still an agent in the ISB, and he wasn't too bad a shot. Yeah, Dan would have been fine.

But no. She got Reilly and . . . Drawing a blank on the male partner's name, Ricki searched around in her memory until it finally crept out of hiding. Jones. That was it. And what kind of name was Jones for a guy who looked like he had a good dose of Asian somewhere in his ancestry? Not to mention that he hadn't said a word. Didn't he talk?

She knew Clay kept glancing in her direction, but she didn't care. After the way he'd been slouching around the last few days with his hands in his pockets and doing his best to avoid her, she was entitled to a couple of minutes of having a mood of her own. She was dealing with his, so he could just deal with hers.

"The ISB is shorthanded, Ricki. We need help, and I'm guessing that Hamilton didn't have a lot of choices," Clay said quietly.

"I know that," Ricki snapped out, then, feeling a twinge of shame at slapping back at Clay for something that wasn't his fault, she slumped down in her seat. "I didn't tell them to go home, did I?"

From the back seat, Anchorman let out a snort of laughter. "That's keeping an open mind, James."

Ricki twisted around in her seat and glared over its back at Anchorman. "Since when did you become a Jonathan Blake fan?"

He lifted his broad shoulders in a shrug. "I'm not, but he isn't here to take a punch at, and I'm a big fan of more help."

"You know I'm not a Blake fan," Clay added. "But you have to be a bit curious."

"About?" Ricki asked.

Clay kept his eyes on the road as he considered it for a long moment. "Blake always sends the agents with the skill sets he thinks are needed for a case. Those two looked like seasoned agents, so what is it about them that Blake thinks we need at the moment?"

"There is that," Ricki muttered, conceding the point only because the same thought had crossed her mind somewhere in the middle of being pissed.

"And last time Blake sent Finn," Clay continued. "You liked working with Finn, didn't you?"

She had, but that had been an entirely different kettle of fish. She and Finn had a tie to each other. Their respective partners had been engaged to each other, and both of them had been murdered. Bringing their killer to justice had been their common goal, and from there a friendship had developed. Well, a kind of friendship. They didn't work for the same agency, and their paths rarely crossed, but Clay was right. She did like the big tough-talking Irishman, even if he did work with Blake. And for all she knew, this Gin Reilly could be one of Finn's cousins from the home country.

Clay turned into the driveway of their rented house and shut off the engine. Feeling the events of the last twenty-four hours weighing down on her shoulders, Ricki dragged herself out of the car and up the porch steps, with Clay, Anchorman and the two special agents just behind her. The front door popped open and Cheron stood on the threshold. The bottom of a long pink robe pooled at her feet as she stepped aside to let them tramp past her into the house.

"Oh, hello. And who are you?" she asked Gin.

"I'm Special Agent Gin Reilly," Gin said with a weary smile.

"And I'm her partner, Special Agent Stephen Jones," the second agent said, politely holding out a hand.

Cheron gave it a brief shake before turning to close the door. "I guess you're the two agents that Hamilton sent. I have some beds made up for you."

As much as she would have liked to tell Reilly and Jones to go find the nearest hotel, Ricki couldn't quite bring herself to be that petty. Besides, she was bone-tired and there would be enough time tomorrow to decide whether or not to call Hamilton and demand he send them back to wherever they'd come from. She glanced at her watch. The glowing dial said it was 3 a.m. Wonderful.

Lifting a hand, she said, "Good night," to no one in particular and headed for the stairs.

Chapter 15

THE RINGING WOULDN'T STOP. Ricki groaned and rolled over, plopping her pillow over her head, but it didn't help. She could still hear the phone. Finally giving up, she groped around on the small nightstand until her hand landed on the rectangular plastic casing. She cracked one eye open and peeked at the display. Eddie.

Quickly scooting up against the wall, she stabbed at the connect button and held the phone up to her ear. "Hey, bud. You're up early."

"It's eight o'clock, Mom. You're always up by eight o'clock." In an instant, Eddie's tone flipped from complaining to alarm. "Is something wrong?"

"No," Ricki assured him. "Just a late night."

"Oh? With Clay?" Now there was a snicker in his voice that had Ricki rolling her eyes.

"That's none of your business, and no. I was out on a case." She reached over and shoved a pillow behind her back. "What's up, bud? How's school?" Eddie had just returned to his prestigious boarding school for gifted kids after spending a few weeks with his father, who'd been recovering from a gunshot wound.

"I guess that's why you sound kind of out of it. What's going on?" Eddie asked.

"Nothing much. Just a bunch of fires that were set in the middle of a road."

"Okay," her son said slowly, drawing the word out in a way that only a teenager could. "Is Anchorman there helping with your case? I mean, investigating fires doesn't sound like his thing, but I've been calling him, and he's not picking up his phone."

"When did you start calling him?"

"Since six this morning. He's always on his way to the diner by then, so he should be answering his phone."

Ricki sighed and switched her cell to the other ear as she wiggled into a more comfortable sitting position. "First of all, bud, I know Anchorman's part of the family, but you shouldn't be calling him at six in the morning. And second, he probably turned his phone off because as it so happens, he *is* here helping me out, and he got to bed as late as I did. Why do you need to talk to him at six o'clock in the morning?" Now it was her turn to sound alarmed. "Is everything all right?"

"I have a big problem going on here. I need him to help with one of my class projects, and I have to know if he can make it to the school on that day."

Ricki sighed. If Eddie needed Anchorman tomorrow, her son was going to be out of luck. "Eddie, when is that day? And don't say tomorrow."

"Next month."

She tried but couldn't hold back a laugh. "And how is this a big problem?"

"Mom, if he can't make it, I'll have to think of something else. Maybe Clay could come? A chief of police is almost as good as a sniper."

"He's a former sniper, and I'm sure Clay would be thrilled to hear he came in a close second." When Eddie made a pouting sound, Ricki shook her head. Despite being almost as tall as his father, it reminded her that her son was still a kid. "Fine. I'll tell Anchorman to turn on his phone, after," she said, raising her voice over Eddie's elated whoop. "After he wakes up and has had some coffee. Which should be in a couple of hours. Deal?"

"Yeah. Deal."

Ricki spent another five minutes listening to Eddie enthusiastically go into details of the latest robot he and his roommate at the school were building. She left him happier than when he called, which with a teenager was always a win. Swinging her long legs over the side of the bed, she stood up and stretched, then grabbed a towel and headed for the shower that Cheron had primly announced was only for the women.

Thirty minutes later she felt a bit more human, and intended to complete the transformation with a strong cup of coffee. She'd noticed the single cup coffeemaker on the counter in the kitchen—something she'd been meaning to invest in herself if she ever had time to get into Tacoma—and quietly walked down the stairs in her stocking feet.

She got three steps past the bottom of the staircase before stopping, surprised to see Agent Reilly sitting at the long island that separated the kitchen from the living space. The FBI agent had a steaming mug in one hand and was tapping away on her phone with the other. She really didn't want to talk to Gin Reilly, but she wasn't about to give up that cup of coffee either, so she nodded when Reilly glanced her way, then continued on to the coffee machine.

"You're up early," Ricki said as she dropped a pod into the slot and pushed the button.

"Your phone woke me up. Then I heard you moving around, so I thought I'd come down and join you."

"Very bold, Agent Reilly."

"Very efficient, Ricki," Gin said. "And I intend to call you Ricki, so you might as well call me Gin."

Ricki lifted her cup out of the machine and took a sip. The woman certainly wasn't shy. But if Gin could be direct, so could she. "Fine. I take it you wanted a private chat for a reason. What is it?"

The FBI agent smiled, her green eyes taking on a sparkle of amusement that transformed her whole expression, giving it a touch of warmth for the first time since Ricki had met her. "Well, to start off, who called you this morning?"

Ricki delayed answering by taking another sip of coffee. "I meant, what do you want to know about the case?"

Gin blinked her eyes in an exaggerated attempt to look surprised. "Oh? The call wasn't about the case?"

"It was my son. Now, about the case?"

Ignoring Ricki's blatant hint to keep it all business, Gin gave her a wide grin. "A son? That's great. Do you have a picture?"

Ricki resisted the urge for all of two seconds before pulling her phone out of her back pocket. Quickly scrolling over to the photos, she pulled one up and turned the screen toward Gin. "Here he is. That's Eddie. He just turned fifteen."

"Wow, good-looking kid."

"So is his father," Ricki said, shoving the phone back into her pocket.

"He looks really tall for fifteen."

Ricki smiled as she picked up her coffee mug again. "So is his father," she repeated. "Bear's a big guy. He played football all the way through college."

Gin sat straight up, her eyes wide. "Wait. Bear? As in Bear James? Did he play for the University of Washington like, I don't know, fifteen years ago?"

"Yeah, he did. Do you know him?" Ricki asked.

The agent shook her head. "Not me. I was still finishing up

high school, but my older brother knew him. At least on the field. Dev played for the University of Colorado." She laughed. "I had no idea that you were Bear James's ex. He was a good player."

"Yeah, he was." Trying not to feel old because Gin Reilly was in high school when she was in college, Ricki smiled. "Did you grow up in Colorado?"

Gin drew her arms in closer to her body and her face lost the animated expression it had held just a second ago. "Dev did. I didn't."

Seeing Gin's strange reaction to her childhood, Ricki let it slide. Instead, she leaned her forearms on the counter and pinned a direct stare on the other woman. "How did you know Bear is an 'ex'? I didn't say he was."

"Ah. Now that was a slip, wasn't it?" Gin's mouth curled up in a rueful smile. "Stephen's always telling me I have to work on that."

"You still haven't answered my question," Ricki pointed out.

"Okay," Gin said. "Here it is. Ricki James. Special agent with the ISB since college, except for a one-year stint you did with the US Marshals when your partner was killed in an ambush. You took some time off, then last year rejoined the ISB." She grinned. "And just for the record, I didn't get into any personal stuff. I had a crush on Bear, along with several other players, and read somewhere that he was divorced."

Amused despite herself, Ricki fought not to smile. "Well, if you're still interested, I can give you his number. And just for the record, I didn't rejoin the ISB, I was reactivated." At Gin's curious look, Ricki shrugged. "Long story. And to be completely accurate, Marie was more than my partner. She was also my roommate in college and my best friend."

"Losing her that way must have been tough," Gin said quietly. "I'm sorry."

Ricki acknowledged Gin's sympathy with a short nod. "I

am too. Now I'd like to know why you were looking into my background."

"Not just your background. I read up on all your cases, too. You do a great job, by the way, and I was checking you out because I like to know who I'm working with."

"So do I," Ricki countered. "Which means it's your turn. How long have you been with the FBI?"

"Since I got out of college, just like you," Gin said. "I worked in the northeast district for a few years then moved over to a special team."

Which, Ricki thought sourly, *is where Blake comes in.* "What kind of special team?"

Gin smiled. "It's not a well-publicized thing. The Bureau likes to keep us pretty close to the vest, but Stephen and I work for the CCU. That's the Critical Crimes Unit. There's about ten teams of partners, and we cover the country."

Ricki frowned. "Cover the country doing what?"

"In a nutshell, we deal solely with any crime that has a good chance of doing widespread damage, or has to be stopped with as little publicity as possible. If the local authorities or our own office is having trouble dealing with it, that's where we come in." When Ricki only frowned, Gin sighed. "Like the Alley Killer."

"The Alley Killer," Ricki repeated slowly. The guy who left gutted bodies in alleys in a half dozen cities. One day he was news with no solid leads, and the next he'd been caught and taken away to a federal holding, never to be heard of since. She paused and lifted an eyebrow. "I wondered about that. Was that you guys?"

"We aren't supposed to talk about our cases, but under the necessity of garnering some trust here, yeah, that was us."

"Do you mean 'us' as in the CCU, or 'us' as in you and your partner?" Ricki asked.

"Let's just leave it at 'us' and move on."

"Okay." Ricki leaned her elbows on the counter. "I know

that Blake sent you, and that he's big on selecting skills to fit a case. So, why you and Stephen?"

"Maybe you can tell me," Gin said, not batting an eyelash at Ricki stating that Blake had sent her and her partner. "Stephen and I have both taken survival training and worked a few cases in the backcountry, but not as much as you have. I have a knack—an instinct I guess might be a better word—for where the bad guys would go. You know, figuring out what their next step will be. Stephen is good with undercover work and with details. He's quick at getting us intel and background information we need to track our suspects down. I'm a good shot, but Stephen is better. He's good at hand-to-hand, but I'm better." She smiled. "You get the idea." Gin pushed her empty cup across the counter. "Can you stick another pod into that machine for me? I need another hit of caffeine." When Ricki picked up the cup, Gin smiled. "And by caffeine, I mean from green tea."

"You don't drink coffee?" Ricki asked. The thought boggled the mind.

"Never have liked the stuff."

Ricki plucked the tea pod out of the rack on the counter and stared at it for a moment. There hadn't been anything in the rack when they'd first come to the house, so she assumed that everything it held now had been bought by Clay and Anchorman, neither of whom would have picked up any tea on their own. Which meant it had been on Cheron's grocery list. She turned and held up the pod in Gin's line of vision.

"How did the guys know to buy tea?"

Not bothering to pretend she had no idea what Ricki meant, Gin met Ricki's stare head-on. "Blake probably got the word here somehow. He usually does when he pulls me for an assignment. Having no tea available is a deal breaker."

"So you don't work directly for Blake?"

Gin shook her head. "Nope. He's an asshole, but a really competent one. I work for Senior Special Agent Todd Barron.

But Blake has a lot of unwritten privileges within the Bureau, so if he wants to 'borrow' a team, he's pretty much allowed to do that." She nodded at Ricki. "I heard through the grapevine that he's pulled that shit on you too. Kind of makes you feel you have no control over your own destiny, or maybe like a paid servant, doesn't it?"

Suddenly feeling a tenuous kinship with the agent, Ricki smiled. "A puppet on a string."

"Yeah, that works too," Gin said. "So, is this the part where we talk about the case? I'd really like to know what you've got."

Ricki finished making Gin's tea, or rather she stood around while the machine made it, then passed the cup across the island. "I don't have squat. A dead body that was shot in the back and then a second shot to the head, execution style. It looks like he was running drugs by using a backpack to carry them across the Canadian border. So he might have been robbed for the coke he had on him, except ten bricks of it were left behind. I took one with me to get tested, and we would have gone back for the rest except the hermit got to it first and burned it up last night. And that's the point where you came in."

"Uh-huh," Gin said. Her eyes narrowed as she watched Ricki. "Who is the hermit?"

"The hermit is some kind of local legend," Ricki said. "We're just borrowing the name for our guy who hangs around in the forest, waiting for people to find a dead body, and then burns up a small fortune in drugs."

Gin picked up a spoon she'd set on the countertop and began to absently stir her tea. "So, you think he's your killer?"

"I don't know," Ricki admitted. "It's a possibility, especially since we don't have any other suspects."

The FBI agent studied Ricki's face for a long moment. "But you don't think so?"

"No. He doesn't pop for me."

"So, he kills the drug runner, takes the drugs, and burns them up?" Gin frowned. "I'm not really seeing that as a reason for Blake calling us in. He could have used someone out of the office in Seattle. We're pretty specialized."

Thinking she and Gin were on the same page on that one, Ricki shrugged. "I don't know. When I called for help, all we had was a crackpot running around in the woods and a dead drug runner."

"A dead drug runner with drugs that were burned up in what?" Gin asked. "Four separate fires? Which is also weird. Why put three or four bricks in each fire? Why not just make one gigantic bonfire and burn them all up at once?"

"No. There were . . ." Ricki felt like a bucket of cold water had been thrown in her face. No matter how tired she was, she should have put two and two together last night. "He put all nine bricks into that fourth fire he started for our entertainment," she said slowly. "Clay counted them. There were nine."

"Okay," Gin said. "And so?" Then she abruptly slid off her stool and stood up. "Oh. Geez. You said that you found ten bricks stacked up at the scene? Is that all you found? Just the ten bricks? So he burned everything up?"

Ricki's expression turned sour. "Yeah. Ten. But we figured the pack he was carrying could have held twice that many. So if all ten are either burned up or waiting to be tested in a lab, then the question is, where is the rest of the cocaine? At least, that's the question I've been asking myself."

Gin immediately picked up on where Ricki was going. "Assuming there really was forty pounds in that backpack, that's ten more bricks of cocaine unaccounted for." She whistled softly under her breath. "That's another half million that he still might be planning to send up in smoke."

"Now how did an old man living in the woods happen to stumble across a million dollars' worth of cocaine? And how did he know that's what Santiago Garcia was carrying in his pack?" Ricki wondered out loud.

The FBI agent picked up her cold cup of tea and took a sip. "I'm still not sure why Blake sent Stephen and I out here to help you, but I'm thinking we're getting close. Tell me what you know about this drug runner."

Chapter 16

"So you were sent here to investigate the drug runner, not to catch his killer?" Clay was sitting on one end of the couch, an ankle propped up on the opposite knee. But his relaxed posture didn't match the sharp note in his question.

"That's what Gin thinks," Ricki said. She had roused Clay and Anchorman out of their beds, while Gin had done the same with her partner. When the three men had filed in, their eyes still heavy from sleep, they had immediately plopped down on the various pieces of furniture scattered throughout the open living space.

They'd gratefully accepted the cups of coffee Gin had passed out, along with bagels she'd warmed up in the microwave. Once they'd looked like they were no longer wandering about in a fog, Ricki had given them a brief rundown on her conversation with Gin, minus their exchange about Blake.

"Our primary focus is to catch whoever killed Santiago Garcia, with the CCU team's help, while their focus is to figure out who sent him here and if there are any others. So we help each other." Ricki paused and put her hands on her hips. "A quid pro quo kind of thing."

"You scratch mine, I'll scratch yours," Anchorman said then lifted a hand to cover a wide yawn. "I'm not seeing the problem here."

Clay fixed his flat cop stare on Gin. "What is a CCU team? Some kind of special unit that operates within the FBI?"

"More or less," Gin said. "And that's about all I can tell you."

Ricki ignored the sharp look from Clay, keeping her attention on Gin. "So we're all on the same page here, and my team has the lead on this case."

Gin nodded. "We know this is your territory, and we'll follow your lead. We'll help you out, and all we're asking in return is that you pass any information on your vic along to us."

"Santiago Garcia," Stephen said in a fluid accent. "What do we know about him, besides the fact he was carrying drugs and got himself killed?"

"Like I told Gin, he's twenty-three years old and the driver's license he had in his pocket was issued by the state of Jalisco, in Mexico," Ricki said with a nod toward the woman, who had taken a seat on a large, cushioned footrest with her legs stretched out in front of her. She didn't bat an eyelash when her partner sat straight up in his seat.

Stephen stared wide-eyed at Gin and then turned his gaze on Ricki. "Did you say Jalisco?" He looked back at Gin. "Did she say that?"

"Yeah," Gin drawled. "Ricki was also nice enough to show me the license. The kid was definitely from Jalisco."

"Well, isn't that an unbelievable coincidence?" Stephen flopped back against the cushions of the couch and shook his head. "Great."

From his position at the other end of the sofa, Clay frowned at him. "Want to fill the rest of us in? What's the deal with Jalisco?"

"You worked homicide in LA, right?" Gin asked him. "When you were there, did you ever run into any gang murders with a CJNG tie?"

"There was one just before I left the department. The vic had a tat with those initials and a crown and a knife on it," Clay said.

Gin nodded. "That's the one. They're big believers in the sword solving everything, and one of the most violent cartels we've run across. They've been tied to some pretty dicey stuff in Mexico. They've even cut off and eaten the body parts of some of their victims. And once they brought down a helicopter with a rocket-propelled grenade. Really bad guys, with a capital *B*."

"Shit," Anchorman said. "Sounds like they would have fit right in with some of the guerrilla fighters I encountered when I was in the Corps."

"Yeah," Gin said. "Sometimes it feels like those types are everywhere. But this particular brand is based out of Jalisco, and over the last few years they've made heavy inroads into the drug trade coming into the Northwest."

Clay and Anchorman looked at Ricki, concern in their eyes. They both knew that her partner and best friend had been killed on the Seattle docks when they'd been escorting a member of the Sinola Cartel who'd been arrested for drug trafficking. She smiled and shrugged, to let them know she was okay with this latest turn. And it wasn't exactly a surprise to her. With the amount of drugs they'd suspected Santiago Garcia was transporting, the odds had been high he was employed by a cartel.

"The execution-style killing also goes with the CJNG style," Gin continued. "Blowing a guy's head to pieces fits right in with them."

Clay shook his head. "Okay. But blowing their own guy's head to pieces and then leaving half—maybe all—of the drugs he was carrying behind? Does that fit in with them?"

"They might have had another two-legged mule to pick up the slack," Gin said with a glance at Ricki.

"That's right." Ricki turned toward Clay. "You counted the bricks in that fourth fire. There were nine, plus the one I took from the crime scene, that makes ten."

"And assuming Garcia had a forty-pound pack, that would hold twenty, which leaves ten more unaccounted for." Clay rubbed a hand over the top of his head. "So our crazy guy has either stashed them somewhere, or . . ." He trailed off, considering it.

"Someone else took them," Ricki said quietly. "Which means this other person could have killed Garcia, or the crazy guy did."

"Or someone we still need to find," Gin pointed out. "Let's say there were two mules, each carrying a forty-pound backpack. That's two million dollars, minus the half million we saw go up in smoke last night. But before it did, and when the mules still had it? Well, that's a lot of money. It would be worth the cartel's time to come looking for it."

Silence fell around the room as each member of the group followed their own thoughts. Ricki finally stirred and her foot started to drum a steady beat against the wood floor. "It doesn't fit. There are pieces we know about this that don't fit this being a cartel hit."

Stephen leaned forward, his hands clasped in front of him. "What pieces?"

"The bullet. A .30-30 Winchester cartridge was found at the scene."

"That's right," Cheron said from the bottom of the stairs. Dressed in her uniform of overalls and a plaid shirt, she looked refreshed as she adjusted her glasses on the end of her nose. "What are you all talking about?"

"We're tossing around ideas about who killed Garcia," Ricki said. "Take a seat and join in. There are still a couple of spots left."

Cheron smiled and walked to the empty chair next to Anchorman's. She sat down as a satisfied gleam crept into the sniper's eyes. "So, is this about the bullet possibly coming from a Winchester 1891 because of the cartridge?" Cheron asked.

"A what?" Stephen looked startled. "Isn't that a game-hunting rifle?"

"Not exactly the semiautomatic or outright machine gun that's favored by CJNG," Gin observed. "That's just plain weird."

Ricki couldn't agree more. She'd felt like the whole thing was, as Gin had said, just plain weird right from the start. It all seemed out of sync somehow. "And there's the second problem. Clay and I backtracked from where we found the body over toward the main trail. It was rough going but doable, so Garcia might have come down from the Copper Ridge Trail, except we came across another track. It looked like it was running parallel to the main trail in both directions."

Gin shrugged. "Okay. That's actually better. It means the drug smugglers would have had even less of a chance of being seen by anyone. So what's the problem?"

"That's rugged terrain back there," Ricki said. "To carve out a way that followed the main trail, or even go chasing after Garcia, and then find your way back after killing him, someone would have to know the landscape and be very familiar with that section of the park."

All the other occupants of the room frowned at once.

"That doesn't sound likely," Cheron finally spoke up, giving voice to the obvious.

"No, it doesn't." Anchorman had said very little up to this point, but now he shifted in his chair. "Whenever my team was in country, we'd usually end up with the job of rooting out the enemy. Sometimes that led us into the backcountry of some pretty wild places. We were good at what we did, but to get us from place to place out there? We'd hire locals."

"Locals?" Gin blinked, then gestured toward the window. "You mean like from here?"

"Why not?" Ricki stated more than asked. "Glacier is the nearest town to the back-door entrance into the park."

Stephen stood up and stretched. "They could have hired anyone. Maybe from Seattle or Spokane. There have to be a lot of people who've been on those trails."

Ricki shook her head. "No, it's not as easy as walking the trails. It takes a lot of experience to hike off them. It would take years to learn the park that well, and to make a track like that. Or even find it if it's left over from the Nooksack or one of the other native tribes that settled into this area. Someone like that wouldn't be living in a city." Ricki paused. "Someone like our crazy guy," she said slowly.

"So he could have been their guide, and then killed them for the drugs?"

"What 'them' are we talking about here?" Clay asked. "We've only found one dead drug runner."

"There might be more," Ricki said. "That hike from the trailhead all the way up into Canada isn't a one-day deal. There has to be a campsite somewhere."

"Maybe they just used one of the regular ones?" Gin suggested. "I mean, as long as they didn't flash their guns around, they'd look like guys going camping and carrying their supplies in a backpack, just like everyone else."

"If they did that, they'd need a permit to post at the campsite," Ricki said. "Or risk a random check by a ranger, and there are a few stations up there where the park rangers can stay while they make sweeps of the campgrounds."

Gin nodded her agreement. "You're right. With two mil in coke stashed in your tent, that would be too risky." She sighed and crossed her feet at the ankles. "That leaves us back with the locals. Or a park ranger." She gave Ricki an apologetic look. "Every service has someone who can be bribed." When

Anchorman grunted, she bit her lower lip to keep from smiling. "Except for the Marines, of course."

"Which leaves us where?" Stephen asked. "Doing background checks on every resident of Glacier? And that's what? One hundred and fifty or so?"

"It isn't so many if we take out any children, elderly people, and relative newcomers," Gin pointed out.

Anchorman also stood, reaching over to draw Cheron up with him. "It might be easier to narrow that down by visiting the local watering hole. Every town, even with a hundred people in it, has a dive bar. Someplace the tourists don't go and where all the local gossip gets hashed over."

"I agree," Clay said. "And in a town this size, it won't be hard to find."

"Maybe it's the Snowmelt," Cheron offered.

"That has a nice bar, honey," Anchorman said, causing Gin's eyebrows to rise. "We're talking about something entirely different." He shrugged. "You all discuss it while Cheron and I scare up a decent breakfast. A warmed-up bagel just isn't going to cut it."

He turned and walked off with the doctor right beside him. Gin stared after him before looking over at Ricki and shaking her head. "Mr. Macho Man is going to cook breakfast?"

Ricki smiled. "Anchorman and I are partners in a diner back in the Bay. He's the cook."

Gin's mouth dropped open. "You own a diner *and* a sniper is your cook?" She glanced at Clay. "Now I know why an LA homicide detective wanted to hang out around there. Interesting place."

Clay's half-smile didn't quite reach his eyes. "Yeah, it is."

Chapter 17

It was half past noon when Ricki stood in front of the tired-looking building, her hands on her hips and her boot tapping on the asphalt of the parking lot. Trust Anchorman to know exactly where the seediest bar in town was.

Tucked away on a small side street, where no tourist would bother to roam, the Last Stop looked like its name. Its wood siding had faded to an ashy gray, and two posts standing out front were stark reminders of a porch roof that was no longer there.

Ricki shook her head and pushed open the door. The loud creak of the hinges immediately drew the attention of the patrons already inside, drinking their day away. She was greeted by a scattering of whistles that came to an abrupt halt when Clay and Anchorman stepped in behind her. Without breaking stride, Ricki walked up to the bar and sat on a stool. Clay took up a position beside her, and Anchorman deliberately sat on the other side of the chief, pointedly ignoring both him and Ricki as he thumped a heavy knuckle on top of the bar.

The whole place was a single room, with booths along one wall and a built-in bar lined with stools along the other. In between them was a scattering of scarred wooden tables flanked by rickety chairs. The man standing behind the bar at the far end pretended not to see them, but couldn't quite hide his sideways glances in their direction as he continued to wipe down a glass he'd plucked from a tray still dripping with water. He carefully added it to the stack on the counter behind him. When Anchorman tapped on the bar top again, he finally looked their way, approaching them with a wide smile.

His gaze immediately went to Anchorman's right shoulder. The sleeve of his shirt was rolled up all the way to the top, leaving a very prominent tattoo of the Marine Corps insignia, with a gun sight in the center, on full display. The bartender ran a nervous tongue over his lips before looking up to meet Anchorman's stare.

"Problem?" Anchorman asked, his tone holding a hint of menace.

"No, no." The bartender's dark hair was slicked back from his face, and he sported a scraggly mustache on his upper lip. His shirtsleeves were also rolled up and the apron tied around his waist had lost any claim to being white a long time ago. "I saw one of those tattoos when I was in the army. On a couple of Marine snipers."

"So? Is it Marines or snipers that you don't like?"

The bartender took a half-step back, his eyes widening as he shook his head. "Just making conversation. What'll you have? It's on the house."

Ricki turned her head to hide her smile. She doubted if she or Clay would be getting any free drinks—unless, of course, one of them suddenly sprouted a Marine tattoo. Anchorman rarely displayed it, but on the short ride over, they'd come up with a plan to cover as much ground as possible, and flashing his sniper tattoo was part of it. Since the three of them had already made an appearance at the Snowmelt, it was a sure bet everyone in town knew who they were and that at least two of them were in law enforcement.

So there was no use in trying to hide that. Which meant their best chance at getting a local to open up was Anchorman. And that tattoo of his was a pretty good conversation piece.

Now all they had to do was look like he had a legitimate excuse to have a drink on his own, and that part of the plan was up to her and Clay.

When the chief took her hand, she smiled, looking all the world as if her entire focus was just on him.

"What would you like, sweetheart?" Clay said, loud enough for most of the surrounding patrons to hear. It was Anchorman's cue to frown and blow out an annoyed sigh.

"I don't know what they're having, but I'll take a beer. Whatever you've got in a long-necked bottle," Anchorman said. When the bartender returned with the beer, Ricki lifted a hand to Clay's cheek, meeting his amused gaze when Anchorman noisily slid off the barstool, his heavy boots hitting the ground with a thud, the sound rolling around the room. It was a good thing this operation didn't call for any kind of subtlety.

The former Marine nodded at the bartender. "What's your name?"

"Everyone in town calls me Jimmy."

Anchorman nodded again. "Thanks for the beer, Jimmy. I think I'll take it over there and give these lovebirds their space."

Once he'd left, Jimmy turned his attention to Clay and Ricki. "And what about you two? What'll it be?"

"Same as our friend," Clay said smoothly. "Two beers." He waited until the bartender returned with the ice-cold bottles before saying anything else. "Nice place. Do you own it, Jimmy, or do you just work here?"

Jimmy wiped his hands on a towel before leaning them against the counter that ran underneath the top of the bar. "Both. I work here and I own it. Why? Are you looking to buy something?"

Clay laughed. "Nah." He inclined his head toward Ricki. "She already owns a diner, and that's enough of a headache."

The bartender looked over at Ricki, his eyebrows raised over dark eyes. "Oh yeah? Is it one of those health food places?"

Ricki shook her head. She'd left her long dark hair loose to spill, smooth and silky, over her shoulders. "No. It's strictly for the locals. There's a resort hotel in town, and all those people go to the fancy restaurant down the street." There wasn't any such restaurant in the Bay, but Ricki was betting Jimmy had never set foot more than fifty miles out of Glacier.

"Well, you don't want to serve up that crap anyway," Jimmy said with a smile, showing a large gap between his two front teeth. "Tastes like cardboard with sawdust on top."

Ricki pretended to smirk at the description as she turned to Clay. "You've eaten there. Is that what you think the food tastes like?"

"Pretty much." He picked up his beer and smiled at the bartender. "I've lived over on the peninsula most of my life," he lied smoothly. "Prefer the smaller towns. How about you?"

While Clay tried the friendly, good old boy approach to pull information out of Jimmy, Ricki took a slow, careful look around. A flyer with big, bold lettering that was pinned to the wall behind the bar caught her eye.

GUIDED TOURS
MOUNT BAKER WILDERNESS AND CASCADES PARK

Underneath was listed a phone number. Ricki silently repeated it, committing it to memory, before picking up her own beer and casually half-turning her body on the stool. She looked over the room. Anchorman was already holding court with a group of men in jeans, flannel shirts, and heavy boots at a table near the back wall. Several other tables were also occupied by men drinking alone.

From the corner of her eye, she caught movement in the last booth on the far right. Turning her head, there was just enough light to make out the single occupant. Slightly overweight with a bald head, he seemed out of place in his business suit and tie in a light shade of blue. He was sitting still with his hands laid on the table, his fingers spread wide apart. His face was in the shadows, so she couldn't tell where he was looking, but since his hands noticeably jerked when she stared right at him, she figured he was watching her and Clay.

An older woman shuffled across the floor, momentarily blocking Ricki's view of the man in the booth. She was slightly bent over as she slowly walked along, guiding a bucket on wheels with the long handle of a mop. She stopped when the man in the corner said something to her, but she only shook her head and continued on her way toward the swinging doors leading into the back. Ricki glanced over at the bartender just in time to catch him watching the exchange between the man and the old woman.

Wondering what that was all about, Ricki turned her head in the opposite direction when the front door opened, letting a bright shaft of light into the dingy room. Gin walked in, only she didn't look like Gin. Her jeans were skintight, and she had on a pair of red boots that matched the red silk of her blouse. The material clung to her every curve, and Gin had left it unbuttoned a good distance down her chest. Her shoulder-length brunette hair was pulled up into a high ponytail and tied with a scarf the same color of red as her blouse and boots. Her bold gaze made a brief sweep around the room, landing on Anchorman. She gave him a broad wink, which he ignored, causing her lips to form into a pout.

"Come on, Snookers," she said to the tall, loose-limbed man who had come up behind her. When he put his arms around her waist, she instantly squirmed away. "Hey, at least wait until we get a table." She took his hand and made a fuss about crossing the room, plopping down in a chair at a table right next to Anchorman's.

While Jimmy was avidly watching the show Gin was putting on, Clay leaned over and whispered in Ricki's ear. "What did Gin do? Go out and pick up some guy?"

Ricki grinned. With worn-out jeans, a slouch, and a messy mop of dark hair over a pair of sunglasses, the man Gin had called "Snookers" didn't look anything like a special agent in the FBI.

"I'm betting that's Stephen," Ricki whispered back. "I'd say he's pretty good at this disguise stuff."

There was a brief silence before Clay said, "Whoa. He's a friggin' genius at it."

They all spent the next thirty minutes dealing with their assignments, probing for information while Gin made a pretense of flirting with both Anchorman and Stephen, giving the ex-Marine an easy way to establish a little male rapport with his smirking drinking buddies.

When Clay struck up a conversation with a newcomer who had taken the stool next to him, Jimmy moved off. He stepped out from behind the bar and walked over to the man sitting in the corner. A short conversation ensued before Jimmy returned to the bar and the man carefully slid out of the booth. Without looking in Ricki's direction, he walked out the door. She nodded at Stephen, who immediately produced a pack of cigarettes from his shirt pocket.

"I'm going out for a smoke," the FBI agent declared to the room in general.

When Stephen passed by the bar, Jimmy called out to him. "You don't have to go outside to smoke. We don't care about that in here."

Stephen only shrugged and jerked a thumb toward Gin. "Talk to her about it. She don't like it when I smoke around her."

"It's a bad habit," Gin yelled back. "And it make my hair stink."

Stephen waved the pack he was holding in the air. "Yeah, whatever."

Once he disappeared out the door, Gin looked over at Anchorman and batted her eyes. "I think I'll freshen up a bit. Do you know where the ladies' room is?"

"I don't have a map of the place," Anchorman snapped and turned his back on her.

Gin got to her feet and glared at him, her hands on her hips. Lifting her chin, she marched off toward the wooden sign on the far wall that said "Restrooms" with an arrow pointing to the back. She wasn't gone long and was already sitting in her seat again when Stephen walked back inside.

She waited until he got to the table then jumped up. Making a show of looking down her nose at Anchorman, Gin loudly stomped her foot. "I don't care for the company in here, Snookers. Let's find another place."

Stephen's mouth twisted into a sneer. "This ain't New York City. There isn't another place."

Gin simply tossed her head and walked past him, heading for the front door. "How about that Snow Top? It said it was a bar and a diner, so we could get some food too."

"The sign outside said Snowmelt, not Snow Top," Her partner said, but Gin had already gone out the door. Stephen followed her, still grumbling under his breath.

Ricki wanted to applaud the two of them but sat with a straight face through another beer before she nudged Clay in the side. "Let's go," she whispered.

Clay dropped two twenty-dollar bills on the counter. "Even if good old Jimmy doesn't like us, that will ensure he won't put up a fuss if we show up here again," he said quietly.

Nodding at Anchorman, who quickly got to his feet, Ricki made a beeline for the front door. She didn't mind hometown bars, even preferred them most of the time, but she'd had her fill of the dim light and musty smell of this one. Stepping out into the cool air, she drew in a deep breath before heading toward the car.

None of them said anything on the ten-minute drive back to the house. Seeing the car that Gin and Stephen had rented parked out front, Ricki smiled. If nothing else, she was sure that Stephen had gotten a license plate for her.

Cheron was again on the porch to greet them, holding the door open as they all filed inside. The doctor followed Anchorman into the kitchen to help with making sandwiches, then cheerfully passed them out as everyone got comfortable either sitting or standing around the kitchen island.

"So, what did you get?" Ricki asked Stephen.

With both his hair and his posture neatly back in place, Stephen smiled. "A license plate." He reached into his pocket and handed a slip of paper to Ricki. "I had the office in Seattle run it on the way back here. It belongs to a Frank Hontel. I've got his address on there too. Hontel is a loan officer at a Bellingham branch of Washington Federal Bank."

"Maybe he's the bartender's banker," Gin said around a bite of a thick ham and cheese sandwich. "Old Jimmy has a safe in his office that would make Fort Knox proud."

Clay's eyebrows lifted in surprise. "He has that kind of safe and he doesn't lock his office?"

Gin pretended to study her fingernails before grinning at the chief. "Oh, it was locked. And not only did he have that high-end safe, there was also a Burberry leather jacket hanging on a hook behind the door. Terrible way to treat that jacket. They run about three grand."

Ricki almost choked on her coffee. "For a jacket?"

"It's a nice jacket," Clay said, then grinned when Ricki looked at him in astonishment. "I might have tried one on a time or two, but I don't own one. I just know that they're nice jackets."

"Great." Ricki rolled her eyes at the thought of Clay

trying on a three-thousand-dollar leather jacket. "Did you get anything helpful out of our closet rich guy, a.k.a Jimmy the bartender?"

"Nothing concrete." Clay's cop demeanor returned. "But he's jumpy. He knew who we were, and he acted like a guy who was waiting for someone to tell him what to do." He glanced over at Stephen. "He kept sneaking peeks at that banker."

"Jimmy had a conversation with him," Ricki said. "He slithered over there when you were busy talking to that guy who sat down next to you. That was just before Hontel left. Without paying his bill."

"Drinks on the house. How nice," Gin said. She winked at Anchorman. "I'm surprised you had to pay for your beer the way everyone was hanging on your every word."

Anchorman shrugged. "They offered. I declined. None of them looked like they were swimming in money."

"Okay," Ricki said. "They didn't have any money, but did they have information?"

"One guy mentioned that the suit in the corner was Jimmy's banker, and he always has a word for Molly."

"Who's Molly?" Ricki and Gin asked in unison.

"The old woman who was mopping the floors. According to my new drinking buddy, Frank Hontel and Molly always act like they don't know each other, but the neighborhood banker always talks to her. My buddy thought it was funny because it's the only time Frank Hontel has a word for anyone besides Jimmy."

Ricki made a mental note to have Dan do a little more research and check that out. "I saw a notice tacked up behind the bar."

Clay nodded. "I saw it too."

Ricki smiled. "I figured you did. It was hard to miss when we were both sitting there staring at it."

"What kind of notice?" Gin asked.

"A flyer, advertising the services of a guide for the Baker Wilderness that surrounds Glacier, and for the park." When everyone around the island grinned, Ricki nodded in satisfaction. "No name was listed, but I got the phone number."

Stephen reached out a hand. "Give it over and I'll have it traced."

Chapter 18

DAYLIGHT WAS SLOWLY FADING AWAY when Ricki walked out of the house and into a world bathed in gold from the setting sun. She walked over and rested a hip on the railing that circled the porch. She kept one foot planted solidly on the planks of the porch's flooring and let the other one dangle in the air as she admired the glowing colors dancing through the trees. She heard the front door open, followed by the steady, measured tread of boot steps on the wood floor.

Ricki smiled to herself. She knew those footsteps. "Hi, Clay." When he stopped beside her, his hands resting lightly on the railing, she looked up at him. "Something on your mind?"

He ran a distracted hand through his hair. "A couple of somethings, actually. I just don't know how to get them out." He inclined his head to the side. "Would you mind sitting with me on the porch steps? That railing will never take my weight, and I feel like I'm towering over you."

"Sure." Ricki stood up and walked over to the steps, sitting on the second one and propping a leg up on the next one down. She curled the fingers of both hands around her raised knee and waited for Clay to settle in next to her. When he didn't say anything, Ricki used her elbow to give him a gentle nudge in the side. "It won't get said until you start talking."

He sighed and stretched his legs out in front of him. "Okay. What did Gin tell you about this CCU section of the Bureau that she works for?"

"She told me it's a special team within the FBI that gets sent out where their skill sets are needed," Ricki hedged, keeping her gaze on the yard in front of them. She didn't want to lie to Clay, but she didn't want to betray Gin's trust either. "And that they aren't supposed to talk about their cases."

Clay turned his head and studied her profile. "But that's not all she told you, is it?"

Knowing she'd never been much of a liar, Ricki gave in and went the more direct route. "No. But she told me in confidence, Clay, and what they do isn't important for our case. What is important are the skills they brought with them, and I mean that for both Gin and Stephen."

Clay crossed his boots at the ankle and leaned back against the top step. "So you aren't going to tell me what this CCU is all about?"

She stared at him for a long moment. "Are you going to tell me what's eating at you?"

He uncrossed and then recrossed his ankles, finally blowing out a heavy breath. "I've been offered another job."

Ricki frowned. Why was that a problem? The DA in Seattle had been making noises the past month about Clay coming onto his investigative team full-time. "You don't want to work in Andre's office?" Andre Hudson was not only the DA but a personal friend to both of them. She knew Clay both liked and respected Andre, so was having a hard time understanding why he'd been so reluctant to talk to her about the job offer.

"It isn't with Andre. It's with Homeland Security."

Clay's quiet statement had her heart skipping a beat. "Homeland Security? Doing what?"

"Tracking bad guys who come in and out of the country."

Suddenly the reason Clay had been brooding about it became crystal clear. "This has to do with Lex," she stated flatly.

The chief let out a harsh laugh. "Yeah, Lex. My brother, the contract killer. The one who was making threats against us just a few weeks ago." He jerked his head backward, toward the house. "The one I'm sure those FBI agents in there know all about, and for all I know, were sent here to keep an eye on me in case I was in contact with him."

"Clay, you can't believe . . ." Ricki's voice trailed off when Clay abruptly turned his head and stared at her. The hard look in his gray eyes plainly said that he *did* believe Gin and Stephen were told to keep an eye on him.

"The FBI wants Lex badly, and I'm certain that they see me as a conduit to get to him." Clay's tone was flat and hard. "They know Lex contacted us during that last case. They know he was in the Bay, and that I'm the reason he was there."

Ricki returned her gaze to the yard. "And you'd rather catch him before the FBI does?"

"He's a contract killer, Ricki. He's dangerous, and he deserves to be locked away. I know all of that. But he's still my older brother, and I want him to have a fair chance to be put behind bars instead of into a grave."

She didn't have any siblings herself, but she could understand that. She really could. But Homeland Security? There had to be another way, although right at the moment she couldn't think of one short of Clay joining the FBI himself, which she knew damn good and well, given his past experience with that agency, he would never do.

She silently mulled it over, fully aware of Clay's intense gaze on her face. There were certainly worse things than working for Homeland Security, and they were sure to have offices in all the different states. "Where is this job located?"

"It would be with their Office of Intelligence and Analysis. That's where the tracking operation lives." He paused. "The job is in New York City." He lifted his shoulders and then let them drop again. "You know the police chief job has gone to part-time. It never should have been a full-time thing in the first place. Not in the Bay. They're better off with two deputies to cover that much area, and a part-time chief."

"It seems to me you've been pretty busy," Ricki said, then pursed her lips when Clay shook his head.

"Mostly helping you solve your cases." He tried for a smile, but it fell flat. "And I love doing that, but they are still your cases. The gig with Andre and the Seattle DA's office is also part-time for the moment, but they're pushing me to come on full-time as head of that team, and I can't keep putting them off. I'm going to have to make a decision on this."

"I see." That's all she could think to say, otherwise her mind was blank.

He drew his legs up and rested his hands on his bent knees. "Look, I'm sorry. I shouldn't have laid this on you while we're in the middle of a case. We can talk about it once we wrap this up and get back home to the Bay."

"Yeah." Ricki stood up, her temper slowly rising. Just like that he was thinking of moving away? "That's a good idea. Let's talk about it later. But I'd like to know one thing. How long have you known about this job offer from Homeland Security?"

Clay also got to his feet and stuck his hands into the back pockets of his jeans. "About a week. Maybe two." When her eyes narrowed, he sighed. "Now you're angry."

Yeah, she was. But she didn't want to have a fight out here on the front porch with Anchorman, Cheron, and two FBI agents sitting in the living room just a few feet away.

"I'm tired," she stated flatly. "Right now I think we both need some space, and there's a case to solve." She composed her expression before glancing over at him. "If you'd rather not work this one because you have other things in your life to take care of, I understand."

"Now you're being snotty, and that isn't like you," Clay said evenly. "I'm not leaving you in the middle of a case."

No, you'll do the polite thing and wait until after it's closed, she thought, then immediately shoved it aside. The case. She needed to concentrate only on the case.

"That's fine. Your choice." She turned to walk up the steps, deftly avoiding his outstretched hand. "I'm going to get some rest. I'm still dragging from yesterday's lack of sleep." She gave him a stiff smile. "Good night."

When she walked back into the house, Anchorman and Cheron were nowhere in sight, but Stephen and Gin were in the living room.

"The sniper and the doctor went out for a walk," Gin announced. "I'd ask you if they're a thing, but it seems pretty obvious."

Ricki shrugged. "Anchorman considers them a thing. Cheron hasn't decided yet."

A spark of amusement lit up Gin's eyes. "Now that must be something new for him."

Despite her sour mood, Ricki's mouth curved up into a smile. "Well, he's been married three times, so yeah, I imagine it is."

"Huh, only three?" Gin laughed.

"Give the guy a break," Stephen muttered, which only made Gin laugh harder.

She was still snickering when Ricki's phone rang. Managing a smile at Gin's obvious amusement, Ricki plucked the phone out of her back pocket. The display said "Dan." Tapping to connect, she held the phone up to her ear. "Hey, Dan. What have you got on our hermit?" She spoke loud enough for Gin and Stephen to hear, which instantly had them quieting down.

"No murders," Dan said. "At least that aren't solved. I'm still tracking down reports from thirty-five to forty-five years ago and checking with the county sheriff's office. But those records aren't digitized, so it's slow going. Luckily for us, the newspapers have computerized most of their back issues, so I'm checking with Bellingham and Spokane to see if any murders around Glacier were reported in those papers. But so far I've drawn a blank. I have a lead on the town clerk who held the job for almost forty years. I'm trying to track her down. She might know something."

Ricki remembered Cheron's suggestion to talk to Jo. At this point, she didn't have anything to lose. "Okay. We'll ask around. Someone still here in Glacier might know something." She thought of Wanda Simms back in the Bay. Wanda was the keeper of all the local rumors, and she would bet Glacier had their own version of the queen of gossip.

"Sounds good," Dan said into her ear. "I'll touch base as soon as I find out anything."

When Ricki hung up, she realized the two FBI agents were looking at her expectantly. She shook her head. "Nothing on the guy yet. We'll start asking around when we get back."

Gin sat up a little straighter. "Back? Where are we going?"

Ricki plopped down in the nearest chair and stared out the front window. Clay wasn't sitting on the porch steps anymore, but she wasn't going to think about that. She shut those thoughts off by focusing her mind on the case. "It makes sense that Santiago Garcia was running drugs through the park and up into Canada."

"Or the other way around," Stephen observed. "Not that it makes any difference. He was still coming through that park."

"Uh-huh," Ricki said. "And whether you're going to

Canada or coming down this way, it's not only a tough hike, it's also a long one."

"You mean it can't be done in one day," Gin said slowly. "You've already told us that."

"Yeah, and that it isn't likely he, and whoever was with him, used one of the standard campsites." Ricki leaned forward, her forearms on top of her thighs. "We need to find that camp."

Gin nodded. "We find that camp, we might find that hermit of yours."

"Why do you say that?" Ricki asked. "We've already found the body he was watching, and he's burned the drugs."

Gin smiled and waved her hand in the air. "But we've all agreed there was probably more than one person running those drugs, and the trail you found was used enough you could see it. I mean it was visible and not completely over-grown, right?"

"Which means it's probably been used more than once," Ricki agreed slowly. "So the hermit might be hanging around to take care of the next group of drug dealers, who would likely use the same trail."

Stephen grunted. "Sounds like this guy has a real grudge against drug runners."

"So he told us," Ricki said absently. "How do you feel about a field trip?"

Stephen's groan was loud and long as he flopped back against the couch. "Not a fan of the great outdoors," he declared vehemently. "Love the scenery, but don't enjoy living in it."

Ricki's brow furrowed in concern. "It isn't the easiest of hikes up there, and over eight miles to the lake. Can you make that while carrying a full pack? And if it's going to be a prob-lem, then now is the time to say so, not when we're out on the trail and we've gone too far to turn back."

Gin rolled her eyes at her partner. "Stop whining. You've

had your share of survival training, and you've been on cases in some rough country." She glanced over at Ricki. "Don't buy into his helpless act here. He'll be fine."

Willing to take Gin's word for it, Ricki shrugged. "Great. I'll let Clay and Anchorman know, and start getting some supplies together. We'll leave first thing in the morning."

Chapter 19

THE MORNING SUN looked weak and slightly anemic as it struggled to warm up the day. Ricki stood by the campfire, a mug of hot coffee in her hand and the collar of her parka zipped all the way up to her chin. She'd stuffed her long pony-tail into her wool cap for some additional insulation and slowly rocked from side to side to keep the circulation in her feet going. She gauged that the temperature was above freezing but it wasn't far from it.

The air in the mountains in November was cold, especially first thing in the morning when the ground had had the entire night to lose the limited heat it had accumulated during the day. Even with the unusual warm streak that they'd been enjoying, it was still cold. Ricki looked up and studied the sky. Their biggest saving grace was that it didn't look like they'd be searching for the drug runners' campsite in the rain or snow.

Stephen emerged from his small one-man tent that was a replica of the other four scattered around the site, three of which were still occupied since Ricki had been the first to stir that morning.

The FBI agent stamped over to the fire Ricki had built, his

hands tucked underneath his armpits and a pained look on his face. "I think my nuts are frozen."

"Gee. Thanks for sharing that." Ricki lifted the coffeepot off the fire and poured out a mug for him. Luckily for Stephen, Anchorman had prepared the pot the night before, so the agent didn't have to put up with her barely drinkable version of coffee. "Here you go. This should help thaw out whatever body part needs it."

"Thanks." Stephen practically grabbed the mug out of her hand and greedily gulped down most of its contents.

He immediately held the cup out, and Ricki refilled it with an amused smile. She'd kept a careful eye on him during the hike into Egg Lake yesterday, relieved to see that Gin had been right. Stephen didn't have any problems making the trip, even if he wasn't a big fan of sleeping outdoors.

She refilled her own cup, which pretty much drained the pot. Thinking she'd start a second one, she didn't get any farther than the container with the water they'd retrieved and treated with purifying tablets before Anchorman called out from his tent on the outside perimeter of the campsite.

"Don't even think about it, Ricki."

Stephen blinked and looked at her as she made a sour face. "What's going on?" he asked.

"Anchorman doesn't like my coffee," Ricki said as the cook wriggled out of his tent.

He walked over to the fire and snatched the coffeepot out of Ricki's hand, then winked at Stephen. "*She* doesn't like her own coffee."

The agent lifted his mug in Ricki's direction. "So she didn't make this?"

Anchorman laughed. "Not a chance. You'd have to drink hers with a spoon."

He walked over to the plastic water jug and filled the pot, then went to Ricki's pack and measured out the coffee. Everyone carried their own gear, and the food had been split up between them, so all the packs were the same weight. More or less.

Ricki had noticed that both Anchorman and Clay had taken extra weight in theirs, while the leaner, less experienced Stephen had been content with the pack he'd been handed. Ricki had wanted to take on some of the weight in Gin's pack since the FBI agent was a good three inches shorter than her, but Gin would have none of that. In the end it had worked out just fine and they'd all made it up to the lake without any delays or mishaps.

In a few minutes, the rich aroma of freshly brewed coffee wafted through the air, drawing the other two out of their tents. Gin appeared first, her gloved hand covering a huge yawn.

"Is there any tea? God, please tell me there's water for tea." She latched on to the cup Anchorman held out with the end of a teabag draped over the side. "Bless you for braving the cold first and getting this going."

Anchorman grinned. "I didn't. Ricki got the first pot on, which is what your partner is guzzling down. This is the second go around. She also put on the water for your tea."

"The second pot is always just as good." When Clay strolled up, Anchorman handed him a steaming mug. The chief gave him a grateful nod, then took up a place on the opposite side of the firepit from Ricki. Neither he nor Ricki noticed the looks exchanged between the other three.

Gin nudged Ricki in the side. "Well, I'm impressed that you not only dragged yourself out of your sleeping bag first this morning, but that you look great." She took a half-step back and studied Ricki, who was standing with one hand wrapped around her mug and the other in the pocket of her jacket.

Ricki looked back at Gin with an amused glint in her eyes. The FBI agent's hair was sticking out in all directions, and there was a crease running down the entire length of her cheek. "You look fine too, but you aren't my type."

Gin made a face at her, then smiled. "Seriously, you look great. What I mean is, being out here really suits you, doesn't it?"

"It always has," Ricki said before looking around the group. "Let's get some breakfast and then start out. I don't know how long it will take us to find that campsite."

"If there is one," Stephen pointed out.

Clay frowned at him. "If there isn't, then we'll have a genuine mystery on our hands. It's eight miles to this point, and another ten or eleven up to Canada. And if I was reading the map right last night, that last five are on a trail that isn't maintained, so it will be much rougher going than the Copper Ridge Trail we took coming into the park."

"You read it right," Ricki said quietly. "There's a lot of places along the way to ambush someone too, so we can't rule out warring groups of drug runners."

"Yeah," Gin said, her tone indicating that the same thought had crossed her mind too. "Let's eat a power bar and get going."

Stephen's face fell. "A power bar?"

"You were expecting one of your gourmet meals out here?" Gin demanded.

"A power bar can't be called a meal at all," Stephen complained.

Ricki started back toward her tent, giving Stephen's arm a friendly pat on the way. "Have two. You can eat the second one on the way to the crime scene."

Thirty minutes later the group started out. Ricki had been surprised the day before when both FBI agents had attached rifles to their packs. Since she'd assumed they mostly worked in an urban environment, she thought they would have preferred pistols. When Gin caught her staring at the rifle, the

FBI agent had grinned and informed her they brought whatever fit the situation.

So with all five of them carrying only a light pack and a rifle across their backs, Ricki set a fast pace. Her GPS compass firmly in hand, she took the lead while Anchorman brought up the rear along with Clay. When they reached the clearing where Ricki and Cooper had come across the two hunters, Ricki didn't stop. She simply adjusted their direction and kept going, so it was barely midmorning when they reached the spot where Santiago Garcia had been murdered.

"This is it," Ricki said quietly. "Let's take a quick break." She pointed northeast. "Then we'll head out that way. Cooper and I came across the footpath at about the halfway point between here and the Copper Ridge Trail."

Stephen removed his rifle and let his pack slip to the ground. "Sounds good to me." He slowly looked around. "This is one isolated place. We haven't seen anyone here since we crossed over the boundary into the park." He kept a wary eye on the heavy growth of trees that enclosed the murder site. "It makes me jumpy."

"Not having a Starbucks in sight makes you jumpy," Gin said. "But you're right. This is really out in the middle of absolutely nowhere." She glanced at Clay. "And you said it's what, ten miles from the Canadian border?"

Clay nodded. "That's right. If you can handle the terrain, it's the perfect place to smuggle drugs into Canada."

"You can carry more on a boat, or in a truck," Gin said. "But this way has a much smaller chance of the runners getting caught and the merchandise becoming a complete loss."

Ricki didn't say anything. She let their conversation flow around her as she slowly circled the tree where they'd found Garcia's body. Her gaze was hard and sharp as it quartered the area, looking for any movement or sound in the forest that didn't belong. She didn't hear or see anything, but that didn't mean the hermit wasn't out there.

"If he's around, he's good," Anchorman said in a low voice. He was standing next to her, his legs braced apart, his gaze tense and alert.

"No question about that." Ricki took one last look around, then walked over to the rest of the group. "We need to move. There's no telling how long this might take."

With Ricki once again in the lead, they headed toward the tree where the bricks of cocaine had been stacked, and from there due east, straight toward the main trail. Traveling cross-country with no established track to follow wasn't easy, and it took them nearly twenty minutes to traverse the quarter mile to where Ricki and Cooper had found the faint path that ran north to south and parallel to the main trail somewhere up ahead.

"This is it," Ricki said, looking in one direction and then another. It definitely wasn't well traveled, but it had seen enough boots tramping along it to leave a definite mark on the ground.

"Great," Gin said, her thumbs hooked around the shoulder straps of her pack. "So, do we split up and go both ways?"

"Until we get the lay of the land, we stick together," Ricki said firmly. She considered their two options before turning north. "Copper Lake is this way. I'm betting they stop closer to that campground."

Once again they all fell in line, with Anchorman and Clay bringing up the rear. Another quarter mile and their "secret" trail veered off to the northwest, putting more distance between it and the main trail. Ricki thought whoever had forged this second trail had done it more for the ease of the hike rather than any panoramic views, but she was still betting they'd come out near Copper Lake.

As it turned out, it was barely another quarter of a mile

along the path before they crossed another track that led off to the west. Ricki frowned at it. It didn't look as well traveled, but it was definitely there. Deciding to keep to the more used route, Ricki continued on, leading the group farther into the backcountry as the forest closed in around them.

Fifteen minutes later the trees thinned out, eventually opening up into a large clearing. Ricki stopped at the edge and stared at the disaster in front of her.

Tents were collapsed, and equipment and trash were strewn everywhere. As the rest of the group came up and got their first look at the scene, Ricki carefully started around the perimeter. Moments later, the whole group split into two sections, each taking an opposite way around the edge of the clearing, their backs to the open space as they carefully monitored the trees surrounding it. When they met on the far side, Anchorman tapped Clay on the shoulder.

"How about you and I do a little recon outside the perimeter while the rest of them check things out around here?"

Clay nodded his assent, and Ricki watched as the two of them disappeared into the trees. "Well, while they're doing that, let's take a look." She walked toward the closest pool of a nylon and polyester blend material, spread out on the ground. By its size, she judged it to be a four-man tent, complete with a ground tarp and rain fly.

She walked over it, stepping carefully to determine if anything had been left inside when the tent had been collapsed to the ground. Given the jagged tear she spotted in the fabric as well as a fiberglass pole that was broken in two, it was obvious that the tent had not been deliberately taken down so much as ripped apart.

There were two more tents, spaced out around the clearing. Gin and Stephen each took one, repeating Ricki's process, while she started her search of the center of the clearing. A round firepit, a good four feet across, took up some of the space. The pit was intact and had a row of coffee mugs perched along the stones that made up the ring. And around it was enough broken gear, meals still sealed in their pouches, and sleeping bags torn apart to stock a small sporting goods store.

While Ricki, Gin, and Stephen were sorting through the mess, Clay emerged from the woods.

He walked over to Ricki, his expression grim. "You need to come see this." When Gin and Stephen joined them, he kept his gaze on Ricki. "We found the last occupants of the camp."

This isn't good, Ricki thought even as she nodded and followed Clay into the trees with the two FBI agents right behind her. About twenty yards in, Ricki spotted Anchorman, standing with his rifle against his shoulder, its barrel pointed to the ground. At his feet was a jumble of arms, legs, and torsos, some contorted into odd angles. Ricki sighed as she surveyed the scene, counting three separate heads. Ten yards away were two more bodies.

"Looks like we've got one Hispanic and two Caucasians," Gin said. "I don't know about those two over there." She glanced over at Ricki. "How do you want to handle this?"

Ricki sighed and pulled out the latex gloves she habitually carried, not surprised when the two FBI agents did the same thing along with Clay. "I'll check for ID on these three if one of you would take the other two. Everyone else spread out and keep your eyes to the ground. Don't destroy any evidence, and mark where you found it." She looked over at Gin and Stephen. "A couple of twigs set in a cross will do. And be sure to take photos before you move anything."

Gin nodded. "Okay."

Ricki looked over at Anchorman. "You'll keep watch?"

"Roger that."

While the two FBI agents started a slow crisscross of the surrounding area and Clay walked over to the two bodies separated from the others, Ricki squatted down next to the trio lying side-by-side. She went through the pockets of the nearest one, a blond male who was on his back and staring with sightless blue eyes up at the trees.

There was a gunshot hole in his chest.

She pulled a wallet out of the unzipped side pocket of the man's jacket. Some of his blood had seeped into the open pocket, encasing the wallet in a cracked and caked coating now that the blood had dried. By the look of him, Ricki estimated that he and Garcia had probably died around the same time.

Dropping the wallet into an evidence bag, Ricki moved on to the next body. It was in the same shape as the first one, but she had to turn it on its side to get to the wallet stuck into the back pocket of the man's jeans. When all five bodies had been searched and any ID retrieved, Ricki and Clay stood up, and the look they exchanged was purely from one cop to another.

"Executed," Clay stated flatly.

"Yeah," Ricki agreed. "But by who?"

Chapter 20

BACK AT THE CLEARING, four of the team members sat in a circle on a clear patch of grass. The two evidence bags—holding five wallets, two rings, and one empty cartridge—were lying in the middle. Anchorman stood nearby, slowly turning as he kept watch for any unexpected two or four-legged visitors.

Ricki pointed at the wallets. "According to their IDs, the vics are all males between twenty-five and thirty-five. Three are from Jalisco, one from Canada, and the other lived right here in Washington."

"In Glacier or somewhere close by?" Gin asked, then frowned when Ricki shook her head.

"Seattle," she said.

Stephen nodded. "That makes sense. Most of the coke is shipped from Jalisco to a city in the US that's near a port of entry. Up here in the Northwest, that would be Seattle."

"Do the drugs mostly go out by boat?" Ricki asked. Since northwest Washington was half water, that seemed like a logical conclusion. *And*, she thought to herself, *something I should already know*. But most of her time was spent at Olympic Park, and there was absolutely no way, or reason for that matter, to smuggle drugs through her park. It didn't border Canada, and a drug runner might find himself facing an actual frozen glacier instead of a quiet town a few hours south of the Canadian border.

"Nope," Stephen replied. "Most of the drugs are taken into Canada by car or some type of motorized transport. Everything from passenger cars to big rigs." He looked around at the forest. "This particular method of smuggling them through a national park is a new one to me."

"Which is probably why Blake sent us here. He must have connected the dots and come up with a possible new drug route into Canada." Gin sighed. "So, we've got dead guys, three from a known transit point for drugs coming into the good old USA, and two others. Maybe one of them was the guide, so we don't need to go looking for one in the town of Glacier after all?"

"Maybe," Ricki said, making Clay smile.

"That's her detective, I-don't-think-so 'maybe,'" the chief said in a loud whisper to Stephen.

The agent stared back at Ricki, his deep brown eyes holding a question. "Okay, fill in the blank. You don't think one of the vics was the guide because . . . ?"

Ricki shrugged. "If we assume the three from Jalisco were the guys trusted to actually carry the drugs, then along with Garcia, that would make four mules. I would have sent at least two trusted guys to protect the four others, which would account for all the vics. As for the guide . . ." She waved a hand toward the empty clearing with its collapsed tents. "And for this kind of knowledge of the park? It has to be someone local, or someone who is here so often all the locals know him." She paused, her lips pressed together into a thin line. "The cartel had to have trusted guys to guard that much, what did you call it? Merchandise?"

"Four million dollars' worth of merchandise," Gin tossed out. "If there were four mules carrying forty pounds apiece."

"I vote with Ricki on this one," Clay put in. "We found two semiautomatic pistols stuck into the back of the belts on the two vics not from Jalisco, which would go with the theory of them being the security contingent for this operation."

From his position as sentry, Anchorman let out a snort. "So, what are you saying? Do you think the other guys would have hauled a cool million each on their backs and not carried a gun?"

Clay shook his head. "No. I think security types carry a weapon at all times. Other people not so much, especially in a campsite, surrounded by cohorts, and out in the middle of nowhere. That alone lends itself to a certain amount of complacency. And while we found pistols stuck into the belts and under the jackets of two of the vics, we didn't find any other guns. Not on the vics or anywhere else in the campsite."

Stephen shook his head. "Nope. Now that you mention it, we came across plenty of food, sleeping bags, pots and pans, even some clothes, but no guns."

"They wouldn't have come up here with just a couple of weapons," Anchorman said. "Even if they were semiautomatics."

"No, they wouldn't have," Ricki said, waiting for Gin's nod of verification. "Which means the mules were killed, along with at least two of their guards, and their guns were taken along with the drugs."

"Do you think there were more than two, and that third one turned on the others?" Gin asked.

"I can't say yet who turned on who, but between Garcia and what we just found, we've accounted for six people." Ricki glanced over at the firepit before looking back at Gin. "There are seven mugs with coffee still in them lined up on the side of the firepit."

"There are seven destroyed sleeping bags too," Stephen added quietly. "I counted them."

"So unless one of the victims was using two cups and two

sleeping bags, we still have someone missing," Gin replied. "I wonder if that seventh person is our killer, or someone who got away," she speculated out loud.

Ricki shrugged. "I don't know. But I'm fairly certain that the hermit wasn't invited in for a cup of coffee."

"So if the hermit killed those people," Stephen said, throwing his arm out in the general direction of the bodies in the woods. "Then someone got away. Otherwise, that missing person is most likely the killer, and the hermit is what then? Some kind of weird vigilante committee of one?"

"That fits," Gin said under her breath, then looked up and said it louder. "That fits. Four mules carrying a million apiece? Well, we figured we saw half a million go up in smoke."

Ricki's eyes narrowed. "Yeah. So where's the other three and a half million dollars' worth of cocaine?"

"That's a good question," Clay said. "So is this one. How are we going to get these five bodies out of here?"

Now that could prove to be a real problem. Ricki stood up and pulled a map out of her day pack. Studying it, she got out her compass and turned to the northeast. Now facing the right direction, she squatted down again and laid the map out on the grass. "I figure we're here. We can either find a route through to Copper Lake ourselves, or have the rescue team backtrack and take the way Cooper and I found to the main trail, then go on to the lake, or some other extraction point that works for the helicopter."

Clay looked up from the map. "Yeah, that sounds good." His mouth twitched at the corners. "And I'm sure glad I'm not the one who will have to call Scott and let him know."

"Who's Scott?" Gin asked.

Ricki picked up the map and started to fold it. "He's the lieutenant in charge of the rescue team. It's also going to take another contingent of park rangers to help out." Ricki winced. "I think I'll let Hamilton make that call."

"Both calls," Clay suggested.

"Good idea," Ricki said with a nod.

"That's all fine and dandy, but what now?" Anchorman asked.

"I'm thinking now we get back to camp?" Gin left it as a question while she slipped her own pack back into place.

Ricki automatically looked up, tracking the position of the sun before doing the more traditional thing and consulting her watch. "We still have some time. There was a cross trail not too far back. I'd like to see where it goes before we leave the area."

Anchorman also looked up at the sky. "We can spare a couple of hours until we have to head back. I don't want us to get caught out here in the dark."

"I'm with the sniper on that one," Stephen said, setting off chuckles from everyone else.

Ricki shoved the folded-up map back into her day pack and shrugged into its straps. "Okay. Let's go."

They all took up the same formation they'd hiked in with, covering the fifteen minutes back to the fork in the trail in silence. Ricki made the right turn and kept walking. It wasn't long before she heard Clay move up behind her, guarding her back.

They made their way along the track, climbing up several small switchbacks as they steadily gained elevation. After a mile in, they hadn't seen anything except glimpses of breath-taking views. Ricki was about to turn them around and head on back when she spotted what was definitely a man-made structure through the trees. Since the path veered in that direction, she just continued to follow along.

It ended in front of a sagging one-story building that was half-cabin and half-shack. The whole structure leaned to the right, giving the appearance that the roof might slide off it with the next puff of wind.

"What in the world is that?" Gin put her hands on her

hips and cocked her head to one side. "And what is it doing out here?"

"I don't know." Ricki walked up to the creaky steps. They actually looked newer than the rest of the cabin they were attached to. Now that she had a closer look, most of the floor-boards on the porch had been replaced as well. Still leery, Ricki tested the first step with one foot, putting increasing pressure on it until she was using her full weight. She turned her head to look at the five people standing behind her and wiggled her eyebrows. "The floor feels sturdy enough."

Despite the skeptical looks she got, she carefully continued up the steps and across the porch, testing each footstep along the way. The door was held shut by a loop of rope running from a nail sticking out from the door over to its twin in the front of the doorframe. Unhooking one end, Ricki gently pushed the door open and stuck her head inside.

The room was a single square of ten feet on each side. A bed frame with no mattress was shoved against one wall, right next to a wooden box that was missing a board in front. The only other piece of furniture was a table, loaded down with cans of food and boxes of matches, along with a whole stack of basic supplies, including a large can of coffee. Ricki walked slowly around the table, stopping on the far side to pick up a box of cartridges. The sound of steps coming across the porch had her looking up as Gin came into view.

"The guys decided to let the lightweights, in a literal sense, do the exploring," Gin said. Her nose lifted into the air and she took an audible sniff. "Smells like more than a few animals have made their home in here, and I'm talking about the kind with fur."

"Can't argue with that," Ricki said. The place really did stink of old feces and who knew what else. She gestured toward the stockpile on the table. "What do you make of this?"

Gin walked over, surprise in her gaze. "I don't know." She

picked up a can of peaches and read the stamp on the top before reaching for another can. "These aren't anywhere near to expiring, and they aren't covered in dust, so I'd say they haven't been here very long."

"Yeah." Ricki looked around. "The whole place has a couple of inches of dust on it, not to mention pine needles that have blown in through the holes in the roof, but this table is clean." She held up the box of shells. "And look what we have here? If it isn't .30-30 Winchester cartridges."

"You don't say?" Gin skirted around the table and looked for herself. "Hmm. Right offhand, I'd say this is somebody's stash of supplies. And the only somebody I've heard of that is skulking around the woods is that hermit of yours."

Ricki frowned. That made sense, but it still didn't add up. A flash of white on the floor caught her eye. Almost buried in pine needles, only a small corner was visible. Ricki took off her glove and bent over to lift the paper between her forefinger and her thumb. She held it up to the light, surprised that it looked like a piece of a check stub—the kind that was attached to a payroll check.

Gin moved closer, her gazed fixed on the ragged scrap of paper. "What's that?"

"I'm not sure." Ricki turned it over. The back was blank, and the only things on the front were some lines and, in the bottom corner, a long number, with a shorter, hyphenated number in front of it in much smaller print. Ricki squinted at it. "This looks like a bank routing number, which would make this longer one a check number, I think."

The FBI agent peered at it over Ricki's shoulder. "Uh-huh. So someone who's been up here lately and has a bank account? Doesn't that kind of rule out the hermit guy?"

"I don't know." Before she could puzzle it out, the sound of a gunshot exploded outside, followed by Anchorman's shout.

"We've got company!"

Chapter 21

RICKI AND GINA both sprang to the boarded-up window and peered through the cracks. Ricki automatically stuffed the check receipt that she'd found into her pocket as she searched for the three team members outside. She couldn't see Clay or Stephen, but she spotted Anchorman kneeling by the side of the porch, his rifle aimed at the trees in front of the cabin.

Ricki grabbed the edge of one of the boards blocking the window and gave it a sharp tug. The rotting wood immediately gave way, and in an instant, she had her rifle barrel through the opening and was looking through her scope. She saw bodies shifting through the trees as Anchorman got off a warning shot.

"Federal agents!" Ricki yelled out, which immediately stopped the shadowy movement of the bodies in the trees. Ricki took in a breath and looked over her shoulder at Gin. "There's too many. We need to get out of here."

"Let's repeat your trick of ripping off boards and go through the back." Gin got up and moved to the rear of the cabin, testing the wall as Ricki watched the shifting bodies keep moving through the trees, spreading out wider and coming in closer.

"Got a board loose," Gin said on a note of triumph.

Ricki heard wood splintering and fired off two shots to cover the sound, with more shots from outside and on both sides of the cabin following suit.

"Okay. Let's go," Gin said. "Stephen will fade off to the left, so I'm betting he and Clay are on that side of the cabin. If you want to let that sniper cook of yours know it's time for a strategic retreat, I'll get the other two guys."

Since she was already on the same side of the cabin that Anchorman was, Ricki simply yelled through the loose boards of the walls. "Anchorman. In the rear. We're out." She waited until she saw him move, then withdrew her rifle from the hole in the window. Keeping low, she took three leaps to get across the ten feet to follow Gin out the makeshift door she'd created in the back.

A wave of relief came over Ricki when Stephen and Clay appeared on her right just as Anchorman popped in from the opposite corner, and the five of them disappeared into the woods. Following a faint trail that led into the woods from the back of the cabin, Ricki and Clay were in front, with Anchorman taking his preferred position as rear guard.

"Which way?" Clay asked when they'd gained some distance from the cabin. Judging by the sporadic gunfire still coming from that direction, Ricki figured they had a few minutes to make a clean getaway. Looking over the lay of the land, she continued to climb up the hill at an angle until she rounded a bend and put a lot of ground between the team and whoever had attacked them.

She took out her GPS compass and followed it, leading the group in an arc to the northeast. But the terrain was unforgiving, so after they'd traveled in silence for another thirty grueling minutes, she headed toward a large pile of boulders. With the hillside at their backs, and the rocks in front of them, it would offer enough shelter for them to regroup.

Ricki walked around to the far side then stopped and

dropped to one knee, her breath coming in quick bursts. It had been a steady climb at a fast clip for the last half hour, and it had taken a toll on her. Even her light pack felt like it weighed a ton. The others also had their heads down, with their breath coming just as hard as hers. It took a few minutes, but once she was taking in air at a more normal rate, Ricki sat on the ground and leaned her back against the rock. A moment later, Clay joined her.

"Are you all right?" he asked.

"I'm good. And you?" When he put a thumb up, Ricki looked around at the others. "Anyone hurt?"

"Just my pride," Anchorman said as he sat cross-legged, one hand on his rifle. "I didn't see them coming until it was almost too late."

"Almost is a lot better than the alternative," Gin declared. "Did you get a look at any of them? Those shots we heard weren't from any hunting rifle. That was a semiautomatic."

"I have to agree with you there, Agent Reilly," Clay said. "Anyone get a good look at them?"

"I only saw shadows of bodies through my scope," Ricki said before looking over at Stephen. "You were on the side closest to them."

Stephen nodded. "Yeah. I didn't see any faces clearly, but a couple of them were sporting a lot of tattoos. They looked like their whole bodies were painted in them."

Ricki exchanged a look with Gin. "What do you think? Would one of the cartels send out guys to check up on their missing drugs?"

"If we're right about the four million dollars, sure they would," Gin said. "And the CJNG is violent enough to have executed their own men at that campsite if they thought they'd been ripped off. *Especially* if they thought they'd been ripped off."

"Enough to go looking for whoever ripped them off?" Anchorman asked.

Gin nodded. "You bet."

Ricki frowned. The whole train of thought brought up a string of unanswered questions, but right now she couldn't puzzle it out. They had to get out of there. Retrieving her map, she spread it on the ground and looked for the best way back to camp. After a few minutes of studying the map, and the topography around them, she straightened up and rubbed a hand across the back of her neck.

"Well, crap." Ricki looked at the faces suddenly turned in her direction. "Our choices aren't good. We can either keep following this deer track we're on and hope it leads us somewhere, or we have to go back the way we came." She pointed to the hill rising behind them. "There's too much of that between us and the main trail—or us and anywhere—to get back to our camp."

The expressions all around her turned grim as everyone bent over the map.

"Well," Gin finally drawled. "We know the way so at least we won't get lost."

Anchorman leaned back against the rock. "Yeah, there is that. And we'll be careful, so we won't get dead either."

"If I were the bad guys, I wouldn't hang around here long. Not when they know we got away, and that we're federal agents." Gin reached over and gave Ricki a light, friendly punch in the shoulder. "That was a good move, James. Letting them know who they were shooting at. Cartel members tend to avoid any federal encounters."

Ricki rolled her eyes. "Gee. Thanks." She glanced over at Anchorman. "Would you take point? You just need to follow the track back to the cabin." At his nod, she switched her gaze to Clay. "And you and I can take Anchorman's place in the rear."

"Stephen and I can do that," Gin said. "This isn't our first op. We don't need to be kept in cotton balls."

"If we get shot at, you'll have to shoot back, so no cotton

balls here," Anchorman put in before Ricki could get a word out. "And I guarantee you that Special Agent James over there is the better shot, which is why she'll take the rear position."

"And again, gee thanks," Ricki said. She wiggled out of her day pack and went rummaging through it for the satphone. She punched in Hamilton's number and waited for him to pick up.

"This is Special Agent in Charge Hamilton."

"It's Ricki. We're in the park, and we have a situation out here."

Chapter 22

ANCHORMAN WALKED into the overgrown space in front of the cabin. Moving to the side of the structure, he gave an all-clear signal to the others waiting in the trees behind the dilapidated structure. Ricki was the first to join him, her rifle ready to be raised to her shoulder at a moment's notice.

"No sign of them?" she asked.

He shook his head. "No. Clay and I went out a hundred feet, all the way around. They're gone." He looked over at her. "It's probably like Gin said, they didn't want to get tangled up with federal agents. Best guess? They're headed back toward Canada."

Ricki sincerely hoped so as she strode over to the porch steps. The door was hanging on one hinge, its lopsided angle blocking the entrance. As Gin crossed the porch to stand behind her, Ricki pushed the door aside and stepped into the cabin.

Half the floor was gone. The boards had been ripped out and tossed into a pile in the corner. The canned goods were lying all over what remained of the floor, with some scattered across the exposed dirt underneath, and the rickety box next to the bed frame had been smashed to pieces. The space was small, so the destruction wouldn't have taken long, but it was thorough.

Gin looked around and shook her head. "Well, I guess they were either looking for something or really didn't like the owner."

"Both, I think." Ricki stared at the gaping hole in the floor, wondering if their attackers had found the missing drugs. Or if the run-down cabin did indeed belong to the elusive hermit who'd taken all the drugs and had stashed them somewhere else. Since neither answer was going to jump out and present itself, she considered a way to find out.

She took off her day pack and set it on the ground, unzipped the top, and rummaged around for some paper and a pencil. Squatting down, she used her pack as a makeshift desk and quickly scrawled out a note. After righting the table, which was miraculously still intact, Ricki used one of the food cans to anchor the note on top of it. She then slung her pack over one shoulder and gave Gin a small push to get her back out the door. Right now the note was the best she could do, and they had bigger problems—like getting out of the park in one piece.

She and Gin rejoined the others and the team once again fell into their line, following the trail in absolute silence. When they reached the point where the two small trails crossed each other, Ricki sent word up the line for Anchorman to stop.

She made her way forward, carefully examining the small trail to the north and then to the south. Nodding in satisfaction, she took the lead as Anchorman dropped to the back with Clay. Ricki walked past the point where they could have turned west and retraced their route to the original crime scene and then taken the now very familiar cross-country hike to their campsite at Egg Lake. But Ricki stayed on the trail followed by the drug runners. Twenty minutes later, they stepped onto the Copper Ridge Trail.

"We'll make better time taking the main trail," Ricki said

to the group that had gathered in a tight circle. "Whoever was shooting at us turned north at that fork. No one has been on the southern section for a while. It wasn't trampled down like the way north."

Stephen looked relieved. "Okay. Now what? We head for Hannegan Pass and back to town?"

Ricki nodded and looked up at the sky as she rubbed her hands together. Although it was barely noon, the temperature had taken a sudden drop, and a bank of dark clouds was rolling in from the west. One thing was certain—it was not going to be a fun hike back to the trailhead.

"We don't have much choice," Ricki said. "Hamilton is in the process of shutting down this entire section of the park, and we don't want to get caught in here carrying rifles. That might get us shot before we can identify ourselves. It's just over six miles to the park's border. We need to make a run for it."

"And all the stuff at our campsite?" Gin asked. "Do we just leave it?"

"Yeah," Ricki said. "Anyone have something there they can't do without?"

With negative head shakes all the way around, Ricki added hers before tightening the straps on her day pack. "Okay then, let's go."

The quick march over the Copper Lake Trail went off without a hitch. When they reached the park border, Ricki closed the gate. She and Hamilton had agreed on that being the signal to any rangers who might be coming up that way looking for them, that they had left the park. She confirmed that with a quick call to the senior agent, then set off with the others on the long journey back to the trailhead.

The plummeting temperature was followed by snow, giving the motivation they needed to keep up the pace. But even so, they took the last few miles in the dark, their head-lamps bouncing off the trees as they moved along the trail.

By the time the parking lot at the trailhead came into

sight, the light snowfall had turned into a thick blanket of white. It was a grateful team who finally stumbled into their rented house, dropping their packs near the front door and collapsing onto the nearest piece of furniture. Cheron came down the stairs, her eyes widening at the sight of exhausted bodies lying everywhere.

"Oh my." She adjusted her glasses then clasped her hands together before walking over and laying a gentle hand on Anchorman's shoulder. "Are you all right?" Her gaze roamed over the rest of the group. "Are all of you all right? Does anyone need medical attention?"

When Stephen lifted his head and gave her a skeptical look, she gave him back a knowing one. "Whether we work with the living or the dead, all doctors go through the same medical schools."

The FBI agent's head fell back down again, and he groaned. "Great. I think my feet are one big blister."

"You need to get your boots off and air your feet out, then I'll look at them," Cheron said. "In the meantime, I'll start some hot cocoa."

"Tea, I'm begging you," Gin croaked.

"Cocoa," Cheron said firmly. "You need the nutrients and the sugar boost." When Gin made a face, Cheron wrinkled her nose. "One cup of cocoa first, and then I'll make tea." At Ricki's loud sniff, the doctor quickly added, "And coffee. I'll also start warming up the stew. There's enough left over to make a good meal for everyone."

"I can help," Anchorman said, struggling to get up, which didn't last long when Cheron placed a hand on top of his head and easily pushed him back down.

"Stay put. I can manage just fine."

Half an hour later, with boots and coats discarded and steaming bowls of stew passed around, Gin looked over at Cheron and smiled.

"Thanks, Doc," the agent said. "This is the perfect

remedy."

"Sometimes the simplest cure is the best one," Cheron replied before glancing over at Ricki. "So, do we talk about it tonight, or wait until morning?"

Ricki popped another bite of stew into her mouth and chewed slowly while she thought it over. "Tonight," she finally decided. "We need a plan for tomorrow."

"Plan?" Stephen shook his head. "All our suspects in this case are either dead or missing."

"We need to find this hermit," Gin declared. "Either he's the one who betrayed those drug dealers and stole their merchandise, which also makes him the most likely killer, or he's been stalking them. But we know he took some of the drugs because he burned half of them in the middle of the highway. And if he took the drugs, he's still the most likely killer. But either way, this hermit knows who the drug runners are and where to find them. If he isn't leading those smugglers through the park, then he knows who is. If we can find that guy, we can shut the operation down."

"Agreed. The hermit, whoever he is, is the key," Ricki said. "And now we know more than we did."

"We do?" Stephen paused with a spoonful of stew halfway to his mouth. "Like what?"

Ricki got to her feet and walked over to set her empty bowl on the kitchen island. "How did they know about that cabin?" she asked before turning around to face the group again. "How did they know?"

"Maybe they followed us there," Stephen offered. "They heard us coming into the clearing and faded back into the trees while we looked over the bodies. Then maybe they figured we might know where the drugs were, so they followed us."

"No way," Anchorman said flatly. "No way were five or six guys moving through those trees and we didn't spot them. They weren't that good."

"Why do you say that?" Gin asked.

"Because I heard them easily enough when they tried to sneak up on us at the cabin," the sniper said. He glanced over at Clay. "The chief heard them too."

Clay nodded. "Anchorman's right. Their ambushing skills in the middle of this kind of backcountry aren't anywhere close to the way the hermit moves through the woods."

"Okay," Ricki said. "If they didn't follow us, then they already knew where that cabin was, and it was their dumb luck and our bad luck that we were already there."

Gin's feet slid off the ottoman she'd propped them up on and hit the floor with a thud. "Which means someone told them. Unless the smugglers were using that cabin to stockpile supplies." She shook her head the instant the words were out. "But that makes no sense. Why not just leave the supplies at the campsite? Why carry them so far out of their way?" She shrugged. "And why trash the cabin?"

Ricki moved to stand next to Gin, her arms crossed over her chest and one foot tapping against the floor. "Those supplies weren't for the smugglers. I think they were for the hermit. Someone is keeping him in basic staples, and from the expiration dates on the cans, I'd say they make a regular run into the park with supplies. And since Glacier is not only the nearest town but where the hermit supposedly came from, then the odds are good his supplier is also from here."

"So if we find this supplier," Gin continued, "he might lead us to the hermit, who could then lead us to the head of the smuggling operation."

"He might not know who that is," Clay pointed out. "This hermit told us that he expects Ricki to track down and catch these guys."

Gin stuck her chin out while her voice took on a stubborn note. "Well, he stole their drugs, and knew where Santiago Garcia's body was, so he sure as hell knows something about this whole operation."

"Maybe that path we followed from the back of the cabin leads to wherever this hermit lives," Anchorman said.

Ricki considered it and then shook her head. "It doesn't make any difference. We don't know how far back that path goes, and we won't be able to get back into the park until the law enforcement unit there declares an all clear." She frowned. "I think we need to start asking questions of some people in town."

"Hey, hang on." Stephen held up his phone. "Now that my brain is thawed out along with my fingers, I just checked my voice mail. It seems the number listed on the guide poster that was in that bar belongs to one James Henry Blighton. It's a landline. My contact sent the address where that phone is located to my email."

"James Henry Blighton?" Clay lifted an eyebrow as he looked at Ricki. "James, as in Jimmy?" He reached into his pocket and brought out his own cell phone. "Want me to call Dan?"

"Yeah, good idea," Ricki said. "Ask him to verify who owns the Last Stop. Let's see if James Blighton is Jimmy's legal name."

As Clay stepped off to the side, Ricki put her hands on her hips. Her eyes narrowed in thought. "We should split up tomorrow and do some footwork." She looked at Gin. "You and Clay can have a talk with Jo."

Gin gave her a puzzled look. "Who's Jo?"

"She owns the Snowmelt," Cheron volunteered. "She's lived in Glacier for decades and knows everyone in town."

The agent nodded. "Okay. And what will Clay and I be talking to her about?"

Ricki gave her a half-smile. "Wanda Simms."

"Who?" Gin asked.

"Wanda Simms," Ricki repeated, barely keeping a yawn in check. "She's the gossip queen in the Bay. Every small town has that one person who knows the history of the town, and everyone who has ever lived in it, and that would include any stories about a resident who fled to the hills and is rumored to have been living there ever since. Maybe Jo can point us to the gossip queen of Glacier."

"Sounds good." Gin gave her a thumbs-up, then sat back down on the couch and lifted her feet onto the ottoman.

"Great." Ricki turned to Stephen. "You and I will head over to the bar and find out what tours Jimmy has been taking out lately. After that, we'll take a look around his house. Maybe we can come up with a reason to get inside."

"No problem," Stephen said. He inclined his head toward Anchorman. "Who'll be taking along Mr. Protection over there?"

Ricki smiled at Cheron. "Hamilton told me on the phone that if the weather is clear enough, they'll try to get a body or two out of that campsite tomorrow. I'm assuming if they do, you'll be heading over to Bellingham?"

Cheron bobbed her head up and down, leaving pieces of her wispy bangs floating away from her forehead. "Yes. Hamilton called me too. But if the weather isn't good enough, I'll make another grocery run. I think we're out of bread."

"Okay. Since we aren't sure exactly where or when the smugglers or the hermit might pop up again, Anchorman will stay with you. That way we'll all have backup with us."

The sniper nodded his thanks at Ricki. "That sounds good."

Clay put his phone away, the flat look of a cop who has picked up a scent was in his eyes. "Dan did a quick lookup. The Last Stop is owned by James Blighton, and I guess we got the straight story about the guy in the bar being his banker. The mortgage note is held by Washington Federal Bank."

"I love it when loose ends start to make some sense," Gin said, lifting a hand to cover a yawn. "But right now, I'm beat. I need some serious sleep if I'm going to apply my well-honed and finely tuned interview skills tomorrow."

With fatigue weighing down on her, Ricki nodded. "I'm all for that."

Chapter 23

THE FOLLOWING morning dawned with the same gray skies as the day before, but the snow appeared to have moved on. Ricki poured a cup of coffee and carried it around the island, taking a seat on the nearest stool. Cheron occupied the one next to hers and was nibbling on a bagel spread liberally with cream cheese.

"Agent Hamilton said you found five more bodies at a second campsite," the doctor said. "Were they all shot?"

Ricki curled her fingers around the steaming mug, using its heat to warm her hands. "It appeared so. Three of them had bullet holes in their chest, and the other two in their backs. From the way the bodies were positioned, I'd say those last two were trying to run away when they were shot, while the other three were facing their killer." She frowned, her forehead wrinkling in thought. "Or maybe killers, as in more than one." She looked at Cheron. "That will depend on what your autopsy shows."

"It usually does." The doctor's smile held just a touch of smugness, which made Ricki laugh.

Sounds from overhead had Cheron hopping off her stool.

"I guess more people are up, so I'd better get started on breakfast."

Ricki's eyes widened, and she quickly raised her mug to hide her grin. "Oh? You aren't going to wait for Anchorman to make it?"

Cheron pulled a spatula out of a drawer and waved it in the air. "Why would I do that? He's tired from all that hiking yesterday, not to mention being shot at." She pointed the flat-headed utensil at Ricki. "All of you are. You should sit down to a good meal before you go off on all those interviews."

Knowing just how high Anchorman set the bar for a good meal, Ricki silently wished the doctor luck with that one. And it wasn't just the meal itself. The diner cook didn't take well to someone else occupying any kitchen that he'd claimed, and he'd certainly claimed this one.

Thinking she might enjoy watching the big man try to find a polite way to order the current love of his life out of his kitchen, Ricki contentedly settled in to enjoy the rest of her coffee before everyone else descended on them.

"We're friends, aren't we, Ricki?" Cheron's question had Ricki blinking in surprise.

"Of course we are," she said, silently wondering what had prompted the doctor to ask such an odd question.

"And friends confide in each other and talk things over, don't they?"

"Yes," Ricki returned cautiously. She really hoped she wasn't in for a chat on the more intimate side of Cheron's relationship with Anchorman. If there actually was one. But, if there was, it would be like discussing the personal details of a brother's life behind his back.

"Okay. That's good." Cheron cracked a dozen eggs into a bowl, then produced a wire whisk and attacked them, stirring vigorously while Ricki watched. "So then it's all right to ask you what's going on between you and Clay?"

Ricki's mouth dropped open. "Going on?"

"Yes." Cheron's practical tone of voice had a wave of heat creeping up Ricki's cheeks. "It's obvious the two of you are doing your best to avoid each other. Although I think that you're a lot madder at him than he is with you." She stopped beating the eggs to look over at Ricki. "So, what did he do?"

Feeling ambushed, Ricki shook her head. "Nothing." When Cheron only adjusted her glasses, Ricki made a face at her. "Remind me not to work with really smart people anymore, and I'm not ready to talk about it."

"Oh." Cheron's look of disappointment was replaced by a startled one at the sound of a loud knock on the front door.

Grateful for the reprieve, Ricki slid off her stool. "I'll get it. You just keep on beating those eggs into submission."

She strode to the door just as Clay appeared at the top of the stairs. At his inquiring look, she only shrugged and opened the door.

Senior Agent in Charge Hamilton was standing there in one of his well-tailored suits, every strand of his dark-brown hair in place. Behind him was Agent Dan Wilkes. The wide eyes and quick shake of the researcher's head were clearly meant to warn her that her boss was not in a good mood. But Ricki could see that for herself just by Hamilton's carefully blank look and formal stance with his hands clasped behind his back. He had on his I'm-the-boss persona.

"Special Agent James?" Hamilton lifted an eyebrow when Ricki stared back at him. "Since the ISB is paying the rent on this house, I'm assuming I can come in?"

Nope. This was not good at all. Blowing out a careful breath, Ricki pinned a smile on her face and stepped aside. "Sorry. You took me by surprise."

"It's a three-hour drive, Agent James, not a cross-country trip." Hamilton stepped into the foyer and looked around while he unwound the scarf from around his neck. "Nice place." He shrugged out of his coat and hung it and the scarf on a nearby hook. He nodded at Clay, who was coming down the stairs. "Chief Thomas."

When Hamilton reached out a hand, Clay shook it, then moved closer to Ricki as the senior agent walked into the living area. "What's this all about?" Clay asked in a low whisper.

"I have no idea," Ricki whispered back, then followed behind her boss. Since Hamilton remained standing, so did she, as he greeted Cheron, then turned to face Ricki.

"Are Special Agents Reilly and Jones here?"

"Yes, sir, they are," Ricki said, her shoulders straight and her back stiff. Maybe the senior agent didn't like the way she was running this case, but she didn't appreciate the prospect of being taken to task in the middle of the living room.

"Oh, get that stick out of your butt, Ricki." Hamilton's expression lost some of its anger as he ran a distracted hand through his hair. "You aren't in the hot seat here, but I can't say the same for those two agents that Blake sent."

She nodded. What had Gin and Stephen done to rile up Hamilton so badly? Whatever it was, she didn't know anything about it. Ricki cast a quick sideways glance at Clay, who only held up his hands, palms out. Apparently Clay didn't know anything about it either.

"What's going on?" she asked bluntly. Might as well get it out in the open.

"I'm having a little problem with Blake not sharing his agenda and turning the ISB's murder investigation into a running gunfight. Not to mention having to shut down the whole northern section of a national park, which I spent the better part of last night hearing about from people back in Washington, DC, with a lot higher pay grades than mine." He pinned his angry gaze on Ricki. "How many times does that make it that you've been shot at in the last week? Not to mention the closing down of a public road while a small fortune of cocaine went up in smoke, which I also heard about from a whole different set of people back in Washington, DC, with those same high pay grades."

Ricki could believe that, although until this moment she hadn't given it any real thought. "I'm sorry, sir, but I don't see how any of that was Reilly's or Jones's fault?"

"I don't either." Gin's voice carried across the living room. Dressed in jeans topped with a cotton blouse and a simple blazer, the FBI agent was standing on the bottom step of the staircase, staring back at Hamilton. She casually walked forward until she was standing directly in front of him. "We were sent here to do a job, and with all due respect, that's exactly what we've been doing."

Hamilton studied her for a moment, then put out his hand. "I'm Senior Agent in Charge Steven Hamilton. And I assume you are Special Agent Gillian Reilly?"

When both Clay and Ricki turned to look at her, Gin went beet red, but her voice remained level. "Gin, sir. I'm either Special Agent Reilly or Gin." She cleared her throat and then squared her shoulders. "I'm not understanding where the confusion is."

"Where's your partner, Agent Reilly? I'd like to talk to him too," Hamilton said.

"I'm here." Stephen bounded down the last two steps, then hurried to stand next to Gin. "Special Agent Stephen Jones."

Hamilton nodded at the introduction, but still made no move to take a seat as he smiled at Anchorman, who had come down the stairs right behind Stephen. "We have some sensitive agency business to discuss," Hamilton said, addressing Ricki. "Is there somewhere private we can talk?"

There was a clattering in the kitchen that had Anchorman heading in that direction. The noise died down and then started up again, finally fading into silence when Cheron appeared with Anchorman in tow. "We were about to go to the grocery store." She looked at her watch. "It should take us about an hour?" She looked at Hamilton as her voice trailed off.

He smiled back at her. "That should be fine. Thank you, Doctor."

Anchorman frowned at the hand she had wrapped around his wrist. "I'd rather stay and hear what's going on."

"Well, that's too bad," Cheron declared, still yanking on his arm. "It isn't any of our business." When he still didn't budge, she hissed at him over her shoulder. "Come on. You're embarrassing Ricki, and you know we'll hear all about it later."

"Fine," Anchorman grumbled. He walked over to the coat hooks and helped Cheron into her parka before grabbing his own. With one last annoyed look at the six people standing in the living room, he ushered Cheron out the door.

The instant the door closed behind them, Hamilton crossed his arms over his chest. "Since Chief Thomas is on loan to the ISB from the Bay's police department, I'm including him in this conversation." He did a quarter-turn of his body to face Gin and Stephen. "Agent James has reported your assistance in this case, and I appreciate that. But this is foremost a murder investigation. A possible smuggling route through the park is a separate issue that should be dealt with separately by the Drug Enforcement Task Force and the DEA. I don't recall it being the purview of the FBI unless they are specifically called in by the task force."

Ricki gave a long, mental groan. Great. They were being dragged into the mud pit of the politics that resulted in the constant territorial pissing contest between the various federal agencies. And there were a lot of those.

"We're here to help Agent James and her team investigate

a murder," Gin said. "The whole drug thing came up as part of it."

Hamilton raised a skeptical eyebrow. "It was that whole drug thing that had Blake picking you and Agent Jones to send here. It wasn't your ability to operate in the backcountry, or to investigate a murder. There are hundreds of FBI agents who could have fit that bill. Imagine my surprise to find out that Blake sent us a CCU team." He crossed his arms over his chest and planted his feet wide apart. "What is it about a single murder that elevated it to the level of a CCU team?"

When Gin remained silent, alarm bells went off in Ricki's head. There was something here she didn't know, and now she gave herself a mental kick for not questioning Gin more closely on that whole CCU thing.

"Agent Reilly," Hamilton said slowly. "What assignment were you working on before you were pulled to come here?"

Gin exchanged a long look with Stephen, then drew in a deep breath. "We were tracking a major drug transit center being run through Portland and, we believed, into central Canada." She narrowed her eyes. "The request came down through channels from the Canadian government."

"Because of an alarming increase in cocaine flooding into central Canada that the government wanted kept under wraps until they knew more about it?" Hamilton smiled when both Gin and Stephen remained silent. "I have my sources too, Agent Reilly. So, the confidential nature of the request put it into the laps of the CCU. And did you consider getting word of a possible smuggling route through North Cascades Park a break in your investigation?"

"It is," Stephen said, speaking up for the first time. "We estimate four million dollars, just on the one drug run."

Hamilton blinked in surprise, then looked over at Ricki. "Four million? What happened to the half million that burned up on the road the other night?"

"We think three of the bodies we found were doing the

heavy work of carrying the drugs, and the other two were guards," Ricki said.

The senior agent still looked surprised, but he nodded. "All right, we'll get to that in a moment." He turned back to the two FBI agents. "So when I mentioned to Blake that it looked like we'd stumbled onto a conduit for drugs into Canada, he pulled you two out of Portland and sent you here. Two birds, one stone, so to speak."

When Gin started to speak, Hamilton stopped her with a look. "Were you investigating a cartel there in Portland?"

Gin nodded, her gaze flashing an apology to Ricki. "Yes. The CJNG."

"I've read some of the inter-agency bulletins. They're dangerous." He unfolded his arms and clasped his hands behind his back. "The ISB is here to solve a murder. If some kind of drug war is breaking out, or a gang of some sort is being sent in as retaliation for the missing drugs, then I'm pulling my agents out of this. We don't get in the middle of a fight with a cartel. That's not what we're trained to do."

"With all due respect, sir," Stephen cut in. There was an urgency to his voice that had Hamilton frowning. "This park is perfect for smuggling drugs in undetected. And to shut that off, Ricki's knowledge and skill in the backcountry, especially here in these mountains, has been a major key in us getting as far into this investigation as we have. We've found their camp in just a couple of trips up there. That's big, sir. We can cut off this route and put a big wrench in the works if we can find their guide. This investigation can make it difficult enough for the cartel that they won't run drugs this way anymore, and that is also huge."

"It's putting my agents at too much risk," Hamilton countered, then frowned at Gin when she laughed.

"I'm sorry," Gin apologized, quickly getting her outburst under control. "It's just that your team here has a Marine sniper on it. Not even the CCU can conjure up one of those."

She glanced at Clay. "Not to mention a chief of police. I doubt if there's an FBI team anywhere in the country that could convince a police chief to join them on an op."

"Anchorman is a retired Marine and is now a cook." Hamilton's mouth twitched at the corners. "And a former sniper. As for the chief, we've found this arrangement to be mutually beneficial."

"Right now the cartel's response is pretty small," Gin said. "If we can solve this murder and let them know that all their drugs are gone, it might convince them that this conduit has too many problems to use again, and we can shut the whole thing down before it gets out of control and you end up with a platoon of federal agencies trampling all over the park." She pointed at Ricki. "We need her skills. We need the skills of this whole weird little team you sent out here. I promise we will solve these murders and shut down drugs being run through this park." When Hamilton remained silent, she added, "And maybe garner a little goodwill with Canada?"

After a long moment, Hamilton smiled. "You make a good case, Agent Reilly." His smile grew a fraction of an inch. "Gin. But before I make any final decision, I need to have a talk with Blake." His gaze shifted between Gin and Stephen. "And the two of you need to be a part of that."

"Glad to, sir," Stephen said. "I would also like to point out that we don't work for Dr. Blake." He let out a sigh. "At least not directly."

"I'm beginning to think Dr. Blake thinks we all work for him," Hamilton said dryly. "We'll get to that call in a minute." He turned to face Ricki. "I need a full report on what you've found, and what your next steps are."

Ricki nodded. Hamilton still hadn't committed to keeping them on this case, but she knew the senior agent well enough to know Gin's arguments had made an impression on him. Which was good, because she really wanted to see this case through. The drug cartel might have taken some shots at them, but she was sure they were operating blind. It was the hermit she was after. Which reminded her about the partial check stub she had in the pocket of her jacket.

She gestured for Dan to follow her. "I have something I need you to look at."

Chapter 24

THE RIDE over to the Last Stop wasn't exactly tense, but it wasn't altogether comfortable either. With Gin and Stephen tied up with Hamilton on that phone call to Blake, she and Clay had taken on the job of conducting the interviews. Ricki worked through her text messages and emails while Clay drove, and neither said a word until the SUV rolled to a stop in the pocket-sized parking lot.

Clay shut the engine off and turned in his seat. "How do you want to handle this? I mean after we answer the question of 'where's the sniper'?"

Ricki made a face before looking around the parking lot. Even though it was small, it was still half-empty. But then it was barely ten in the morning, so it was just as surprising there was anyone there at all. She just hoped that one of the cars taking up space belonged to Jimmy, the local bartender and mountain guide. "I'm sure the entire town knows we're law enforcement by now," she said to Clay. "I think asking some straightforward questions is the best approach."

The chief glanced across the small, mostly empty lot. "Hopefully it's early enough to catch Jimmy here alone, and off guard." He stuck his hands in his jacket pockets and waited for Ricki to take the lead.

When she walked through the door, Ricki headed right to a stool at the bar. Taking a seat, she casually looked around. Two of the tables were occupied, each with a pair of men, and there was only one patron at the bar, sitting at the end farthest away from the front door. But the space behind the bar was empty. Ricki looked down to the far end, where a man with a ball cap pulled down over his eyes with the ends of a scraggly haircut poking out around the edges, drank from a tall bottle of beer. He didn't return her stare but kept his eyes down and his shoulders hunched over.

Swiveling around on her stool, Ricki immediately caught the eye of one of the men sitting at a table. The white hair on his head was thinner than his bushy beard, which reached halfway down his chest. The plaid shirt he had on looked to be a half size too big for him, and a heavy pair of hiking boots stuck out from beneath the table. He nodded and grinned back at her, showing a wide gap between his two front teeth.

"Hey there, missy," he called out, then leaned to the side to get a better look at the front door. "Where's that sniper friend of yours?"

Ricki tried to keep from grinding her teeth together even as she pasted on a smile. "He has some things to take care of today."

A thick gray eyebrow lifted high on the old man's forehead. "And you don't, missy? From what I hear, you're a big-time detective or something."

"Or something," Ricki muttered under her breath as Molly shuffled out of the back hallway, pushing her bucket and mop in front of her.

She stopped mid-step when she spied Ricki and Clay. Abandoning her bucket of soapy water, she slowly made her way to the bar. Stepping behind it, Molly kept walking until she was facing Ricki over the rough wooden top.

"What can I git you?"

Ricki glanced at Clay, who immediately gave the older woman a friendly smile. "It's a little early yet. If you have any coffee, that will be fine."

Molly shook her head, sending her limp gray curls bouncing around her ears. "If you want coffee, why'd you come into a bar? There's a diner jist down the street. They got plenty o' coffee."

Clay's smile didn't fade one bit as he settled his forearms on top of the bar. "I'm here, so this coffee will be fine."

Molly shrugged. "Don't got no cream or sugar," she warned before looking at Ricki. The woman's face had a network of deep lines running across her forehead and down her cheeks. Everything about her looked worn down, from her frizzy hair in various shades of gray to her slightly stooped shoulders. Molly had the air of a woman who was waiting for old age. Except for her eyes. They were a startling shade of green, like a piece of jade that had been put into the wrong setting. And she didn't blink once as she stared Ricki down. "What do you want, missy?"

Thinking that must be the local, catch-all nickname for any unknown woman, it had a more condescending ring to it coming from Molly than it had from the man at the table. Hearing the underlying challenge loud and clear, Ricki made sure her tone wasn't as friendly as Clay's. "I'm Ricki, or Special Agent James, whichever you prefer." She lifted her shoulders in a shrug that matched the one Molly had used. "Not 'missy.' And I'll have a ginger ale."

When Molly moved off, Clay leaned closer to Ricki and lowered his voice. "Looks like Jimmy isn't here."

"That's fine for the moment. Maybe we can catch him at his house. I wanted to talk to Molly anyway."

"Why?" Clay asked.

"I'm not sure." Ricki sighed and watched the old woman

carefully pour out a large mug of coffee. "She's another puzzle piece that doesn't add up."

Clay glanced over at the mop sticking out of the bucket that the old woman had left in the middle of the floor. "It seems pretty straightforward to me."

Ricki was spared having to answer when Molly made her way back down the bar.

"Here you go." She set a glass filled with ice and an amber-colored soda in front of Ricki, then slid a coffee mug over to Clay. "Can I git you anything else?"

It seemed Ricki's little challenge had worked because Molly sounded much more casual and the belligerent expression on her face had disappeared.

"You're Molly, aren't you?" Ricki started out. When the woman nodded, Ricki did too. "I saw you when we were here the other day. Do you work here?"

"I clean." Molly pursed her lips. "What do you do, Agent Ricki?"

Ricki met the challenge in the green eyes staring back at her with a grin. "I investigate crimes in the national parks. Do you have a last name, Molly?"

The old woman let out a rusty laugh. "I haven't needed it in so long, I don't use it anymore. Molly is fine. Everyone in town knows who I am." She picked up a wrinkled dishcloth and ran it across the top of the bar. "Are you here investigatin' some crime that happened in North Cascades?"

"A body was found in the park a few days ago. I think it was in the papers," Ricki said.

Molly smiled. "Our paper don't come out until Wednesday, but I heard about it. Folks are sayin' someone killed him. You know, like a murder."

"Murdered or not, all deaths in the park have to be investigated," Ricki said easily.

Molly dropped her eyes as she kept wiping down the counter. "Something about him dealing drugs." Molly's nose wrinkled up. "I don't understand who he was sellin' drugs to way out there."

"I wouldn't know about that. I'm only here to investigate a death in the park," Ricki said.

Molly's gaze snapped up to hers. "Now that's hard to believe. I heard you was out there with the county law when drugs were burnin' up on the road."

"You can't believe everything you hear, Molly," Clay said.

She looked over at him and frowned. "That's a nice smile you got there, mister. And a pretty face. But that won't do you no good with me. I fell for those once, and it got me nothin' but grief."

When Molly set her cloth down and took a half-step backwards, Ricki quickly nudged Clay with the toe of her boot.

Understanding the silent message, Clay stepped off his stool. "Our sniper friend wanted me to give that gentleman over there a message, so I'd better do that." Despite Molly's warning, he smiled at her before turning it on Ricki. "Ladies." With a slight nod, he picked up his coffee mug and strolled across the room.

"Glacier seems like a nice town," Ricki said. She picked up her glass of soda and studied the color for a moment. "Reminds me of the town I live in."

"Where's that?" Molly asked, stepping forward again and putting her palms on the counter that ran underneath the bar.

"A place called the Bay," Ricki replied. "On the other side of the Puget Sound from Seattle."

"You got a big park out there too?" Molly asked.

"Olympic Park," Ricki supplied. "I grew up there." When Molly only grunted at that, Ricki continued. "How long have you lived in Glacier, Molly?"

"A long time."

"And how long have you worked for Jimmy Blighton?"

"A while now. I needed the work," Molly said. "He's been

good to me. Lets me eat some meals here without chargin' nothin'."

"That's very nice of him." Ricki pretended to look around. "Where is he? With the bar open, I expected to see him here."

Molly dropped her cloth again. "He asks me to open the place sometimes. If he has somethin' to do."

"Like what?" Ricki asked, her gaze growing sharper along with her tone of voice. "What is Jimmy doing this morning that he can't open up his own place?" Ricki pointed to the flyer still pinned to the wall. "Is he taking some hikers out on a guided tour?"

Molly glanced at the flyer, then shook her head. "That's old. He don't do that no more. He's got the bar goin' good now, so he don't need to do any side work." She stepped back, a leery look in her jade-colored eyes. "I got to get back to takin' care of my own business now. If you need a refill on that soda, you jist come back here and git it. No charge for a refill."

Ricki lifted her glass. "Thanks. I'll do that." She watched as Molly moved off, the shuffle prominent in her step as she retrieved her mop and bucket before disappearing down the back hallway.

Picking up her soda glass, Ricki wandered over to the table where Clay was sitting. He pushed out a chair in an invitation to sit down. Ricki took the seat and smiled at the white-haired man who'd been looking for "the sniper."

"This is Special Agent Ricki James," Clay said, his head inclined in her direction. "Ricki, this is Big Mack and Pac-Man."

The older man grinned. "A nickname I picked up when I drove a big rig."

She smiled back at him. "Let me guess, you had a Mack truck."

He slapped his palm on the table as he croaked out a

laugh. "That's right, Agent James. I had a Mack. Loved that truck. Sold it to my nephew when it was time to give up life on the road." He patted the center of his chest. "My old ticker started having a problem with fried food and fast women." He laughed again and pointed to his friend sitting next to him. "This here is Pac-Man." Big Mack gave him a poke in the side with a bony finger. "Because he likes to eat. The man will gobble up anything you put in front of him."

Pac-Man, who towered over his friend and must have tipped the scales at a good three hundred pounds, ducked his head as he touched a finger to the brim of his cap. "Ma'am."

"She ain't no ma'am," Big Mack objected. "She's a special agent, with a police chief and a sniper for friends. That takes her out of the sissy 'ma'am' category."

"Um, thanks, I think," Ricki drawled.

Her response had Big Mack going off into another fit of laughter before settling down. "The chief here says you have some questions to ask. Well, Pac-Man and I would be happy to help you out. So ask away, Agent James."

"Have you heard about the dead body that was found in the park?" Ricki immediately tossed out.

Pac-Man nodded while Big Mack rolled his eyes. "Probably heard about it before he got to that morgue over in Bellingham. All the dead bodies in the park go there."

Knowing the gossip mill in small towns, Ricki only nodded. "What else did you hear?"

"That he was carrying a pack full of drugs." Big Mack paused to take a sip of his beer. "Don't take no college degree to figure out he was probably runnin' 'em up to Canada."

"Okay," Ricki said. "Anything else?"

"Well, that and some crazy person shot the guy and took the drugs."

"A crazy person?" Ricki repeated. "You heard there was a crazy person who shot the man found dead in the park?"

Big Mack shrugged. "The whole town is talkin' about it."

"That's right," Pac-Man said with another duck of his head. "I heard it over at the hardware store. Some guy who's been living out in the park like some kind of human Bigfoot or something."

"Yeah. Like that," Big Mack agreed. "What do you know about that?"

Ricki shook her head. "I've never met anyone like that." And it was mostly true. It wasn't as if she and the hermit had been introduced.

Big Mack's face fell, and his lower lip quivered. "I guess that it probably can't happen." He looked up at Ricki with sad eyes. "I've lived here going on thirty years. Now and again I'd hear a rumor about some wild man living up in those mountains, but for all the times I've hiked and camped out in the Mt. Baker wilderness and in the park, I ain't never seen any wild man." He sighed as he raised his beer bottle to his mouth. "Makes a helluva a story, though, don't it?"

"It does," Ricki agreed. "I was wondering where Jimmy was. Molly said he had something to do today."

"For the last couple of days," Big Mack volunteered. "But that isn't unusual. He doesn't always come in during the week 'cause that's his slow time. So he has Molly open up, or one of the other guys."

"I've run the bar for Jimmy," Pac-Man spoke up. "It ain't hard to do. Only time it's busy is on one, maybe two Saturday nights and that's only if the Snowmelt is full. Then folks will come over here."

"Yeah, the place isn't exactly jumpin' most of the time," Big Mack cut in. "I guess that's why that banker comes around real regular. Every Thursday afternoon like clockwork. Must be keepin' an eye on things. Makin' sure Jimmy can make his loan payment." The elderly man leaned forward and dropped his voice to a conspiratorial whisper. "Although I had a loan on my Mack truck when I first bought it, and I never had no banker come around to my place and ask about it. Makes me think Jimmy might be behind on his note."

"Maybe he should start taking people out on guided tours again," Ricki said.

Big Mack blinked, taking a moment to fix his watery eyes on Ricki. "He still does. That's usually where he is when he ain't here."

Ricki lifted an eyebrow. "Oh? Molly said he didn't do that work anymore."

Pac-Man made a tsking noise in his throat while Big Mack let out an audible snort.

"Ah. That woman ain't here most of the time." The old trucker tapped a finger against the side of his head. "Jimmy gave her a job here about five years ago, and she's been cleanin' the place up ever since."

Pac-Man solemnly nodded, his gaze earnest when he looked at Ricki. "It was real nice of Jimmy to help her out like that. Real nice."

Big Mack put his hand over his heart and raised his eyes to the ceiling. "It's a straight-up miracle. The first time Jimmy Blighton has ever done somethin' nice for a fellow human being."

Chapter 25

THE SNOWMELT WAS BUSIER than Jimmy's run-down bar, but there were still several tables and booths available when Ricki and Clay arrived just as the lunch shift went into full swing. Jo was behind the hostess stand up front, dressed in the same jeans and plaid shirt outfit she'd had on the first night they'd come in. Only now her shirt was sporting a pattern in various shades of green instead of yellow.

She greeted them with a wide smile and plucked two menus out of the box next to the old-fashioned cash register. "Glad to see you. You're going to like our lunch special today."

"I don't doubt it," Ricki replied. "Can we have a booth nearer the back?"

Jo didn't even blink an eye at the request, but nodded, directing a small wiggle of her eyebrows toward Clay. "You sure can."

They followed her down the long aisle, but when Jo stopped at a cozy booth for two, Ricki shook her head and pointed at a bigger one a little farther down. "How about that one?"

"Sure," Jo said easily. "Are you expecting someone else? I can be on the lookout for them if you want."

"We were hoping you could sit and talk with us for a while." Ricki said while Clay slid into the booth. "We have some questions we'd like to ask you."

Jo hesitated for a moment before she turned up the wattage on her smile. "Sure. That's not a problem at all. I'll get someone to watch the front for me and then we can sit and chat." She set the menus down on the table. "Meanwhile, you two look this over and see if anything appeals to you."

When Jo hurried off, Clay picked up the menus and handed one to Ricki. "We'd better order some lunch to make her time worthwhile."

Ricki nodded and opened the menu. "Yeah. I think Glacier is a lot like the Bay when it comes to seasonal business. There probably isn't much by way of tourists coming through here in the winter."

Clay looked at her from over the top of the menu. "Probably not," he agreed quietly. "Not much going on."

Ricki didn't look away. "Kind of like the Bay in that respect too, isn't it? Not much going on."

Jo bustled up, wiping her hands on the apron tied around her waist. "So, I'm all set." She stopped next to the booth, slowly looking from Ricki to Clay. "I can come back a bit later if you aren't ready for those questions yet."

"Now is fine." Ricki broke off the staring match with Clay and smiled at Jo. She scooted closer to the wall, leaving a space for the blonde woman to slide into the booth.

With a sigh, Jo took the offered seat, then sent Ricki a wary glance. "Are you two fighting about something?"

"No," Ricki said quickly. "Just a difference of opinion." She shrugged as if it had already passed. "We live in a small town ourselves, Jo. So we know how the gossip mill works. I'm assuming you've heard about the dead body that was found up in the park?"

"Quite a few of them, I guess," Jo said, her smile trembling. "It's scary to think someone is going around murdering people. Do you know who it is?"

Ricki shook her head. "Not yet, but we're still in the early stages of our investigation."

Jo nodded and turned her head to look down the length of her restaurant. "We don't have anything to worry about, do we?" There was a tremor in her voice, and the gaze she turned back on Ricki looked troubled. "I wouldn't want anyone in town to get shot."

"How do you know the victim was shot?" Clay asked.

The owner's mouth twitched up into a smile. "It's Wednesday, Chief Thomas. Our paper came out this morning." She shrugged. "But I'd already heard it. Like Ricki said, the gossip mills in small towns are real fast."

Since quite a few park rangers had been on the extraction mission, and a number of them likely lived in the area, Ricki didn't doubt that word was out before the body even got to the autopsy table. It also wasn't what she had come here to talk about. "How long have you lived in Glacier, Jo?"

Jo blinked at the sudden change in subject, then sank more comfortably into her seat. "All my life. I married a local boy, so I just stayed on. My Donald, that would be Donald Bain and he was my husband. Anyway, Don and I made ends meet by running a gift shop and doing handiwork and other odd jobs until we saved up enough money to buy this old building. We lived in it for a few years while we were fixing it up, and eventually we got enough money to open the Snowmelt. It's had its ups and downs, but this old place did real well for us. And it kept me going after my Don passed away a few years back."

"I'm part-owner of a diner back home." Ricki smiled. "It's had a few ups and downs too, so I know what you mean." She twined her hands together and rested them on the table. "Since you've lived here all your life, you must be familiar with other incidents in the park, or even around town, where someone was killed."

Jo's expression sobered. "Accidents in the wilderness area outside the park. Couple of them were from being shot, but that's because you can hunt on that land." Her brows scrunched together as she thought it over. "In the park, I think it's mostly from falls, or freezing to death because they were foolish enough to go hiking up there in the winter and got caught in a big storm. Not anyone was shot, though, that I recall. There's no hunting allowed in there."

"No, there isn't," Ricki said. "So you can't think of anyone in the area who was attacked or murdered in all the time you've lived here?"

Her eyelashes fluttered for a moment before her gaze focused back on Ricki. "Now that's a real odd question, Agent James. Why would you want to know that?"

"Lots of people with fancy degrees work in every agency," Ricki said easily. "And they don't just do profiles on people but on communities too. They look for things like a regular string of burglaries over the years, or any other specific kind of crime. It helps establish the probability of a criminal coming from the community."

"So, if there's been a murder here every so often, then the killer probably lives in the town?" Jo asked. "That kind of thing?"

"Something like that."

Jo's smile returned. "Well, then I guess we're safe enough, because I don't recall anyone being murdered in the park." She partially deflated again with a sigh. "Now the wilderness area is a different story. We've had some murders there." She lifted her head and looked at Ricki. "But that's not where you found this latest body, is it?"

"No, it isn't," Ricki said.

Jo leaned forward and set her elbows on top of the table. "What about that crazy man? Couldn't he have done that murder?" At Ricki's bland look, Jo only shrugged. "I heard about him. Folks coming in here have been talking about it."

"I've heard the rumors about some guy living out in the park like Bigfoot," Ricki said, repeating what Big Mack had said just an hour ago. She leaned back and studied Jo's face. "You've lived here quite a while. Have you ever heard of someone who was living in the park? Maybe someone from Glacier or one of the other towns near here who went to live off the grid?"

The older woman chuckled. "A lot of people have said they were going to, but I don't know anyone who actually did it."

Ricki frowned, pretending to think something over. "I'd like to put the whole 'crazy man as a killer' thing to rest. The rumors are saying he supposedly has lived in the park for years. Is there someone in town who would be the person to ask about that? I know back where we come from, there's a woman who knows everything that ever went on in our towns. If you have one of those, then maybe she can confirm, or better yet deny, there ever was any such person."

"We had one," Jo said. "Mabry Garner. She must be coming up on a hundred by now, but I'm not sure if she's even still alive. She went to live with her son and daughter-in-law a few years back. Somewhere near Granite Falls, as I recall."

Ricki silently tucked that information away. "Well, that's too bad." She pulled her cell phone out of her parka and scrolled over to a notes application. "I'm just going to put in a few notes about these more traditional questions I have to ask, if you don't mind."

"No, I don't mind," Jo said. "Fire away, and then I really need to get back to work. But I'd like to ask you something first."

Ricki set her phone down and folded her hands on top of it. "Okay."

"What happened out on the road the other night?"

"There was a fire." Ricki cocked her head to one side. "Someone had set a bonfire in the middle of the road."

"Now, why would they do that?" Jo wondered.

"I don't know," Ricki said. "It's not my case. We were only there as an extra pair of hands."

"Not your case?"

Ricki shook her head. "Nope."

Jo pursed her lips and stared at the unoccupied space across the table. "So you don't know what was burning?"

"Why?" Ricki countered. "What do you think was burning out there?"

"I heard it was drugs."

"Did you?" Ricki said softly. She waited, watching Jo squirm in her seat. "Where did you hear that?"

"Well, now," Jo said, "that I do remember. Jimmy from the Last Stop bar a block down told me. I dropped in there one night to have a drink someplace other than here." Her arm swept out to the side. "It's good to change it up every once in a while. And besides, we share customers, so I know most of the folks who hang out at that bar." When Ricki didn't say anything, Jo cleared her throat. "Okay. Now, about your questions?"

Ricki got out her phone again, and this time turned on the record button and set the phone between them. "This will be faster than taking notes," she said when Jo simply stared at the phone. "So, have you noticed any strangers in town?"

"No. I mean, of course there are strangers in here. But no one I would consider suspicious looking or anything," Jo said.

"How about any unsuspicious-looking people who were asking around about a guide service?" Ricki asked. "Have you come across or heard about anyone like that lately?"

Jo adamantly shook her head, making her ponytail sag down to her neck. "No. Not this late in the season. If someone is asking for a guide now, they shouldn't be hiking up in those mountains. We've already got storms coming through here."

"So Jimmy hasn't taken any parties out lately?"

The older woman blinked. "Jimmy? I don't know. Whenever he disappears for a few days, that's usually what he's doing. But I don't know about lately. He usually stops making guide trips in September. He says it gets too wet and cold after that." She chewed on her lower lip for a moment. "Why are you asking about Jimmy?"

"We were over at his bar this morning, and he wasn't there. I thought maybe he was on a guide trip."

"Oh." Jo made a move to slide out of the booth. "Well, I don't know for sure that he isn't. I mean, it's late in the season and all, but the weather's been pretty good. Maybe he thought it would be okay. I need to get back to work. If you have any more questions, maybe you could stop in again tomorrow?"

Maybe, Ricki thought as she watched Jo make her escape. If she wasn't too busy tracking down one James Blighton.

Across the table, Clay put down the menu he'd been pretending to read. "You know, I'm not that hungry."

"Me either," Ricki said. "And we have a lot of work waiting for us."

Clay nodded. "Yeah. Checking up on Reilly and Jones, helping Anchorman and Cheron put the groceries away."

"Making sure Hamilton didn't decide to yank us off the case," Ricki said, taking up the narrative.

"And I'm thinking we should track down Jimmy Blighton."

She smiled at him. "Chief, I like the way you think."

Chapter 26

CLAY TOOK the wheel while Ricki pulled up Jimmy's home address that Dan had sent to her email. Thanks to the GPS built into the dashboard of Clay's truck, she had the exact location of the house. As Clay followed the directions chirped out by the automated voice in the tracking software, Ricki made a call to Gin to let them know where they were going and when they would check back in.

Five minutes later, Clay slowly passed by a driveway that was little more than two ruts in the dirt covered with a thin layer of gravel. Ricki stared at the house, set back from the street and partially hidden by several towering trees. Behind it was an old barn, its wide doors shut.

"I don't see anyone, or a vehicle of any kind," Ricki said.

Clay let his truck roll to a gentle stop far enough down the sparsely populated road to be out of sight of the house. "Do we know what Jimmy drives?"

"No, we don't." Ricki stepped out of the truck and stood with her hands on her hips, considering the various angles they could take to reach the front of the house with minimal exposure to anyone who might be watching from inside. When Clay joined her, she pointed toward the center-left of the cluster of trees in front of the house. "I think that line would give us the best approach."

Clay considered it for a moment before nodding. "Agreed." He glanced over at her. "Do you have your pistol with you?"

"Under my parka." Ricki unzipped her jacket and pulled out her Glock. She was better with a rifle, but she could hit what she aimed at with a handgun too.

They moved forward, walking five feet apart and their weapons held down at their sides. Ricki kept the house within her line of vision, stopping when they reached the edge of the small stand of trees.

There was a good twenty feet of cleared-off space between the tree line and the house. The structure wasn't large. From the front it was hard to gauge how far back it reached, but there was no second floor, and Ricki guessed there was only one bedroom in the rear of the house. From her vantage point she could easily see the paint peeling away from the outside wall in large patches, as well as the missing steps that should have led up to the porch. The whole place had the same dilapidated air as the Last Stop.

Jimmy must like the shabby look, Ricki thought before glancing over at Clay. He gave a short, quick nod, which she returned, then the two of them stepped forward together.

The house remained silent as they approached the front. Blinds were drawn over the two windows on either side, and a floorboard groaned with a loud creak when Ricki stepped onto the porch. With their presence announced, she lifted her hand and gave a sharp rap against the door, then leaned slightly forward, listening for any movement coming from inside.

When no one appeared, she knocked again, and this time called out. "Jimmy? It's Special Agent Ricki James and Chief Thomas. We'd like a word with you."

The silence continued for another thirty seconds before

Ricki shrugged. "If he's in there, he doesn't seem inclined to come to the door."

"Want to take a look around?" Clay asked.

Ricki turned away from the door. "Oh, yeah. We have to take into consideration that Mr. Blighton might be in trouble."

Clay grinned. "Absolutely. And we wouldn't want to leave him in distress."

"Of course not." Ricki jumped down the two feet from the porch to the ground. "I'll take the right if you'll go left."

The chief immediately turned and slowly walked toward the left-hand corner of the house while Ricki headed in the opposite direction. Halfway to the back, she came across another window, covered with curtains that had seen better days. Ricki cupped her hands to the glass and peered inside through one of the larger rips in the curtains' fabric.

The room was sparsely furnished with a double bed and a tall dresser. Half of its drawers were open with clothes hanging over the side, and another pile was haphazardly stacked on a straight-backed wooden chair. The bed was unmade and the walls were bare, adding to the room looking more like a prison cell than a cozy retreat. All that was missing were bars on the windows.

Still seeing no sign of life, Ricki kept on walking toward the back of the house. She rounded the corner at the same time that Clay did. Seeing his questioning look, she shook her head.

"There wasn't anything but a messy bedroom." She turned to look over the rear of the house. Through a narrow window, she could see an old white refrigerator that matched one sitting outside on the back porch with all of its doors missing. Since they had no reason to enter the house, Ricki studied the barn.

It might have been painted red once, but now it was a weather-worn gray. On a rainy day, it would have faded right into the background, and there were a lot of rainy days on the western side of the Cascade Mountains.

"What do you think?" Clay asked.

Ricki looked over at him. Clay's gaze was also on the barn. "We're here, so it's worth a look," she said.

They crossed the overgrown patch of land extending out from the house. As they got closer to the tall, wide doors of the barn, Ricki saw the heavy-duty lock on the door. She walked up and examined it, lifting it with one hand as she studied its shiny gold surface.

"New," she murmured before looking over at Clay. "This lock is new."

Clay leaned in to get a closer look. "Then it's the only thing around here that isn't older than dirt. Wonder what Jimmy has in there that needs a brand-new lock?"

"Good question." Ricki let the lock drop back into place. "Let's do a walk around. Maybe there's a missing board somewhere."

It only took ten minutes for them to check the exterior of the barn, but luck wasn't on their side. No missing boards, or any other crevices wide enough to give them a peek inside. As they headed back to the truck, Ricki shook her head in disgust.

"Everything else Jimmy owns has holes in it, so you'd think that old barn would be no exception."

"Looks like he kept it in pretty good shape," Clay agreed. "But without a warrant, there's not much more we can do."

She blew out a breath and stuck her hands in her pockets. "I know. I guess we'll have to find him the hard way. With good old-fashioned footwork."

Clay shrugged and then stifled a yawn. "It's not as if we haven't done a lot of that on other cases." When they were settled back into the truck, he looked over at her and lifted an eyebrow. "Where to? Do you want to make another pass at the bar? Molly or Pac-man might have a sudden improvement in their memory of the last time they saw Jimmy."

Ricki shook her head. "No. Let's go back to the house, grab some lunch, and bring the others up to date." She snapped her seatbelt in place and leaned back against the seat. "And see if we still have a case to pursue. Hamilton might have left word that he's taking the ISB off the case, which would mean you, Anchorman, and Cheron too."

Clay put the truck into gear and pulled out onto the road, executing a neat three-point turn and heading back toward town. "If he was going to do that, he'd have already told you himself."

"Probably," Ricki agreed.

When they reached the Airbnb, the SUV that Cheron had rented was parked out front and both Stephen and Gin were occupying chairs on the wide porch.

"How'd the morning hunt go?" Gin called out as Ricki and Clay approached the house.

"Interesting," Ricki said. She climbed the three steps and took up a position near the railing. Leaning against it, she gave Gin a quizzical look. "It's too cold to be hanging out on the front porch. What's up?"

"It was a good place to be while your boss was having a talk with Blake," Gin said. "They were giving off a little too much heat for my pay grade."

"And mine," Stephen put in. "But I have to admit, I did enjoy the thought of Blake taking a verbal thrashing. That's got to be a rare thing."

Ricki grinned. "Sorry I wasn't here."

"I'll record it next time and play it back to you," Gin said. "By the time Hamilton and Dan left, we were too settled in here to move. So, what did we miss? Find out anything interesting?"

"It seems we've lost one of our less colorful locals. Jimmy is missing in action," Ricki said.

Gin's eyes narrowed and she slid forward to sit on the edge of her chair. "As in, he's nowhere to be found?"

"Not that anyone will admit to," Ricki said.

"How long has he been missing?" Gin demanded. "Do we know?"

"I got the impression he lives at that bar, unless he's out playing mountain guide for the tourists. And neither Molly nor a couple of regulars at the Last Stop have seen him since the first time we showed up there asking questions."

Gin's forehead puckered in thought. "So that was what, two days ago?"

Clay, who had been standing near the top of the steps, moved across the porch and took an empty chair on the other side of Gin. "That's about right. And that means that no one's seen him since we were ambushed up in the park."

The FBI agent's eyes widened as her gaze shifted from him to Ricki. "You think he's been the guide for the drug smugglers?"

Ricki crossed her booted feet at the ankles. "It's a possibility. The timing of his disappearing act certainly fits."

Stephen frowned. "But we didn't say anything to anyone in the bar that we were planning a trip into the park, so he wouldn't have gone there because of us."

"True," Ricki said. "So if that's where he went, then he'd already planned on hiking in, especially if he was going to lead a group in or meet up with one." She silently navigated her way through several possibilities. "I think whoever ambushed us at that cabin was just as surprised to see us there as we were to see them."

"I second that," Clay said. "I think we saw each other at about the same time. If they had really intended to ambush us, they would have spread out more, cut off our escape route, and then come at us from different sides."

"Yeah, you're right," Stephen conceded. "So, how do we track down our absent bartender?" He looked out past the porch toward the sea of trees with the mountains rising behind them. "There's lots of ground to cover out there."

"I don't think he'd stay out there long. His comfort zone is around here," Gin said.

Ricki nodded. Gin was right. "Both Molly and Jo said that Jimmy rarely leaves the bar, except to take out guided tours. And only then during the season. According to Jo, once winter sets in, it gets too cold and wet for him to go out anymore." She angled her body so she was facing Stephen. "Information is always a good thing. Do you think you could look into his background, and more specifically into his bank accounts?" She paused to think it through. "And get a description of his vehicle and its plate number. We also need to know if he has any relatives in the area. You can work with Dan. See what the two of you can come up with as fast as you can."

When she mentioned working with Dan, Stephen's face lit up. "Yeah. Maybe he can pass along some research hints he picked up with the CIA."

"That are legal," Gin drawled before frowning at Ricki. "Are you looking for something in particular?"

"Anything that will justify us getting a search warrant."

"To search what?" Gin asked.

Ricki uncrossed her ankles and stood up. "His house and mostly his barn." Her mouth flattened into a thin line. "Everything else he owns is held together with nothing more than spit and a couple of patches of paint, except for that barn. It's airtight and has a shiny new lock on the doors."

Gin smiled. "Really. Now isn't that interesting. Do you think he got spooked and ran, but will hopefully come back for whatever is stashed away in that barn that requires a shiny new lock?"

"Right now, all I think is that he's missing," Ricki said. "Are Anchorman and Cheron back from the store?"

Stephen stood up and stretched his arms over his head. "They are. He mentioned something about lunch while we were helping to carry in the groceries." He dropped his arms back to his sides and stamped his boots to get the circulation going again in his feet. "Cheron mentioned that she got a call from Hamilton while they were on their way back here and Hamilton was headed for Seattle. He told her that the forecast is clear for tomorrow, so the recovery would be delayed until then, and they were arranging for a team to go in and retrieve the bodies." He hunched his shoulders inside his thick coat. "A fully armed team, I guess, from what she said. Which takes a little longer to arrange, and that's why they're going in tomorrow instead of today."

Glad that the senior agent hadn't asked her to make another hike into the park to meet that armed team, Ricki walked over to the front door. "Okay. We'll plan on a trip into Bellingham and the morgue tomorrow or the day after, depending on when Dr. Robbins is ready for us. In the meantime, I'll see if Anchorman can make something quick for lunch. Then we'll head into town to do a basic canvass around the bar. Maybe we'll come across someone who can tell us where Jimmy might be."

Chapter 27

ANCHORMAN'S LUNCH of thick ham and cheese sandwiches with a side of fruit salad was consumed in record time. Stephen, who Gin declared was the slowest eater on the entire planet, took half his sandwich with him to eat on the way into town. This time Ricki drove the SUV while Clay took the time to check in with his deputies back in the Bay. When Ricki pulled into a parking spot at the end of a block of small businesses and retail shops, the chief put his phone away and Stephen wrapped the remainder of his sandwich in a paper napkin before setting it on the console between the front seats.

Ricki twisted around so she could see the two FBI agents sitting behind her. "It's a small town, so we should split up and work alone. We're more likely to make a connection if there's just one of us talking to a local resident. Two of us might make them feel ganged up on."

She looked out the side window toward the main street of the town. "Gin, you and Stephen take this side of the street and anything on the blocks to the west. Clay and I will start on the other side and work our way east. The body found up in the park should have been reported in the local paper this morning, so we let's stick with just that and see where it goes."

She glanced at her watch. "There aren't that many businesses on any of the blocks, so plan to either meet back here or check in with me an hour from now."

At everyone's nod, Ricki exited the car. She and Clay walked across the street as Gin disappeared into the nearest shop and Stephen continued to the one next door.

"Text me the name of any place you go into, and I'll do the same," Clay said. "That way we won't double up on any of them."

Ricki nodded as they walked up to a small ski shop with a few racks of apparel running down the center. Through the front window they could see the lone clerk sitting on a stool behind the counter, her eyes glued to her cell phone.

Long brown hair was pulled into a ponytail that hung from the top of her head and flopped over on her shoulder, which was left partially bare by a sagging T-shirt. Even through the window Ricki could see her chewing vigorously on what was likely a giant wad of chewing gum. Clay immediately shook his head.

"You take this one. I'll take the snowboarding shop next door."

Ricki silently mouthed the word "coward" at him, then grinned when he didn't hesitate to answer, "absolutely." Still smiling, she texted the name of the shop to him before pushing open the door, setting off a tinkling noise from the old-fashioned bell hanging above it. The girl looked up, gave Ricki the quick once-over, then went back to scrolling through her phone.

Half-annoyed and half-amused, Ricki unzipped her parka. When the clerk looked up again, her gaze zeroed right in on the gold badge hooked to Ricki's belt. She quickly straightened up on her stool, her teeth gnawing on her lower lip as Ricki walked up to the counter.

"Hi." Ricki waited for a moment while the clerk stared back at her. "I'm Special Agent Ricki James."

"Like with the FBI?" the clerk blurted out.

Thinking that getting into an explanation about the different agencies in the federal government would be a waste of time, Ricki let it pass. "Something like that."

The girl's hand flew to her mouth. "Are you here about the dead guy? It was in the paper this morning. They found a dead guy up in North Cascades Park. That's like a federal thing, isn't it? I mean, since it's a national park and all." Without waiting for an answer, she waved a hand in front of her and kept going. "I don't know any dead guys. I mean, guys who I thought were alive and now they're dead. That's why you're here, isn't it? I mean, I heard some FBI types showed up at the fires someone set on the road, but they didn't stay long. I guess there was a note or something? And then someone shot an arrow at one of the police officers, who chased after the guy, but he got away."

Ricki sorted through the rambling account, trying to pick out the highlights. "I think we need to start again. I'm Special Agent Ricki James," she said slowly, holding out her hand. "But it's fine to call me Ricki if you'd like. And you are . . . ?"

"Oh." The clerk's cheeks flushed as she timidly reached over to take Ricki's hand to give it a limp shake. "I'm Meghan. Meghan Kroner." She hesitated, then shrugged. "You can call me Meghan."

"Thank you," Ricki said with a polite nod. "To answer your first question, yes, I'm here about the dead hiker who was found in the park." She paused, waiting, but Meghan didn't say anything else. Filing that away to think about later, Ricki moved on. "You also mentioned the note left at the scene of the fires?"

Meghan blinked. "Note?"

"Yes. You said a note was left?"

"Oh yeah. Yeah." The young clerk bobbed her head up and down, sending her ponytail into a swirl of motion. She impatiently pushed it back over her shoulder as her voice dropped into a conspiratorial whisper. "I heard it was pinned to a tree by an arrow. Kind of like a Robin Hood sort of thing. You know, like a warning to the evil sheriff from the guy trying to help the poor people."

Positive that Sergeant Crowder wouldn't appreciate being cast in the role of the "evil sheriff," Ricki leaned against the counter and gave the girl an encouraging smile. "Wow. I hadn't heard that." Mostly because it wasn't true. The note was nailed to a tree, and an arrow was shot at the fourth fire.

"Well, you weren't there very long, were you? My sister dates a friend of one of the deputies who was out there, and he said you didn't show up until almost everything was over, and then you left with some other people."

"I did leave with some other people," Ricki said, not bothering to go into any more explanation than that. "So, a note pinned to a tree? Like I said, wow."

Meghan grinned. "Yeah. Weird, huh?"

"Any idea who the Robin Hood guy is?"

"Oh, it was probably the hermit," Meghan said in such a matter-of-fact tone, Ricki blinked in surprise. "Or maybe a guy I went to high school with. Some of them are still hanging around, and most of them do some bow hunting every year."

"Who's the hermit?" Ricki asked.

Meghan rolled her eyes. "I don't know. He's supposed to be some old guy who lives in the forest and never dies, or some shit like that. Everyone in town knows the story, but no one has ever seen him. And I've never heard him doing any good deeds for anyone, so he isn't anything like Robin Hood. I don't think he really exists at all."

Oh, he exists, Ricki thought, but went along with Meghan's shrug. "Anything else happen at that fire that I wouldn't know about?"

"I don't know." Meghan's mouth pursed as she considered it. "That's about all I heard."

"And you haven't heard anything at all about the dead hiker?"

The clerk shook her head. "Nope. Just that some rangers found him off the main trail, and they took him out of there on a helicopter." She shrugged again. "But that's how they get most of the people who get hurt or killed in an accident out of the park."

After a few more questions, it was obvious she wasn't going to get anything else out of Meghan, so Ricki thanked her for her help and made her way out to the sidewalk. She checked her phone for business names that Clay had sent her. She passed up the next two establishments and went into the third one on the block. Slowly they worked their way through all the businesses on the east side, then checked in with Gin and Stephen at the hour mark.

Since the two FBI agents were still working their assigned area, Clay and Ricki continued. It was another hour before they ran out of real estate and businesses. Meeting outside the last one, they returned to the starting point, where Gin and Stephen were leaning against the hood of the car, waiting.

No one said much until they were enclosed in the SUV and on their way back to the house.

"Interesting thing," Gin piped up from the back seat as Stephen reached for his wrapped-up sandwich on the console. "Everyone had heard about the dead guy found in the park, but no one seemed to know much more than that. One helpful fellow even showed me the article about it in the local paper, and that's pretty much all it said." Gin lifted her hands in the air and ran them apart in a parallel line as if she were reading the headline of a newspaper. "Dead guy found in the park. Probably an accident." She dropped her hands back into her lap. "I'd say that's pretty impressive on the part of the rescue team. Apparently none of them did any talking."

A little surprised herself, Ricki didn't share that with Gin. After all, she'd started out as a park ranger before joining the

ISB as an investigative agent, so she wasn't about to trash the guys in a service she'd been very proud to be a part of. "So, nobody mentioned that he was shot or might have been running drugs," Ricki stated.

"Nope," Gin said. "Not a word. And when Stephen and I compared notes, no one he talked to mentioned anything other than an accident either. How about you? Did anyone mention the gunshot or the drugs to either of you?"

"Not to me," Clay said. "I got the same story you did."

Ricki met Gin's gaze in the rearview mirror. "I didn't hear about the gunshot wound or drug running either. What about the fires? Did anyone bring up the fires set on the highway?"

Gin glanced over at Stephen, who shook his head. "No. What did you hear?"

"The clerk in the first store I went into brought it up on her own. Her name's Meghan Kroner, and she knew about the fires, and about the note. She swears it was pinned to a tree by someone acting like Robin Hood. She thinks it might be one of the boys she went to high school with."

"Really?" Gin's dry tone had Ricki smiling.

"Yeah, really. And she said that a very brave deputy chased the Robin Hood wannabe back into the forest. I suspect the brave deputy was the friend of her sister's boyfriend, who is the person Meghan heard the whole story from."

"The friend of . . . who now?" Gin ended on a snort. "Small-town gossip. Isn't that special?"

"Funny thing, though," Ricki went on. "Meghan didn't know anything about the drugs being burned in that last fire, so I'm guessing the friend of her sister's boyfriend was actually one of the deputies directing traffic away from the fire and did a little embellishment of his role to impress Meghan."

"Every guy likes to be the hero," Stephen said. He crumpled up the now-empty napkin and tucked it into his coat pocket. "When was the first time we heard a local bring up the drug connection?"

"This morning. Molly mentioned it," Ricki said. "And so did Big Mack, who also had something to say about the hermit."

"Was Big Mack the gentleman Anchorman was drinking with the other night at the bar?" Gin asked. "Because I didn't hear him bring up the hermit to Anchorman."

Ricki silently chewed on that for a moment. "Jo told me she was at the Last Stop later that same night, and she also brought up the drugs and the hermit. Big Mack did too, and so did Meghan, for that matter, although she thinks the hermit is just a myth. Big Mack sounded as if he was leaning that way too."

"But the drugs," Gin said, homing in on that. "Did anyone else mention the drugs after we left the bar?"

"Doesn't sound like it." Ricki tapped a finger against the steering wheel. The bar seemed to be the connection for knowing things the rest of the town didn't. And at the center of that bar stood one Jimmy Blighton. "We need to find Jimmy."

Chapter 28

RICKI WOKE to the sound of a knock on her bedroom door. She looked over at the watch she'd set on the bedside table the night before. The dial glowed, its hands pointing to 7 a.m. Calling out, "Come in," she scooted until she was sitting up, tugging on her pillow until it acted as a barrier between the thin T-shirt on her back and the cold bedroom wall.

Gin stuck her head around the corner of the door. "I'm assuming you're alone?"

Wishing everyone in the house didn't know about the strained relationship between her and Clay, Ricki fixed an annoyed glare on Gin. "Yes. I'm alone. Not that it's any of your business. What do you want at"—she paused to point-edly glance at her watch again—"seven o'clock in the morning?"

Gin laughed. She stepped in and closed the door behind her. "I can't believe a country girl like you sleeps in late."

"It's not like I get up every morning and milk the cows," Ricki snorted out. "And I can't believe a city girl like you doesn't sleep in late."

"I didn't grow up in a city."

Curious, Ricki pressed her lips together and watched the

FBI agent for a long moment. "Okay. Where did you grow up?"

"Long story." Gin smiled as she walked over and sat on the edge of the bed.

Ricki quickly moved her long legs out of the way before they got trapped under the FBI agent's butt. "Gee. Make yourself at home."

"Thanks. So. I thought we'd have an exchange of information," Gin said. She lifted one leg and propped it on the bed, curling it in front of her. "Did you say you were going to talk to Hamilton last night?"

"And so?" Ricki asked.

The FBI agent looked down and pretended to study her fingernails. "Well, it so happens I got a call from Blake, and he had something interesting to say."

Her curiosity piqued, Ricki bent her legs beneath the blankets to sit cross-legged as she kept her eyes on Gin. "Like what?"

"Are you going to share too?" Gin reached over and tapped one finger against the blanket covering Ricki's knee. "It has to be a mutual thing."

Ricki nodded. "Fine. You go first. What did Blake have to say?"

Satisfied with that, Gin smiled. "Rumors. He's had his ears to the ground. Or rather, agents he's placed on task forces have had their ears to the ground," Gin qualified. "And they're hearing rumblings about the CJNG cartel losing track of one of its drug shipments, which is code for someone stole it."

"I don't suppose the rumors had the name of this thief?" Ricki asked.

"The *guía*, according to Blake's informant." There was a note of satisfaction in Gin's voice. "The guide."

Ricki's breathing quit for a beat. "You're kidding? The guide stole it?"

"That's the rumor going around the drop sites. And the add-on to that is that the cartel sent people to track the guide down."

"Since Jimmy is missing, I wonder if he was the guide and those cartel types managed to find him." Ricki remembered to suck in a deep breath.

Gin nodded. "I was wondering the same thing. Now, what did Hamilton have to say?"

"Nothing that big, more like a confirmation." Ricki unwound her legs and stretched them out again. "I'm sure this is waiting for Stephen in his email, but Dan found an interesting deposit in Jimmy's bank account. A twenty-thousand-dollar deposit made the day after we were ambushed. Into his account at Washington Federal."

"That's the same one our banker buddy in the bar works at," Gin said then blew out a low, soft whistle. "A payoff?" Her eyebrows drew together as her mouth pulled down into a frown. "Wait a minute. If Jimmy is the guide, then why would the cartel pay off someone they suspected of stealing their drug shipment? At least according to the intel that Blake gave me. That doesn't make sense."

Ricki sighed and threw the covers back. "I didn't think so either. So what we've got is another piece of a puzzle that doesn't fit together." She dropped her legs over the far side of the bed and stood up. "I'm going to take a shower, then I'll meet you downstairs and we can brief the others over breakfast."

It took a half hour to get everyone around the kitchen island. Bowls of creamy eggs and fried potatoes were passed around, while a gallon of liquid caffeine jolted tired systems awake. Gin stuck with her tea while Ricki had her hand curled around a large mug of coffee.

"Judging by the way Jimmy lives, and the state of his bar, twenty thousand would be a good chunk of change," Clay said. "But it makes me wonder where the rest of it is."

Cheron blinked and set her forkful of eggs back onto her plate. "What rest? Do you mean more money?"

"More money is right," Gin said. She blew across the top of her teacup before taking a small sip. "If he's been their guide all along, then he would have been paid a lot more money, and a lot more often than the one time. The cartel would also think he took the merchandise and killed off everyone else."

"How do you know that?" Clay asked.

"Blake told me." When Clay made a sour face, Gin hurried on, recapping the information that the profiler had passed along to her.

"Maybe their regular guide was one of the dead men you found at their camp." Cheron picked up her fork again and popped the bite of eggs into her mouth. "So it was Jimmy's first time as a guide."

"The doctor has a point," Stephen said. "Jimmy could be the one who's been taking those supplies to that cabin we found. If those were for the hermit, then the cartel could have offered Jimmy that twenty thousand to take them there. Especially if the cartel believes the hermit is responsible for killing their crew and stealing the drugs. The odds are good that word that this hermit burned up half a million of their merchandise on a public road has gotten back to them. They're going to come looking for the guy who did that."

"Maybe," Ricki said, making Clay and Anchorman laugh while Stephen's face collapsed into a frown.

"Okay," the FBI agent said, scowling at Gin, who was grinning at him. "What's wrong with that theory?"

"How would they know?" Ricki asked. "How would they know that Jimmy has been taking supplies to the hermit? It's not as if he's taken out an advertisement about it. And if the cartel had no way of knowing that, then the whole theory falls apart."

"But Jimmy did have flyers about his services as a guide. I

saw a couple up at some of the outdoor shops I went into today. Maybe it's like the doctor said. Their last guide was killed, so they needed another one just to go up and check things out. Then they stumbled across Jimmy and got lucky."

"If it was Jimmy's first gig as their guide, then how did he know where the drug runners' camp was?" Gin asked. She glanced over at Ricki. "Yeah. I see what you mean. Too many holes and unanswered questions."

"I'd still bet that little pissant is in it up to his neck," Anchorman declared. "So, what's the plan for today? Am I still taking Cheron over to the ME's office in Bellingham?"

Ricki was spared an answer when Cheron shook her head. "They'll be bringing the bodies down today, so they likely won't get to Dr. Robbins in time for him to do much. I spoke with him just before you all came downstairs, and he feels tomorrow would be better."

"Okay," Ricki said. "Then Anchorman can take you tomorrow." She looked at the former Marine. "Today, I think you and Stephen should go hang out at the Last Stop. See if that banker comes in. According to your drinking buddy, Big Mack, he shows up every Thursday like clockwork. If he does, call me." She looked at Clay. "And you should go have a solo early lunch at the Snowmelt. Jo likes that smile of yours, and she might be prone to being a bit more talkative if you're alone."

"And what will you and I be doing?" Gin asked.

"Canvassing the area. Dan emailed me the make, model, and license plate of Jimmy's truck," Ricki said. "We need to find it. Hamilton is also putting out a be-on-the-lookout bulletin with the state police. But like you said, this is his comfort zone, so I'm betting wherever he's holed up, it's close to his home."

With breakfast out of the way, the team broke up. Clay took his phone to the living room to return calls until it was time for him to head to the Snowmelt, and Stephen hung out in the kitchen to help Anchorman with the cleanup. Ricki and Gin checked their service weapons, then retrieved their parkas from the hooks in the foyer and went out the front door.

"What are we looking for?" Gin asked as Ricki set the SUV into motion.

"A black 2005 Ford pickup." Ricki dug out a slip of paper from her pocket and handed it to Gin. "I wrote down the plate number."

The agent smoothed out the paper and anchored a corner in the center console so they could both see the letters and numbers. She leaned back in her seat and sighed as Ricki started a slow drive along the streets to the business district. "Well, this beats taking a ten-mile hike into the park."

"Suit yourself," Ricki answered. "I prefer the hike to driving the streets."

"Going up and over that Hannegan Pass is not my idea of fun, but yeah, it beats a dark alley at night, and sure smells a whole lot better." Gin peered out the side window, squinting at a dark Ford truck parked alongside the road. "Do you know what bothers me most about this case?"

"There's only one thing?" Ricki mumbled, then glanced at Gin with a sigh. "No, I don't. What bothers you the most about this case, Agent Reilly?"

"Like they taught us—follow the money. If whoever took those drugs sold them, then where's the money? Because twenty thousand is chicken feed compared to the street value of that coke. And if the drugs haven't been sold yet, where did the thief stash them?"

"Good questions," Ricki said. "Do you know what bothers me most about this case?"

Gin laughed. "No, Agent James. What bothers you the most?"

"If the guide, or whoever took the drugs, shot all the runners and the guards, how did he get four backpacks that weighed forty pounds each out of the park?" She tapped a finger against the steering wheel. "We know he split up Santiago Garcia's pack, leaving half of the cocaine behind. But we didn't find any drugs left behind at the main camp. Just the dead bodies."

"Maybe those dead bodies weren't all the runners and guards," Gin said. "Maybe some of those were in on it too and they carried the drugs out."

"That big a group would have been noticed by someone," Ricki pointed out. "They only went off the trail after they were in the park. Until then, they would have been seen by anyone else out hiking that day. And the whole idea of this little operation of theirs was not to attract any attention."

Gin leaned forward when another dark pickup came into sight. "Does everyone around here own a pickup?" she half-jokingly complained. When the plate number didn't match, she leaned back again. "I don't know. Like you said, there're a lot of loose ends and unanswered questions in this case, and from the way Blake described the chatter that his sources are hearing, the cartel is sounding as confused as we are."

Having no response to that, Ricki turned onto the main highway and headed east. "Let's look at the section of town with most of the single-family houses."

Another hour passed, and they once more came up on the main highway. Ricki sat at the crossroads, letting the engine idle as she rested her forearms on top of the steering wheel. She finally turned east, shrugging at Gin's questioning look. "Let's take a look along the highway, and then around the parking lot at the trailhead. If he is the one bringing basic supplies to the hermit, then maybe he's also holing up with the guy."

They didn't see any abandoned trucks along the way, and when they got to the parking lot, it was empty. Tired and frustrated, Ricki ran a hand over her cheek, shoving aside a thick lock of hair that always worked its way out of her ponytail. "If he's dumped his truck, it could be anywhere."

"I still think he's nearby," Gin said. "But I hear what you're saying. Even around town, it wouldn't be hard to hide a truck. The whole place is pretty remote."

Ricki started up the SUV again just as a heavy raindrop splattered against the windshield. Within minutes the sky opened up.

"If the temperature drops, we're going to end up driving in a lot of slush," Ricki said.

"So I guess that's all the search we're going to get in today," Gin replied. "I'd just as soon sit back at the house with my feet up and watch the slush through the living room window, with a glass of wine in my hand."

"Make that a beer and it sounds like a good idea," Ricki agreed.

She drove carefully out of the lot, avoiding the potholes that were already filling up with muddy water. They hadn't quite reached the paved road when her cell phone rang. She used one hand to dig it out of her parka. Not recognizing the number, she handed the ringing phone to Gin. The FBI agent tapped the connect button and set the phone on the center console.

"This is Special Agent Ricki James."

"Hey, Agent James. This is Sergeant Crowder. We met at a fire a few days ago."

"I remember, Sergeant. What can I do for you?"

"Well. We got a call to come out to National Forest Road 3040. Do you know where that is?"

Ricki frowned. "Not right off the top of my head, but I'm sure I can find it. What's going on?"

"I saw an alert this morning to be on the lookout for a black pickup belonging to a James Blighton. And to notify you if we had any information on it."

Ricki exchanged a quick look with Gin, who silently held a thumb up. "Great. Is it off Road 3040?"

"No. We didn't find the truck. But we did find its owner."

Chapter 29

THE RAIN KEPT UP, coming down in a steady fall of ice-cold water, thoroughly drenching the police and emergency responders who'd been summoned to the crime scene. The early darkness of winter had already descended on the area, so the crime scene was lit up by a half dozen pairs of head-lights, outlining shimmering figures moving through a trans-parent sheet of rain.

Ricki adjusted the hood on her parka, pulling it tight around her face as she stood on the edge of a dirt road that was rapidly dissolving into a sea of mud. She braced her feet apart to counter the gusts of wind and kept her hands in her pockets as she waited for Sergeant Crowder.

She watched the eerily lit scene moving in front of her, ignoring the rain dripping off her shoulders and soaking her jeans. Since the Sergeant stood a head above most of the other officers milling around, he wasn't hard to spot. The young deputy who'd stopped her from the other side of a strip of crime scene tape had reached the sergeant and was gesturing back at Ricki as he talked to his superior officer.

Crowder immediately looked up. He quickly scanned the crowd, and when he spotted her, waved for her to join him.

Ricki picked her way through the bodies milling around. The sergeant waited until she'd come up next to him, then turned and walked farther up the road, toward an area that was beyond the reach of the police cruisers' headlights. Here a half dozen officers held up flashlights next to their heads, aiming the narrow beams toward a single point in the center.

There were fewer people up here, and a makeshift shelter of a tarp nailed to several trees had been set up in an area ten feet away from the edge of a pullout that some long-ago road crew had carved into the side of the dirt road. Ricki followed the lieutenant across the pullout and into the trees before stopping next to the temporary shelter. Underneath it was a body, dressed in jeans, boots, and a heavy coat. It was lying face down on the forest floor, with a large single hole in its back.

"ID in his pocket says he's James Blighton, and the picture on the ID matches the vic," Crowder said. "We also had one of the local EMT guys come up and identify him. Says the vic owns a bar in Glacier."

"That's right," Ricki confirmed, her gaze traveling the length of the body. There was a technician kneeling next to Jimmy with the word "Forensic Team" emblazoned across the back of his rain poncho. "Do we have a time of death?"

Crowder shook his head, sending droplets of rain flying in an outward spiral. "Not until we get him to the ME. You aren't going to get a doc way out here, and especially not in this weather." He glanced over at Ricki. "The deputy who checked your credentials said there were two of you. So where's your friend?"

"She's around." Ricki walked over to the body and sank down to her knees, not caring about the water and mud beneath them. She leaned over to get a better look at the bullet hole. "Are there any other wounds?"

"Not that I could see," the tech answered. He slipped a plastic bag over one of Jimmy's hands and secured it with a zip tie.

Ricki got to her feet again and rejoined the sergeant. "You said some sightseers found him?" She looked around. She hadn't seen any hiking trails leading into the forest from the pullout. And there wasn't anything around the spot where the body was lying, except for a lot of trees. "How did they see him from the road?"

"They didn't," Crowder said. "According to their statements, the driver needed to take a leak. So he pulled over and walked into the trees for a little privacy and practically stumbled over the body." The sergeant pointed at a small pile of branches off to one side. "He was covered with those when we got here, but most of his legs were sticking out. Whoever tried to conceal the body didn't do a good job of it." He crossed his arms over his chest. "Got any ideas who that might be?"

"I wish I did," Ricki said. "It might solve a lot of things."

"Would those fires and all that cocaine burning up be one of them?"

She shivered as the cold from her wet jeans crept up her spine. "Yeah. Along with who murdered the guy we found in the park ten days ago."

Crowder nodded. "I heard rumors that wasn't an accident." He inclined his head toward the body lying on the ground. "Same bullet hole in the back?"

"And one in his head for good measure. Did Jimmy have anything else on him besides his ID?"

"Not much," the sergeant said. "There were a couple of pictures that looked like they were taken inside a bar, about ten dollars, all in one-dollar bills, and a business card."

Ricki frowned. "A business card? Whose business card?"

Crowder took a step forward and tapped the forensic tech on the shoulder. "Hey, Jay, hand me the evidence bag with that business card in it, and the one with the pictures."

Without looking up, Jay reached into a waterproof satchel and pulled out two small plastic bags. He handed it to the sergeant, then continued his careful examination of the body.

Crowder stepped back and handed both bags to Ricki. She held one up with a gloved hand and peered through the plastic.

"Fun Time Travel," she read out loud. The address was listed in Bellingham. Ricki turned the card over. The back was blank—no additional phone number or name had been written on it. She handed the plastic bag back to Crowder. "It looks new."

"Yeah, I don't think he's had it very long."

Ricki nodded and held up the second bag. The first picture was a shot of Jimmy, mugging for the camera as he stood behind the counter in his bar. But it was the second photo that caught her attention. Now Jimmy was standing in front of the counter, one arm around the shoulders of a younger-looking, smiling Molly. Ricki flipped the bag over, noting the date written on the back of the picture was from two years ago. Frowning, she studied the front of the photo again. Both Jimmy and Molly looked relaxed and happy. A stark contrast to the two individuals Ricki had met. "The only person he was ever nice to," Ricki muttered.

"He was only nice to who?" the sergeant asked.

Ricki briefly closed her eyes, sending up a silent wish that she would somehow be miraculously cured of her habit of voicing her thoughts out loud. "Jimmy. I was told he wasn't a very friendly guy, and the only person he liked enough to help out occasionally is the woman in that picture." She handed it back to Crowder, who stared down at it.

"You don't say. Who is she?"

"Her name is Molly," Ricki said. "She wouldn't give me her last name. She's the cleaning lady at the Last Stop."

"I've driven past that place," Crowder stated. "That's the victim's bar?"

"Yep. That's the one." Ricki looked back at the satchel Jay kept near his feet. "You didn't find a cell phone on him?"

The lieutenant shook his head again. "No cell phone.

That wallet was all he had on him. No set of keys either. Not for a house, or his bar, or a truck. So I figure whoever brought him here must have also dumped his truck somewhere, since you reported it as missing."

It sounded reasonable, but the absence of keys wasn't the most urgent of her problems at the moment. She also had no suspects that she could actually identify. The only one she'd had was lying dead on the ground. "Since this is Whatcom County, I'm assuming the body will go to Dr. Robbins? He's the ME in Bellingham."

"Yeah, I know him, and you assume correctly," Crowder confirmed. "And aside from the wallet, we don't have much else to go on except the body. The tourists drove right over any tire tracks that would have been on that pullout, and we didn't find anything else in the area that might have been dropped or left by the killer." He peered into Ricki's face. "So, you're saying this James Blighton was a suspect in your murder?"

"A solid person of interest," Ricki confirmed. "He probably would have been upgraded to a suspect if I'd had a chance to talk to him."

Crowder hooked his thumbs underneath his belt. "Well, someone made sure that wasn't going to happen."

"It seems like it."

The sergeant leaned forward to peer directly into Ricki's face. "I'm asking if you come across any information that could help us out here, that you share it. And we'll do the same."

"No problem, Sergeant. Always happy to share," Ricki said. She stamped her boots to bring some feeling into her feet. "I'll let you get back to this." She nodded her thanks. "I appreciate the call."

"Anytime," Crowder said before going to stand next to Jay.

Ricki made her way out of the trees and back down the short stretch of road. When she reached the SUV, she found Gin already sitting in the front seat, the heater on full. Ricki climbed into the driver's seat and, feeling a little lightheaded at the sudden blast of warmth, waited a moment to let it pass. Once she felt steady again, she peeled off her wet gloves and set them on the dashboard.

"Find out anything?" she asked Gin.

"Besides the fact that it's very uncomfortable sitting in a puddle of water?"

Since her own seat was rapidly becoming soaked with the runoff from her jeans and parka, Ricki gave her a tired smile. "A hazard of living in the Northwest. Was there anything else?"

"Just one thing. The general consensus among the cops who are here is that the crazy man who set the fires is the same one who killed Jimmy Blighton."

Ricki wasn't surprised at that. The thought had also crossed her mind that the hermit was behind Jimmy's murder. "Funny, Crowder didn't mention that to me."

"Yeah, it really is funny, because according to one of the officers, they've already put in a request to Fish and Wildlife for a list of the hunting permits of anyone who's reported a kill using archery or crossbow equipment. And that's a direct quote from the guy, since I have no idea what the difference is between archery and crossbow equipment."

"Well, if the hermit is trying to live up to the Robin Hood comparison, he'd be using a longbow of some sort," Ricki said. "And Crowder never mentioned asking for that list either."

"So what *did* the sergeant mention?" Gin asked.

"That all they found on Jimmy was his wallet. And the only things in it were ten, one-dollar bills, his ID, and a couple of pictures," Ricki said. "Both of the pictures were taken inside the bar, and one of them was with Molly."

Gin's eyebrow winged upward. "Molly? Really? I'm getting the feeling there's a closer connection between Jimmy and Molly than her just being his cleaning lady."

"I can get on board with that," Ricki said. She straightened up in her seat "Which is something we can look into tomorrow. Right now I'm tired, wet, and hungry, so I vote we head back to the house, get into some dry clothes, and see if anyone else has something to report."

The FBI agent immediately reached over and buckled her seat belt. "I'm all for that."

Chapter 30

CLAY'S TRUCK was already parked in front of the Airbnb, so Ricki pulled the SUV up beside it and turned off the engine. By the time she and Gin sloshed their way to the porch steps, Cheron was already standing in the open front door, two steaming mugs in her hand.

"Good heavens. Get inside before you both drown." She stepped back and used one of the mugs to gesture at the porch chairs. "Sit down there and take those boots off."

"I will if you give me that tea," Gin said. "I can smell it from here."

"Boots first, then you can have your tea inside," Cheron said firmly.

Ricki wanted the coffee Cheron was also holding too much to argue with her. She plopped down on the closest chair and leaned over to tug at the muddy tangle and wet knots that used to be bootlaces. It took her a full minute, but she finally triumphed in loosening them up. She lifted her ankle and balanced it on her opposite knee as she tugged the boot off, repeating the process with her second boot. At least the sturdy footwear had done its job. Her socks were still dry.

She picked the boots up with one hand and snagged the

mug of coffee out of Cheron's hand with the other as she stepped inside. Dropping the boots next to the door, Ricki flipped the hood of her parka back and unzipped it, then tossed the thoroughly wet coat onto one hook, leaving it to drip dry onto the tile floor. With her dry shirt, dry socks and wet pants, she left Gin to her own struggles and headed straight for one of the tall stools next to the kitchen island. She figured her soaked jeans would do the least amount of damage there.

Anchorman took one look at her and shook his head. "What did you do? Get out of the SUV and beat the bushes looking for Jimmy?" He shoved a small plate across the linoleum top of the island. Ricki snatched up the hot biscuit dripping in butter and gratefully bit into it.

"Almost," she said around bites.

Clay walked over and sat down next to her as Gin staggered across the room and collapsed onto the third stool.

"Food," she pleaded. "I'm begging for food."

The Marine-turned-cook chuckled and slid a second plate in her direction, raising an amused eyebrow when she lifted the biscuit, chomped down, and half of it disappeared.

Turning back to his stove, he draped a dishtowel over one shoulder. "Now that you two have made an appearance, dinner will be ready in an hour."

"An hour?" Gin gave him the evil eye while she licked the butter off one of her fingers. "That's just plain cruel."

"It will give you time to clean up," Cheron told her calmly.

"What kept you so long?" Clay asked, ignoring the other two. He reached over and tweaked the end of Ricki's ponytail, which was still dripping water down her back. "And had you standing out in the rain long enough to get this wet?"

"We got a call from Sergeant Crowder." Ricki rolled her shoulders back and forth before sliding off the stool. Right about now, a hot shower sounded like heaven.

Clay's eyes widened in surprise. "The state policeman from the fires?"

"Yeah. He'd seen the BOLO that Hamilton put out for Jimmy's truck, so when he identified the dead body, he called me." She looked around. "Where's Stephen?"

"Upstairs, working on his computer," Clay said. "What dead body? Are you saying Jimmy is dead?"

"Bullet hole in the back," Ricki confirmed. "Some tourists found him on one of the forest roads." A shiver ran up her spine and had her turning toward the stairs. "We'll fill everyone in after I've had a quick shower and gotten into some dry clothes."

"A very hot, quick shower," Gin qualified as she slid off her stool and followed Ricki up the stairs. "And I'm using the guys' shower, so if anyone has to go pee, take it outside."

Ricki literally peeled her clothes off in the bathroom and spent a glorious fifteen minutes letting the hot water chase the last of the ice out of her body. Wrapped in a large fluffy towel, she dashed to her bedroom and took out dry clothes, then lay the wet ones over a chair that she placed next to the heating vent. She took the extra ten minutes to blow-dry her hair, which she rarely did, and only bothered with now because she'd had her fill of wet hair hanging down her back.

Pulling it into its usual ponytail, she padded down the hallway in fresh wool socks. She waved at Stephen, who was sitting on the living room couch, his laptop open on the coffee table, then stopped in the foyer to examine her boots. She'd also brought tennis shoes with her, but she preferred her boots. They were still soaked, but someone had taken the time to wash the mud off while she'd been upstairs.

Grateful, she looked over at the island and found Clay's gaze on her. She held up one boot, then smiled a thanks when he shrugged. She then set it down again, walked across the space separating them and sat down on her stool. Leaning over, she gave him a quick kiss on the cheek.

"Thanks."

He smiled back at her. "You're welcome."

"Oh." Cheron fairly beamed at them from across the island. "Did you two make up?"

Anchorman reached over and latched on to her arm and not so gently pulled her in his direction. "I need some help over here."

"With what?" Cheron looked puzzled but dutifully turned to stand beside him.

Stephen looked up from his computer screen. "What are you two fighting about?"

"We aren't fighting," Ricki said firmly, then breathed a quiet sigh of relief when Gin came down the stairs. "So, what do we want to do first? Eat or catch up?"

"Both," Clay stated.

Anchorman nodded and handed a platter piled high with baked chicken breasts to Cheron. "Here. Put that out on the island, and we'll let everyone dish it up buffet style." He began filling serving bowls with mashed potatoes and green beans, along with more biscuits and a large soup bowl brimming with gravy.

Ricki hopped off her stool and went to retrieve silverware while Clay took care of the plates and glasses.

Cheron took bottles of ice water out of the refrigerator and set them at the end of the counter. "You all need to drink some water before you have a beer." When there was a groan behind her, she swiveled around and was met with Anchorman's innocent look.

"Water," she repeated firmly, waiting for his nod before returning her attention to the food-laden island. "Everyone, come get a plate. I have a dead body I need to hear about."

"We have such great dinner conversations." Stephen shook his head as he pushed up from the couch.

"I doubt if it's so different at your house. I know for a fact that Carrie enjoys talking murder," Gin declared. When her partner gave her a sour face, she made a comical one right back at him.

Ricki nudged Gin with an elbow as they loaded up their dinner plates. "Who's Carrie?"

"Stephen's wife," Gin whispered back. "She's great. You'd really like her."

Ricki stopped her forward motion down the buffet line and stared at Gin. "I didn't know he was married. He's not wearing a ring."

"He usually doesn't on ops. And we haven't gotten around to exchanging personal stories."

"You knew about my divorce," Ricki muttered. "And I showed you Eddie's picture." Her eyes narrowed on Gin's face. "Do you have any kids? Does Stephen?"

"Nope and nope, and you're holding up the line, James." Gin pointed at the food with the fork she was holding in one hand. "Keep moving. We have a briefing to get to. Stephen told me he has some big, as in really big, news for us, and I'd like to hear it."

Distracted from Gin's personal life, Ricki got her stockinged feet going again. Yeah, she'd like to hear some big news too.

Once everyone was settled, there was no work talk for a good fifteen minutes as everyone dug into their food while it was still hot. It wasn't until Anchorman and Clay were making their second pass at the makeshift buffet that Ricki set her own plate aside and scooted forward in her chair.

"I guess I can start." She paused for a moment to get her thoughts in line, and to wish she had a whiteboard to make a timeline and keep everything straight. "I got the call from Crowder just as we were about to head back here. He'd been called out for a dead body on Road 3040, about five miles east of here. The sergeant stated that a car of sightseers stopped for a bathroom break and stumbled across the body. It was approximately ten feet from a pullout in the road, and partially covered in branches. ID in the wallet confirmed it was Jimmy Blighton."

"Well, shit," Clay said, injecting a good amount of feeling into the word. He glanced over at Anchorman. "I guess that explains why he didn't show up at the bar today."

"No one showed up," Stephen clarified. "Not the bartender, not the banker, not the cleaning lady." He held his hands out, palms up. "Nada."

"Huh. That's weird. Who was running the bar?" Gin reached for the last of her second biscuit and popped it into her mouth as her gaze bounced from Stephen to Anchorman.

"Pac-Man. He said he got a call from Molly, who got one from Jimmy last night, who asked her to open up. But she was under the weather, so she called Pac-Man." Anchorman shrugged. "Running that bar seems to be a community affair, with everyone acting on a Scout's honor kind of system."

"Jo didn't have much to add either," Clay said, giving Anchorman an annoyed look when the ex-Marine gave him a hard poke with his elbow.

"Losing your touch there?"

Gin's mouth curved upward as she quickly put her two cents in next to Anchorman's. "That would be very odd, since you have such a pretty face."

"What I *did* get out of her," Clay ground out, pointedly ignoring both Gin and Anchorman, "is that she's lived here her whole life, and the only time she gets out of town anymore is when she goes into Bellingham or Seattle twice a week to pick up supplies. Apparently Glacier isn't on anyone's regular delivery route."

Stephen snorted out a laugh. "I believe that. The bar was low on beer, so I asked Pac-Man when they were expecting their next delivery, and he said the same thing. Jimmy had to go into Bellingham every week or so in his own truck to pick up his order." He looked over at Ricki. "Which I'm assuming we haven't found yet, since you haven't mentioned it."

Ricki shook her head. "No truck. And according to Crowder, no keys. But Jimmy did have a business card in his wallet that looked brand new, so he hadn't been carrying it long. It was for a travel agency in Bellingham."

Clay leaned back against the couch and frowned. "It sounds like old Jimmy was planning a trip."

"Very out of character, according to Gin." Ricki gestured toward the FBI agent who grinned back at her.

"That's right," Gin confirmed. "If Jimmy was planning a trip, I'd say it was more of a get-out-of-Dodge kind of thing than some normal vacation he takes every year."

"Jimmy also had a couple of photos in his wallet," Ricki continued, wanting to finish up and get to Stephen's really big news. "One of them was of him and Molly."

"Weird relationship those two have," Gin remarked. "I mean, she's his cleaning lady. But he gives her a place to stay and lets her eat at the bar for free."

"I've got that on my back burner, simmering," Ricki said. She turned slightly in her chair to face Stephen. "So now we're at the point of hearing your really big news. Please tell me it will lead us to another suspect."

Stephen's expression grew thoughtful. "I don't know about that, but it will give us a name for a suspect we already have."

Ricki's nerves tingled as the room went silent and all eyes were glued to Stephen. "The check stub?" she guessed.

"Give the lady a point," Stephen said with a grin. "It is indeed all about the check stub you found up at the cabin. It turns out my buddy back at Quantico knew someone in the accounting office for the State of Washington, and she likes my buddy enough that she looked up the check number. That payment was issued as a regular disability check to one Walter Modonsky. That's about all she could tell from the check register. We would need to tag someone in the eligibility unit to get any more details on Walter Modonsky."

Ricki's heart rate picked up. A name. They finally had a

name for the hermit. The stub could belong to whoever was leaving the supplies at the cabin, and they would have to rule that possibility out, but her every instinct told her that Walter Modonsky and the hermit were the same person. "Background check?"

Stephen picked up a single sheet of paper lying next to his laptop. "This is all I could find. Walter Modonsky. Birthdate July 1, 1955, which makes him sixty-seven years old. He was born in a hospital in Bellingham. Two parents listed on the birth certificate and five members of the household according to the census counts during his childhood years. I found the two parents, both deceased, and two sisters. One passed away twenty years ago from cancer, and the other one is living in Springfield, Illinois. But Walter lived his entire life in the area, mostly in Deming, then made the very bold move of relocating twenty miles up the road to Glacier."

"So he lived here?" Ricki's gaze narrowed. Now how was it that Walter Modonsky moved to a town with fewer than two hundred people, and no one here could remember him?

"For two years, anyway," Stephen said. "That's how many years he filed taxes with an address in Glacier."

"And then what?" Gin demanded. "Did he do his famous 'poofing' act after that?"

Stephen waved the paper he'd been reading from in the air. "More or less. That's the last known interaction he had with anything traceable, as far as I can tell. Dan hasn't been able to find anything else either. No driver's license, no credit card, no arrests or any kind of criminal history, and no tax returns beyond those two years when he was nineteen and twenty. And to go along with all of that, no known residence either, once he turned twenty. Like I said before. Nada. After 1975, the guy's a ghost."

Ricki drummed a finger on the arm of her chair. That clinched it with her—there couldn't be two guys like that in the same area. Modonsky was the elusive hermit. "No one's completely a ghost. Especially when they get disability checks from the state."

"Get them where?" Clay asked quietly. "I doubt if the State of Washington is leaving them nailed to a tree."

"They don't." Stephen leaned over and tapped a few keys on his laptop. "The checks are mailed to a PO box in Deming that's still under his parents' name. Both deceased."

Gin rolled her eyes. "Well, unless the whole ghost gig runs in the family, then clearly they aren't the ones picking up the checks, so who is?"

"We'll need to make the trip to Deming and ask the post-master," Ricki said. "We passed through it on the way here. It's off the 542. I'd guess it's about the same size as Glacier, so there's probably only one post office."

"That would be correct," Stephen said, tapping away on his keys. "According to my research, there's more kids in the local high school than there are in the whole town, so the school district must pull from a pretty wide area."

"If the guy ever went to high school, it was a long time ago," Anchorman said. "And we need to find this jerk today." He pointed his fork at Ricki when she opened her mouth. "And don't tell me he isn't a jerk, or a prime suspect. He took a shot at you."

"So did the cartel," Ricki pointed out. "Then the question is, which one killed Santiago Garcia and the five others up at the camp? The cartel, with its track record of killing anyone who gets in their way? Or Walter Modonsky, a.k.a. the hermit, who we have no evidence has ever killed anyone?"

Anchorman put his fork down on his plate with a loud clang. "Except when DJ first told us his dad's story about this hermit, he said the guy fled to the mountains because he'd killed someone."

Anchorman's further tirade on the matter was interrupted by a loud thump against the wall, the impact hard enough to make the glass in the front window shudder. Five bodies hit the ground, with Clay and Anchorman immediately scrambling to the front foyer, where they'd left their guns. Ricki and 'n both crawled onto the couch while Stephen reached up 1 scooped his laptop off the coffee table.

Ricki reached over and turned off the table lamp while Gin did the same with the one on her side of the couch. At the same time, Cheron switched the kitchen lights off, throwing the entire first floor into darkness. Ricki cautiously peered over the edge of the couch, looking out into the night that hung like a black curtain just beyond the porch.

She didn't see anything. Not even the hint of a movement.

When she looked at Gin, the FBI agent gave a negative shake of her head. Frustrated, Ricki looked in the direction of the foyer and hissed, "Turn on the porch light." A moment later, the area immediately in front of them was flooded with light that penetrated another two feet out into the yard. She couldn't see much beyond that, but at least whoever was out there would have a harder time sneaking up on them.

"I know the back door is locked," Cheron whispered from somewhere in the dark. "I locked it myself."

"That's good," Ricki said, then slid off the couch. Staying low, she made a sprint for the foyer, where Anchorman was crouched next to the front door, one hand on his rifle, the other on the door handle. She picked up her rifle from where she'd left it in the corner next to the coat hooks, then took the box of shells that Anchorman passed to her. Clay came up behind her, his Glock in his hand.

"We could wait them out, see what their next move is," the chief said. "But if it's the cartel out there, I'm surprised they haven't raked the whole front with bullets by now."

"Something hit the side of the house," Ricki said, her voice low and tight. "I don't think it was a bird, but it didn't sound like a bullet either."

"Nope, it didn't," Anchorman said. "Besides, these walls aren't that thick. I think a bullet might have come right through them, especially if it had been shot from a semiauto-matic." He looked back at Ricki and Clay. "We need to go out and have a look."

Ricki nodded her agreement. "I'll take left. Clay can take right. You hold the middle and cover us."

The former sniper grinned back at her. "Nothing different there. I'll open the door on three and set down some fire for you two to get out there." He reached up and turned off the porch light.

Ricki's muscles bunched as she held her breath and waited for Anchorman's soft count. On three, the ex-Marine whipped the door open and slid out onto the porch, still on his knees. He left enough space on either side of himself to let Ricki and then Clay slip by him as he got off a volley of shots into the trees.

Ricki kept low, making her way along the porch. She hadn't gone far when she spotted the thin shaft of wood sticking out from the wall. Making her way to it, she reached up as far as she could but still couldn't touch it. Taking a deep breath, she stood up long enough to give it a good yank. It didn't budge, remaining solidly embedded in the wall. But in that brief moment, Ricki spotted the paper attached to the shaft.

A message delivered by an arrow? She smiled grimly to herself. Now who did that remind her of? Standing again, she carefully removed the paper that was bound to the shaft with a bit of string. Ricki crawled back to Anchorman, who was no longer shooting, but had his eyes to his scope as he slowly quartered the area.

"I've got what Modonsky wanted delivered," she said. Clay stopped his forward progress and looked back at her. She waved the rolled-up piece of paper at him even though the odds were small that he could see it in the dark. "We got a message."

When Ricki heard his footsteps coming back her way, she

ducked inside the house. She kept her rifle with her as she walked into the living room, then carefully placed the gun in a spot where it couldn't do any damage on its own. Sitting on the couch, she unrolled the paper as Anchorman and Clay made their way back inside.

"Where did you find that?" Gin asked.

"Attached to the arrow that hit the house." Ricki recognized the spidery scrawl. It was the same one that had appeared on the note left at the fire.

Agent Ricki James:
Your time is running out
Look to the banker's ties

Ricki silently handed the note to Gin, who read it, then passed it along to the others.

"What does that mean?" Gin demanded. "Especially that bit about the banker's ties?"

"I don't know." Ricki sighed and tucked an errant lock of dark hair behind her ear. Walter Modonsky was not only an enigma but a real pain in her side. Along with the fact he might also be a killer. Who apparently knew the banker. "But isn't it lucky we planned on paying Mr. Hontel a visit tomorrow?"

Chapter 31

"I'm getting sick and tired of threats from this guy," Gin stated. She stopped outside the doors of the Washington Federal Bank in Bellingham and unzipped her parka, making sure her gold badge was visible.

Ricki had already done the same, and she couldn't agree more with Gin's sentiment about Walter Modonsky. But she didn't voice that out loud as she pulled open one side of the glass doors. The lobby looked like every other bank branch she'd ever been in, with teller counters for the customers on one side, and individual desks, cubicles, and offices for the string of bank employees on the other. Ricki stopped in the middle of the lobby to get her bearings and adjust to the heat inside, which was a stark contrast to the frigid morning air beyond the front doors.

A middle-aged woman dressed in a neat business suit got up from her desk and approached them, her high heels ringing with a clipped staccato beat against the floor. Her brown hair was neatly styled, and she wore a name tag with the words "Account Manager" under her name. The manager's gaze immediately dropped to Ricki's badge. When she lifted it again, her lips were curved up into a friendly smile.

"Can I help you?" She nodded to include Gin in the offer.

"We'd like to speak with Mr. Hontel. Is he in?"

The woman's smile held firm. "Do you have an appointment?"

Ricki's gaze lowered to the name badge. "Linda, isn't it?"

The manager nodded. "That's right. And you are Officer . . . ?"

"Special agent," Ricki corrected, making her own smile as Linda's faded. "Both of us are special agents, and we'd like to speak to Mr. Hontel."

The manager's eyes cut to one of the offices along the side wall. Ricki's gaze followed hers just in time to see the banker from the Last Stop closing the blinds over the tall pane of glass that faced the front lobby.

Gin was also looking at the now-shuttered office and, without taking her gaze off it, she lifted her shoulders in a casual shrug. "I'm Special Agent Reilly with the FBI, and I see Mr. Hontel is already preparing his office for our visit." She turned her head and gave Ricki a bland look. "We wouldn't want to keep him waiting."

"Of course not," Ricki said to the flustered manager. She didn't know which had knocked the woman for more of a loop, Gin's cheeky declaration, or her announcement that she was with the FBI.

Thinking it must be nice not to be continually asked if you were investigating a theft in one of the park's gift shops, Ricki turned to the right and stepped onto the carpeted area that led to Hontel's. The plaque on the outside had his name and the title "Commercial Loan Officer." Ricki took that in as she pushed open the door, half-surprised Hontel hadn't thought to lock it.

The man behind the desk looked up from his computer, and even managed a fair imitation of appearing to be startled at her sudden appearance in his office. He slowly got to his feet and leaned his hands against the desk. "Can I help you?"

"Hello, Mr. Hontel," Ricki said pleasantly. In the dimly lit Last Stop, she hadn't noticed the long strands of thinning brown hair that were combed over the top of his head, or the bulbous nose framed at the apex by two heavy eyebrows. He was about her height and was dressed in a brown suit that looked like it had come right off a rack at a discount store.

Ignoring his question, Ricki made her way to one of the two chairs positioned in front of the desk and sat down while Gin closed the office door, then stood in front of it, her feet braced apart.

Hontel gave Gin a wary look before returning his attention to Ricki. "I'm sorry. Have we met?"

Ricki shook her head as she slowly looked around. There wasn't much to the office. It was a square space, not particularly large, with an L-shaped desk and a single picture hanging above it. A potted plant occupied one corner, and aside from the two visitor chairs, that was pretty much the entire office. "We haven't met, but we have seen each other."

The slightly rotund man ran a nervous hand down the front of his blue-checkered tie. "We have? Then I need to apologize, because I don't recall seeing you."

"No?" Ricki smiled and tilted her head to the side. "I was at the Last Stop bar on Monday." When she read the clear denial leap into his eyes, she let her smile drop away. "That was four days ago, Mr. Hontel. I doubt if you've forgotten it."

He sat down in the leather chair, keeping his palms flat on the desk. He finally turned to his computer and tapped on the keyboard. "Ah yes, it's here on my calendar. I was in Glacier at the beginning of the week, checking up on a property we have a mortgage on. Several properties in that area, actually." Hontel turned to face Ricki again, folding his hands in front of him. "But I have to apologize. It's very dark inside the Last Stop, and I wasn't there long. I'm afraid I simply don't remember seeing you there."

Ricki shrugged. "Do you recall seeing Molly?"

His forehead creased when he frowned. "Molly?" He briefly closed his eyes, looking as if he were trying to search his memory. "Molly. Oh yes. I believe Mr. Blighton mentioned her once or twice. The woman who cleans the bar, as I recall."

"That's right." Ricki studied him for a moment. "Mr. Blighton? That's very formal for someone you drop in on every Thursday. Except for this week. Any reason you came in on a Monday instead?"

The man's face went slightly pale, but he kept his tone polite. "It fit my schedule better. I always make a weekly trip to the area. As I said, the bank has an interest in several properties there." He cast a sideways glance at Gin. "Now, I'm going to have to insist that you tell me who you are, and what this is all about."

"I'm Special Agent Ricki James, with the National Park Service."

Hontel's shoulders visibly relaxed, and a hint of amusement crept into his gaze. "Ah. A theft in a gift shop, perhaps?"

"Sometimes," Ricki said amicably. "But this time we're looking into a death in the park."

"And a possible drug connection," Gin spoke up. "I'm Special Agent Reilly, with the FBI."

Hontel slumped back against his seat, his eyes wide as he stared at Gin. "FBI? Oh God."

I guess your local informants didn't tell you that, Ricki thought, waiting until the banker's breathing had evened out again. "Our leading suspect has turned up dead, Mr. Hontel. Which is why we're paying you a visit this morning. It seems he had an account here at this bank."

Now Hontel's face lost all its color and his hands had a death grip on the edge of the desk. "Dead? Jimmy's dead?"

So now it was Jimmy, not Mr. Blighton. Wasn't that interesting? "His body was found yesterday, but the police can't release any details until they notify the next of kin. They've asked us and the FBI to help track that information down," Ricki said without blinking an eye. "So we're here asking for your help."

"I don't know." Hontel's voice trembled. "I mean, that would be personal information on his account. You'd need a warrant, or at the very least a death certificate." The banker made a visible effort to pull himself together. "I'm sure the police won't have a problem obtaining either one of those."

"We'll be stopping by the county morgue next," Ricki smoothly assured him. "We know Mr. Blighton had a business loan and a personal account with your bank. Did he have any other accounts? Perhaps a savings account under a different name?"

"He only has the two," Hontel snapped out. "He would need proper identification to open an account under a different name. We have rules that must be followed."

"Did he ever wire any money outside the country?" Gin asked.

"I wouldn't know, and once again, you'll need a warrant or a death certificate, along with the permission of the next of kin."

"Which you won't tell us, will you?" Gin said.

The banker stood up and crossed his arms over his chest. "Since I can't help you, I believe our business is concluded. If you obtain that warrant, any one of the managers or officers here will be happy to assist you."

Ricki stood as well, letting her jacket fall away just enough for Hontel to get a good look at the Glock nestled in her shoulder harness. "Thank you for your time."

"Certainly," the banker said before sitting down again and turning back to his computer in a clear signal of dismissal.

Gin opened the office door and stepped out, grinning at all the faces that immediately turned away, accompanied by a sudden burst of activity at all the surrounding desks. Ricki nodded at Linda as she and Gin passed her on their way to the front door.

Once they were out on the sidewalk, Gin stuck her hands in her pockets, then glanced over at Ricki. "What now?"

"Let's drop in on the Fun Time Travel agency. It's just around the corner," Ricki said.

They walked along in companionable silence, their parkas once again zipped up and concealing both their badges and their weapons. No use in starting a panic out on the street.

"I noticed Mr. Hontel didn't have to look up anything to know how many accounts Jimmy had at that bank," Gin said. She stopped in front of a store window and stared at a fitted long-sleeved dress in hot pink.

Ricki gave her a puzzled look. "You don't strike me as the type to be into fashion."

"When you grow up without any kind of flash, a pretty dress can mean a lot," Gin said. "But that isn't my color."

The stark feeling behind the simple statement left Ricki's mouth hanging open. "No flash? What does that mean?"

Gin shrugged. "Oh, the latest tennis shoes, or a brand-new dress for a dance rather than a hand-me-down. That kind of thing." She turned away from the store window and continued walking. "So, what do you think about Hontel knowing all about Jimmy's accounts right off the top of his head?"

"I think that's as big a red flag as him doing that switch from 'Mr. Blighton' to 'Jimmy' in nothing flat." Ricki paused. "He seemed genuinely upset to hear that Jimmy was killed. But not enough to ask how he died. Which makes me wonder if he cares more about Jimmy being killed or the fact that we know about it."

Gin nodded. "I noticed that too. I'm assuming he already had a good idea of what might have happened to poor Jimmy."

"And who might have made it happen," Ricki added.

"I don't see him for the murders," Gin admitted. "But I like him for laundering the money."

"I have to agree." Ricki sighed. "But despite the great act he tried to put on, I think he already knew Jimmy was dead."

When Gin stopped in her tracks, Ricki did too. "Why is that?" the FBI agent demanded.

"Because he didn't show up at the bar yesterday. Big Mack told us he comes in every Thursday like clockwork. Except for this week. He came in on a Monday. A week after Santiago Garcia was shot, according to the ME, and two days after the rescue team got back to their respective bases after the body was extracted."

Gin grunted and started walking again. "Which would fit with your theory about small-town gossip and the spread of wildfires having something in common."

"Yes, they do. An amazing amount of speed." Ricki stopped in front of a small picture window with the name "Fun Times" painted across it, along with an ocean below the words and an airplane soaring above them. Judging by its miniature size, the travel agency appeared to be a one-man shop. A middle-aged man sporting a blue sport coat and brown plaid pants leaped up from his desk the minute they walked in the door.

"Good morning, ladies. Good morning. Won't you have a seat?"

He quickly crossed the small space and herded Ricki and Gin toward two chairs in front of a table that held a computer. He perched one hip on the edge and beamed down at them. "Now. Where is it you'd like to go?" He gave them a broad wink that Ricki immediately dropped into the category of "smarmy," along with a toothy smile. "Someplace warm, I'll bet. Am I right?"

Ricki unzipped her jacket and lifted her badge off its belt clip. She held it up until it was only a few inches away from the smirking man's nose. "I'm Special Agent Ricki James, with the National Park Service, and this is Special Agent Reilly with the FBI."

Okay." He peered a little closer at her badge, then looked past her to give Gin the once-over. "Two lady special agents. I have to say that's a first for me. I'm Willie Sanders, owner of Fun Time Travel." He slid his hip off the table and skirted around it to sit in the desk chair on the other side. "Did some criminal book a getaway trip with us?"

"I don't know," Gin said, her tone as dry as dust. "Does that happen often around here?"

Completely unfazed, Willie gave her another wink, then leaned back in his chair and steepled his fingers together. "Not that I know of. So, what can I do for you two lovely ladies today?"

"We're interested in a trip booked by a James Blighton," Ricki said.

"Jimmy?" Willie blinked in surprise. "Now what can he possibly have done to attract the attention of two lady cops?"

"We aren't at liberty to discuss that," Ricki said. "But I'm sure you're familiar with the term 'aiding and abetting'?"

Gin lifted an eyebrow. "I believe in Washington that makes someone as culpable as the criminal, doesn't it?"

"As far as I know," Ricki said. When Willie's expression turned sour, Ricki sent him a flat, hard look. "Now, we'd just like to know when and where he booked that trip for."

Willie sighed and ran a bony hand through his dark hair. "Okay, whatever. No need to make any threats."

"Not a threat, Mr. Sanders," Gin assured him. "Just a general discussion on the law."

His mouth flattened out into a thin line. "Yeah. Sure. Anyway, Jimmy didn't book anything. He was looking at Jamaica and Tahiti. Said he'd be in later this week with his decision. I was expecting to see him today."

"And when was he last in here, Mr. Sanders?" Ricki asked.

"Just this past Tuesday. Said it was a spur-of-the-moment kind of thing and he was looking to leave in the next week or so. He was even willing to pay the higher price for a last-minute booking." Willie let out a noisy sigh. "But I'm guessing he won't be in today, will he?"

Chapter 32

ANCHORMAN LOOKED up from his seat outside the ME's autopsy room. He held the sports section of a newspaper open in front of him while the rest of the edition was stacked at his feet. It didn't surprise Ricki that the silver doors leading to the inner chamber were closed. Anchorman had certainly seen his fair share of blood and torn-apart bodies during his deployments, but he still couldn't stomach the sterile atmosphere of an autopsy.

The desk next to Anchorman's chair was empty. "Where's Crystal?" Ricki asked, thinking the lab tech was probably assisting Dr. Robbins and Cheron.

"Upstairs running bullets through some kind of enhanced microscope, or something like that." Anchorman nodded at Gin. "Hey, Reilly. How was your morning running around with a fellow agent?"

Gin laughed. "Since my partner is a fellow agent, not all that unusual." She glanced at the closed doors. "How was your morning in the autopsy?"

"Outside the autopsy," Anchorman clarified. "I'm not much on watching a body get cut up on purpose."

"I don't think the former owner cares too much anymore,"

Gin said. "And might care a lot more about us finding answers. How long have you been waiting out here?"

Ricki walked over and poked at the paper in Anchorman's hands. "Long enough to talk Crystal into scaring up an actual printed paper. I'm surprised she knew what it was."

The Marine-turned-cook heaved a theatrical sigh. "She did give me a pitying look, and has been treating me like her grandfather ever since."

"You probably act like it," Gin said. "Sitting in front of doors and guarding your woman is a bit on the prehistoric side."

Anchorman shrugged. "Don't really care, and I'm not going to change." He folded up his sports section and laid it on top of the rest of the paper. "So, did you two get anything out of the banker?"

"Enough to believe he's in it up to his eyeballs," Gin said, her voice sharp enough to cut ice. "At least for the money. Nothing concrete. Just a strong feeling."

"Neither one of us thinks he's good for the murders," Ricki finished for her. "We'll get into details when we get back to the house and the whole team can hear them." She glanced at the closed doors. "Any updates on the autopsy, or what Crystal has to say about the bullets?"

Anchorman shook his head, then stood up when Crystal came walking into the room. She stopped and stared at the newcomers, her gum snapping in her mouth.

"I don't know if all of you are supposed to be here." She walked over to her desk and pulled up a log on her computer screen. "I'm only showing Dr. Cheron and Agent James on the log." She pointed at Anchorman. "I let you take the place of Agent James, but now she's standing right there." She smiled at Ricki then gave Gin a pointed look. "And I don't know you at all, so two of you should probably wait in the front lobby." She frowned. "How did you get in here, anyway?"

Gin smiled and pointed to the gold badge clipped to her belt. "I showed the guy at the lobby desk this." She reached into her back pocket and removed a leather case, then casually flipped it open so Crystal could see her credentials. "And then I showed him this."

Ricki raised a hand to hide her grin when Crystal didn't look the least bit impressed. "Okay. Great. You're FBI. But you still aren't on the expected visitors' log."

"Gee. Sorry I missed that," Gin said.

When it looked like the FBI agent was about to say something even more sarcastic, Ricki stepped in front of her, blocking her view of Gin. "Crystal, we have six dead guys in your morgue, and maybe a seventh related to the same case. It's going to take more than just Dr. Garrison and I to work on this."

"Oh." Crystal considered it for a moment, then jerked her head toward Anchorman. "I didn't think he was an investigator. I thought he was some kind of bodyguard for Dr. Garrison."

"He's that too," Ricki said, keeping a straight face when Anchorman shot her an annoyed look over the lab tech's head. "Did you find out anything from examining the bullets?"

As a distraction, the question worked pretty well. Crystal's stubborn expression dropped away, to be replaced by her face lighting up with enthusiasm. The lab tech might have been on a whole other planet when it came to the way she dressed and how she looked at the world, but she loved her work. Which gave Ricki a wide swath of common ground with the younger woman.

"Interesting," Crystal declared. "Totally mag. All the cartridges were .30-30 Winchesters, so I'm thinking the shooters used the same kind of rifle. Probably the Winchester 1891, or a later version of some kind."

Ricki and Gin exchanged a startled look. Shooters? As in plural?

Lost in her own world, Crystal didn't notice the stunned look on all three faces staring back at her. "But there were two different striation patterns on the bullets. It was a nine and three split on those."

"Hang on, hang on," Gin said. "What does that mean? Nine bullets came from one rifle, and three came from another?"

Crystal's head bobbed up and down, the light catching on the row of rhinestone studs in her ears. "That's exactly right. Not all the bullets were intact enough to examine, but most of them were. A shot in the back, and a shot in the head. Seven bodies, with twelve recovered bullets I could examine, all shot from two different guns. Of course, I don't have any weapons to compare them to, but I can do that once you find something." She paused to suck in a deep breath. "Now, as far as the cocaine is concerned—"

She stopped midsentence when Ricki shoved a hand in front of her face.

"Hold on there. Two different guns? Can you tell us which bodies were shot with which gun?"

"Of course I can." Crystal plopped down in her desk chair and started tapping away on her keyboard. "I've already started a report. Let's see." She squinted at the screen for a moment, then reached into her desk drawer and plucked out a pair of glasses. Unlike the rest of her, they were very plain looking with bulky solid black frames. "Okay. Striation number one was on the bullets from bodies two, three, and five. All the rest had striation number two on them and came from a different gun, so that would be bodies number one, four, six, and seven."

Gin huffed out a breath. "So which bodies were which?"

Crystal gave a look that clearly stated what she thought of Gin's IQ. "They're numbered in order, of course. Number one was the first body we received. Two through six all came in at once, and number seven is the latest one."

Ricki quickly translated that from numbers to names. "So striation number one came from bullets and bodies found at the camp, while number two came from Santiago Garcia, Jimmy, and two of the bodies from the camp."

Crystal gave an audible sniff. "That's what I said."

"And all the bullets came from a hunting rifle, not an automatic pistol?" Gin asked. When Crystal nodded, the FBI agent looked over at Ricki. "Well, isn't that a kicker?"

"Yeah," Ricki said with a slow nod. "Yeah, it is." She returned her attention to the lab tech. "You were about to say something about the cocaine?"

"Oh, yeah." Crystal's attention returned to the computer screen. "Okay. Only one tested for it in his blood, and that was body number seven. The others were clean. And only the first body had any on his clothes. The others did not." She looked up from her screen. "That's all I've got so far. I'm waiting on Dr. Robbins for anything else he needs a quick look at, and I need to get these to the bigger lab to confirm what I've found." She gave Ricki a smug grin. "And they will. Confirm my findings, I mean."

When the doors to the autopsy room opened, Crystal swiveled around in her chair. "Hey, Dr. Garrison. There's a whole gang of your friends out here."

Cheron smiled at the lab tech. "Yes. I can see that. Dr. Robbins and I have concluded our work, so you can all come in now." She peered at Anchorman through the lenses of her oversized glasses. "The body's all covered up, so you'll be fine."

"Great," he muttered under his breath when Crystal snickered, but followed behind Ricki and Gin, letting the door swing shut on the lab tech's amused look.

Dr. Robbins was staring at his iPad, frowning at the screen.

"I see Crystal has found that the bullets came from two different weapons."

Cheron's mouth formed into an O. "She did? So all the drug runners were killed with one weapon, and the last victim with another?"

Ricki shook her head. "Not exactly. There's a mix in there. We can go over it later. Did you find anything else?"

"Not really," Dr. Robbins said. "All died from gunshot wounds, and Crystal's report stated only one, the last victim, had any drugs in his system, although I didn't see any sign of long-term abuse, so if he had a habit, it was a relatively new one." The doctor scrolled through several pages on his iPad. "Time of death for that last victim is twenty to twenty-four hours before he was brought in." He stopped to do some more scrolling. "And the other five who were brought in together also all died at the same time. Approximately twelve days ago."

Ricki mentally counted the days backwards. "So, hang on here. You're saying that those five victims died on the same day as the first victim, Santiago Garcia?"

The doctor frowned as he once again consulted his iPad. "That would be correct, Agent James."

"I concur," Cheron said. "And I just went over Crystal's preliminary report." Her gaze met Ricki's as she adjusted her glasses. "Whoever fired the weapon that created the second set of striations on the bullets was present at every single murder."

"But he had help at the camp," Ricki said. "Someone else was there."

Chapter 33

"Two shooters?" Clay ran a hand across his cheek. "And the tech is sure about that?"

Ricki nodded at the group gathered around the kitchen island. "Crystal is a little off the beaten path at times, but she's good at what she does. She found two sets of striations, and can match each set to each body." She leaned over the blank piece of paper she'd laid on the countertop in front of her. After drawing three circles all in a line, she made two more farther away and at an angle to each other.

"This is where we found the bodies at the camp." While the others crowded closer, she pointed to the first circle in the line. "This is who Crystal's report refers to as body number two. He was standing next to bodies number three and four when they were all killed." She tapped a finger on the other two circles, farther away. "And these are bodies five and six. Now, bodies number two and five were killed by one shooter, and the rest of them by the other."

Clay was leaning over the counter, studying the drawing. "So the shooters must have lined all five up, and the first three were shot while two tried to run, and then they were shot, with their killers taking out one each."

"That's how I see it," Ricki said, straightening up on the stool. "They probably took out the guards first, along with one of the mules, and then shot the other two mules when they tried to run."

"Which is why the guards never got a round off," Anchorman said. "Still, that's some good and really fast shooting with a leverage action rifle."

Gin sighed. "Yeah, like maybe the kind that comes with a lifetime of practice living off the grid. Which brings us back to Walter, the hermit."

Ricki knew that. And certainly everything pointed to him, but the elusive hermit didn't sit right with her as a killer. He'd had multiple opportunities to shoot any of them but hadn't done it, settling for warning notes instead. Even at the fires, that arrow only flew toward the gasoline-soaked pile he'd built when no one was close enough to get hurt. No. It didn't fit. They were missing something.

We need to talk to him.

When Gin nudged her in the side, Ricki looked up to find five pairs of eyes staring back at her.

"Who do we need to talk to?" Gin asked.

Realizing she'd voiced out loud the words she'd thought were only in her head, Ricki shrugged. "The hermit. I mean Walter Modonsky. We need to talk to him."

Stephen lifted a hand to stifle a yawn and shook his head. "How do we do that? Take an ad out in the local paper?"

Gin moved restlessly on her stool, finally clasping her hands in front of her as she looked at Ricki. "Which bothers me about this hermit. If he's spent all his life living in the mountains, how does he get around in the civilized world so easily? I mean, he shows up at a public highway to set off fires, then here at the house to deliver a message by arrow. But when we discover his supply stash, he's nowhere to be found."

"He might have been there at the cabin," Anchorman stated. "If I had seen a unit of guys coming down the trail, all armed with semiautomatics, I wouldn't have shown myself either."

"He could have said something when we ended up back at the cabin," Gin argued. "When all the guys with the really scary guns had disappeared."

"Our guns are scary too," Clay put in. "And the only other times he's let us know he was around, there were only one or two of us there. We had five at the cabin, all armed. I wouldn't have liked those odds either."

"I'm telling you, he's our guy," Gin insisted.

"Which means he's got the rest of the drugs stashed somewhere," Stephen said. "And that's what we need to find."

But Clay shook his head. "He hates drugs. He told us that himself. So the most likely scenario is that he's already destroyed them, which means there isn't anything to find."

Ricki let the argument flow around her as she stared down at the paper with its circles. They'd already concluded that Santiago Garcia had been using one of the seven coffee mugs at the campsite, which meant he'd probably been there when the guide, and whoever his partner was, had rounded them all up. Then when the shooting started, Garcia had run, along with the other two mules, only he'd gotten away. Which meant one shooter had chased after him, and that would explain Garcia being shot on the same day as the others. But why leave half the drugs in his pack behind? She frowned, then slid off the stool, her sudden movement effectively silencing everyone around her.

"Okay. Let's go over what we know and see if we can come up with a direction to pursue." Ricki tapped the paper with the circles. "We start with the drug runners. We know there was a group, probably with the CJNG cartel out of Jalisco, running drugs through the park and up to Canada." She added her nod to the others'. "And the only way they could get through the park on a path that was off the main trail was to have someone who knows the area like the back of his hand guide them through."

"Which means a local," Stephen said. "Or someone who has lived in the park for a really long time."

Clay blew out a breath. "But we know there had to be two, because we have two shooters working together." He turned his head and looked at Gin. "What are the chances that one of the drug runners and the guide hooked up and stole the drugs together?"

The FBI agent shook her head. "Knowing how the cartel operates? Not good. Anyone who's been a member of the CJNG would know that stealing those drugs would sign his death warrant, and that the cartel would never stop looking for him." Gin paused and looked around the table. "And the cartel's reach is very wide. They would have found any former member who betrayed them."

"I agree," Ricki said. "The type of guns used to do the killing don't match a cartel member. Whoever partnered up were two locals. Hunters."

"I also think whoever they are would have wanted to keep a close eye on our investigation," Gin said slowly. She placed her palm on top of the paper Ricki had drawn on. "We've probably met them at some point since we arrived in town."

"Which doesn't narrow it down much for the second partner, assuming Modonsky is in on it," Stephen complained. "We've interviewed half the town at this point. I mean, he could be a busboy at the Snowmelt, or one of the shop owners or clerks that we talked to."

"A partner who lives in town would explain how Modonsky seems to move about so easily," Clay stated. "We only talked to the hermit up at the park. We never spoke to whoever shot the arrows. That could have been his partner, and we just assumed that was also the hermit."

"Which would mean the partner is the one who shot Jimmy, and that would be with the gun that produced the second set of striations that Crystal identified. So he was also the one who chased Garcia through the woods and caught up with him," Ricki said.

"Which would make the partner a younger guy," Stephen observed. "Modonsky is an expert in the forest, but from our information, he's no spring chicken. I can't see him sprinting through the woods after a panicked twenty-three-year-old."

Clay leaned over, placing his forearms on the counter as his gaze went flat. "Which would fit Jimmy. It also fits that the only people who knew about the vics being shot, and the drug connection, all spent time at Jimmy's bar. Which makes that bar the source of information."

"Or the information was fed to Jimmy to spread around," Gin said quietly. She glanced over at Ricki. "All along the finger for all of this mess has been pointed at Modonsky, the so-called hermit." Steady green eyes met Ricki's dark-blue ones. "How did you hear about this hermit in the first place?"

Ricki wet her lips. She hated ratting out a fellow park ranger, but Gin was right. It was DJ who had made sure to clue her in on the story of the hermit. "One of the rangers who volunteered for the rescue mission, Darren Jenson."

Clay's gaze also shifted over to Ricki. She could see the apology in his eyes. "That's right. It was Jenson. And if he fed Jimmy the story, then Jimmy might have become a loose end. Jenson is also in good enough shape to chase Garcia through the forest."

Unhappy, but having no choice but to consider the affable DJ as a suspect, Ricki sighed. "And no one would question a ranger taking a shift up in the northern section of the park, which would give him the means to drop off the supplies for Modonsky. It isn't as if he would have to account for all his time up there, or punch in on a time clock."

"I can run a check on him, see if there's anything wonky in his background or his financials," Stephen volunteered.

"Can you also run one on the banker while you're at it?"

Ricki asked. "Someone is going to have to launder the money if the two partners ever get around to selling the drugs."

"OTSW: the basic business requirements of the drug trade," Gin said. She lifted a hand and counted off the letters. "Obtain the drugs, transport the drugs, sell the drugs, wash the money."

Her partner nodded. "That could be the connection between our players. Modonsky and this ranger obtain the drugs, Jimmy uses his truck and the excuse of making a beer run to transport them, and our friendly neighborhood banker puts the money in the washer and launders it right into some offshore account."

"Which means there has to be a record somewhere in that bank's accounting system of that money going in and being wired out to a foreign country."

Gin shrugged. "Or it might be listed as a business-to-business loan, with the bank only acting as an intermediary."

Ricki's head was pounding. She could feel the beat crawling up at the base of her skull. "Before we neatly wrap all this up in a bow, let's do the background searches and see what else we can turn up." She pointed at Clay. "How did the interview at the post office go?"

"About what we expected," Clay said. "A very nice woman named Jeanie runs the place, and she's been there almost twenty years. She told me she receives a cashier's check once a year to pay for the rent on the box. She leaves a notice in the box every June, and the next week the check appears in a sealed envelope addressed to her. She also said she inherited the routine from the man who ran the post office before her, who has since passed away."

"I don't suppose the helpful Jeanie ever saw anyone pick up anything from that box?" Gin asked, then sighed when Clay shook his head.

"Nope. She's never seen anyone go near it, and they've

never had a request to change the lock, so I'm guessing it uses the same key that Modonsky's parents used."

"Surveillance cameras?" Stephen asked.

Clay only chuckled. "Not a chance. And Jeanie claims it would be next to impossible to figure out if anyone local was picking up Modonsky's mail. They get a visit from almost everyone in the area, to either pick up something or mail out something. It wouldn't take much for anyone to slip anything out of the box when no one was around, or they were too busy to notice."

The throbbing in Ricki's skull beat a little harder. She rubbed the base of her neck in a futile attempt to ease it off as her gaze shifted to Stephen. "How about at the high school? Tell me we have a picture of Walter Modonsky."

"The clerk there was also very helpful," Stephen said. "And better yet, there were shelves right there in the office lined with every yearbook the school has ever put out. I started with 1973, figuring he was eighteen that year, so the most likely one he would have graduated in. A Walter Modonsky wasn't listed anywhere in it that I could find. But when I went back one year, I hit pay dirt."

Ricki's heart rate jumped. It was about time they had some luck in this case. "What did you find?"

"Well, there was a placeholder for Modonsky's class picture his junior year. He must have missed his picture day. But he was listed in the picture for the school's archery club."

"Archery?" Ricki's wide grin met Gin's satisfied smirk. "Is that so?"

Stephen's grin was as wide as Ricki's. "Uh-huh. But it wasn't a great shot, so I sent it to Dan to have it cleaned up some and blown up into a larger print, isolating just Modonsky."

"Did Dan give you a timeline on that?" Ricki asked.

"He's working on something for Hamilton, but he said he should have it tonight or first thing in the morning."

She wished she had it in her hand right now, but the wait would be worth it. Finally, a picture of the hermit. Her cell phone pinged, indicating an incoming email. She quickly dug it out and tapped on the screen, reading the message from Hamilton. Barely repressing her glee, she held the phone up high for the whole group to see. "Hamilton came through with the warrant for us to search Jimmy's property. The house, the barn, and his bar." She tucked her phone away. "Two of us can take the house and the barn, and the other two the bar. Anchorman, you stay here with Cheron."

Chapter 34

"WHAT DO you think Gin and Stephen will come up with at the bar?" Clay asked. Beneath the windproof protection of her parka, Ricki's shoulders lifted into a shrug. They were walking through the trees, preferring to take the same path to Jimmy's house that they had the last time they were here rather than the much more open and exposed gravel driveway.

"I doubt if they'll find a big stockpile of cocaine," she said. "Whoever killed him would have secured that by now, provided Jimmy ever had it in the first place."

Clay gave her a curious look. "So you think someone is trying to set him up for the murders?"

She shrugged again. "I don't know. But I think someone is being set up, and I know we have two shooters. Which tells me it's the second shooter trying to point the finger somewhere else."

"Out of all our potential suspects who are still alive, which is coming down to three—Modonsky, Hontel, and DJ—I'm sorry to say that DJ seems to be the most likely."

Ricki was afraid of that too, but only by a process of elimination. Hontel wasn't capable, and she simply didn't think it was Modonsky. Which only left DJ. But she was having a hard time swallowing that one too. "Why do you say that?" she finally asked.

Clay stuck his hands in his pockets as he adjusted his stride to hers. "Mostly because he's the smartest of the three of them. From your description, Hontel doesn't sound like the brightest bulb in the box, and Modonsky never even made it through high school. Which leaves DJ, as much as I hate to admit it."

"Yeah. Me too." Ricki reached out a hand to pull Clay to a stop. "Hang on." She peered through the trees toward the house. "There's Molly."

The older woman had stepped outside onto the small porch. She had on her usual shapeless dress in a flat brown. It was topped by a fluffy coat that was the same color as her dress and had a rip along one sleeve.

Molly paused to reach overhead, clasping her hands together as she stretched out her back. Then she bent over and pulled her thick wool socks right up to the bottom of her kneecaps. She made her way to the last step, then turned and picked up an ax that was left leaning against one of the porch posts.

With the ax in her hand, she slowly turned around, her back stiff as she faced the wall of trees that surrounded the house. Ricki watched her scan slowly from side-to-side, and was startled when Molly looked right at her.

Shaking the jumpy feeling off, Ricki moved forward with Clay right next to her. Once she'd cleared the trees, she stopped again and lifted a hand in greeting.

"Hello, Molly. I'm surprised to see you here," Ricki called out. When the woman didn't say a word, Ricki continued forward. "I thought you'd be at the Last Stop."

Once Ricki and Clay got closer, Molly switched the ax from one hand to the other. Seeing it, Ricki's smile stayed in place, but she did stop.

"I live here," Molly blurted out. "Not at the bar."

Ricki looked at the ax in her hand. "Are you going to chop some wood?"

The older woman looked down at her hand and frowned, as if she wasn't sure how the ax had gotten there. She held the ax out and let it fall to the ground as she flexed her fingers back and forth. "I can't chop wood no more. I got arthritis in my hands, so Pac-Man is coming over to help me out."

"That's very nice of him," Ricki said. "Maybe while he's doing that, my friend here and I can search through the house?"

When Molly shook her head, Ricki held out her phone. "I have a search warrant here that will let me do that. It means we're allowed to come into the house. Is that okay with you?"

"What's that mean? A search warrant?" Molly frowned at the phone Ricki was holding up. "That's a legal thing, ain't it? Does it mean Jimmy said it was okay? Because Jimmy owns the house. I don't own it."

Ricki didn't say anything for a long moment. She wasn't sure Molly knew about Jimmy being killed, which might make things a lot more difficult.

Molly's shoulders slumped over. "You go ahead and look around if you want to. I got work to do." She pointed to a bucket and mop next to the porch. "I got to clean off that mop and scrub out the bucket before I have to go over to the bar again. So you go ahead and do what you want." She turned her back on them and grabbed up the mop and bucket, then toted them away, disappearing around the corner of the house.

"What do you think?" Clay said.

"I think the door is open and we have a warrant."

He followed her into the house. "Yeah, but I meant about Molly. Do you think she really doesn't know that Jimmy is dead?"

"I don't know," Ricki said. "When we're through with the

house, I'll go out back and ask her." While Clay did a slow walk around the living room, Ricki put her hands on her hips and studied the small space. It looked different from what she'd imagined. Given the state of the back bedroom, she assumed the rest of the house would look the same. But for all its compact size, it was neat and tidy. Two pillows were arranged on the sofa, and the furniture and tables all appeared to be dust free.

Ricki left the living room and wandered down a back hallway. She stepped into a narrow bathroom with a tub and shower combination on one end. It too was scrubbed clean, and all the towels were hung in their proper places. Ricki peeked into the medicine cabinet and saw nothing unusual. The only drug in it was a bottle of aspirin.

She continued down the hall to the only bedroom. Someone had picked up in there as well. All the drawers and the small closet held men's clothes. She didn't spot any of Molly's signature loose-fitting dresses until she opened another tiny closet in the hallway. She went into the kitchen where a low cot, with several blankets neatly folded on top, was pushed against one wall. Clay was standing in front of the half-sized window, looking out into the yard.

"I guess Molly sleeps in here," Ricki said quietly. "And does most of the housework too, if I had to guess. She's kind of like a live-in maid, or an indentured servant." Ricki folded her arms across her chest and let out a snort of disgust at the idea.

"Uh-huh." Clay turned his head and looked back over his shoulder. "Is it my imagination, or is she moving a lot better than she did just a few minutes ago?"

Ricki stepped over to the window and peered through the dirty glass. Molly did look better as she crossed over the back to pick up a hose. But when she bent to turn the spigot, she slowly stood up again, rubbing her hand as her shoulders slumped over.

"It must hurt to use a mop with that arthritis in her hands," Clay murmured. He glanced over at Ricki as Molly's hand moved to the small of her back. "I think indentured servant pretty much covers it."

Ricki watched as Molly looked over in their direction, still rubbing her back. She finally set the bucket upright and began hosing it out. "Let's go take a look in the barn."

They walked across the dirt patch in back that passed for a yard, moving toward the barn. Molly abandoned her bucket and followed them, being sure to keep at least six feet behind.

"Why do you want to look in there?" she asked when Ricki stopped to study the heavy lock on the doors. "No one goes in there except Jimmy. He keeps his truck in there."

Ricki turned around and smiled at the older woman. "What else does he keep in there, Molly?"

Molly shrugged. "I don't know. I don't go in there."

"So you don't have a key to this lock?"

"No." Molly shook her head, sending her frizzy hair flying in several directions. "Jimmy doesn't want me to go in there. So I don't."

Ricki looked toward the house. "Maybe he keeps the key in the kitchen, or his bedroom?"

Molly frowned. "No. There's one key and Jimmy has it." She chewed on her lower lip. "If you want to git in that bad, there might be some loose boards round back."

Having already explored that option on their previous trip, Ricki shook her head. "How about bolt cutters? Does Jimmy have any bolt cutters, Molly?"

Jimmy's permanent houseguest looked at Ricki and grinned. "He's got them." She pointed at the oversized doors. "They're in the barn."

While Ricki stared at the woman in exasperation, Clay put a hand on her shoulder. "I have some in the truck," he murmured before striding off.

Keeping a close eye on Molly, Ricki leaned back against the wooden walls of the barn. "Have you seen Jimmy lately?"

Molly rolled her eyes. "If I did, I woulda been seein' a ghost."

Surprised, Ricki nodded. "I wasn't sure anyone had been out here to let you know."

"Everybody in town knows," Molly said with a shrug. "The hermit shot him."

Ricki lifted an eyebrow but otherwise didn't move. "Is that what everyone in town is saying? That the hermit shot him?"

"He mighta shot himself," Molly said. "He weren't too good with a gun." Clay appeared around the corner of the house, carrying a pair of bolt cutters in one hand. He'd unzipped his parka, and the badge attached to his shirt flashed under a narrow beam of sunlight. Molly took several steps back. "I got to git to my work." She didn't wait for an answer but scurried away as Clay walked up to the barn.

The chief stared after her retreating figure. "Was it something I said?"

"It might be that badge you're wearing," Ricki said cryptically, shaking her head when Clay sent her a questioning look. "Let's get inside and see what Jimmy thought was worth a padlock."

With a nod, Clay stepped up to the doors and settled the bolt cutters into place. The muscles in his arms strained as the powerful jaws on the cutter did their job, slicing through the curved metal bar of the lock. Setting the tool aside, Clay lifted the lock away and swung open the doors.

The interior was dark and damp from several shingles missing in the roof, but it still had the slightly sweet smell of fresh sawdust. The large open space in the center was empty. Wherever Jimmy's truck was, it wasn't where he usually kept it.

Ricki walked across the floor, sending sawdust flying around her boots. She walked off to the side, where there was a storage closet. Opening the door revealed a walk-in space, with several buckets stacked together in one corner. Over them hung an array of mops and brooms, right next to another pair of bolt cutters and several rusty saws. With nothing else to see, Ricki returned to the open space.

Clay stood in the middle, staring down at the floor. "Find anything interesting in that storage area?"

"Nope." Ricki looked around, then slowly walked to the rear of the barn, her head down. When she turned and made her way back to Clay, there was a frown on her face. "This sawdust is brand new, but I don't see any tire tracks."

"Me neither," Clay said. "And didn't Molly tell us she never came in here?"

"That's what she said."

Clay squatted down and ran a hand along the floor, scooping up sawdust as he went. "So, either Jimmy drove his truck out of here and then came back and covered the floor with fresh sawdust just before he was killed, or someone is trying to cover something up."

"Someone who had a key to the padlock," Ricki said. "The key that Molly told us Jimmy carried with him."

When Clay continued to run his hand back and forth over the floor, Ricki went back into the storage area and returned with two brooms. She handed one to Clay. "Here you go. I'll take the other side."

Carefully they moved the sawdust aside, examining each floorboard underneath. Ricki was almost to the end of her first pass when Clay let out a sharp whistle.

"Over here. I've got something."

She walked over and joined him, looking over his shoulder as he squatted down next to a heavy dark patch on the floor.

"Maybe Cheron has something with her that can test for blood," Clay said. "But right offhand, I'd say we found the spot where Jimmy was killed."

Chapter 35

Ricki hung up her cell phone. "Cheron and Anchorman are on their way over with Cheron's luminol and a blood collection kit. They'll be here in a few minutes." She looked down at the dark stain covering the floor between her and Clay. "Assuming this is Jimmy's blood, then it's obvious someone moved the body after he was killed."

"Which would take some muscle," Clay said. "Especially if he was hoisted into the back of a pickup truck."

"That the killer would have driven to the dump site," Ricki added, taking up the narrative, "and then driven off and ditched somewhere." She gazed toward the wide-open double doors leading into the barn. "And then what? The killer walked from wherever he ditched the truck back here to pick up his own ride?" She shook her head. "Even though there's a BOLO out on it, no one has seen that truck, so it can't be close by. The killer would have had a long walk."

Clay stuck his hands in his pockets and rocked back on his heels. "Something else to add to the list of what's skewed sideways about this case."

"Hello? What are you doing?" Molly stood in the open doorway, squinting into the semi-darkness inside the barn. She pointed at the small piles of sawdust pushed to the side to expose the floor. "You shouldn't be sweepin' up. Jimmy don't like that."

"Molly," Ricki called out, "do you know anything about this?" She pointed at the stain and watched as Molly craned her neck but otherwise didn't budge.

"I don't see nothin'. What is it?" Molly asked.

"You can come closer and get a better look at it," Ricki said.

This time the older woman vehemently shook her head and took a step backward. "No. No. I never go in there. Jimmy don't like it."

Ricki slowly walked over to the open door, stopping a few feet away from the entrance. "He won't mind now, Molly. Jimmy's dead. You told me so yourself."

Molly took another cautious step backwards, keeping a close eye on Ricki. "Don't make no never mind. I'm not supposed to go into the barn." Having made that declaration, Molly turned and almost ran right into Anchorman. When he reached out to steady her, she made a terrified squeak, accompanied by a quick sidestep to avoid his outstretched hand. "No, no. Stay away." She skirted around him and quickly fled toward the house. Opening the tattered screen door, she disappeared inside.

Anchorman rubbed a hand underneath his chin as he stared at the closed screen door. "I haven't seen that reaction from anyone in a long time, and back then I was carrying a very nasty-looking rifle."

"You're a big man," Cheron said in a practical tone. "You probably just startled her." She adjusted her glasses as she looked past Ricki into the interior of the barn. "Now where is this possible bloodstain?"

Ricki pointed at Clay, and once Cheron walked past her, a black backpack slung over one shoulder, Ricki reached out and stopped Anchorman who was following along behind.

"Have there been any more arrows or other weird things going on at the house?" she asked in a low voice.

"No." Anchorman kept his answer soft enough it wouldn't carry to Cheron, who was kneeling on the wood floor as she searched through her backpack. "Should I be on guard for something specific?"

"I haven't heard anything, but I don't like this." Ricki kept her gaze on the doctor as she tucked a stray lock of hair behind her ear. "We need a reason to send Cheron home."

The former Marine snorted as his gaze also drifted over to the doctor. "Have you got something that will make her go back to the Bay? Because I haven't come up with anything short of hog-tying her and driving her back there myself. So far, nothing I've said has made her budge an inch."

Not the least bit surprised, Ricki sighed. There were too many odd things about this case, and way too many dead bodies popping up for her to be comfortable having the doctor around. She'd put in a call to Hamilton, but that might take a while. He'd sent her an email last night stating that he'd be out of town on a major consult with the district covering the southeast and might not get back to any requests for a day or two. Still, when she got back to the house she would make the call and leave him a message. A day or two's delay was better than nothing.

"Definitely blood," Cheron announced, her voice echoing through the large, empty space in the barn. "I'll take a sample, but I'm also going to put in a call to Dr. Robbins. I'm hoping he'll send Crystal here to process this scene."

Ricki and Anchorman walked over, stopping when Cheron held out a hand. "Don't walk in any farther. Who knows what could be hiding in all this sawdust?"

"Contaminated sawdust," Ricki pointed out. "The roof leaks pretty badly."

Cheron looked up at the small shafts of light that

peppered through the shingles overhead. "Yes, well, still, I'd like a trained forensic technician to take a look."

"Fine by me," Ricki said. "What about the size of this stain? Is it enough blood to be the murder scene?"

"I can't say for sure, of course," Cheron stated. "But given the size of the bloodstain, and that a fair amount of it would have seeped through and into these floorboards, I'm comfortable in saying that someone was killed here. Naturally, we won't know exactly who until we match this blood to a body in the morgue."

"And if there's no match there, then we're still missing a body," Ricki said.

The doctor accepted Anchorman's hand and let him pull her to her feet. "I'd say that's true." She looked around. "There isn't anything more I can do here." She reached into her backpack and handed Anchorman a small roll of crime scene tape. "If you would put this across the front door once we have all closed up, I'll step outside and call Dr. Robbins." She shook a warning finger at Clay. "Now, you be careful where you step, Chief."

"I will," Clay assured her, an amused smile pulling at his mouth as the doctor hurried off. "Where to now?" he asked Ricki.

"Anchorman will stay with Cheron," she said, which had the big man immediately doing an about-face and striding after the doctor. "And you and I will touch base with Gin and Stephen to check up on how they're making out with their search of the bar."

Since Anchorman had come right up the driveway, he and Cheron were gone within minutes. Meanwhile Ricki and Clay walked back to the truck. When they reached the front of the house, Molly came bursting out the door, her arms around a bulging plastic garbage bag.

She hurried toward them in her half-walk, half-limp gait, stopping at the point where she was blocking their way. "Can you give me a ride to the bar?" Despite the fact she was breathing heavily from her exertion, there was a determined look in her eyes. "I'm moving in there fer a while. I'm not stayin' here." When Ricki lifted an eyebrow, Molly's chin jutted out. "When I first walked up to that old barn, I heard you say that was blood on the floor. I ain't stayin' no place where there's blood on the floor."

Ricki looked at Molly for a long moment. The woman stood, radiating an odd mixture of defiance and fear. "Okay, Molly. We'll be happy to give you a ride."

Molly first sagged with relief and then quickly straightened up, tightening her hold on the garbage bag, before scurrying off in the direction of the truck.

"Are you sure about this?" Clay asked.

She honestly didn't know, but it was the only other place Molly had to go, and she didn't want the older woman to sleep outside because she was afraid to stay in the house. "Our FBI friends will have already searched the bar and taken anything of interest out of it, so it should be fine. At least I won't be lying awake tonight wondering if Molly is freezing to death under a tree somewhere." She shrugged as she followed Molly to the truck. "I didn't notice any shelters in town for someone with nowhere to go."

Clay bumped her lightly with his arm. "You're a good person, Ricki James."

Ricki shook her head. She didn't think not wanting someone to freeze to death was a big deal, but she gave him a return arm bump and kept walking. When they reached the truck, Molly had climbed into the bed in the back and was wedged into the corner behind the driver.

"You need to sit inside with us, Molly," Clay said.

"I'm stayin' here. You jist drive. I'll be fine." Molly hunkered down even more and drew her knees up to her chest.

Clay opened his mouth, then shut it again. "I shouldn't be

doing this," he muttered loud enough for Ricki to hear before stomping his way to the front of the truck.

Sure that arguing with Molly wouldn't do them any good, Ricki climbed into the passenger seat and checked her cell phone for any messages from Gin. Clay got behind the wheel, then also glanced at his cell before dropping it into the center console and starting up the truck.

Spotting a text from Gin, Ricki read it out loud as Clay guided the truck onto the road. "Gin wants us to meet them at the bar, and she's sent for a locksmith." Ricki noted the time of the text then looked at the clock on the dashboard. "Who should be arriving in about twenty minutes, according to Gin's timeline."

Clay nodded, then looked at his phone when it rang. So did Ricki. The name of the district attorney of Seattle flashed onto the screen.

"Want me to get that?" Ricki asked.

"No." Clay reached over and tapped on the decline icon. "I'll call him back."

"He might need your help on a case."

"It's not about a case," Clay said without taking his eyes off the road.

Ricki leaned back against her seat and forced herself to relax. Clay and the DA didn't have just a business relationship; they were also friends. Andre could have been calling him about anything. But since Clay already knew what it was about, she was pretty sure the possibilities were narrowed down to one—his departure for Homeland Security and New York. If it were anything else, he would have told her.

Carefully refraining from crossing her arms over her chest, she was unaware of her boot tapping against the floor as she stared out the side window. The rest of the ride was thankfully short and passed in a charged silence.

As soon as the truck parked in front of the Last Stop, Molly scooted toward the tailgate. She climbed over it, carefully stepping onto the ground before snatching up her garbage bag and limping toward the front door. Ricki got out and took the time to look around, surprised that there weren't any other vehicles in the parking lot. She walked past Clay, who was waiting on the porch with its missing roof, and stepped through the door that Molly had left wide open.

Molly stood by the bar, looking around at the completely empty room. When Ricki walked inside, she jerked her head toward the small hallway leading to the back. "There's a storeroom back there with a cot in it. That's where I'll be." With a death grip on her garbage bag, she clomped in that direction. Ricki walked over to the bar and read the large note that had been left on top.

I didn't have any keys to lock up. Sorry. Pac-Man

SINCE NOTHING LOOKED out of place, it appeared that leaving the Last Stop unlocked the night before hadn't done any harm, so Ricki continued toward the same back hallway Molly had taken. She heard Gin's voice coming from an open door on the right, just past the one that Molly was opening with a key she'd taken out of the pocket of her jacket. Ricki frowned for a moment, staring as Molly disappeared through the open doorway, then moved on down the hallway toward the voices coming from the now-dead Jimmy's office.

"I had ten bucks that said the locksmith would get here first."

Ricki leaned against the door jamb and smiled. "You lose then."

Gin looked over from the desk chair she was lounging in and made a face at Ricki. "Well, that sucks." She frowned at the sudden noise filtering in through the wall. "Is that Clay? What's he doing?"

Clay stepped up behind Ricki and peered over her shoulder. "I'm right here. That's Molly. She's going to sleep in the storeroom next door."

"Why?" Stephen asked. He was leaning against the wall, one ankle crossed over the other. "Did something happen at Jimmy's house?"

"It looks like he was killed in the barn, then dumped at the other crime scene," Clay said. "Molly's too spooked to stay there now."

Ricki tilted her head toward the wall Jimmy's office shared with the storeroom. "Tell me you've already searched in there."

"We did once we found a key shoved into the back of the office desk," Gin confirmed. "But we didn't find anything much." She swiveled the chair around and pushed a box of shells across the small desk. "Found these in one of the drawers."

Chapter 36

RICKI STARED at the box of .30-30 Winchester cartridges. "Interesting coincidence."

"So is the missing, very expensive jacket," Gin said. "I don't suppose Jimmy had it on when he was found?"

"Nope." Ricki shook her head. "He didn't have on any jacket at all."

"If someone took it, then they knew what it was worth," Stephen said.

Ricki's phone beeped with an incoming email. Since it was from Dan, she immediately opened it, her gaze narrowing as she scrolled through the screen. "Dan has dug up some background on DJ. It seems his father grew up in Deming, but DJ did not. He was born in Seattle and grew up there, with a few years spent in Portland. Until he was assigned to the North Cascades Park three years ago, he was living in Boulder, Colorado, and working out of the Rocky Mountain District." She looked up from her screen, feeling a trickle of relief. "Dan also pulled his personnel file. During his three years here, he's usually assigned to the southern section of the park. With that kind of record, I'm not sure how he could have spent enough time to know the north section, where all the bodies were found."

"There's still the fact that he made sure he told us about the hermit, and volunteered for that rescue mission even though he supposedly doesn't know much about that part of the park," Clay pointed out.

"I'm aware of that," Ricki snapped back at him. She quickly closed her mouth and bit the inside of her lower lip to keep it that way.

When Clay shrugged and said, "I'll go wait for the locksmith," she could have kicked herself.

Damn it. She was still mad about his whole "I want to go to New York and chase after Lex" thing, but she didn't have any right to bite his head off. Especially not in front of other members of the team. If he wanted to keep secrets, that was his business.

Stephen pushed away from the wall and stuck his hands into his coat pockets. "I'll go keep the chief company."

Gin leaned back and drummed a finger against the desk, not saying anything until Stephen's footsteps had faded away into silence. "You two have been glaring at and tiptoeing around each other for days. I don't suppose you'd care to tell me what's going on?"

As much as it would have been great to vent to someone, Ricki shook her head. She really liked Gin, but she didn't know the FBI agent well enough to dump her personal life out in a heap at her feet. "I'll apologize."

"Yeah, well, that's all great and good, but you both have the rest of us walking on eggshells around you. So do more than apologize. You need to fix it or put it aside enough that it doesn't affect the team or our case."

"I'll take care of it," Ricki said evenly. She and Gin both turned their heads at the thump of heavy boot steps heading their way.

"It sounds like the locksmith has arrived," Gin said.

Stephen strolled in the door, hesitating until he saw Gin's nod. A thin, lanky man with bright-red hair and carrying a tool bag came in right behind the FBI agent. He looked around and laid two fingers against his forehead as he kept walking in the general direction of Gin and Ricki, then continued on right over to the large safe.

"Fancy-looking model," he said, setting his tool bag next to his feet. "More show than security, though." He kneeled down to study the combination lock, humming off-key under his breath. After several minutes, he sat back on his heels and grinned. "Old-fashioned. No electronics, just a combination of iron, steel, and a heavy-duty lock. It shouldn't take too long to get through it." He pulled a drill out of his bag, then glanced over at Stephen. "If I run out of juice, where do I plug this puppy in?"

The locksmith, who introduced himself as Sam over the high whine of the power drill, applied steady pressure as he kept on humming his tune. Ricki and Gin both retreated to the quieter, more open bar area, where Clay sat at a table enjoying a beer. Ricki supposed she should mention he shouldn't be drinking on the job, but since the ISB wasn't paying him, it wasn't worth the argument.

She shrugged, thinking they could both use a drink, and got a bottle for herself as Gin wandered outside. She carried it over to the table where Clay was sitting and pulled out a chair, painfully aware that if she waited for an invitation, she might be waiting a very long time.

She sat for a moment, her fingers running over the label on the bottle she was holding. "I'm sorry," she finally said quietly. "I shouldn't have snapped at you like that. Thinking a park ranger might be behind all this touches a nerve."

Clay nodded then looked over at her, his gray-eyed gaze capturing hers. "Yeah, I get that. But it isn't why you snapped at me."

Ricki sucked in a slow breath. "No. It's not. It's you

deciding to leave, and it's you keeping secrets." When he opened his mouth, she held up a hand. "But we agreed to put it aside until we solved this case. I didn't keep my end of that bargain, and I'm sorry for that. You don't have to be here, but you are because you know I need you, and I want you to know I appreciate that. But the way I'm acting . . ." She paused and continued to look him square in the eye. "The way *we're* acting is affecting the rest of the team, and I can't have that."

Clay raked a hand through his hair, then sat back, stretching his long legs out underneath the table. "I want to make a couple of things clear. You can be as mad as you want, Ricki, but I'm not going to walk off on you in the middle of a case. And if you think I would, then you don't know me at all. That, and I haven't made my mind up yet about going to New York. I was being honest about that. Andre is pressing me for an answer, but I've already told him I'm not giving him one until you and I have talked this over, and that won't be until we hunt down this killer."

Ricki raised her eyes to the ceiling in exasperation. "Why didn't you just say that in the truck?"

"I don't know." Clay took a long sip of his beer and then grinned. "What if we agree that both of us have a reason to be pissed off at the other, and call it a draw? And we'll talk about it after we're back in the Bay. Then we can lay all our cards on the table."

Feeling much lighter, Ricki grinned back at him. "With 'cards' being some kind of stand-in for our thoughts and feelings?"

Clay gave a comical wince. "Ouch. Don't say that to a guy. 'Cards' works fine."

"Great." Her snarky response was cut short by a triumphant shout from the back room.

"We're in!"

She and Clay got to their feet in unison and headed for the back hallway just as Gin pushed open the front door.

"I heard him," she called out, following Ricki and Clay down the hall.

The three of them crowded into the small office space, where Sam stood in front of the now wide-open door to the safe.

"There you go, folks," he said with a slight flourish of his arm. "Not much in there, so I'm not sure it was worth all the fuss, but she's open." He leaned over and squinted at an oblong object wrapped in plastic. "What's that?"

Stephen clapped a hand on the locksmith's shoulder and pulled him back to give Ricki enough room to step in front of the safe. She also bent over slightly and studied the white brick. It was wrapped in plastic except for a two-inch hole cut out of the top, over a sizable divot.

As Stephen escorted the curious locksmith out of the room, Ricki looked over her shoulder at Clay. "I guess we know why Jimmy's tox screen came out positive for cocaine. It looks like he was trying out the product."

Gin crowded in behind her. "That's all that's in there? Just the one brick?"

"That's it," Ricki confirmed. "But it's enough to peg Jimmy as being involved in all of this."

"Yeah," Gin said. "But which part? I'm betting he's not the one washing the money—we'll leave that to our friendly neighborhood banker. And I'd bet a year's pay that Jimmy didn't have the juice to sell all that coke, so that leaves his role as obtaining them, which would make him one of the shooters. Or maybe he drove the getaway truck and took the drugs to some safe hidey-hole, or maybe straight to a distribution point?"

"Shooter or getaway truck," Ricki repeated. "Since Jimmy's lived here all his life and knew the surrounding area well enough to offer his services as a guide, I'm going with the shooter."

Gin nodded her agreement. "Okay. That's two of the four slots filled. What's next?"

"Dinner and some rest," Clay said. "It's been a long couple of days. And if there's a plan to draw Modonsky out, then I need to recharge before I take another hike into the park."

The FBI agent grimaced, then added a small groan. "That hike is probably inevitable, but I'm not looking forward to it either."

Ricki reached in and pulled the brick of cocaine out of the safe and handed it to Gin. "Since this is your major concern, you can keep tabs on it." She waved a hand toward the door. "Let's go hit Anchorman up for dinner and then get some sleep."

Chapter 37

RICKI WAS SITTING at the kitchen island, enjoying a second cup of coffee and listening to Cheron give Stephen a very serious account of how she came across the bodies left behind by a serial killer in Utah. The perpetually gray skies outside their rental house had relented enough to let a few stray beams of sunshine come through the windows. Not enough for the house's occupants to abandon their wool shirts and parkas, but the unusual sight of sunshine in the Cascades in November was enough to lift everyone's spirits just a little.

When Anchorman winced at a particularly harrowing part of Cheron's story, Ricki smiled. Leaving the Marine to the small torture chamber of his own making, she picked up her coffee mug and wandered into the living room, then sat on the couch next to Clay.

"Checked in with your deputies lately?" she asked.

He chuckled as he propped up one boot on the opposite knee. "Yeah. I think Jules is enjoying bossing Ryan around," he said, referring to his one full-time deputy and the younger intern in his three-person department. "He's making Ryan do all the paperwork."

"You mean the paperwork that you habitually dumped on

him?" Ricki turned an amused gaze on Clay. "And what paperwork are we talking about here? Is there a sudden crime spree in the Bay?"

"Two jaywalkers, both tourists," Clay said. "And someone ran the only red light in town. Also a tourist."

"Sounds like a very dangerous place," Gin laughed. She was sprawled out in a chair on the opposite side of the coffee table.

"Once Crystal gets here, do you want to come out to the crime scene?" Ricki asked. She smiled at Stephen. "One or both of you?"

Gin shook her head. "Nope. We need to check in with our boss and let him know we found at least one brick and a link to the rest of the missing cocaine."

Stephen looked up from his laptop. "He's also having that twenty thousand in Jimmy's bank account traced, so he might have an update for us. Have you got Dan working on anything?"

"There's nothing more anywhere on Walter Modonsky, and I still feel he's the key to all of this," Ricki said. "So I asked Dan to run down another source. Mabry Garner."

"The gossip queen of Glacier?" Clay smiled. "The one Jo told us about?"

Ricki nodded. "That's her. According to Jo, she's close to a hundred, and went to live with her daughter and son-in-law in Granite Falls. Since the legal records don't have anything much on Walter Modonsky, I'm hoping Mabry will remember him from the time he lived in Glacier. Before he fell off the map."

The sound of an engine drew her gaze to the window. An SUV pulled up to the house, and Crystal jumped out of the passenger's side, then turned and reached in to grab a large backpack. Threading her arm through one strap, she hefted it onto her shoulder. Slamming the car door shut, Crystal waved an enthusiastic goodbye to whomever was behind the tinted windows. Ricki blinked when the SUV backed away and drove off as Crystal walked toward the porch.

"Cheron," Ricki called out. "Your lab tech is here."

"Oh, wonderful." Cheron wiped her hands on a dishtowel and hurried to the foyer. She opened the door before Crystal had a chance to knock.

Gin leaned over the arm of her chair and whispered to Stephen, "Keep in mind, she's good at her job."

Ricki got to her feet and gave Gin a warning look as she waited for Cheron and Crystal to appear. The lab tech swaggered in a moment later, walking straight to the island and dumping her backpack on top. She nodded at Anchorman, who was rinsing off dishes at the kitchen sink, then turned and looked over the group in the living room.

Cheron made a dramatic sweep of her arm toward the tech. "Everyone, this is Crystal. She's Dr. Robbins' top lab technician."

That was certainly news to Ricki. As far as she knew, Crystal was the only lab tech who reported directly to the ME. Which, she supposed, would make her the best. *And the worst,* Ricki thought with a silent smile.

"Crystal," Cheron happily continued, "you know Ricki, of course. And you've also met Gin and Anchorman." When the lab tech nodded, Cheron pointed to Stephen. "That's Stephen Jones. He's also with the FBI."

Crystal stepped forward and stuck her hand out. "So, I'd guess you're part Asian? Maybe Chinese?"

While Ricki did an inner groan, Stephen merely nodded. "Vietnamese. My mother."

"You're a handsome guy," Crystal said. Her mouth curved up into an appreciative smile. "What's the rest of you?"

"Iowan."

Crystal looked impressed. "The Native American tribe that settled around the Grand River basin? I've read up on some of their history. That's totally cool."

"That would be totally cool," Stephen agreed. "But I was referring to the state. My dad is from Iowa. He still owns a farm there."

"Oh." Crystal's smile fell, but she managed a polite nod. "A farm is cool too."

"Yes, well," Cheron interrupted, turning Crystal's attention away from Stephen. "And this is Clay. He's—"

That was as far as Cheron got before Crystal's eyes fairly bugged out of her head, and she let out a low whistle. "Wow. You are like, movie star good-looking."

When Clay shot Ricki a look that clearly said "Help," Ricki grinned and stepped forward, cutting off Crystal's immediate line of sight to Clay. "He's a policeman, Crystal. A chief of police, actually."

The lab tech's mouth dropped open. "No shit? Wow. We don't have any guys on the Bellingham force that look like that." She turned to face Cheron, who frowned back at her. "You said you were starting up a lab in the same town as all these guys. Do you need a lab tech?"

When Cheron only blinked at the young woman, Ricki tapped Crystal on the shoulder. "Did I see your ride here drop you off?"

She bobbed her head up and down, then reached into her pocket. Drawing out several sticks of gum, she began to expertly unwrap them using only one hand. "Oh yeah. That was my boyfriend. I would have introduced him, but he had to get back."

"Uh-huh. And will he be coming by to take you back to Bellingham?" Ricki asked.

Crystal nodded again as she popped the sticks of gum into her mouth. "Oh yeah. No worries. He'll be here first thing in the morning." She smiled. "I don't own a car. It's my part in reducing my carbon footprint."

Gin lifted a skeptical eyebrow. "So your boyfriend drives you around? How's that working out for *his* carbon footprint?"

"It's still only one car instead of two," Crystal stubbornly maintained. "Anyway, I'm going to need to bunk here tonight." She peeked around Ricki to look at Clay. "Got any space available in your room?"

Clay's eyes narrowed. "I thought you said that was your boyfriend who dropped you off?"

"He is, but we have a flexible arrangement." Crystal glanced over at Stephen and winked. "How about you?"

The FBI agent gave her a polite smile. "My arrangement isn't so flexible. I'm married." He pointed at Gin. "To her cousin, so there is no chance my wife wouldn't hear about you bunking down in my room."

Ricki stared at Gin, partially stunned. "Your cousin? Your partner's wife is your cousin?"

Gin nodded. "Carrie. I told you about her."

"You didn't mention she was your cousin." Ricki put her hands on her hips as her gaze narrowed on Gin's face. "Anything else you want to share?" Ricki frowned when that closed look in Gin's eyes slammed down once again. Feeling as much as seeing her discomfort, Ricki quickly shifted the group's attention back to Crystal. "What about Anchorman? Do you have any offers to make to him?"

Crystal laughed, then reached out and gave Ricki a light punch in the arm. "Man, these guys are too easy." She looked at Stephen and then Clay with a wide grin. "Come on. You're all too old for me." She jerked her thumb over her shoulder, toward the kitchen. "Especially him."

"And I'm thanking the Lord for small favors," Anchorman shot back.

"I'm already sharing a room with Gin," Cheron said, along with a pleading look at Ricki.

Throwing her hands into the air, Ricki gave in for the sake of peace all around. "Fine." She looked at Crystal. "You can bunk in with me, but it's going to be an air mattress on the floor."

Crystal frowned. "I'll flip you for the bed."

"No," Ricki said firmly. "Unless you put anything higher than a two in front of your age, you'll take the air mattress, and I'll keep the bed, thank you very much."

The tech's lower lip stuck out for a second and then she gave it up and simply shrugged. "Fine. So where's this crime scene?"

"Good question. We should get out there before the entire morning burns away." Ricki looked over at Gin. "Last chance to tag along?"

"Nope," Gin said. "However, I will set up the air mattress in your room." When Ricki rolled her eyes, Gin laughed. "You're welcome. Happy to help."

"Let me grab my bag, and we'll go," Cheron said.

A few minutes later, they were all piling into the SUV. Crystal's eyes widened when Anchorman climbed into his seat, holding his rifle.

"What do you need that for? I don't like guns."

"That's too bad," Anchorman said as he buckled his seatbelt. "We're searching for a killer, so the rifle is coming with us."

"No one else is bringing a gun along," Crystal stoutly declared. "Maybe you're just paranoid."

Cheron politely cleared her throat. "Well now, I do believe several of them have a weapon harness on, so they're all carrying. But don't worry. They won't use them unless it's absolutely necessary."

The tech's mouth dropped open, and she looked around the cab of the SUV. "Okay. How many of you are carrying guns?" When three hands immediately lifted into the air, she crossed her arms over her chest and flopped back against the seat. "Oh, great."

"Are you telling me when you go out to a crime scene, the police officers there aren't carrying guns?" Anchorman demanded.

"I don't do a lot of field work," Crystal mumbled.

"Oh great," Clay said under his breath, mimicking Crystal and earning him a discreet poke in his arm from Ricki.

"We'll be in and out in no time," Ricki told her. "And it's part of our job to carry a gun."

Crystal gave Anchorman an accusing look. "Not yours. Cheron told me you're a cook who works at Ricki's diner and comes along to help only when she's shorthanded."

"When I come along to help, I'm not coming as the cook," Anchorman said calmly. "It's because I was in the Marines." When Crystal blinked at him, he smiled. "As a sniper."

"Holy shit." Crystal sank farther down into the seat, her head dropping until her chin was touching her chest. When Ricki swiveled around and glared at Anchorman, he grinned. Okay. Maybe the young tech deserved that for taking a swipe at all the guys' egos, but she still expected them to be the adults in the room.

"It's only a five-minute drive, Crystal," she said. "And they're just trying to pull your string. Ignore them."

"Fine with me," the tech mumbled.

Crystal didn't say another word until they pulled up in front of Jimmy's barn. Ricki frowned as she stepped out of the car. The crime scene tape Cheron had asked Anchorman to string across the door was on the ground, and one side of the oversized doors was partially ajar. She knew very good and well that they had made sure to close it. They'd even secured the doors by simply shoving a narrow piece of wood through the handles. Now, that piece of wood was lying on the ground, and she didn't think the wind had put it there. Not wanting to alarm Crystal, she walked to the front of the car where Clay was already waiting.

"A door is open," he said in a low voice.

"Yeah, I saw that." Ricki waved at Anchorman, who trotted up to join them. "The door's open and it shouldn't be.

Keep Cheron and Crystal behind us, and the car between them and the house."

"Will do," Anchorman said. He turned around and walked back to where Cheron was talking to Crystal while Ricki and Clay walked toward the barn. Clay kept an eye on the house as Ricki yanked open the barn door, her gun drawn. She was immediately hit with a smell that was strong enough to make her eyes sting. It was also one she knew very well. And by the surprised gasps behind her, so did Crystal and Cheron.

Bleach. *Shit.*

As the doctor and lab tech ran toward the barn, Ricki stepped inside. The odor was strong, but not overpowering, and there was no mistaking where the bleach had been dumped. It was all over the crime scene.

"Who the hell did that?" Clay asked out loud as he came up beside Ricki.

"Oh my, oh my." Cheron skidded to a stop, her hands on her cheeks. "It's destroyed."

"Right down to the dirt," Crystal agreed. "I've never heard of anyone pouring bleach on a crime scene." She turned horrified eyes to Cheron. "What do we do now?"

"What we do is you two go outside with Anchorman. Ricki and I will check out the rest of the barn," Clay said.

Crystal took another look at the scene and vigorously nodded her agreement. "I think that's good, and then we're going to get out of here, right?"

"That's right," Ricki said. *But not before we check out the house, too,* she amended silently. While Anchorman shepherded Cheron and Crystal toward the door, Ricki and Clay turned to face the dark interior. They'd only gone two steps when a voice rang out.

"Stop where you are. All of you."

Chapter 38

EVERYONE FROZE, except for Crystal, who threw herself at Cheron. The doctor patted the young tech's back and glared into the darkness. "You're scaring her to death."

A shadowy figure moved through the dark at the far end of the barn. Anchorman instantly countered by shifting his position to stand between the figure and the two women clinging to each other.

"I said don't move."

"Fine," the former Marine snapped out. "Then you don't move either."

"Where's the old woman?"

Ricki frowned. The old woman? There was only one that she knew of who hung around Jimmy's place. "She's moved into the Last Stop."

There was a loud snort that echoed through the rickety building. "That ratty bar? What did she do that for?"

Ricki slowly relaxed. Crossing her arms over her chest, she tilted her head to the side. "You seem to know a lot about what goes on in Glacier. About Molly, and this place of Jimmy's, and that the Last Stop is a bar. How long have you been keeping track of your old hometown, Mr. Modonsky?"

The figure moved forward, coming out of the shadows enough to form into a tall, thin man with a long beard, dressed in overalls and holding a gun that was clearly aimed in their direction.

"That wouldn't be a Winchester 1894, by any chance, would it?" Ricki asked.

"It's good for hunting. Has been for more than a hundred years. Are you Agent James?" The hermit gestured at Clay with the barrel of his gun. "Who is that with you?"

"This is Clay Thomas. He's the chief of police in the Bay."

"I know where that is. Who's the other fellow? The one that walks like a military man?"

"You have a good eye, Mr. Modonsky. That's Anchorman. He was in the Marines," Ricki said, keeping her tone polite. "He needs to take the other women out of here."

Walter shook his head. "I don't think so." He raised his voice, irritation bleeding through the words. "And you, quit your blubbering. I don't kill women."

Crystal's sobs immediately subsided into sniffles, her arms clamped around Cheron's waist.

"How about men? Do you kill men, Mr. Modonsky? Because wherever you show up, there also seems to be a dead body."

"Oh my God," Crystal wailed, the sound abruptly cut off when Cheron slapped a hand across her mouth.

"How do you know my name? No one besides my wife has known my name for forty years."

Ricki lifted an eyebrow. His wife? "That's odd, because we couldn't find any marriage certificate with your name on it, Mr. Modonsky."

He let out another snort. "We married ourselves, and I've considered her my wife for forty-eight years. We were together for forty-five of those, but she's gone now."

"I'm sorry," Ricki said softly.

"And I didn't kill any of those men."

The underlying anger in his voice rang through the barn. From the corner of her eye, Ricki saw Clay's shoulders tense up and his stance widen. One wrong word and this would not end well for any of them.

"Okay. You didn't kill anyone," Ricki said. "Can you tell me who did?"

"I've been telling you," Walter said.

"All you've told me is to look for the ties to the banker," Ricki pointed out reasonably. "And I'm assuming you were referring to Hontel?"

The gun pointed at them lowered an inch. "At least you got that far."

"And there were two shooters up at that camp, weren't there?" Ricki went on. "One of them chased Santiago Garcia through the forest before killing him, then unloaded half the cocaine in his backpack and took the other half with him. Isn't that right?"

"Mostly right," Walter said. "But you still have a ways to go."

"How long has the cartel been running drugs through the park?"

There was a long sigh from the other end of the barn. "About a year, near as I can figure. I watched them for a while. I didn't like it, but they kept to themselves, so I just watched them. And then the killing started." He shook his head. "I knew they were camped there. I was staying at the lower cabin because I intended to check on them. That's when I heard the shots. By the time I thought it was safe to take a look, they were just leaving. Taking those backpacks with them and abandoning everything else. I knew one of them was missing, so I destroyed the rest of the camp and went looking for him the next morning. Followed a trail and ran into those two idiot hunters." He went silent for a long moment. "Did you catch those two?"

"We did," Ricki said. "Put them under arrest and shipped them out of the park."

"That's a good thing." He shifted the barrel of his gun slightly. "Well. Got what I came to find out, so I'll be going. I have other things to do. You put those killers behind bars too, so I won't have to do anything to them. Or you, if you waste any time trying to catch me."

"If you didn't kill anyone, we aren't interested in catching you, Mr. Modonsky. But if you know who did kill those men, you need to tell me now," Ricki said.

"I can't," he stated flatly. "You'll have to figure it out on your own."

"Is Jimmy the one who was leaving supplies up at the cabin?" Ricki asked, rapidly shifting her line of questioning to keep him talking.

"Not telling you that either," Walter said.

"Because if he was, I'm sorry to inform you he was murdered two, maybe three days ago. Right here, as a matter of fact."

There was another short period of silence before Walter said, "I know."

Ricki's eyes narrowed. "You knew? Did you put the bleach on the floor? Because that's not helping your story that you haven't killed anyone."

"I didn't put the bleach there. It's nasty stuff and stinks to high heaven." Walter stepped farther into the light, but not enough that Ricki could make out his features. "Now, all of you move over to the side and face that wall." When no one moved, the sound of a hammer dropping into full cock position made a terrifying noise in the dark.

Ricki unfolded her arms and held her hands up. "Okay, okay. We're moving." She nodded at Clay and Anchorman, who slowly moved to the left, bringing Crystal and Cheron with them until they were all pressed up against the wall.

Walter Modonsky slowly walked toward the barn door,

keeping his gun trained on them and the hood of his jacket pulled down low over his forehead. He didn't say another word, but the minute he'd backed out of the barn, the doors slammed shut. Ricki, Clay, and Anchorman all raced forward, but not before Walter got the piece of wood jammed back through the door handles.

"Stand back," Clay said. He and Anchorman each lifted a heavily booted foot and rammed it into the door. The wood keeping the doors from opening splintered into small pieces as the doors swung open, one of them sagging as it banged against the side with enough force that the upper hinge came loose. Ricki raced into the dirt yard along with Anchorman and Clay, her gun drawn, but the hermit was nowhere to be seen.

"And poof," she said under her breath, gazing all around the yard. "Isn't that just great?"

Chapter 39

IT WAS a disgusted group that tromped into the house, with Cheron still keeping a comforting arm around Crystal. Ricki peeled off her jacket and unbuckled her shoulder harness, hanging both of them on a hook in the foyer before stalking into the living room and flopping down on one of the chairs.

When Clay got settled on the couch, she looked over at him, her blue eyes radiating annoyance. "How does he do that? Just poof out of sight like that?"

Clay shrugged. "Years of practice, I guess." He pushed himself off the couch and walked toward the kitchen. "Does anyone want a beer? I intend to actually finish this one."

"Still on duty," Ricki said. "But help yourself."

"Thanks, I will."

Behind her, Ricki heard the refrigerator door open and then shut again, followed by the tread of footsteps coming down the stairs.

"I have Crystal settled on the air mattress," Cheron declared. "But I think she needs to go home."

Anchorman lifted the bottle of beer that Clay had tossed him. "I'll second that."

Cheron put her hands on her narrow hips and looked

from Anchorman to Clay and then back again. "One of you should drive her."

Both men immediately protested as Cheron stood patiently and waited them out.

"Well," Gin said from her sprawled-out position in her favorite chair. She gestured toward Stephen, who was occupying one of the stools at the kitchen island, his laptop open in front of him. "Don't mind us. But it would be nice to know what's going on." She glanced at the ceiling. "What happened to our lab tech?"

"The hermit happened," Anchorman said with a shrug. "He wasn't much considering all the hype about the guy, but he managed to really spook the kid."

"He was enough to keep you standing still at gunpoint," Cheron pointed out. She walked over to the couch and took a seat next to Clay. "Both of you," she said, giving the chief a pointed look.

Gin's mouth was wide open when she turned her head to look at Ricki. "The hermit was there? At the barn?"

Ricki nodded, still feeling put out by the whole thing. "One Walter Modonsky, in person. He was there when we arrived, and might or might not have dumped bleach all over our crime scene."

"Bleach?" Gin said, clearly astonished. "Well, that's bad. Really bad."

Cheron made a distressed sound deep in her throat. "Ruined is what it is. Completely ruined."

"Luckily when it comes to Jimmy's murder, we have a crime scene to spare," Gin said. She was sitting up straight, her hands gripping the arms of the chair. "What did he say? Anything? Did he kill all the drug runners? How about the coke? Does he have the coke?"

"It was pretty much a no across the board," Ricki replied. "At least that's what he says. He claims they were all dead when he got there, and he found Garcia's body just before those hunters did."

"And he won't tell us anything about who did kill those six men, plus Jimmy Blighton, or who even took the drugs," Clay said. "Although we know for a fact he took ten bricks, so who's to say he doesn't have them all?"

Ricki looked at him, her forehead wrinkled as she silently chased a thought lingering in the back of her mind. There was something about what Clay had said that didn't sit right with her. But she couldn't catch it before Stephen swiveled around on the stool until he was facing the group in the living room.

"I'm sorry to add to your crappy day," the FBI agent said. "But since you didn't answer your phone, Dan called me." He focused on Ricki. "First, he wanted you to know that Mabry Garner passed away three months ago. And her daughter said it was a lovely memorial. He also said if there's anything else you need, just give him a call."

Ricki's mouth pulled down at the news. Mrs. Garner had a memorial service three months ago?

"And I have some news about that twenty thousand," Stephen announced.

Her attention immediately diverted from her own jumbled thoughts, Ricki leaned forward in her chair. "What news?"

"It wasn't a payment from a cartel, or any other drug-related enterprise. It came through another bank from an account owned by our friendly banker, Mr. Hontel." Stephen turned back to his computer screen. "And it gets better. Hontel deposited almost fifty thousand into that same side account of his yesterday, which he then wired to an account in the Cayman Islands this morning."

"Where did that money come from?" Ricki asked.

"I don't know, but it's about the worth of a two-pound brick of cocaine," Gin said. "Give or take. I'm thinking he got one just like Jimmy did, only Hontel cashed his in instead of snorting it up his nose."

"Not enough for us to get a warrant to search his place," Ricki said. "But it's a start."

Stephen looked over his shoulder and grinned. "And this will be the finish. Take a look at this." He picked up his laptop and walked it over to the coffee table. Setting it down, he tapped on the keys as Ricki, Clay, Anchorman, and Cheron gathered in closer. "The boss sent me this footage, taken at Hontel's second bank, where he has that same personal account."

The black-and-white video showed customers coming and going through the bank's front door. About thirty seconds in, the slightly rotund and balding figure of Frank Hontel came into the frame. He pushed open the glass door and stepped through it before holding it politely while an elderly woman walked into the bank. Once he'd let go of the door, Hontel quickly passed out of the camera range. Stephen looked at his audience, a gleeful smile on his face. "Well? How about that?"

"Well what?" Anchorman asked. "The guy needs to ditch the comb-over and either lose thirty pounds or buy bigger clothes. He looked like a stuffed sausage in that jacket."

Stephen beamed. "Exactly. The jacket. I might not have caught it but for the fact Senior Special Agent Todd Barron, who is our boss, is a clotheshorse. Gin caught it too." When he was met with silence, he patiently replayed the tape, stopping it at the best full view of Frank Hontel.

When you grow up without any flash. Gin's words echoed in Ricki's mind. Flash. She leaned in closer and stared at the screen. "The jacket." She glanced over at Clay. "He's wearing that three-thousand-dollar jacket that belonged to Jimmy. And a couple of sizes too small for him, too."

Clay's eyebrows shot up. "Yeah. He is." He exchanged a grin with Ricki. "Now, I wonder where old Frank got that?"

"It's enough to at least bring him in for questioning," Ricki declared. "Along with his interesting bank deposits."

"For the murder," Gin agreed. "But I doubt if you'll get a federal warrant to search his place for the drugs without something more."

"But that jacket should be enough to get the local law enforcement a look at his place," Clay said. "All we need is a warrant. And some local law enforcement to go along with it." When Gin gave him a speculative look, he shook his head. "I'm not local enough. He hasn't done anything in my jurisdiction."

"But I know someone who is," Ricki said. "Crowder." She got out her phone and scrolled through her contacts. When she found his number, she hesitated before tapping on it. "We still need that warrant, and Hamilton is out of town." She looked at Clay. "What about Andre?"

Clay immediately reached into his back pocket for his own cell phone. "His area is Seattle, but I'm sure he knows the DA in Bellingham."

Ricki nodded and stepped into the kitchen to call Crowder, a plan already forming in her mind. It only took five minutes for the sergeant to understand and agree to meet Ricki at Frank Hontel's place, the location of which she would text to him as soon as she had it. "I need a home address," she told Stephen as she walked back into the living room.

The FBI agent lifted a half sheet of paper off the coffee table and waved it in the air. "I already gave it to Clay. Here's your copy."

"Thanks." She quickly sent off a text to Crowder, then moved to take Clay's empty spot on the couch, next to Cheron. "I need a favor."

Cheron adjusted her glasses and smiled. "What's that?"

"Someone needs to drive Crystal back to Bellingham tonight. She shouldn't stay here. She's too shook up."

The doctor nodded her agreement. "That would be an

excellent idea. Maybe we could drop her off on our way to search this Mr. Hontel's home?"

Ricki glanced down at the paper she was still holding. "He lives in an apartment, I think. And here's the favor. I need you to drop her off and then head back to the Bay."

"Why?" Cheron's chin hardened into a stubborn line. "I'm part of the team, so I should stay and—"

"Part of being a team is doing what's best for it. You know that," Ricki cut in. "Crystal needs to get home so she doesn't fall completely apart, and from this point on, the team is going to be in full hunting mode." She didn't gentle her voice, knowing that would never work with Cheron. Instead, she kept to a brisk, practical tone. "You know that isn't your strong point, and you might be a distraction." Now she lowered her voice to a whisper. "Especially for Anchorman, and you've seen how Modonsky can sneak up even on him. We'll need to be very careful."

The doctor's shoulders slumped as the defiance faded out of her gaze. "That's true." She took in a deep breath and closed her eyes.

Her lips moved silently in a chant she'd started practicing recently whenever she needed to calm down. A habit probably spurred on by dealing with Anchorman. Maybe Cheron should pass it along to the man's three ex-wives. Ricki grinned at the thought.

"All right," Cheron said when she opened her eyes. "But we'll need the car."

"The SUV is the only vehicle big enough to carry all of us," Ricki said just as Clay stepped back into the room. "You'll have to take Clay's truck."

The chief stared at Ricki. "Take Clay's truck where?"

Ricki cleared her throat and got to her feet so she was on the same level as Clay. "Cheron needs to drive Crystal home and then head back to the Bay."

"You're asking me if Cheron can drive my truck—and

we're talking about my fairly new, unscratched truck here—to Bellingham and then to the Bay?"

The doctor popped up off the couch, her hand held out. "That's right. And I'll need the keys, please."

Reaching slowly into his pocket, Clay removed a set of keys and dropped them into the doctor's outstretched hand. "There you go." As Cheron hurried toward the stairs, Clay sent Ricki a look that promised payback before turning his head to stare at Anchorman, who was still sitting on the couch. "If she gets one scratch on my truck, you're paying."

The ex-Marine scrunched up his face in a pained look, but he nodded. "Understood."

Blowing out one last annoyed breath, Clay glanced back at Ricki. "Andre said to give him a couple of hours and he'll have our warrant."

Ricki's smile dripped with satisfaction. "Which is just about what it will take to drive to Bellingham, so we need to get going." As the rest of the team shifted into high gear, Ricki dropped onto the couch and tapped on Dan's number. When he picked up, she rattled off a request, then took in a slow breath.

"And I also would appreciate it if you'd set up a meeting between Ranger Darren Jenson and me here in Glacier tomorrow afternoon."

Chapter 40

THE APARTMENT complex Frank Hontel lived in was large, spread out, and located in a solid middle-class section of the city. Its brick facade would have fit in anywhere in the state, and the landscaping along the walkway leading to the three-story structure was a solid green without any pops of color in it. A deputy made a side trip to the parking slot assigned to apartment 321 and found a compact black car with license plates matching Hontel's vehicle occupying the space.

With verification that the suspect was home, Sergeant Crowder gave a solid rap on the door, then stepped back so whoever put their eye to the peephole could get a good look at him and his uniform. "Mr. Hontel? I'm Sergeant Crowder with the Whatcom County Sheriff's Department. We need to speak with you, sir." When he was met with nothing but silence, he turned up the volume on his voice a notch. "I'd appreciate you answering the door, Mr. Hontel. I'd hate to disturb your neighbors by standing here and shouting for the next hour."

Within moments there was the scraping sound of metal chains and locks being disengaged. The door opened enough for Frank Hontel to peer through a six-inch crack.

"What can I do for you, Officer?"

The sergeant smiled and stuck a folded paper through the crack, poking it straight into Hontel's chest. "I need to give you this."

Frowning, Hontel automatically grabbed the paper. "What is it?"

Crowder placed a beefy palm on the door and gave it a hard shove, pushing a startled Hontel back several feet. "It's a search warrant. And I'll need you to come down to the station to answer a few questions."

"Search warrant?" Hontel goggled at the two officers who came in right behind Crowder. "Why? This must be a mistake. I haven't done anything wrong."

"We're investigating a murder that happened in Glacier a few days ago. Our job is to serve the warrant, search the place, and collect you, in that order. Deciding right and wrong is above my pay grade." Crowder walked right toward Hontel, who scrambled to back up several steps. Satisfied the banker was out of the way, the sergeant jerked a thumb over his shoulder. "But you can talk it over with them. They have a few questions of their own."

Hontel's gaze flew past the sergeant. When it landed on Ricki, with Gin right beside her, he froze. "I've already talked to you. I told you I don't know who's Jimmy's next of kin, or about any money he wired out of the country."

"How about money *you* wired out of the country?" Gin asked. "Specifically, to the Cayman Islands. Fifty thousand is a lot of cash, Frank. Where did it come from?"

While Gin continued to pepper the banker with questions, Ricki slowly walked around the living room. Most of the room was taken up by a couch, two chairs, and a coffee table, clustered around a wall with a shelving unit and entertainment center holding a TV.

She walked over to one shelf and studied the row of pictures. A young boy of about ten had his hand on a small girl's shoulder. They were standing with two adults in front of a small tract house. *Family,* Ricki silently guessed, seeing the adult Frank Hontel in the face of the boy and in the grown man standing behind him. The same group showed up in the next picture on the shores of a lake, and again in a third photo taken in front of a cabin.

Ricki started to turn away when she paused, frowning. She picked up the third picture and studied it carefully. She knew that cabin. The two small square windows had boards across them now, but she would swear that was the cabin where the hermit picked up his supplies.

She carried the picture over to where Hontel was standing. He was alternating between shouting at Gin and the sergeant. Clay emerged from the back bedroom carrying a jacket over his arm. He held it up for Hontel to see.

"I found it. Hanging right there in his closet with his off-the-rack suits." Clay gave the garment a gentle shake. "That's a bad setting for a Burberry jacket."

"Where did you get the money for that, Frank?" Ricki asked. "Maybe from the same little income source that let you send fifty thousand to the Cayman Islands, or afford getaways to the beach or a private cabin?"

"That's not family money," the banker sneered. "There is no family money. We were only driving by that lake, and we didn't have to pay for that cabin. My great-grandfather was a logger, and he built that cabin and homesteaded that land. It still belongs to us, no matter what the government says."

"Is that right?" Ricki murmured with a last look at the picture. When she raised her eyes again, it was to pin Hontel with a hard stare. "And how about the jacket? Did that come from your great-grandfather, too?"

"A friend gave it to me," he snapped.

"Now that wouldn't have been Jimmy by any chance, would it?" Gin drawled. "I think the good sergeant here is going to want to ask you some questions about the timing of that gift. And I'd like to know what you did with your brick of cocaine." She crossed her arms as the color drained out of Hontel's face and a line of sweat popped up on his brow. "Now, your buddy Jimmy was snorting his away when he could have sold it. A brick like that would bring in close to 50k." She bared her teeth in a nasty smile. "Wouldn't it, Frank?" She looked slowly around. "I wonder if we'll find any residue around here, or on some of your clothes."

When the banker collapsed onto the floor and sobbed, Ricki once again left him to Gin as she walked away to answer her cell phone. It was Dan. She stepped into the hallway to get out of range of Hontel's increasingly loud wails.

"What is it, Dan? What have you got for me?"

"Ranger Jenson will be at your place tomorrow afternoon between three and four," the researcher said.

Ricki's expression drooped around the edges. She hoped nothing would come of that interview, but she had to cover all her bases. "What about my call?"

"No problem getting hold of Margaret Modonsky, Walter Modonsky's only surviving sibling. And her married name is Dunmore, by the way. It was late, but I gave her a call, and she's willing to talk to you at eight tomorrow morning, Pacific time. That would be ten in the Midwest. How did the warrant work out?" he asked, and Ricki could hear the smile in his voice. "I got a call from DA Hudson. He wanted to keep Hamilton in the loop." Ricki winced when Dan laughed. He didn't wait for her response but only said, "I'm sure you'll be hearing about this," before he hung up.

She was sure of it too, and her annoyance showed on her face when she turned around and found Crowder standing right behind her.

"I was only waiting for you to finish up. I wasn't eavesdropping," he said. When she rolled her eyes, he laughed. "I wanted to thank you for expediting the search warrant and for giving us this collar. I have a feeling Frank Hontel is going to sing like a canary."

Ricki wrinkled her nose at the loud wails coming through the open door of the apartment. "I think you're probably right, Sergeant, and the collar was always yours."

The big man shook his head and indulged in his habit of sticking his thumbs into his belt. "We found that body in a national forest, not on state or county land."

"True," Ricki said, finding her smile. "But we found the actual murder scene in Glacier, and that is covered by the county, so the collar is yours."

Crowder chuckled. "And so is the paperwork, I guess. How about your murders up in the park? Having any luck?"

"Some. I'm hoping for a breakthrough tomorrow."

Crowder nodded, and his gaze took on a feral gleam. "Then I'll just say good luck, and good hunting. If you need any help, call me."

Ricki nodded her thanks. "I'll do that, Sergeant."

Chapter 41

Ricki stood in front of the couch, looking out the large picture window at the world outside, which had turned into a snow globe overnight. A small storm had passed through sometime after midnight, leaving behind a fairy-dusting of snow on the trees, the ground, and the cars parked on the street. All that was needed to complete the picture was a doe gracefully walking across the landscape. Enjoying the quiet of the moment, Ricki continued to sip her coffee while she waited for Clay to grab a mug of his own and join her.

"Still building a picture in your head?" he asked, as he stopped and stood beside her.

She glanced up at him. "Picture?"

He smiled. "When you're putting the pieces of a puzzle together, you get quiet. Like you were after we came back back from Hontel's apartment last night." He took a long sip from his steaming mug as he watched her. "Like you are now."

Her gaze returned to the idyllic scene outside the window. "I've never been the chatty type."

"No," Clay acknowledged. "But you are good at puzzles and patterns. What are you thinking?"

She turned from the window and watched Anchorman puttering away in the kitchen, his expression showing the same intensity as when he had a lock on a target. "That some people are always who they are, no matter what role they're playing." She nodded at the former Marine working away in the kitchen. "Whether they're being a sniper or a cook. And some people are like chameleons. They take on the character of the role, no matter what it is."

Clay laughed softly. "So, some leopards never change their spots and others do nothing but change them, or something like that?"

She grinned. Trust the chief to strip it all down to its simplest element. "Yeah. Something like that."

"And who is the spot-changer in the puzzle you're assembling?"

"I think for this all to make sense, there has to be more than one person who knows that park like the back of his hand." She looked at the iPad she'd brought down with her and was now laying on on the coffee table. "And I'm hoping Margaret Modonsky Dunmore can tell us who that is." She checked her watch, then picked up the iPad. Navigating over to the FaceTime app, she put in the phone number Dan had sent her.

It only took a few seconds for a face to appear on her screen, telling her that Margaret Dunmore had been waiting for her call. Ricki smiled at the comfortable face beaming back at her.

"Good morning, Mrs. Dunmore. I'm Special Agent Ricki James with the Investigative Services Branch of the National Park Service."

Brown eyes crinkled in amusement. "My, isn't that a mouthful? Hello there, Special Agent Ricki James. I'm Margaret Modonsky Dunmore, of the Family Acres farm near Springfield, Illinois." She laughed. "Ha. See? Anyone can have a title." Margaret's face moved closer to the screen. "You are very pretty to be some kind of investigator. Do you carry a gun, dear?"

Liking the woman with her pure-white hair and friendly smile, Ricki quirked an eyebrow. "When it's necessary."

"And I'll bet you hit whatever you aim at, don't you?"

Ricki laughed. "As a matter of fact, I do."

"Ah, well then." Margaret's smile faded a little. "And will you be aiming at my baby brother? Not that I would entirely blame you. Walt was always a stubborn handful. But I thought he was dead these past fifty years, so hearing he's still alive has been a bit of a shock."

"Then you haven't seen or heard from your brother in all that time, Mrs. Dunmore?" Ricki asked.

"You can call me Maggie. Everyone does. And I'll be calling you Ricki, because I'm over seventy and saying your whole title is too much for me to have to bother with." When Ricki smiled, Margaret did too before she sighed. "But to answer your question, Ricki, no, I haven't seen or heard from my brother in almost fifty years. Actually, forty-eight to be exact. He disappeared when he was twenty years old. I remember it because he vanished just a month after my wedding. My husband and I were already in Illinois, working on his daddy's farm, when my mama called and said no one had seen or heard from Walt for a few weeks."

"The story I was told was that your brother killed someone and fled when the police came to arrest him," Ricki said, stopping when Margaret vehemently shook her head.

"I heard that pile of bull crap, too. From my mama, may she rest in peace. She called and told me about that stupid rumor. It didn't start making the rounds until a good five years after Walt disappeared. It upset my mama, because if anyone was killed, it was Walt. That was the only explanation we could come up with. Someone had killed my brother and dumped his body in the woods where it would never be found." She let out a snort. "I should have known better.

Should have known he went to defend that girl's rights. He was crazy about that chit from the moment he laid eyes on her."

Ricki's nerves started to tingle, and off to the side, well out of Margaret's sight, both Clay and Anchorman shifted their weight, coming to full attention. "What chit would that be, Maggie?"

Maggie lifted a heavily veined hand and waved it in the air. "Oh, some young thing that came to Glacier to spend the summer with her cousin—who was every bit as silly as she was, as I recall. But the cousin was tight with that Bain kid. Back then she went by Lynnie or something like that, and I don't recall the boy's first name, but he and Walt were friends. That's how my brother met Mary. And I certainly remember her name. Just sixteen years old and a cheeky little thing. Wore tight shorts and even tighter tops, and she had her eye on Walt right from the start. He was a very handsome boy and could have had his pick of the litter, if you know what I mean."

"Mary," Ricki repeated. "What was Mary's last name?"

The older woman's face scrunched up. "Oh dear. I just don't remember. There was something funny about it, but I can't quite put my finger on it."

"That's okay," Ricki soothed. "Who was violating the girl's rights?"

"What?" Maggie blinked rapidly, looking confused until suddenly her expression cleared. "Oh. That thing my brother was always going on about." She laughed, a surprisingly deep, infectious sound that had even Clay and Anchorman smiling. "It was over some bit of land her grandfather had laid claim to. Or maybe it was her great-grandfather, I don't know. One of those people. Anyway, she was always going on about it, claiming the government had taken it away from the family, and they had a right to it because they had homesteaded the place. I think they even took it to court. I don't remember exactly why." Maggie sighed. "My memory isn't as good as it used to be."

"I think your memory is just fine, Maggie," Ricki said slowly. "Did this Mary ever mention this homestead being in the middle of North Cascades Park?"

Maggie clapped her hands in delight. "Why, yes. That was it. Walt told me that Mary said her great-grandfather—yes, that was it—her great-grandfather . . . well, he built a cabin up there before it became a park, so he'd homesteaded the land." Maggie shook her head. "I told Walt that you can only homestead unclaimed land, and all that area was owned by the federal government, so they weren't homesteading, they were squatting."

"A cabin. In the park," Ricki repeated. "And Walt knew where it was?"

"Oh sure. My brother loved the outdoors. He was an excellent hunter, with a rifle or a bow. He was even teaching Mary how to hunt."

I'll bet he taught Mary a lot, Ricki thought. "This Mary . . . does the last name Hontel sound familiar to you?" Ricki held up a warning hand as Gin and Stephen came down the stairs. The two FBI agents quietly stood in the foyer, their necks craned to catch every word broadcasting from Ricki's iPad.

"Well now," Maggie laughed. "Aren't you the clever one? That's it. If you just took that 'n' out, they would have been the hotels. That's what I used to think was so funny about it."

"Yeah, that is kind of funny," Ricki agreed, her smile no longer reaching her eyes. "Do you know what happened to Mary?"

Maggie's mouth turned down at the corners. "That's kind of funny, too. My mama told me she heard the girl had left town to marry a boy from California or someplace like that. I don't believe mama ever saw her again, but then why would she? With Walt gone, there was no reason for her to come around anymore. It could be the reason Walt left, now that I think on it. He might have been heartbroken that she just upped and married someone else." She hesitated, then drew in an audible breath. "How much trouble is Walt in?"

Ricki wished she could say none, but that would be really stretching it since at this point, she wasn't sure. So she went for honesty. "I don't know, Maggie. But I'm going to do everything I can to help him out."

Maggie's relief was all over her face. "That's good, and I appreciate it. Walt will too once he gets his head out of his butt." Her chin trembled, but her eyes were clear when she looked straight into the screen. "The next time you see him, you tell him to call me. You have my number."

"I'll do that, Maggie," Ricki said with a smile. "And thank you. You've been a big help."

"Glad to hear it. Oh, and there's one more thing I should have mentioned about Mary before I go. Farm chores don't wait on anyone." She laughed. "But it's about that girl. She introduced herself as Mary Hontel, but since her mother's name was also Mary—which was, of course, a ridiculous thing—Walt always called her by the same nickname her family used."

"Would that be Molly?" Ricki asked.

"Like I said, Ricki. You really are the clever one. Goodbye now." Maggie's smile was back just before the screen went blank. Ricki leaned against the couch cushions, a satisfied gleam in her eyes.

"Why don't you look as stunned as the rest of us?" Gin demanded, taking a seat in her favorite chair. "Molly Hontel? So we're talking about good old Frank's sister? The one who cleans the Last Stop bar and who you spotted in that family photo?"

"Both the same person," Ricki confirmed, then shook her head. "I should have seen it. Walter Modonsky even told us to look for the ties to the banker. He wasn't talking about drugs or money. He was talking about family." She looked over at

Clay and Anchorman. "And when he said he can't tell us who the shooters were? He meant because one of them was the woman he considered his wife."

"Which means what?" Anchorman demanded. "That the old buzzard won't rat out his wife because she might get put behind bars, but he's perfectly fine if *you* put her there?"

Ricki shrugged. "That sounds right if you're the old-fashioned type, and I'm betting that Walt is."

"Okay. What do we do now?" Gin asked. "Head out to the bar and pick her up? Because I'm seeing a problem here."

"Yeah." Ricki rubbed a hand down the side of her cheek. "The odds are good her brother has already warned her." She spied Stephen, standing near the island, his laptop under his arm. "Can you look up something for me? We need to move fast. And while you're at it, we'll need a warrant to conduct a search for the drugs, and since that's what you and Gin are here for, a federal judge will do just fine."

Chapter 42

The SUV pulled into the parking lot. Five bodies were out of the car as soon as it rolled to a stop. They met in front of the vehicle, all of them carrying pistols that were loaded, drawn, and ready.

"Clay and I will go in," Ricki directed in a short, clipped tone. "Anchorman, you cover the back door. Gin and Stephen, you stay here and cover the front. Everyone be careful. Molly might be our second shooter."

As Anchorman trotted around the side of the building, Ricki counted to ten before she and Clay walked to the front door, each holding their guns up at chest level. Clay turned the handle and nodded to Ricki to let her know the door was unlocked. She counted to three, then Clay shoved open the door and Ricki stepped inside. She swept the barrel of her gun across the interior as Clay followed her in.

There wasn't anyone in the bar area. An eerie silence had Ricki's fingertips tingling with nerves. She waited as Clay checked the space behind the bar, then they started to advance again into the back hallway.

The door to the storeroom had a padlock on it, so Ricki passed it by and continued to the office. The door was open and the space empty. She exited back to the hallway just as Clay emerged from the small bathroom across from the office.

"No one," he said. He inclined his head toward the back door. "I'll let Anchorman know we're clear."

Ricki nodded and holstered her gun as she walked back into the front area with its empty tables and booths. She went directly to the front door and signaled the all clear to Gin and Stephen, shaking her head when Gin called out to ask if Molly was inside.

As the two FBI agents crossed over to the front door, Ricki ducked back inside and stood with her hands on her hips, slowly surveying the room. When her gaze passed over the bar, she spotted a piece of lined notebook paper lying on top. She walked over and leaned against the rough wooden top of the bar, letting out a short laugh when she read the note.

"What's so funny?" Gin asked. When Ricki held up the note, Gin snatched it out of her hand, glanced at it, then looked over at Ricki. "You have got to be kidding me."

"What does it say?" Stephen asked just as Clay and Anchorman came in from the back hallway.

"What does what say?" Clay looked startled when Gin thrust the note into his hands. He sighed before reading it out loud. "'Goodbye. I'm going to hit the road. Nice to have met you. Molly.'" He handed the note to Anchorman, who then passed it to Stephen. "That's a new one on me. I can't remember a suspect ever leaving me a goodbye note."

"Wonderful," Ricki said. "That's one for the books."

"Do you think the banker actually warned her?" Stephen asked. "I was sure he'd make a deal to ID the second shooter to save his own ass. But then, that was before we found out that the second shooter was his sister."

"I'm sure Hontel demanded a lawyer then called his sister the minute his lawyer arrived," Ricki said. "He probably used the lawyer's cell phone and talked to Molly before we even got back from Bellingham."

"Which was also before we knew Molly was his sister," Stephen said.

"Yeah, well, let's see if anyone else got warned," Ricki said. "We need to make another stop."

～

Ricki got out of the SUV and looked to the far end of the parking lot. The paneled van was parked in its parking place, so there was a very good chance they weren't too late after all. With the team following close behind, she strode through the front door of the Snowmelt, startling the young woman wearing a waitress uniform and stacking menus on the hostess station.

"I'm sorry," the waitress apologized. "We don't serve breakfast, and lunch doesn't start for another hour."

"We're here to see Jo," Ricki said. When the waitress looked like she was going to protest, Ricki pointed to the gold badge at her waist. "It really wasn't a request. Can you please tell me where she is?"

The young women's eyes widened and then fixed on the gun harness beneath Ricki's open parka. "She's in the office. Back there. Through the kitchen."

As Ricki strode off, she heard Anchorman's low voice behind her, talking to the waitress.

"Now, I'm just going to stand right here until Agent James finishes having her talk with your boss. And I'd appreciate it if you'd stand here and keep me company."

Ricki kept on walking, straight through the double doors that led into the kitchen. A man in a chef's hat looked up, freezing in place as she walked toward him.

"Where's Jo's office?" she asked politely, smiling her thanks when the chef silently held up a hand and pointed to a door in the back.

When Ricki walked in, Jo was at her desk, counting out a

stack of bills. When she looked up, Ricki saw the fear leap into her eyes.

"Why, Ricki, this is a surprise." She gestured toward the neat pile of money. "I'll be with you as soon as I finish preparing this bank deposit. Why don't you and your friends go make yourselves comfortable at your usual table?"

She's going to need that deposit to pay her bail, Ricki thought, but she smiled when she took a seat in the chair next to Jo's desk.

"I really can't have you in here right now," Jo said, her gaze shifting to include the other three people crowding in behind Ricki. "If you'll just—"

"You know, Jo," Ricki cut in. "It's the little things that usually trip people up. Like telling me to go chase down Mabry Garner when she passed away three months ago—with a very nice memorial service, according to her daughter. Now, since she was the gossip queen of your little town here, probably for most of her very long life, then I'm betting that the service and burial took place right here in Glacier. So I had to wonder why you didn't know that."

"It slipped my mind," Jo said quickly. "I've been so busy, I simply forgot." She dropped her eyes to her desk and slowly shook her head. "It isn't easy for a widow to run a business. Sometimes it can be overwhelming."

"Widow." Ricki pursed her lips, pretending to think it over. "Bain." She looked over at Stephen. "Wasn't that the name listed as the owner of the Snowmelt?"

Stephen smiled. "Yes, it was. Dan and Jocelyn Bain."

"That's my name," Jo said. "Jocelyn is a mouthful, so I shortened it to Jo a long time ago."

"How long ago?" Ricki asked. "Did you stop using Lynnie after you were married? Or after your close friend and cousin Mary Hontel stopped coming around?"

"M-M-Mary?" Jo stuttered out. "What makes you think I have a cousin named Mary?"

Ricki leaned back in the chair, letting one boot tap on the

tile floor. "Let's see. Who told me that? Was it her brother, Frank? No. Not Frank. He's too busy right at the moment explaining himself to the county sheriff's deputy that has him under arrest. Since the town gossip has passed on, who else would remember your cousin Mary?"

Gin leaned forward and said in a loud whisper, "I believe we heard it from Maggie."

When Jo went pale, Ricki nodded in satisfaction. "That's right. Maggie Dunmore, formerly Maggie Modonsky. I'm sure you remember the Modonskys? That would be Maggie and her younger brother, Walter. The man your cousin ran off with when she was sixteen years old." When Jo remained silent, the sound of her rapid breathing filling the small office, Ricki folded her hands and rested them on top of the desk. "No? Maybe you only remember him by his local nickname, 'the hermit'?"

"You talked to Maggie," Jo said in a small voice. "That can't be true. She's been gone from around here for decades."

Ricki shrugged. "Sorry, but we did. And we also have a warrant to search your house and business." When Jo sniffed, Ricki's smile grew broader. "Which will include your delivery van that's parked outside. No one in town is going to rob you, Jo. So I imagine that van is a pretty safe place to keep something."

"No," the restaurant owner said in a soft voice. "This is wrong. It's all wrong."

"We found the brick of cocaine in Jimmy's safe," Ricki said. "And the money Hontel got for selling his. But I'm betting that was just a good faith gesture for one of the four partners in this little scam you were part of. I'm guessing we'll find a lot more in your van."

"No. No." Jo shook her head. "I mean, I'm just holding it for someone else. That's all. I didn't do anything. I'm just holding it for a friend."

"I think this is where you get read your rights." Ricki got

up and nodded at Gin, who stepped forward and stood over Jo.

"You have the right to remain silent," Gin said as tears rolled down Jo's cheeks.

"I'm just holding it. I don't know where it came from," Jo wailed as Gin kept reciting the Miranda rights. "She just asked for a favor. You have to believe me."

"Stop talking until I'm finished," the FBI agent said. "Now, answer this question and then you can talk all you want. Do you understand these rights?"

"I understand, I understand," Jo sobbed. "I just need *you* to understand, too." She looked horrified when Gin held up a pair of zip-tie handcuffs. "What are you doing?"

Gin leaned down until she was just a couple of inches away from Jo's face. "Answer Agent James's questions, and we'll wait on these handcuffs. And I'll take the keys to that van, unless you prefer that we break into it?"

Jo's sniffles increased as she opened a desk drawer and handed a set of keys to Gin. The FBI agent took them and did an about-face, winking at Ricki as she and Stephen headed out the door.

Ricki sat down in the visitor's chair again and stared at Jo. "You helped carry the drugs out of the park."

"No, no," Jo said. "Molly did that."

"Four runners with backpacks, and four of you. We know you were there," Ricki said, delivering the lie with enough authority to have Jo cringing. "Oh, I forgot to mention that we found the four runners and their guards. They were all dead. From gunshot wounds fired from the same type of rifle Jimmy owned. And Walt too, for that matter. I'm betting he taught his wife how to shoot that same gun."

"They weren't married," Jo said, her mouth trembling. "It made Molly mad that they were never properly married."

"Did she shoot those drug runners?" Ricki asked. "There were two shooters. Was Molly one of them?"

When Jo's shoulders slumped and she nodded, Ricki's gaze narrowed on her bowed head. "Were you the other shooter?"

Jo's head jerked up. "No. It was like you said. Molly and Jimmy had the guns. Molly worked for those horrible people. She showed them how to get through the park without being seen, and sometimes Jimmy helped her. Molly knew everything about that park since she'd been living there for so long, and Walt had taught her how to hunt for food. Molly planned everything. Frank and I only carried the drugs out. No one was supposed to get hurt, but after they lined them all up, Molly and Jimmy just started shooting." Jo closed her eyes, but the tears continued to leak out from under her eyelids. "No one was supposed to get hurt. We were only going to tie them up, that's all. But Molly said that shooting them was kinder." Jo's eyes opened and she turned a watery, pleading look on Ricki. "She's crazy. Why else would she say that?"

"Oh, I don't know," Ricki drawled. "Maybe being tied up and left out to freeze to death, or as an easy meal for some four-legged predator, didn't sound so good to Molly either."

Jo stared at her. "I . . . I . . . ." Unable to get past that, her whole body collapsed inward. "What do you want me to tell you? I want to make a deal."

"Where's Molly?" Ricki demanded.

"At the bar?" Jo ventured, then recoiled at the quick flash of anger in Ricki's eyes.

"Don't lie to me. I have seven dead bodies in the morgue, so don't you lie to me. Where's Molly?"

Stephen stuck his head into the office, bracing one hand against the doorframe. "Gin wanted me to let you know that one of the backpacks is missing, and another one only has eight bricks in it."

Ricki frowned. Eight would be half of one backpack, less the two given to Hontel and Jimmy, with the remaining ten bricks having gone up in smoke on the highway. That meant a full backpack was missing, with a million dollars' worth of cocaine in it.

"Was Molly here?" she asked. "She came here and took one of the backpacks, didn't she?" When Jo didn't say anything and only continued to sob, Ricki blew out an exasperated breath. "Frank called her, you know."

Jo's tears slowed down enough for her to gape at Ricki. "What?"

"Her brother, Frank," Ricki repeated. "After he was arrested, he called his sister to warn her. I'm wondering why you were still hanging around. Molly didn't warn you?"

"Frank called her?" Jo shook her head, then swiped at the tears on her cheeks. "She didn't say anything. That little bitch. She takes her share and tells me that with Jimmy gone she's got nowhere to go, so she's going back to Walt." The tears stopped flowing as Jo's face contorted in anger. "Her brother calls and tells her we've been found out, and she doesn't say one damn word to me?"

Walt. Ricki knew it. Disappearing into the park would be the safest place for Molly. After all, it had worked fine for almost fifty years.

Getting to her feet, Ricki looked over at Stephen. "She's all yours, along with the drugs. We have a killer to catch."

Chapter 42

RICKI DROPPED her light pack onto the ground. The tents erected by the rescue team ten days before were still standing in a neat row on one side of the campsite, which she considered a minor miracle.

It had been close to noon when Stephen had dropped them off at the trailhead leading up to Hannegan Pass. By the time they'd navigated the eight miles up to Egg Lake, the sun had disappeared along with any lingering twilight, and they'd finished the hike with headlamps and a prayer. It had also helped that between the equipment abandoned by the rescue team, plus the gear and supplies left behind by the hunters, they didn't have to bring much with them.

The temperature had dropped like a bomb once the sun had gone down, and threatened to dip below freezing before it made its appearance again. Ricki stood at the edge of the campsite, looking out into the darkness. With no light other than what was being given off by the fire, they were surrounded by a sea of black, with only the creaking of branches testifying to the existence of a forest around them.

People in the city don't know how dark it can get out here, Ricki thought. Her gaze drifted upward to a sky that was as black as the area spreading out from the campsite. Not one star penetrated the thick cloud cover overhead.

"Here." Gin held out a tin mug, steam rolling over its top like a boiling cauldron. "I thought you might like something warm."

Ricki took the mug between her gloved hands. "Thanks." She glanced back toward the fire. Clay and Anchorman were sitting on the ground, having an animated discussion about the Seattle Seahawks and the state of football in general.

Bear would be right at home here, surrounded by forest and talk of football. Ricki shrugged at the random thought. Oddly enough, although football was such a big part of Bear's life, it wasn't an interest she'd shared with her ex, though over the years she'd learned to appreciate the sport. Still, she'd rather watch a good baseball game, preferably with a hot dog and a cold beer.

"What are you thinking so hard about over there by yourself?" Gin asked.

Ricki laughed. "My ex-husband."

"Okay," Gin said. "A little weird, but then this whole place is a little weird."

"Only if you aren't used to it."

The FBI agent smiled. "And I guess you are. Before all the fireworks start tomorrow, I wanted to tell you a couple of things."

When she paused, Ricki gave her a sideways glance. "Is it something about the case?"

"No," Gin said. "Not really. You had enough on your plate, and I didn't want to add any more, but I got a call on the satphone I brought along. It was Stephen. He said that a couple of CJNG members showed up in town right after we left."

Ricki blinked. "Where? In Glacier?"

"Yeah." Gin's smile didn't last long. "They weren't hard to spot in a town that size. So Stephen did what he does best with that human chameleon trick of his and passed himself off as a local. He told them that he heard there was a whole passel of guys who came out of the park and hightailed it to Seattle. But he had Sergeant Crowder come pick up Jo, so that's where you'll find her, and he'll drop the drugs off at Hamilton's office." When Ricki continued to stare at her in disbelief, Gin shrugged. "Stephen is tailing the CJNG guys. We still have an op that needs to be finished, so I won't be staying in Glacier when we get back. I'll be on my way to join my partner. I just wanted to tell you how much I've enjoyed getting to know you, Ricki James."

Still slightly dazed, Ricki shook her head to clear it and then held out her hand. "Same here, Gin Reilly."

As Gin clasped Ricki's hand in her own, her smile returned. "Oh, before I forget, Stephen also wanted me to thank you for not making him come along on this hike again. I think my partner has had his fill of the outdoors for quite a while."

Ricki smiled. "Well, someone had to take care of the stash of cocaine we uncovered, and getting Jocelyn Bain locked up." She gave Gin a quick nudge with her elbow. "You didn't have to come either. It might have been better if you'd stayed with Stephen."

"Yes, I did have to come," Gin countered quietly. "A deal is a deal. You helped us with our drug case, which will make Blake and the other powers that be at the agency very happy. In return, we help you catch whoever is littering your park with dead bodies." She shook her head. "I just didn't expect it to be Molly. So I'm guessing all that hunched-over, arthritic old lady stuff was just an act, along with the way she talked?"

"You weren't there when we found the blood on the barn floor at Jimmy's place, but Molly did a pretty good quickstep across that yard trying to get away from Anchorman. It didn't exactly match up with the way she shuffled around every other time she saw us," Ricki said dryly.

"Is that when you began to suspect her?" Gin's curious gaze met Ricki's thoughtful one.

She took a long sip of coffee then shook her head. "Not the way you mean. There wasn't a suspect who sat right. The only thing we knew for sure was that someone had to be helping the drug runners get through the park without being seen, and had to know where that cabin was, and be able to chase Santiago Garcia through the forest and off the trail. Whoever it was had to have an excellent knowledge of the park. Walter clearly did, but what did we see him actually do? Talk to us without showing himself and then poof into thin air when he could just as easily have shot us, then made sure we would never have been found. And then there was sending all that coke up in flames. None of that fit the actions of a killer. So there had to be someone else. Someone connected to the Last Stop, because it seemed anyone who hung out there knew more about the crimes than anyone else in town."

"So, what are you saying? That you had Big Mack and Pac-Man on your suspect list?" Gin laughed.

"I considered it," Ricki said with a straight face before she broke down and grinned. "But I didn't think of Molly. Not until Walter mentioned a wife. Over forty years out here? His wife would have known as much about the park as Walter did. And he never said she'd passed on. All he said was that she hadn't been with him for the last few years. Anyway, even then I didn't key in on Molly. I thought it might be someone still lurking in the shadows, and we just hadn't uncovered her yet."

"And she would need to have some basic survival skills too," Gin said. "Like hunting for food or living without deodorant. Molly's act was good enough that she seemed helpless."

"Uh-huh. Something like that."

Gin scuffed the toe of her boot into the dirt. "Your partner . . . her name was Marie, wasn't it?"

Coming out of left field the way it had, Gin's question

made Ricki's stomach clench, but she managed a silent nod. Even after all this time, the thought of how Marie died still hurt.

"Is it true she was murdered by her own unit? And that you almost died too?"

"Something like that," Ricki said again, softly, then delivered her standard answer whenever she was faced with questions about her former partner and best friend. "I don't talk about it."

"But I'll bet you get asked about it a lot." Gin kept her gaze straight ahead, staring into the darkness. "And that's the weird part. You still get asked about it, but then you're constantly being told it's all over. They're dead now, or locked up, or whatever, so just move on. But no matter how fast you move, there are some things that always stay with you."

There was something in Gin's tone that had Ricki keeping quiet. There was pain and hesitation, neither of which she'd ever associated with the straightforward, tough FBI agent.

"I guess you heard your boss call me Gillian?" Gin finally said. When Ricki nodded, she did too. "Yeah. I don't use it."

Not knowing what to say to that, Ricki kept it light. "Too Irish for you?"

"Well, there is that," Gin said. "But no, that's not the reason. It's because my father really liked the name."

There was a long silence while Ricki simply waited her out.

"I changed it to Gin when I was sent to Nebraska. To live with my aunt. She's my mother's sister. Not related to my father at all." Gin cut off her choppy dialogue and dug her boot farther into the dirt. "My brother Devon was sent to my uncle's place in Denver. Uncle Todd was Mom's older brother, and he didn't have any kids. I was ten and Devon was fourteen. I guess it was a good thing there were only two of us. We might have run out of relatives."

Feeling a wrench for Gin, who'd been separated from her

only sibling, Ricki sighed. "I'm sorry. That must have been really tough."

Gin let out a short, bitter-sounding laugh. "Yeah. Not as tough as staying in Cleveland, though. When your father is Byron Reilly, it's hard to stay under the radar."

Ricki was about to put a comforting hand on Gin's shoulder, but it froze in midair. Byron Reilly? It was close to a couple of decades since that name was splashed all over the news, but it wasn't one you'd ever forget. Or one she'd ever linked up with Gin. Ricki made a small choking sound before she could control it, which had Gin giving her a quick glance along with a brittle smile.

"Oh. I see you've heard of him."

The Black Cross Killer? Who hadn't heard of one of the worst serial killers who'd ever been caught? Byron Reilly had gained his nickname because of the small cross he always burned into the flesh of his victims. He'd gone undetected for decades and had only been caught after he'd pulled his oldest son into his sick games. It had taken the police years to discover that Charles Reilly had been his father's partner, which was the reason the Black Cross Killer had destroyed so many lives. There were actually two of them. It had been a sensation in the press when it was revealed that the son's first kill had been . . .

Ricki's mind slammed to a halt. Gradually realizing how heavily she was breathing, she forced herself to take in air slowly, and then let it out in small bursts.

"Yeah," Gin said, as if Ricki had spoken out loud. "My half brother killed my mom, among a hundred others, while our mutual father looked on and applauded."

"And you saw it," Ricki breathed out.

"Devon and I both saw it, and that's how they were caught. I guess my old man thought his younger children would join in on the family business." Gin said flatly. "So I know what it is to live with the ultimate betrayal by someone you should be able to trust without question. And to have it follow you everywhere." She turned and looked squarely at Ricki, shadows from the firelight flickering over her face. "I don't tell that to many people, and I'm going to trust you to keep it to yourself. But I thought you should know you aren't alone in having to live with knowing that kind of betrayal really does exist in this world."

Ricki removed one of her gloves and again held out a hand. Gin looked at it a moment before pulling off her own glove and clasping Ricki's hand with her own. "You're all right, James."

"You too, Reilly." Ricki looked over at the fire, where the two men were still engrossed in their football discussion. "Let's get some rest. We have a killer to track down tomorrow."

Chapter 43

THE MORNING DAWNED cold and dreary, with the gray clouds overhead dropping a sprinkle of snow as a harbinger of what was headed their way. Ricki stamped her feet to keep the blood flowing as she checked her rifle. She still had her Glock in a holster sitting on the small of her back, but this was the mountains, where a rifle was best when hunting game—no matter how many legs it might have.

Clay and Anchorman were finishing their coffee while Gin stood waiting, her hand gripping the strap of the rifle nestled along her back.

It was a few minutes past seven, with barely enough light to call it daytime, but they needed to get going before Mother Nature made the trail to Walter's cabin impossible to hike. Or at least what Ricki hoped was the trail to Walter's cabin.

The path leading away from where he kept his supplies might go nowhere, so it was a gamble. But she thought it was a logical one. The only way Walter and Molly could have stayed undetected for so long was if they kept clear of the main trails, which meant staying to the west. And that was exactly the direction that path had been heading in.

It didn't take long for them to backtrack to the Copper Ridge Trail, and then find the almost invisible cut-through to the parallel trail discovered by the drug runners. Or likely shown to them by Molly. When they reached the point where the trail crossed with another one, Ricki turned left, heading for the cabin with its pile of unclaimed supplies.

When they came out of the trees and into a small clearing, Ricki expected to see the lopsided cabin. Instead, there was nothing but splintered boards and mangled tin cans spread out in a wide arc in a foot-high pile of rubble.

"Holy hell." Anchorman stopped beside her and stared at the disaster. "What did that crazy old bastard do? Blow up the cabin?"

Clay let out a low whistle while Gin stood with her mouth open.

"So which one do you think did this?" Gin asked. "Molly or Walter?"

Anchorman let out a snort. "Whichever one is crazier."

"That's a toss-up." Clay met Ricki's gaze. "I guess we keep going?"

Surveying the damage, Ricki nudged a piece of jagged wood with the toe of her boot. There wasn't any reason to linger here, so she gave an affirmative nod to Clay's question. "The other path started out from the back." She walked around the rubble, with Gin right beside her.

"I can't believe they blew up that cabin and no one heard or saw anything," the FBI agent said.

Ricki shrugged. "There isn't anyone out here this time of year, so who was going to hear it?"

"Geez. All you people are crazy," Gin said, then fell silent as they reached the trail leading out and began to climb.

The sky continued to drop a soft dusting of snow in small spurts, reminding them it was there but dissolving into an icy sheen of water as soon as it touched the ground. The instant melt added to the misery of the climb, keeping the ground at their feet and the parkas on their backs slick with moisture.

The team kept going, gaining height, losing a little, and then gaining some more. As they drew nearer to a crest, Ricki slowed the pace down, stopping every hundred feet of trail to listen. They were almost at the top when she heard it. Voices. Raised enough for the sound to carry, but not enough to make out the words.

Halfway around a long, gradual bend in the trail, the voices became more distinct, and their volume louder. Ricki halted and dropped to one knee, straining to hear what was being said as the others behind her followed suit.

"You give that to me. It's mine!"

Despite its high shriek, there was no mistaking Molly's voice.

"You have no right to bring this poison into our home, Molly," Walt shouted back. "You bring this evil into our house. An evil you killed for. You killed all those men, and then you killed Jimmy."

Molly's voice rose another notch, with loathing dripping from every word. "This isn't any house, you old piece of shit. It's nothing more than a shack looking over a cliff. That's all I've ever had with you. A shack. And Jimmy was snorting our profit away right up his fat nose and bragging about it. He wouldn't shut his mouth, so I shut it for him."

"He was kin, Molly," Walt spat out. "Jimmy was kin. You have to be colder than the winter freeze to kill your own blood."

While the husband and wife raged on, Ricki shifted her body into a low crouch and slowly crept around the curve. Deciding to use the natural cover at hand, she lifted an arm and left the narrow path, disappearing into the forest along with the rest of the team.

They wove their way slowly between the trees, stepping over rotting logs and walking carefully to make as little noise as possible, letting the wind knocking the branches high above them cover the sound of their movement. Still a good ten feet inside the tree line, Ricki peered into the cleared-off patch of land that rose up a hill on one side and ended in a steep drop-off on the other. Dotted with old tree stumps, it was topped with a cabin standing at its center.

The peace of the hilltop being gently dusted with a thin layer of snow was broken by the two combatants, grappling together as one dragged the other toward the edge of the small plateau.

"It's mine," Molly repeated, a death grip on the padded straps of a large backpack that Walter held in his hands.

He didn't say a word, but kept walking toward the edge, dragging the backpack and the clinging Molly along with him. When Molly lost her grip on the straps, she recoiled for a moment before flinging herself through the air and landing on Walter's back. Her hands formed into claws as she raked them across his face. Off-balance, Walter let out a string of curses as he staggered forward, coming dangerously close to the edge of the cliff.

Ricki stepped out into the open, firing a single shot into the air to get their attention centered on her rather than each other. "Stop!" she yelled out, sprinting toward them. "Federal agents."

Shock caused Molly to lose her grip and slide onto the ground. She staggered back a few steps as Walter, freed from her weight, leaped forward. In one smooth swing of his arm, he tossed the backpack over the edge just as Ricki moved between him and the wildly infuriated woman he called his wife.

As Anchorman and Clay grabbed hold of the man and wrestled him to the ground, Molly slapped her hands on either side of her head and sank to her knees with a loud wail.

"What did you do? You stupid old man, what did you do?" She leaned over as if she were in pain. "That was mine. Mine!

It would have given me a life. I could have had a real house, with heat and a bathroom, and meals not warmed up from a can or from something I had to shoot myself." She rocked back and forth, angry tears streaming down her cheeks. "I've had nothing for most of my life, and all because of you wanting to live out here. You had no right to throw my money away. No right."

"I told you what the price was for coming back," Walter panted out as he lay spread-eagled on the ground.

"I hate you," Molly screamed out as the two men jerked Walter back up to his feet. "I hate you."

As Gin moved between Anchorman and Clay to put the zip-tie cuffs on the man they were holding between them, Molly slowly got to her feet, her eyes blazing as she stared at the spot where her fortune had disappeared forever. She turned her head and looked at the man she'd run away with forty-eight years ago and spit at him. "It's mine," she said in a high-pitched wail that sent a nervous jitter up Ricki's back. And then Molly screamed it. "Mine."

Without another sound she took a long step forward then broke into a run, heading straight for the edge that ended with a vertical drop of a hundred feet.

"No!" Ricki yelled. She dropped her rifle and dived for Molly, her hand barely grazing a denim-covered leg before she hit the ground. Her momentum kept her sliding forward. She barely registered Molly's blood-curdling, high-pitched scream as the old woman threw herself outward, over the edge, dropping out of sight in the blink of an eye.

Desperately scrabbling for any handhold, Ricki arms were stretched out in front of her as she skidded across the ground on her belly. She shoved the heels of her hands into the slick dirt with its veneer of snow, trying to slow herself, but her hands, wrists, and then her forearms were suddenly cutting through the air in the empty space beyond the edge of the cliff. A scream rose in her throat only to be abruptly cut short when her whole body was jerked to a sudden, brutal stop.

Feeling like her limbs had been torn off, she grimaced in pain. She turned her head and caught a split-second glimpse of Walter dropping her legs to the ground, then saw him stagger backwards before her vision was blocked by a broad chest.

Strong arms locked themselves around her, and Clay's anguished voice floated somewhere over her head. "Shit, Ricki. Shit." He dragged her upright until her feet were off the ground. "You have a crappy habit of having a run-in with cliffs."

Clamping her firmly to his chest, he carried her backwards, away from the edge. He didn't stop until he bumped up against a post stuck into the ground in front of the cabin.

While Gin raced over toward a limp Ricki, Anchorman laid a hand on Walter's shoulder. The man everyone called the hermit was panting, and tears leaked from his eyes as he stared at the spot where Molly had disappeared.

"You've earned a pass, old man," Anchorman said quietly. "You can go on your way, and no one will stop you, or you can come back with us. Ricki will see that you aren't hassled with any charges, and so will Clay. And if they can't swing it, then I'll bring you back here myself, and believe me when I say no one will stop me. So the choice is yours."

Walter shook his head, looking at the former Marine with watery eyes. "There's no choice to make. I have nothing to go back to." He looked over at the drop-off and his voice trembled. "My only family chose to die rather than live with me."

Anchorman's hand tightened on Walter's shoulder. "If there's one sure thing I learned all those years in combat, it's that you can't be responsible for everything, because shit happens." He waited until Walter looked back at him. "You're only responsible for learning to live with the choices people make, old man. Not for the choice itself."

Walter drew in a slow, deep breath. "I'll think on it, son. And you can stop calling me an old man. I could still whup your ass if I put my mind to it."

Anchorman grinned. "Maybe you could, Walter. Maybe you could. Let's see how Ricki is doing."

Epilogue

RICKI WAS SITTING on a porch step, leaning against Clay as she watched Anchorman talk to Walter while Gin cleaned off her dirty and bruised hands.

"I'm telling you," Gin said, her voice bordering on testy, "all of you are batshit crazy."

"Maybe," Clay said, keeping one arm firmly around Ricki's shoulders. "But we make a good team."

"We do," Anchorman stated. He looked at Ricki for a long moment before tilting his head toward Walter. "He's thinking about coming back with us. But he thinks he has no reason to."

Ricki ignored the pain in her hands and legs as she smiled up at the hermit. "You have family, Walter. That's enough reason."

The older man shook his head, making droplets of water jump away from his beard. "The last of my family is lying at the bottom of that valley." His gaze drifted over the cabin behind Ricki's back. "It's going to make it hard to live here. I'll be needing to find another spot."

"In the middle of winter?" Ricki lifted an eyebrow. "You've spent enough winters in the Cascades to know you'll

351

be lucky to survive with a shelter already built. Without one, you won't make it. And your stash of supplies has been blown to hell and back. Why did you do that?"

"I didn't. Molly did," Walter said. "I always have a stick or two of dynamite, to help get the stumps out when I need to. Molly knew where it was. She said she was leaving. Going to Canada, and she wouldn't tolerate anyone else using her cabin." He sighed and looked down at his feet. "Not even me. The next thing I know, she's blowing the thing up."

"Did Molly bring you those supplies?" Ricki asked, surprised again when Walter shook his head.

"Jimmy did. He's Lynnie's cousin. Molly showed him where the cabin was when he got old enough to keep her secret."

"Lynnie?" Gin blinked. "You mean Jo? She and Jimmy were related to each other?"

A shadow of a smile flitted across Walter's lips. "She was Lynnie back when we all ran together. Jocelyn Blighton Bain. She, Molly, and Jimmy were cousins of a sort. Molly on Jo's father's side of the family, and Jimmy on her mother's." He shrugged. "When she and Don got married, everyone was blood family except me. I guess it was always that way." He turned his head to look off into the distance again, but not before Ricki caught the sheen of moisture in his eyes.

"You have family, Walter," she said slowly. "I talked to Maggie. She thought you'd been murdered long ago, and was very happy to hear that you were still alive."

Walter's mouth opened as his jaw dropped to his chest. "Maggie?" He got the one word out and then frowned. "Murdered? Why would she think that?"

"I don't know." Ricki smiled. "Why don't you ask her yourself?"

"Maybe I'll do that," Walter said slowly. "I should clear that up, shouldn't I?"

Anchorman gave him a quick slap on the back. "It's the

least you can do for family. We'll help you find a place to stay and get settled."

Now Walter frowned, but there was a definite sparkle in his eyes. "No need for that, son. I've got a house in town. It even has a barn to keep my truck in."

"A barn . . ." Gin gaped at him. "Are you saying that the house Jimmy and Molly were living in was actually yours?"

Walter shrugged. "What's mine was also Molly's, so it's more like Jimmy was living in Molly's house. And working in her bar."

"Well, shit," Anchorman said. "You own that dive too? And a truck?"

Walter gave Anchorman a poke in the arm. "How did you think I was getting around town, son? Use your head. Or do you leave that to the womenfolk?" He looked up at the sky, leaning his head back as he studied the clouds. "If we're going, we'd better get to it. We might make it back before that storm coming in dumps a heap of snow at our feet."

As Gin and Anchorman accompanied Walter to his cabin to help him pack a few things, Clay stood up and held his hand out to Ricki. She took it and let him pull her to her feet, wincing at the jabs of pain shooting up her legs and into her hips.

Clay's concern showed in his eyes. "Are you all right enough to walk out of here?"

"Moving around will help keep me from stiffening up," Ricki said. She squinted as she looked over the ground near the edge of the plateau. "Where's my rifle?"

"Gin set it over here." Clay pointed to the other side of him, where her gun was propped up against the side of the porch. "Are you sure about this? Walking ten miles is a lot more than just moving around to loosen up, even if I do carry your pack."

Ricki made a face. "I'm tough, Clay. I'll make it, and you don't need to carry my pack."

"Maybe not," he said easily. Putting a finger under her chin, he turned her face toward his. "But I'm going to anyway because I meant what I said, Ricki. We make a good team. And that's how I want it to stay."

Ricki stared at him, seeing the confidence in his gaze. "What does that mean, Clay?"

He leaned down and kissed her softly before drawing back with a smile flickering on his mouth and in his eyes. "Lex is going to have to take his chances with whatever agency is chasing after him. If he wants to talk to me, he knows where I am. In the Bay. With you." As the others came out onto the porch, Clay picked up her rifle and ran a finger down her cheek. "Are you ready to go?"

Ricki felt the warmth bubble up inside her, breaking out into a

contented smile. He was right. They were a good team. "Yeah. Let's

get out of here."

∾

IT WASN'T until the next afternoon, as she was enjoying a last mug of coffee on the porch of the Airbnb, that Ricki got around to checking her voice mails. The first one made her smile, and she was still grinning when she tapped on the number and it was answered on the other end.

"Hi, DJ. This is Ricki James. I'm sorry I didn't make our meeting yesterday." She listened for a moment as she watched Clay load up the SUV.

"No, nothing's wrong. Everything's cleared up and we're heading home. I'll do that, thanks, and you take care of your-self too."

After hanging up and tucking her cell phone back into her pocket, Ricki raised the mug to her lips. It had been a close thing, and she and Clay still had some things to sort out, not to mention that Lex was still lurking somewhere in the background, but right at this moment, life was pretty good.

THE END

THANK you for reading *Hiding In The Shadows*! Next up, Ricki is called to Yellowstone National Park, where a small group is staging their annual re-enactment of the first legal arrest of a poacher operating in the then newly formed national park. But instead of the actors playing out a scene from another time, they all end up dead, including someone close to Special Agent Cooper. The devasted agent calls Ricki, asking her to come to Yellowstone and help catch a determined killer in ***Colder Than Ice***. Now on pre-order through Amazon. Grab your copy today by clicking below! http://getbook.at/ ColderThanIce

If you'd like to know read more about Ricki—please sign up for CR Chandler's email list! In addition to being the first to be notified about any new releases, or content only sent to people signed up to receive the author's newsletter, you'll also be able to download a **free** Ricki James book—only available to anyone who signs up on the email list. Backcountry Murder follows one of the first cases Ricki solved as a new ISB agent —before she came to the Bay—and includes the story of the first time she met Anchorman. You can sign-up for the email and to receive your **free** book here! CLICK HERE FOR FREE BOOK!

Made in the USA
Middletown, DE
26 October 2022

13553311R00201